1988

THE GRAYWOLF

SHORT FICTION SERIES

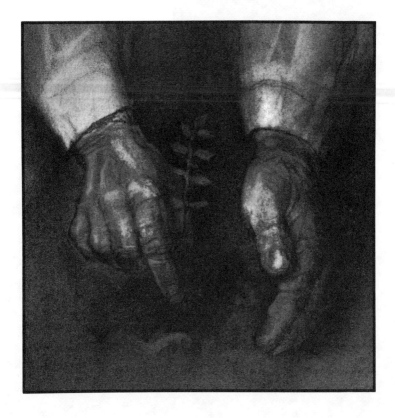

SAINT PAUL / 1988

Full Measure

MODERN SHORT STORIES

ON AGING

Edited by Dorothy Sennett

Foreword by Carol Bly

GRAYWOLF PRESS

Graywolf Press receives generous donations from private and governmental sources, including the Minnesota State Arts Board and the National Endowment for the Arts. Graywolf is a member agency of United Arts, Saint Paul.

Library of Congress Cataloging-in-Publication Data

Full measure.

(Graywolf short fiction series)
1. Aging—Fiction.   2. Short stories, American.
3. Short stories, English.   I. Sennett, Dorothy,
1909–   II. Series.
PS648.A37F85   1988   813'.01'08355   87-83080
ISBN 1-55597-105-9

Published by GRAYWOLF PRESS,
Post Office Box 75006, Saint Paul, Minnesota 55175.
All rights reserved.

Second Printing

Acknowledgments

WARREN ADLER. "The Angel of Mercy," Copyright © 1977 by Warren Adler is from *The Sunset Gang* (Viking Press, 1977). Reprinted by permission of the author.

CONRAD AIKEN. "Mr. Arcularis," Copyright © 1950 by Conrad Aiken *The Short Stories of Conrad Aiken*, Alfred A. Knopf, 1950.

LOUIS AUCHINCLOSS. "Suttee," Copyright © 1970 by Louis Auchincloss. Reprinted by permission from *Second Chance: Tales of Two Generations* (Houghton-Mifflin Co.).

ARTHENIA J. BATES. "A Ceremony of Innocence," From *Seeds Beneath the Snow* Copyright © 1969 by Arthenia Bates. Reprinted by permission of Howard University Press, Washington, D.C.

SAUL BELLOW. "Leaving the Yellow House," From *Mosby's Memoirs*, Copyright © 1957 by Saul Bellow. Reprinted by permission of Viking Penguin Inc.

CAROL BLY. "Gunnar's Sword" From *Backbone*, Copyright © 1976 by Carol Bly. First published in The American Review. Reprinted by permission Milkweed Editions.

HORTENSE CALISHER. "The Middle Drawer," Copyright © 1948, 1975 by Hortense Calisher. First published in *The New Yorker*. Reprinted by permission.

RAYMOND CARVER. "After the Denim," Copyright © 1981 by Raymond Carver. Published in *What We Talk about When We Talk about Love* (Alfred A. Knopf, 1981). Reprinted by permission of author.

JOHN CHEEVER. "The World of Apples," Copyright © 1966 by John Cheever. Reprinted from *The Stories of John Cheever* by permission of Alfred A. Knopf, Inc.

Table of Contents

IV

V

Preface

A short story, said Frank O'Connor, is the lonely voice of a "submerged population."* The people in this collection speak with the lonely voices of one of the great submerged populations of our time, the elderly. Clearly, these voices must be heard, and contemporary writers have heard them.

Responding to O'Connor's challenge that in a short story " . . . a whole lifetime must be crowded into a few minutes," modern writers have found old age to be fertile ground, offering that significant moment which " . . . enables us to distinguish present, past and future as though they were all contemporaneous."

Selecting these stories and coming to terms with the necessary omissions from this enormous field have been less perilous tasks than one might suppose. I wanted my old people to be of our time—ordinary, easily recognizable, sharing the commonality of age—and yet to reveal themselves, through the

*Frank O'Connor, *The Lonely Voice: A Study of the Short Story,* (Cleveland and New York: Meridian Books, The World Publishing Company, October, 1965), Introduction.

eyes of a broad range of gifted observers, in all their extraordinary differences. Moved by these drives, I found that the stories selected themselves. As the collection grew, I felt each newcomer resonating, "bouncing off" the rest, receiving and releasing energy and light.

What I hoped to achieve by this mingling of characters, beyond the enjoyment of the stories for themselves, was to show how differently good writers perceive old people. Like Chaucer's "goodly company," old people are "people of all kinds . . ." We are you, grown old.

Although we survivors are vulnerable, we are tough. We may have lost a great deal, but we know that to survive we must hang on to something. We understand not only that life ends, but that it renews itself, and in renewal lies survival. Let me recount some ways of renewal.

We survive in our attachment to living things. In Joyce Carol Oates' "A Theory of Knowledge," we see Professor Weber, an old philosopher, struggling through a haze of confused memories to validate the ideas he wants to pass on. Yet it is not through large statements, but rather through an act of simple humanity, that he achieves dignity. During the night, roused by the screams of a battered boy, the old man moves with great pain and courage to rescue him. To be this kind of survivor, it is enough for one to love a vagrant, nameless child.

We survive in our attachment to places. In James Fetler's endearing "The Dust of Yuri Serafimovich," an ancient Russian wanderer (former seaman, veterinarian—now half-derelict), has just passed his naturalization test, owing to the generosity of the examiner, who knows Yuri has to become a citizen to receive his pension.

During all his wayfaring, Yuri has carried with him a bucket of dirt from his native city, Murmansk. After his papers come through, he takes the bucket to the San Francisco Zoo. " . . . Serafimovich was shuffling from compound to compound, from railing to railing, and each time he stopped he plunged his hand into the tin box and scattered dust among the beasts. . . . Dust to the elephants, dust to the imprisoned cats. Like a planter, the old man was sowing his dust." Finally he has given up the Russian Imperial Flag.

We survive in the things we loved in our youth. In Grace Paley's "Dreamers in a Dead Language," we meet Faith's father, Mr. Darwin, "one of the resident poets of the Children of Judea, Home for the Golden Ages, Coney Island Branch." He has written "still another love song," and Faith's lovers court her through her father, offering to get his poems published.

In a letter to the manager of the Home, Mr. Darwin says, "Dear Goldstein. Are we or are we not the People of the Book? Books mean mostly to you Bible, Talmud, etc. To me and my generation, idealists all, book means B O O K S. . . . "

We survive in the connectedness of generations. In Hortense Calisher's "The Middle Drawer," Hedwig Licht, aged two, " . . . stared mournfully into the camera with the huge, heavy-lidded eyes that had continued to brood in her face as a woman, the eyes she had transmitted to Hester. . . . "

We survive in those we love profoundly. In Arturo Vivante's "The Soft Core," Giacomo alternately resents and venerates his dominating eighty-year-old father. But when his father has a stroke, " . . . Strangely now, Giacomo found that he *could* talk to his father, easily, affably, and with pleasure, and that his voice was gentle. When his father was well, he couldn't, but now he was reaching the secret, soft core — the secret, gentle core that is in each of us. And he thought, *this* is what my father is really like; the way he is now, this is his real, his naked self. . . . "

These story-tellers make us feel the last years of life as funny, pathetic, painful, tragic (often, all at once), and, above all, as complex. Through their art, they free the voices of the aging, the survivors of living. Great art defines us, and makes us survivors.

Since every writer hopes to become old, his stories should make us sense the old person he is to become. In the words of Simone de Beauvoir:

"We must stop cheating; the whole meaning of our life is in question in the future that is waiting for us. If we do not know what we are going to be, we cannot know what we are; let us recognize ourselves in this old man or that old woman. It must be done if we are to take upon ourselves the entirety of our human state. And when it is done we will no longer acquiesce in the misery of the last age; we will no longer be indifferent, because we shall be concerned, as indeed we are."*

DOROTHY SENNETT
November, 1984

*From the Introduction to *The Coming of Age.* (New York: G.P. Putnam's Sons, English translation 1972 by Andre Deutsch, Weidenfeld and Nicolson).

Foreword

It is surprising that twenty-three stories about old people should make bright reading. Being conventional, I started through *Full Measure* in my persona (that buttoned cassock of the personality): I was a high-minded learner about old age, all set to be compassionate and all willingness to be instructed.

Of course, no one is remiss in practising compassion or docile learning, yet what a waste it would be to approach this particular anthology with only those churchy virtues! The best way to read *Full Measure* is leisurely, richly, to sink into it the way we sink ourselves into adventure stories. Here are twenty-three stories full of psychological and physical danger, and we can read them for the action, for the particular occasions of the forty-odd characters, for their ingenuity or valor or bad luck or ghastly decision making. I found myself taking note of their doings, the way a midshipman might read letters from recent graduates now out on the great waters. Whatever these characters are coming to, beset by, licked by, or able to alter—all that lies ahead. I found myself fascinated by how well or how poorly these story people took hold: I made role models out of some of them.

Literate people of course resist expressions like "role models," but the idea of modeling oneself on others means we trust our willpower and intend to use it. If we choose to model the tiniest aspect of our behavior on someone else's it means we have decided to shape our lives ourselves. That is a realistic, cheering thought.

An example: thousands of writers who have spent part of their childhood in intellectual pursuit while their brothers and sisters were simply being sociable report having taken *Little Women's* Jo as their role model. Since Jo gave all those solitary hours to scribbling little stories in the attic, she validated devotion to a skill (writing, in this case) which doesn't pay off in the short term. How obvious it sounds! Yet sociologists have told us that if children don't see other children or adults making short-term sacrifice for long-term goals they usually miss developing the ethical muscle to make sacrifices themselves. We are a simpler species than we pretend: we don't find it glamorous to say, "I learned by copying."

For a moment let's consider this possibility: what if thousands of rigid, egotistical professors, given to making others adopt their all-encompassing thought systems, were to read Joyce Carol Oates's "A Theory of Knowledge," and learn by copying? If we resist admitting to role modeling as older children or teenagers, we are likely to resist it all the more strongly when thinking of role modeling for seventy- and eighty-year-olds. Professor Weber was the essential type of people who fail to develop their feeling side: it made him the more frantic to sell his ideation to others. Then—within this story—he makes two huge changes in his style. First, he learns to do what psychotherapists and social workers call Active Listening: he actually hears a child's need to be saved. He doesn't do it unconsciously, either: he knows he has become sensitized in a new way. Second, having listened, he believes in the child's need. He doesn't pooh-pooh it, nor take the child's signals merely as signs of lower-class behavior—the kind of "denial" so favored by chill, advantaged people. Weber acts. Despite his frailty, he struggles across farmland to the barn where the child has been tied down and tortured. He saves him. It is a marvellous instance of someone's learning too late to abandon what T. S. Eliot called (in "East Coker") our intellectual "equipment always deteriorating / In the general mess of imprecision of feeling." What is the *precise feeling* to aim at? It is to confess that someone's scream is indeed a scream, and that a scream is a scream for help. Just as I have always found it distressing that Mozart wrote beautifully so young—that James Joyce finished *Dubliners* in his twenties—it is proportionally cheering that this Professor Weber, and the rest of us, can come to consciousness and bravery in our old age.

Not everyone in *Full Measure* learns psychological or physical heroism. Some of the characters are piteous or offensive or both, yet their stories are oddly lively. We are in the presence of people who are being as inventive as they can. Some of them are merely canny, but they keep their eyes open, and are as hospitable to life as they can manage. Inventiveness and enthusiasm in everyday life are everyone's goals, with changes in the game rules as we age. What matters is being up for the game, whatever the rules. There are some children—we all know one or two—who burst into tears when they learn that in Monopoly you may not pick up the silvery shoe and fly from Go to Go to Go, avoiding all the rent-charging landfalls. Most children have more fibre: they like the game rules because limitations mean challenge, and challenge means adventure.

What are the rules for the old-age game, then? As you go along this track, you get some kit: you gain savvy in practical things; you learn the flare of connecting things with ideas. You learn to connect past ideas with present ideas. You learn to ask, given these past and these present ideas, what changes are possible? You get a kinder humor.

On the down side, you receive noticeably less respect from most forty- and fifty-year olds. They can tell that you are retreating from their shallow, muscley, profitable projects! You receive audible scorn from teenagers, who still use words like "old geezer" and "old bag," because the way teenagers ward off fearful scenarii (such as old age for us all) is with scorn. What else? You get increasing pain, which in turn makes it hard to stick to your goal of not being querulous.

Some of the people in *Full Measure* do a marvellous job of the old-age part of their lives. Others, especially Miss Verney in Jean Rhys's "Sleep it Off, Lady," are brave and funny about some of their projects, and hopelessly feckless about others. I shall never forget Wallace E. Knight's hero in "The Resurrection Man," because he passionately devises a way to kill and bury himself before enduring the full wrath of a terminal illness. He has enormous mechanical ingenuity—a quality common to protagonists in nineteenth-century fiction, but now rare except in spy and detective fiction. The Resurrection Man's story is pure adventure.

We might miss the interesting qualities of character in these stories because our literary habit is to think of individual *character* as the focus of fiction about the "real" part of life—ages eighteen through sixty. When we read about people who are aged 7 to 17, we tend to discount some of their individuality. That is because we stereotype youth: we think of stories about youth as amalgams of environmental influences which will shape the characters' later, "real" life. For every reader who has gone through *A Portrait of the Artist as a Young Man* paying attention to Stephen's individual personality there are likely hundreds who read the book as informal sociology—as a study of a severe, anti-expressive environment. Too bad. In the same way, one can read about characters aged 61 to 100 as if they were only case studies to do with old age, not people.

Dorothy Sennett, however, by virtue of putting together this astonishing anthology, and explicitly in her Preface, begs us not to stereotype old people. The question is: can a book actually stop people from stereotyping? *Full Measure* is a hearty, funny, serious, tough book—but can it actually stop its readers from stereotyping?

We know how much and how little literature can do. It points out victims, gives us some clear images of their sufferings, and leaves us with either of two responses: if we are sensitive, we feel shamed and a little blamed. If we are insensitive, we feel "the slight flutter" that Chekhov mentioned, in "Gooseberries"; we pause in our constant attending to our own affairs long enough to feel a little ethical flutter, a little *frisson*—and that's all. When it comes to making ethical change, the classic tools of fiction are first, focus, and second, shame and blame. They are pretty good tools. We think of Dickens, of Woolf at her best, and of Lawrence when he is on solid footing, and of all the muckrakers of all time. Generation after generation of writers offer their Horrible Examples. Readers, generation after generation, acknowledge the given injustices and cruelties, and then return to their ordinary indifference.

The secret social-skill finding here is that *shaming and blaming does not work at all.* Even peace workers, who love shaming and blaming more than most groups, who tirelessly parade their accusing signs in front of armories and arsenals, who regale us with virtuous exclamations like "I just can't understand how people can . . .!"—even they are trying the new, twentieth-century "interpersonal skills." Peace workers attend an ever-increasing number of workshops in which they deliberately learn from social workers and therapists how to set up conversations between adversaries in which the goal is to break down stereotyping habits, and replace them with "shared meanings," empathy, "partialization," and dozens of other cognitive procedures designed to halt inaccurate abstraction and subjective inference. I have deliberately used these social-work terms because they are the language of a new body of skills for change. They are *not* simply new horrible jargon for the Socratic method, as literary conservatives sometimes maintain: they are the new, if horrible, jargon for new, marvellous social change.

Dramatic use of these anti-stereotyping workshops has been made by the Center of Psychological Studies in a Nuclear Age, under the aegis of the Harvard Medical School at Cambridge Hospital. The Center actually takes high-level Soviet, American, and Third World physicians and others, puts them into workshop groups which spend whole days learning and practising therapeutic process.

Since social workers and therapists are onto new skills, we will learn them, too. We may spend some time bristling about it, first: then we will learn. Literature has much to offer in return: when it is not precious or fashionably fragmentary—when it takes on the big subjects—it can handily package a lot of human experience for social scientists. If teachers and students in graduate schools of social work were to use *Full Measure* as a text, I would suggest they read the book through once for pleasure and once for professional insight. When starting the second reading, they might make a list of the forty-five or forty-six elderly characters in the book. To the right of this list there would be three columns, respectively entitled Very Good Personal Qualities Which Actually Improve with Age, Special Efforts Which People Must Make When They Are Old, and Circumstances Which Enhance or Degrade Life Quality. For example, Professor Weber, in Oates's story, would have his new humility and swift life-saving work listed in the first column. Dr. Morris, in Bernard Malamud's "In Retirement," needs, for his Special Efforts Old People Must Make, simply to stop lusting after young women. Every one of the twenty-three stories in the book offers items for the third column—circumstances which help or damage our lives.

Most people studying therapy and social-work skills are two, if not three, generations younger than the clients they expect to serve. That means they need all the vicarious, mentally-imaged experience of middle age and old age they can lay hand to. They can't learn nearly so fast from their student-interviews with clients as one might think: literally hundreds of quarter-hours are wasted in generalizations, and in inaccurate, prematurely drawn conclusions. It takes most interviewees—as anyone knows who has collected oral histories—ages before they tell *the actual details of their lives*—those details which are the true source of meaning for themselves and for those working with them. An example: we are supposing that a middle-aged son of a dying mother is trying to discover his own change of feeling. Here is the kind of interview he might have with a student social worker:

> Interviewer: Let's see. You said that this last visit seemed different to you somehow. Can you say a little more about that?
>
> Client: Yes, she was different. Just really different. (Pause) Or anyway, I felt different towards her. I mean, what with the way she used to be so much. The way she always was with me when I was a kid. That all seemed different—*felt* different anyhow. Oh, I guess all it means is she is older and sicker.

It might take an inexperienced interviewer *hours* to develop that man's conversation to anything so specific as the following—taken from Richard Stern's story, "Dr Cahn's Visit":

> For the first time in his adult life, Will found her beautiful. Her flesh was mottled like a Pollock canvas, the facial skin trenched with the awful last ditches of self-defense, but her look melted him. It was human beauty. Day by day, manners that seemed as much a part of her as her eyes—fussiness, bossiness, nagging inquisitiveness—dropped away. She was down to what she was.

The paragraph illustrates a surprising subtlety in many middle-aged caretakers of the very aged: these middle-aged children go on being angry at their parents, perhaps, but they also make out a kinder underlayment to their parents' personalities. Richard Stern speeds up our ability to ask:

"Yes, I was feeling the same old such-and-such but what *else* was I feeling?" It is the great anti-stereotyping query.

Literature is the business of providing scenes so that readers can vicariously live them, but the fact is, beyond that, writers generally don't know how to make adults change. Readers read all the wonderful truths and say, "Oh, how accurate that is! I can relate to that, all right! Oh, how true of life that is! How he or she wonderfully points out virtues and evils!" but people don't change so quickly from all that reading as people change from learning twentieth-century interpersonal skills. Therefore, I hope that social workers will use these stories in their group-dynamics classes, in their dyads and triads, in their role-modeling exercises, in their comparisons of text learning and practicum learning. We are all of us convinced that Yeats was right:

> An aged man is but a paltry thing
> A tattered cloak upon a stick—unless
> Soul clap its hands and sing, and louder sing
> For every tatter in its mortal dress.

The question is: exactly *how* do we take in the fact of physiological loss and convert some of our conscious sense of that loss to spiritual gaiety? For such transformation we need both the genius of literature and the genius of therapeutic process—best of all, used together.

We'll want our humor, of course. Here we are, scared to get so old as Saul Bellow's Hattie, whose skin doesn't feel so much like her own skin any more as it feels simply like a container of her real self. What's more, Bellow tells us, her skin feels "much slept in."

That is going to take some humor—living in a skin much

slept in, trying hard to keep growing up, trying to maintain what decency we have and to acquire a little more, trying to learn more gaiety for every loss—while all the time we are floating closer to a universe that is more and more laid bare to us.

Here is a book of fellow travellers.

CAROL BLY

FOR MY SON

Full Measure

MODERN SHORT STORIES ON AGING

I

Leaving
the Yellow House

THE NEIGHBORS—there were in all six white
people who lived at Sego Desert Lake—told one another that
old Hattie could no longer make it alone. The desert life, even
with a forced-air furnace in the house and butane gas brought
from town in a truck, was still too difficult for her. There were
women even older than Hattie in the county. Twenty miles
away was Amy Walters, the gold miner's widow. But she was a
hardier old girl. Every day of the year she took a bath in the icy
lake. And Amy was crazy about money and knew how to manage it, as Hattie did not. Hattie was not exactly a drunkard, but
she hit the bottle pretty hard, and now she was in trouble and
there was a limit to the help she could expect from even the best
of neighbors.

They were fond of her, though. You couldn't help being fond
of Hattie. She was big and cheerful, puffy, comic, boastful, with
a big round back and stiff, rather long legs. Before the century
began she had graduated from finishing school and studied the
organ in Paris. But now she didn't know a note from a skillet.
She had tantrums when she played canasta. And all that remained of her fine fair hair was frizzled along her forehead in

small gray curls. Her forehead was not much wrinkled, but the skin was bluish, the color of skim milk. She walked with long strides in spite of the heaviness of her hips, pushing on, round-backed, with her shoulders and showing the flat rubber bottoms of her shoes.

Once a week, in the same cheerful, plugging but absent way, she took off her short skirt and the dirty aviator's jacket with the wool collar and put on a girdle, a dress, and high-heeled shoes. When she stood on these heels her fat old body trembled. She wore a big brown Rembrandt-like tam with a ten-cent-store brooch, eye-like, carefully centered. She drew a straight line with lipstick on her mouth, leaving part of the upper lip pale. At the wheel of her old turret-shaped car, she drove, seemingly methodical but speeding dangerously, across forty miles of mountainous desert to buy frozen meat pies and whisky. She went to the Laundromat and the hairdresser, and then had lunch with two martinis at the Arlington. Afterward she would often visit Marian Nabot's Silvermine Hotel at Miller Street near skid row and pass the rest of the day gossiping and drinking with her cronies, old divorcees like herself who had settled in the West. Hattie never gambled any more and she didn't care for the movies. And at five o'clock she drove back at the same speed, calmly, partly blinded by the smoke of her cigarette. The fixed cigarette gave her a watering eye.

The Rolfes and the Paces were her only white neighbors at Sego Desert Lake. There was Sam Jervis too, but he was only an old gandy-walker who did odd jobs in her garden, and she did not count him. Nor did she count among her neighbors Darly, the dudes' cowboy who worked for the Paces, nor Swede, the telegrapher. Pace had a guest ranch, and Rolfe and his wife were rich and had retired. Thus there were three good houses at the lake, Hattie's yellow house, Pace's, and the Rolfes'. All the rest of the population—Sam, Swede, Watchtah the section foreman, and the Mexicans and Indians and Negroes—lived in shacks and boxcars. There were very few trees, cottonwoods and box elders. Everything else, down to the shores, was sagebrush and juniper. The lake was what remained of an old sea that had covered the volcanic mountains. To the north there were some tungsten mines; to the south, fifteen miles, was an Indian village—shacks built of plywood or railroad ties.

In this barren place Hattie had lived for more than twenty years. Her first summer was spent not in a house but in an Indian wickiup on the shore. She used to say that she had watched the stars from this almost roofless shelter. After her divorce she took up with a cowboy named Wicks. Neither of them had any money—it was the Depression—and they had lived on the range, trapping coyotes for a living. Once a month they would come into town and rent a room and go on a bender. Hattie told this sadly, but also gloatingly, and with many trimmings. A thing no sooner happened to her than it was transformed into something else. "We were caught in a storm," she said, "and we rode hard, down to the lake and knocked on the door of the yellow house"—now her house. "Alice Parmenter took us in and let us sleep on the floor." What had actually happened was that the wind was blowing—there had been no storm—and they were not far from the house anyway; and Alice Parmenter, who knew that Hattie and Wicks were not married, offered them separate beds; but Hattie, swaggering, had said in a loud voice, "Why get two sets of sheets dirty?" And her and her cowboy had slept in Alice's bed while Alice had taken the sofa.

Then Wicks went away. There was never anybody like him in the sack; he was brought up in a whorehouse and the girls had taught him everything, said Hattie. She didn't really understand what she was saying but believed that she was being Western. More than anything else she wanted to be thought of as a rough, experienced woman of the West. Still, she was a lady, too. She had good silver and good china and engraved stationery, but she kept canned beans and A-1 sauce and tuna fish and bottles of catsup and fruit salad on the library shelves of her living room. On her night table was the Bible her pious brother Angus—the other brother was a heller—had given her; but behind the little door of the commode was a bottle of bourbon. When she awoke in the night she tippled herself back to sleep. In the glove compartment of her old car she kept little sample bottles for emergencies on the road. Old Darly found them after her accident.

The accident did not happen far out in the desert as she had always feared, but very near home. She had had a few martinis with the Rolfes one evening, and as she was driving home over the railroad crossing she lost control of the car and veered off the crossing onto the tracks. The explanation she gave was that she had sneezed, and the sneeze had blinded her and made her twist the wheel. The motor was killed and all four wheels of the car sat smack on the rails. Hattie crept down from the door, high off the roadbed. A great fear took hold of her—for the car, for the future, and not only for the future but spreading back into the past—and she began to hurry on stiff legs through the sagebrush to Pace's ranch.

Now the Paces were away on a hunting trip and had left Darly in charge; he was tending bar in the old cabin that went back to the days of the pony express, when Hattie burst in. There were two customers, a tungsten miner and his girl.

"Darly, I'm in trouble. Help me. I've had an accident," said Hattie.

How the face of a man will alter when a woman had bad news to tell him! It happened now to lean old Darly; his eyes went flat and looked unwilling, his jaw moved in and out, his wrinkled cheeks began to flush, and he said, "What's the matter—what's happened to you now?"

"I'm stuck on the tracks. I sneezed. I lost control of the car. Tow me off, Darly. With the pickup. Before the train comes."

Darly threw down his towel and stamped his high-heeled boots. "Now what have you gone and done?" he said. "I told you to stay home after dark."

"Where's Pace? Ring the fire bell and fetch Pace."

"There's nobody on the property except me," said the lean old man. "And I'm not supposed to close the bar and you know it as well as I do."

"Please, Darly, I can't leave my car on the tracks."

"Too bad!" he said. Nevertheless he moved from behind the bar. "How did you say it happened?"

"I told you, I sneezed," said Hattie.

Everyone, as she later told it, was as drunk as sixteen thousand dollars: Darly, the miner, and the miner's girl.

Darly was limping as he locked the door of the bar. A year before, a kick from one of Pace's mares had broken his ribs as he was loading her into the trailer, and he hadn't recovered from it. He was too old. But he dissembled the pain. The high-heeled narrow boots helped, and his painful bending looked like the ordinary stooping posture of a cowboy. However, Darly was not a genuine cowboy, like Pace who had grown up in the saddle. He was a late-comer from the East and until the age of forty had never been on horseback. In this respect he and Hattie were alike. They were not genuine Westerners.

Hattie hurried after him through the ranch yard.

"Damn you!" he said to her. "I got thirty bucks out of that sucker and I would have skinned him out of his whole pay check if you minded your business. Pace is going to be sore as hell."

"You've got to help me. We're neighbors," said Hattie.

"You're not fit to be living out here. You can't do it any more. Besides, you're swacked all the time."

Hattie couldn't afford to talk back. The thought of her car on the tracks made her frantic. If a freight came now and smashed it, her life at Sego Desert Lake would be finished. And where would she go then? She was not fit to live in this place. She had never made the grade at all, only seemed to have made it. And Darly—why did he say such hurtful things to her? Because he himself was sixty-eight years old, and he had no other place to go, either; he took bad treatment from Pace besides. Darly stayed because his only alternative was to go to the soldiers' home. Moreover, the dude women would still crawl into his sack. They wanted a cowboy and they thought he was one. Why, he couldn't even raise himself out of his bunk in the morning. And where else would he get women? "After the dude season," she wanted to say to him, "you always have to go to the Veterans' Hospital to get fixed up again." But she didn't dare offend him now.

The moon was due to rise. It appeared as they drove over the ungraded dirt road toward the crossing where Hattie's turret-shaped car was sitting on the rails. Driving very fast, Darly wheeled the pickup around, spraying dirt on the miner and his girl, who had followed in their car.

"You get behind the wheel and steer," Darly told Hattie.

She climbed into the seat. Waiting at the wheel, she lifted up her face and said, "Please God, I didn't bend the axle or crack the oil pan."

When Darly crawled under the bumper of Hattie's car the pain in his ribs suddenly cut off his breath, so instead of doubling the tow chain he fastened it at full length. He rose and trotted back to the truck on the tight boots. Motion seemed the only remedy for the pain; not even booze did the trick any more. He put the pickup into towing gear and began to pull. One side of Hattie's car dropped into the roadbed with a heave of springs. She sat with a stormy, frightened, conscience-stricken face, racing the motor until she flooded it.

The tungsten miner yelled, "Your chain's too long."

Hattie was raised high in the air by the pitch of the wheels. She had to roll down the window to let herself out because the door handle had been jammed from inside for years. Hattie struggled out on the uplifted side crying, "I better call the Swede. I better have him signal. There's a train due."

"Go on, then," said Darly. "You're no good here."

"Darly, be careful with my car. Be careful."

The ancient sea bed at this place was flat and low, and the lights of her car and of the truck and of the tungsten miner's

Chevrolet were bright and big at twenty miles. Hattie was too frightened to think of this. All she could think was that she was a procrastinating old woman, she had lived by delays; she had meant to stop drinking, she had put off the time, and now she had smashed her car—a terrible end, a terrible judgment on her. She got to the ground and, drawing up her skirt, she started to get over the tow chain. To prove that the chain didn't have to be shortened, and to get the whole thing over with, Darly threw the pickup forward again. The chain jerked up and struck Hattie in the knee and she fell forward and broke her arm.

She cried, "Darly, Darly, I'm hurt. I fell."

"The old lady tripped on the chain," said the miner. "Back up here and I'll double it for you. You're getting nowheres."

Drunkenly the miner lay down on his back in the dark, soft red cinders of the roadbed. Darly had backed up to slacken the chain.

Darly hurt the miner, too. He tore some skin from his fingers by racing ahead before the chain was secure. Without complaining, the miner wrapped his hand in his shirttail saying, "She'll do it now." The old car came down from the tracks and stood on the shoulder of the road.

"There's your goddamn car," said Darly to Hattie.

"Is it all right?" she said. Her left side was covered with dirt, but she managed to pick herself up and stand, roundbacked and heavy, on her stiff legs. "I'm hurt, Darly." She tried to convince him of it.

"Hell if you are," he said. He believed she was putting on an act to escape blame. The pain in his ribs made him especially impatient with her. "Christ, if you can't look after yourself any more you've got no business out here."

"You're old yourself," she said. "Look what you did to me. You can't hold your liquor."

This offended him greatly. He said, "I'll take you to the Rolfes. They let you booze it up in the first place, so let them worry about you. I'm tired of your bunk, Hattie."

He raced uphill. Chains, spade, and crowbar clashed on the

sides of the pickup. She was frightened and held her arm and cried. Rolfe's dogs jumped at her to lick her when she went through the gate. She shrank from them crying, "Down, down."

"Darly," she cried in the darkness, "take care of my car. Don't leave it standing there on the road. Darly, take care of it, please."

But Darly in his ten-gallon hat, his chin-bent face wrinkled, small and angry, a furious pain in his ribs, tore away at high speed.

"Oh, God, what will I do," she said.

The Rolfes were having a last drink before dinner, sitting at their fire of pitchy railroad ties, when Hattie opened the door. Her knee was bleeding, her eyes were tiny with shock, her face gray with dust.

"I'm hurt," she said desperately. "I had an accident. I sneezed and lost control of the wheel. Jerry, look after the car. It's on the road."

They bandaged her knee and took her home and put her to bed. Helen Rolfe wrapped a heating pad around her arm.

"I can't have the pad," Hattie complained. "The switch goes on and off, and every time it does it starts my generator and uses up the gas."

"Ah, now, Hattie," Rolfe said, "this is not the time to be stingy. We'll take you to town in the morning and have you looked over. Helen will phone Dr. Stroud."

Hattie wanted to say, "Stingy! Why you're the stingy ones. I just haven't got anything. You and Helen are ready to hit each other over two bits in canasta." But the Rolfes were good to her; they were her only real friends here. Darly would have let her lie in the yard all night, and Pace would have sold her to the bone man. He'd give her to the knacker for a buck.

So she didn't talk back to the Rolfes, but as soon as they left the yellow house and walked through the super-clear moonlight under the great skirt of box-elder shadows to their new station wagon, Hattie turned off the switch, and the heavy swirling and battering of the generator stopped. Presently she became aware of real pain, deeper pain, in her arm, and she sat rigid, warming the injured place with her hand. It seemed to her that she could feel the bone sticking out. Before leaving, Helen Rolfe had thrown over her a comforter that had belonged to Hattie's dead friend India, from whom she had inherited the small house and everything in it. Had the comforter lain on India's bed the night she died? Hattie tried to remember, but her thoughts were mixed up. She was fairly sure the deathbed pillow was in the loft, and she believed she had put the death bedding in a trunk. Then how had this comforter got out? She couldn't do anything about it now but draw it away from contact with her skin. It kept her legs warm. This she accepted, but she didn't want it any nearer.

More and more Hattie saw her own life as though, from birth to the present, every moment had been filmed. Her fancy was that when she died she would see the film shown. Then she would know how she had appeared from the back, watering the plants, in the bathroom, asleep, playing the organ, embracing—everything, even tonight, in pain, almost the last pain, perhaps, for she couldn't take much more. How many twists and angles had life to show her yet? There couldn't be much film left. To lie awake and think such thoughts was the worst thing in the world. Better death than insomnia. Hattie not only loved sleep, she believed in it.

THE FIRST ATTEMPT to set the bone was not successful. "Look what they've done to me," said Hattie and showed visitors the discolored breast. After the second operation her mind wandered. The sides of her bed had to be raised, for in her delirium she roamed the wards. She cursed at the nurses when they shut her in. "You can't make people prisoners in a democracy without a trial, you bitches." She had learned from Wicks how to swear. "*He* was profane," she used to say. "I picked it up unconsciously."

For several weeks her mind was not clear. Asleep, her face was lifeless; her cheeks were puffed out and her mouth, no longer wide and grinning, was drawn round and small. Helen sighed when she saw her.

"Shall we get in touch with her family?" Helen asked the doctor. His skin was white and thick. He had chestnut hair, abundant but very dry. He sometimes explained to his patients, "I had a tropical disease during the war."

He asked, "Is there a family?"

"Old brothers. Cousins' children," said Helen. She tried to think who would be called to her own bedside (she was old enough for that). Rolfe would see that she was cared for. He would hire private nurses. Hattie could not afford that. She had already gone beyond her means. A trust company in Philadelphia paid her eighty dollars a month. She had a small savings account.

"I suppose it'll be up to us to get her out of hock," said Rolfe. "Unless the brother down in Mexico comes across. We may have to phone one of those old guys."

IN THE END, no relations had to be called. Hattie began to recover. At last she could recognize visitors, though her mind was still in disorder. Much that had happened she couldn't recall.

"How many quarts of blood did they have to give me?" she kept asking. "I seem to remember five, six, eight different transfusions. Daylight, electric light . . . " She tried to smile, but she couldn't make a pleasant face as yet. "How am I going to pay?" she said. "At twenty-five bucks a quart. My little bit of money is just about wiped out."

Blood became her constant topic, her preoccupation. She told everyone who came to see her, "—have to replace all that blood. They poured gallons into me. Gallons. I hope it was all good." And, though very weak, she began to grin and laugh again. There was more hissing in her laughter than formerly; the illness had affected her chest.

"No cigarettes, no booze," the doctor told Helen.

"Doctor," Helen asked him, "do you expect her to change?"

"All the same, I am obliged to say it."

"Life sober may not be much of a temptation to her," said Helen.

Her husband laughed. When Rolfe's laughter was intense it blinded one of his eyes. His short Irish face turned red; on the bridge of his small, sharp nose the skin whitened. "Hattie's like me," he said. "She'll be in business till she's cleaned out. And if Sego Lake turned to whisky she'd use her last strength to knock her old yellow house down to build a raft of it. She'd float away on whisky. So why talk temperance?"

Hattie recognized the similarity between them. When he came to see her she said, "Jerry, you're the only one I can really talk to about my troubles. What am I going to do for money? I have Hotchkiss Insurance. I paid eight dollars a month."

"That won't do you much good, Hat. No Blue Cross?"

"I let it drop ten years ago. Maybe I could sell some of my valuables."

"What valuables have you got?" he said. His eye began to droop with laughter.

"Why," she said defiantly, "there's plenty. First there's the beautiful, precious Persian rug that India left me."

"Coals from the fireplace have been burning it for years, Hat!"

"The rug is in *perfect* condition," she said with an angry sway of the shoulders. "A beautiful object like that never loses its value. And the oak table from the Spanish monastery is three hundred years old."

"With luck you could get twenty bucks for it. It would cost fifty to haul it out of here. It's the house you ought to sell."

"The house?" she said. Yes, that had been in her mind. "I'd have to get twenty thousand for it."

"Eight is a fair price."

"Fifteen. . . . " She was offended, and her voice recovered its strength. "India put eight into it in two years. And don't forget that Sego Lake is one of the most beautiful places in the world."

"But where is it? Five hundred and some miles to San Francisco and two hundred to Salt Lake City. Who wants to live way out here but a few eccentrics like you and India? And me?"

"There are things you can't put a price tag on. Beautiful things."

"Oh, bull, Hattie! You don't know squat about beautiful things. Any more than I do. I live here because it figures for me, and you because India left you the house. And just in the nick of time, too. Without it you wouldn't have had a pot of your own."

His words offended Hattie; more than that, they frightened her. She was silent and then grew thoughtful, for she was fond of Jerry Rolfe and he of her. He had good sense and moreover he only expressed her own thoughts. He spoke no more than the truth about India's death and the house. But she told herself, He doesn't know everything. You'd have to pay a San Francisco architect ten thousand just to *think* of such a house. Before he drew a line.

"Jerry," the old woman said, "what am I going to do about replacing the blood in the blood bank?"

"Do you want a quart from me, Hat?" His eye began to fall shut.

"You won't do. You had that tumor, two years ago. I think Darly ought to give some."

"The old man?" Rolfe laughed at her. "You want to kill him?"

"Why!" said Hattie with anger, lifting up her massive face. Fever and perspiration had frayed the fringe of curls; at the back of the head the hair had knotted and matted so that it had to be shaved. "Darly almost killed me. It's his fault that I'm in this condition. He must have *some* blood in him. He runs after all the chicks—all of them—young and old."

"Come, you were drunk, too," said Rolfe.

"I've driven drunk for forty years. It was the sneeze. Oh, Jerry, I feel wrung out," said Hattie, haggard, sitting forward in bed. But her face was cleft by her nonsensically happy grin. She was not one to be miserable for long; she had the expression of a perennial survivor.

EVERY OTHER DAY she went to the therapist. The young woman worked her arm for her; it was a pleasure and a comfort to Hattie, who would have been glad to leave the whole cure to her. However, she was given other exercises to do, and these were not so easy. They rigged a pulley for her and Hattie had to hold both ends of a rope and saw it back and forth through the scraping little wheel. She bent heavily from the hips and coughed over her cigarette. But the most important exercise of all she shirked. This required her to put the flat of her hand to the wall at the level of her hips and, by working her finger tips slowly, to make the hand ascend to the height of her shoulder. That was painful; she often forgot to do it, although the doctor warned her, "Hattie, you don't want adhesions, do you?"

A light of despair crossed Hattie's eyes. Then she said, "Oh, Dr. Stroud, buy my house from me."

"I'm a bachelor. What would I do with a house?"

"I know just the girl for you—my cousin's daughter. Perfectly charming and very brainy. Just about got her Ph.D."

"You must get quite a few proposals yourself," said the doctor.

"From crazy desert rats. They chase me. But," she said, "after I pay my bills I'll be in pretty punk shape. If at least I could replace that blood in the blood bank I'd feel easier."

"If you don't do as the therapist tells you, Hattie, you'll need another operation. Do you know what adhesions are?"

She knew. But Hattie thought, *How long must I go on taking care of myself?* It made her angry to hear him speak of another operation. She had a moment of panic, but she covered it up. With him, this young man whose skin was already as thick as buttermilk and whose chestnut hair was as dry as death, she always assumed the part of a child. In a small voice she said, "Yes, doctor." But her heart was in a fury.

Night and day, however, she repeated, "I was in the Valley of the Shadow. But I'm alive." She was weak, she was old, she couldn't follow a train of thought very easily, she felt faint in the head. But she was still here; here was her body, it filled space, a great body. And though she had worries and perplexities, and once in a while her arm felt as though it was about to give her the last stab of all; and though her hair was scrappy and old, like onion roots, and scattered like nothing under the comb, yet she sat and amused herself with visitors; her great grin split her face; her heart warmed with every kind word.

And she thought, People will help me out. It never did me any good to worry. At the last minute something turned up, when I wasn't looking for it. Marian loves me. Helen and Jerry love me. Half Pint loves me. They would never let me go to the ground. And I love them. If it were the other way around, I'd never let them go down.

Above the horizon, in a baggy vastness which Hattie by herself occasionally visited, the features of India, her *shade*, sometimes rose. India was indignant and scolding. Not mean. Not really mean. Few people had ever been really mean to Hattie. But India was annoyed with her. "The garden is going to hell, Hattie," she said. "Those lilac bushes are all shriveled."

"But what can I do? The hose is rotten. It broke. It won't reach."

"Then dig a trench," said the phantom of India. "Have old Sam dig a trench. But save the bushes."

Am I thy servant still? said Hattie to herself. *No,* she thought, *let the dead bury their dead.*

But she didn't defy India now any more than she had done when they lived together. Hattie was supposed to keep India off the bottle, but often both of them began to get drunk after breakfast. They forgot to dress, and in their slips the two of them wandered drunkenly around the house and blundered into each other, and they were in despair at having been so weak. Late in the afternoon they would be sitting in the living room, waiting for the sun to set. It shrank, burning itself out on the crumbling edges of the mountains. When the sun passed, the fury of the daylight ended and the mountain surfaces were more blue, broken, like cliffs of coal. They no longer suggested faces. The east began to look simple, and the lake less inhuman and haughty. At last India would say, "Hattie—it's time for the lights." And Hattie would pull the switch chains of the lamps, several of them, to give the generator a good shove. She would turn on some of the wobbling eighteenth-century-style lamps whose shades stood out from their slender bodies like dragonflies' wings. The little engine in the shed would shuffle, then spit, then charge and bang, and the first weak light would rise unevenly in the bulbs.

"Hettie!" cried India. After she drank she was penitent, but her penitence too was a hardship to Hattie, and the worse her temper the more British her accent became. *"Where the hell ah you Het-tie!"* After India's death Hattie found some poems she had written in which she, Hattie, was affectionately and even touchingly mentioned. That was a good thing—Literature. Education. Breeding. But Hattie's interest in ideas was very small, whereas India had been all over the world. India was used to brilliant society. India wanted her to discuss Eastern religion, Bergson and Proust, and Hattie had no head for this, and so India blamed her drinking on Hattie. "I can't talk to you," she would say. "You don't understand religion or culture. And I'm here because I'm not fit to be anywhere else. I can't live in New York any more. It's too dangerous for a woman my age to be drunk in the street at night."

And Hattie, talking to her Western friends about India, would say, "She is a lady" (implying that they made a pair). "She is a creative person" (this was why they found each other so congenial). "But helpless? Completely. Why she can't even get her own girdle on."

"Hettie! Come here. Het-tie! Do you know what sloth is?"

Undressed, India sat on her bed and with the cigarette in her drunken, wrinkled, ringed hand she burned holes in the blankets. On Hattie's pride she left many small scars, too. She treated her like a servant.

Weeping, India begged her afterward to forgive her. *"Hattie, please don't condemn me in your heart. Forgive me, dear, I know I am bad. But I hurt myself more in my evil than I hurt you."*

Hattie would keep a stiff bearing. She would lift up her face with its incurved nose and puffy eyes and say, "I am a Christian person. I never bear a grudge." And by repeating this she actually brought herself to forgive India.

But of course Hattie had no husband, no child, no skill, no savings. And what she would have done if India had not died and left her the yellow house nobody knows.

Jerry Rolfe said privately to Marian, "Hattie can't do anything for herself. If I hadn't been around during the forty-four blizzard she and India both would have starved. She's always been careless and lazy and now she can't even chase a cow out of the yard. She's too feeble. The thing for her to do is to go East to her damn brother. Hattie would have ended at the poor farm if it hadn't been for India. But besides the damn house India should have left her some dough. She didn't use her goddamn head."

WHEN HATTIE returned to the lake she stayed with the Rolfes. "Well, old shellback," said Jerry, "there's a little more life in you now."

Indeed, with joyous eyes, the cigarette in her mouth and her hair newly frizzed and overhanging her forehead, she seemed to have triumphed again. She was pale, but she grinned, she chuckled, and she held a bourbon old-fashioned with a cherry and a slice of orange in it. She was on rations; the Rolfes allowed her two a day. Her back, Helen noted, was more bent than before. Her knees went outward a little weakly; her feet, however, came close together at the ankles.

"Oh, Helen dear and Jerry dear, I am so thankful, so glad to be back at the lake. I can look after my place again, and I'm here to see the spring. It's more gorgeous than ever."

Heavy rains had fallen while Hattie was away. The sego lilies, which bloomed only after a wet winter, came up from the loose dust, especially around the marl pit; but even on the burnt granite they seemed to grow. Desert peach was beginning to appear, and in Hattie's yard the rosebushes were filling out. The roses were yellow and abundant, and the odor they gave off was like that of damp tea leaves.

"Before it gets hot enough for the rattlesnakes," said Hattie to Helen, "we ought to drive up to Marky's ranch and gather watercress."

Hattie was going to attend to lots of things, but the heat came early that year and, as there was no television to keep her awake, she slept most of the day. She was now able to dress herself, though there was little more that she could do. Sam Jervis rigged the pulley for her on the porch and she remembered once in a while to use it. Mornings when she had her strength she rambled over to her own house, examining things, being important and giving orders to Sam Jervis and Wanda Gingham. At ninety, Wanda, a Shoshone, was still an excellent seamstress and housecleaner.

Hattie looked over the car, which was parked under a cotton-wood tree. She tested the engine. Yes, the old pot would still go. Proudly, happily, she listened to the noise of tappets; the dry old pipe shook as the smoke went out at the rear. She tried to work the shift, turn the wheel. That, as yet, she couldn't do. But it would come soon, she was confident.

At the back of the house the soil had caved in a little over the cesspool and a few of the old railroad ties over the top had rotted. Otherwise things were in good shape. Sam had looked after the garden. He had fixed a new catch for the gate after Pace's horses—maybe because he could never afford to keep them in hay—had broken in and Sam found them grazing and drove them out. Luckily, they hadn't damaged many of her plants. Hattie felt a moment of wild rage against Pace. He had brought the horses into her garden for a free feed, she was sure. But her anger didn't last long. It was reabsorbed into the feeling of golden pleasure that enveloped her. She had little strength, but all that she had was a pleasure to her. So she forgave even Pace, who would have liked to do her out of the house, who had always used her, embarrassed her, cheated her at cards, swindled her. All that he did he did for the sake of his quarter horses. He was a fool about horses. They were ruining him. Racing horses was a millionaire's amusement.

She saw his animals in the distance, feeding. Unsaddled, the mares appeared undressed; they reminded her of naked women walking with their glossy flanks in the sego lilies which curled on the ground. The flowers were yellowish like winter wool, but fragrant; the mares, naked and gentle, walked through them. Their strolling, their perfect beauty, the sound of their hoofs on stone touched a deep place in Hattie's nature. Her love for horses, birds, and dogs was well known. Dogs led the list. And now a piece cut from a green blanket reminded Hattie of her dog Richie. The blanket was one he had torn, and she had cut it into strips and placed them under the doors to keep out the drafts. In the house she found more traces of him: hair he had shed on the furniture. Hattie was going to borrow Helen's vacuum cleaner, but there wasn't really enough current to make it pull as it should. On the doorknob of India's room hung the dog collar.

Hattie had decided that she would have herself moved into India's bed when it was time to die. Why should there be two deathbeds? A perilous look came into her eyes, her lips were pressed together forbiddingly. *I follow*, she said, speaking to India with an inner voice, *so never mind*. Presently—before long—she would have to leave the yellow house in her turn. And as she went into the parlor, thinking of the will, she sighed. Pretty soon she would have to attend to it. India's lawyer, Claiborne, helped her with such things. She had phoned him in town, while she was staying with Marian, and talked matters over with him. He had promised to try to sell the house for her. Fifteen thousand was her bottom price, she said. If he couldn't find a buyer, perhaps he could find a tenant. Two hundred dollars a month was the rental she set. Rolfe laughed. Hattie turned toward him one of those proud, dulled looks she always took on when he angered her. Haughtily she said, "For summer on Sego Lake? That's reasonable."

"You're competing with Pace's ranch."

"Why, the food is stinking down there. And he cheats the dudes," said Hattie. "He really cheats them at cards. You'll never catch me playing blackjack with him again."

And what would she do, thought Hattie, if Claiborne could neither rent nor sell the house? This question she shook off as regularly as it returned. *I don't have to be a burden on anybody*, thought Hattie. *It's looked bad many a time before, but when push came to shove, I made it. Somehow I got by.* But she argued with herself: *How many times? How long, O God—an old thing, feeble, no use to anyone?* Who said she had any right to own property?

She was sitting on her sofa, which was very old—India's sofa—eight feet long, kidney-shaped, puffy, and bald. An underlying pink shone through the green; the upholstered tufts were like the pads of dogs' paws; between them rose bunches of hair. Here Hattie slouched, resting, with knees wide apart and a cigarette in her mouth, eyes half-shut but farseeing. The mountains seemed not fifteen miles but fifteen hundred feet away, the lake a blue band; the tealike odor of the roses, though they were still unopened, was already in the air, for Sam was watering them in the heat. Gratefully Hattie yelled, "Sam!"

Sam was very old, and all shanks. His feet looked big. His old railroad jacket was made tight across the back by his stoop. A crooked finger with its great broad nail over the mouth of the hose made the water spray and sparkle. Happy to see Hattie, he turned his long jaw, empty of teeth, and his long blue eyes, which seemed to bend back to penetrate into his temples (it was his face that turned, not his body), and he said, "Oh, there, Hattie. You've made it home today? Welcome, Hattie."

"Have a beer, Sam. Come around the kitchen door and I'll give you a beer."

She never had Sam in the house, owing to his skin disease. There were raw patches on his chin and behind his ears. Hattie feared infection from his touch, having decided that he had impetigo. She gave him the beer can, never a glass, and she put on gloves before she used the garden tools. Since he would take no money from her—Wanda Gingham charged a dollar a day—she got Marian to find old clothes for him in town and she left food for him at the door of the damp-wood-smelling boxcar where he lived.

"How's the old wing, Hat?" he said.

"It's coming. I'll be driving the car again before you know it," she told him. "By the first of May I'll be driving again." Every week she moved the date forward. "By Decoration Day I expect to be on my own again," she said.

In mid-June, however, she was still unable to drive. Helen Rolfe said to her, "Hattie, Jerry and I are due in Seattle the first week of July."

"Why, you never told me that," said Hattie.

"You don't mean to tell me this is the first you heard of it," said Helen. "You've known about it from the first—since Christmas."

It wasn't easy for Hattie to meet her eyes. She presently put her head down. Her face became very dry, especially the lips. "Well, don't you worry about me. I'll be all right here," she said.

"Who's going to look after you?" said Jerry. He evaded nothing himself and tolerated no evasion in others. Except that, as Hattie knew, he made every possible allowance for her. But who would help her? She couldn't count on her friend Half Pint, she couldn't really count on Marian either. She had had only the Rolfes to turn to. Helen, trying to be steady, gazed at her and made sad, involuntary movements with her head, sometimes nodding, sometimes seeming as if she disagreed. Hattie, with her inner voice, swore at her: *Bitch-eyes. I can't make it the way she does because I'm old. Is that fair?* And yet she admired Helen's eyes. Even the skin about them, slightly wrinkled, heavy underneath, was touching, beautiful. There was a heaviness in her bust that went, as if by attachment, with the heaviness of her eyes. Her head, her hands and feet should have taken a more slender body. Helen, said Hattie, was the nearest thing she had on earth to a sister. But there was no reason to go to Seattle—no genuine business. Why the hell Seattle? It was only idleness, only a holiday. The only reason was Hattie herself; this was their way of telling her that there was a limit to what she could expect them to do for her. Helen's nervous head wavered, but her thoughts were steady. She knew what was passing through Hattie's mind. Like Hattie, she was an idle woman. Why was her right to idleness better?

Because of money? thought Hattie. Because of age? Because she has a husband? Because she had a daughter in Swarthmore College? But an interesting thing occurred to her. Helen disliked being idle, whereas Hattie herself had never made any bones about it: an idle life was all she was good for. But for her it had been uphill all the way, because when Waggoner divorced her she didn't have a cent. She even had to support Wicks for seven or eight years. Except with horses, Wicks had no sense. And then she had had to take tons of dirt from India. *I am the one,* Hattie asserted to herself. *I would know what to do with Helen's advantages. She only suffers from them. And if she wants to stop being an idle woman why can't she start with me, her neighbor?* Hattie's skin, for all its puffiness, burned with anger. She said to

Rolfe and Helen, "Don't worry. I'll make out. But if I have to leave the lake you'll be ten times more lonely than before. Now I'm going back to my house."

She lifted up her broad old face, and her lips were childlike with suffering. She would never take back what she had said.

But the trouble was no ordinary trouble. Hattie was herself aware that she rambled, forgot names, and answered when no one spoke.

"We can't just take charge of her," Rolfe said. "What's more, she ought to be near a doctor. She keeps her shotgun loaded so she can fire it if anything happens to her in the house. But who knows what she'll shoot? I don't believe it was Jacamares who killed that Doberman of hers."

Rolfe drove into the yard the day after she moved back to the yellow house and said, "I'm going into town. I can bring you some chow if you like."

She couldn't afford to refuse his offer, angry though she was, and she said, "Yes, bring me some stuff from the Mountain Street Market. Charge it." She had only some frozen shrimp and a few cans of beer in the icebox. When Rolfe had gone she put out the package of shrimp to thaw.

People really used to stick by one another in the West. Hattie now saw herself as one of the pioneers. The modern breed had come later. After all, she had lived on the range like an old-timer. Wicks had had to shoot their Christmas dinner and she had cooked it—venison. He killed it on the reservation, and if the Indians had caught them, there would have been hell to pay.

The weather was hot, the clouds were heavy and calm in the large sky. The horizon was so huge that in it the lake must have seemed like a saucer of milk. *Some milk!* Hattie thought. Two thousand feet down in the middle, so deep no corpse could ever be recovered. A body, they said, went around with the currents. And there were rocks like eye-teeth, and hot springs, and color-less fish at the bottom which were never caught. Now that the white pelicans were nesting they patrolled the rocks for snakes and other egg thieves. They were so big and flew so slow you might imagine they were angels. Hattie no longer visited the lake shore; the walk exhausted her. She saved her strength to go to Pace's bar in the afternoon.

She took off her shoes and stockings and walked on bare feet from one end of her house to the other. On the land side she saw Wanda Gingham sitting near the tracks while her great-grandson played in the soft red gravel. Wanda wore a large purple shawl and her black head was bare. All about her was—was nothing, Hattie thought; for she had taken a drink, breaking her rule. Nothing but mountains, thrust out like men's bodies; the sagebrush was the hair on their chests.

The warm wind blew dust from the marl pit. This white powder made her sky less blue. On the water side were the pelicans, pure as spirits, slow as angels, blessing the air as they flew with great wings.

Should she or should she not have Sam do something about the vine on the chimney? Sparrows nested in it, and she was glad of that. But all summer long the king snakes were after them and she was afraid to walk in the garden. When the sparrows scratched the ground for seed they took a funny bound; they held their legs stiff and flung back the dust with both feet. Hattie sat down at her old Spanish monastery table, watching them in the cloudy warmth of the day, clasping her hands, chuckling and sad. The bushes were crowded with yellow roses, half of them now rotted. The lizards scrambled from shadow to shadow. The water was smooth as air, gaudy as silk. The mountains succumbed, falling asleep in the heat. Drowsy, Hattie lay down on her sofa. Its pads were like dogs' paws. She gave in to sleep and when she woke it was midnight; she did not want to alarm the Rolfes by putting on her lights so took advantage of the moon to eat a few thawed shrimps and go to the bathroom. She undressed and lifted herself into bed and lay there feeling her sore arm. Now she knew how much she missed her dog. The whole matter of the dog weighed heavily on her soul. She came close to tears, thinking about him, and she went to sleep oppressed by her secret.

I suppose I had better try to pull myself together a little, thought Hattie nervously in the morning. *I can't just sleep my way through.* She knew what her difficulty was. Before any serious question her mind gave way. It scattered or diffused. She said to herself, *I can see bright, but I feel dim. I guess I'm not so lively any more. Maybe I'm becoming a little touched in the head, as Mother was.* But she was not so old as her mother was when she did those strange things. At eighty-five, her mother had to be kept from going naked in the street. *I'm not as bad as that yet. Thank God! Yes, I walked into the men's wards, but that was when I had a fever, and my nightie was on.*

She drank a cup of Nescafé and it strengthened her determination to do something for herself. In all the world she had only her brother Angus to go to. Her brother Will had led a rough life; he was an old heller, and now he drove everyone away. He was too crabby, thought Hattie. Besides he was angry because she had lived so long with Wicks. Angus would forgive her. But then he and his wife were not her kind. With them she couldn't drink, she couldn't smoke, she had to make herself small-mouthed, and she would have to wait while they read a chapter of the Bible before breakfast. Hattie could not bear to sit at table waiting for meals. Besides, she had a house of her own at last. Why should she have to leave it? She had never owned a thing before. And now she was not allowed to enjoy her yellow house. *But I'll keep it,* she said to herself rebelliously. *I swear to God I'll keep it. Why, I barely just got it. I haven't had time.* And she went out on the porch to work the pully and do something about the adhesions in her arm. She was sure now that they were there. *And what will I do?* she cried to herself. *What will I do? Why did I ever go to Rolfe's that night—and why did I lose control on the crossing?* She couldn't say, now, "I sneezed." She couldn't even remember what had happened, except that she saw the boulders and the twisting blue rails and Darly. It was

Darly's fault. He was sick and old himself. *He* couldn't make it. He envied her the house, and her woman's peaceful life. Since she returned from the hospital he hadn't even come to visit her. He only said, "Hell, I'm sorry for her, but it was her fault." What hurt him most was that she had said he couldn't hold his liquor.

FIERCENESS, swearing to God did no good. She was still the same procrastinating old woman. She had a letter to answer from Hotchkiss Insurance and it drifted out of sight. She was going to phone Claiborne the lawyer, but it slipped her mind. One morning she announced to Helen that she believed she would apply to an institution in Los Angeles that took over the property of old people and managed it for them. They gave you an apartment right on the ocean, and your meals and medical care. You had to sign over half of your estate. "It's fair enough," said Hattie. "They take a gamble. I may live to be a hundred."

"I wouldn't be surprised," said Helen.

However, Hattie never got around to sending to Los Angeles for the brochure. But Jerry Rolfe took it on himself to write a letter to her brother Angus about her condition. And he drove over also to have a talk with Amy Walters, the gold miner's widow at Fort Walters—as the ancient woman called it. The Fort was an old tar-paper building over the mine. The shaft made a cesspool unnecessary. Since the death of her second husband no one had dug for gold. On a heap of stones near the road a crimson sign FORT WALTERS was placed. Behind it was a flagpole. The American flag was raised every day.

Amy was working in the garden in one of dead Bill's shirts. Bill had brought water down from the mountains for her in a homemade aqueduct so she could raise her own peaches and vegetables.

"Amy," Rolfe said, "Hattie's back from the hospital and living all alone. You have no folks and neither has she. Not to beat around the bush about it, why don't you live together?"

Amy's face had great delicacy. Her winter baths in the lake, her vegetable soups, the waltzes she played for herself alone on the grand piano that stood beside her wood stove, the murder stories she read till darkness obliged her to close the book—this life of hers had made her remote. She looked delicate, yet there was no way to affect her composure, she couldn't be touched. It was very strange.

"Hattie and me have different habits, Jerry," said Amy. "And Hattie wouldn't like my company. I can't drink with her. I'm a teetotaller."

"That's true," said Rolfe, recalling that Hattie referred to Amy as if she were a ghost. He couldn't speak to Amy of the solitary death in store for her. There was not a cloud in the arid sky today, and there was no shadow of death on Amy. She was tranquil, she seemed to be supplied with a sort of pure fluid that would feed her life slowly for years to come.

He said, "All kinds of things could happen to a woman like Hattie in that yellow house, and nobody would know."

"That's a fact. She doesn't know how to take care of herself."

"She can't. Her arm hasn't healed."

Amy didn't say that she was sorry to hear it. In the place of those words came a silence which might have meant that. Then she said, "I might go over there a few hours a day, but she would have to pay me."

"Now, Amy, you must know as well as I do that Hattie has no money—not much more than her pension. Just the house."

At once Amy said, no pause coming between his words and hers, "I would take care of her if she'd agree to leave the house to me."

"Leave it in your hands, you mean?" said Rolfe. "To manage?"

"In her will. To belong to me."

"Why, Amy, what would you do with Hattie's house?" he said.

"It would be my property, that's all. I'd have it."

"Maybe you would leave Fort Walters to her in your will," he said.

"Oh, no," she said. "Why should I? I'm not asking Hattie for her help. I don't need it. Hattie is a city woman."

ROLFE COULD NOT carry this proposal back to Hattie. He was too wise ever to mention her will to her.

But Pace was not so careful of her feelings. By mid-June Hattie had begun to visit his bar regularly. She had so many things to think about she couldn't stay at home. When Pace came in from the yard one day—he had been packing the wheels of his horse-trailer and was wiping grease from his fingers—he said with his usual bluntness, "How would you like it if I paid you fifty bucks a month for the rest of your life, Hat?"

Hattie was holding her second old-fashioned of the day. At the bar she made it appear that she observed the limit; but she had started drinking at home. One before lunch, one during, one after lunch. She began to grin, expecting Pace to make one of his jokes. But he was wearing his scoop-shaped Western hat as level as a Quaker, and he had drawn down his chin, a sign that he was not fooling. She said, "That would be nice, but what's the catch?"

"No catch," he said. "This is what we'd do. I'd give you five hundred dollars cash, and fifty bucks a month for life, and you let me sleep some dudes in the yellow house, and you'd leave the house to me in your will."

"What kind of a deal is that?" said Hattie, her look changing. "I thought we were friends."

"It's the best deal you'll ever get," he said.

The weather was sultry, but Hattie till now had thought that it was nice. She had been dreamy but comfortable, about to begin to enjoy the cool of the day; but now she felt that such cruelty and injustice had been waiting to attack her, that it would have been better to die in the hospital than be so disillusioned.

She cried, "Everybody wants to push me out. You're a cheater, Pace. God! I know you. Pick on somebody else. Why do you have to pick on me? Just because I happen to be around?"

"Why, no, Hattie," he said, trying now to be careful. "It was just a business offer."

"Why don't you give me some blood for the bank if you're such a friend of mine?"

"Well, Hattie, you drink too much and you oughtn't to have been driving anyway."

"I sneezed, and you know it. The whole thing happened because I sneezed. Everybody knows that. I wouldn't sell you my house. I'd give it away to the lepers first. You'd let me go away and never send me a cent. You never pay anybody. You can't even buy wholesale in town any more because nobody trusts you. I'm stuck, that's all, just stuck. I keep on saying that this is my only home in all the world, this is where my friends are, and the weather is always perfect and the lake is beautiful. But I wish the whole damn empty old place were in Hell. It's not human and neither are you. But I'll be here the day the sheriff takes away your horses—you never mind! I'll be clapping and applauding!"

He told her then that she was drunk again, and so she was, but she was more than that, and though her head was spinning she decided to go back to the house at once and take care of some things she had been putting off. This very day she was going to write to the lawyer, Claiborne, and make sure that Pace never got her property. She wouldn't put it past him to swear in court that India had promised him the yellow house.

She sat at the table with pen and paper, trying to think how to put it.

"I want this on record," she wrote. "I could kick myself in the head when I think of how he's led me on. I have been his patsy ten thousand times. As when that drunk crashed his Cub plane on the lake shore. At the coroner's jury he let me take the whole blame. He said he had instructed me when I was working for him never to take in any drunks. And this flier was drunk. He had nothing on but a T shirt and Bermuda shorts and he was flying from Sacramento to Salt Lake City. At the inquest Pace said I had disobeyed his instructions. The same was true when the cook went haywire. She was a tramp. He never hires decent help. He cheated her on the bar bill and blamed me and she went after me with a meat cleaver. She disliked me because I criticized her for drinking at the bar in her one-piece white bathing suit with the dude guests. But he turned her loose on me. He hints that he did certain services for India. She would never have let him touch one single finger. He was too common for her. It can never be said about India that she was not a lady in every way. He thinks he is the greatest sack-artist in the world. He only loves horses, as a fact. He has no claims at all, oral or written, on this yellow house. I want you to have this over my signature. He was cruel to Pickle-Tits who was his first wife, and he's no better to the charming woman who is his present one. I don't know why she takes it. It must be despair." Hattie said to herself, *I don't suppose I'd better send that.*

She was still angry. Her heart was knocking within; the deep pulses, as after a hot bath, beat at the back of her thighs. The air outside was dotted with transparent particles. The mountains were as red as furnace clinkers. The iris leaves were fan sticks —they stuck out like Jiggs's hair.

She always ended by looking out of the window at the desert and lake. *They drew you from yourself. But after they had drawn you, what did they do with you? It was too late to find out. I'll never know. I wasn't meant to. I'm not the type,* Hattie reflected. *Maybe something too cruel for women, young or old.*

So she stood up and, rising, she had the sensation that she had gradually become a container for herself. You get old, your heart, your liver, your lungs seem to expand in size, and the walls of the body give way outward, swelling, she thought, and you take the shape of an old jug, wider and wider toward the top.

You swell up with tears and fat. She no longer even smelled to herself like a woman. Her face with its much-slept-upon skin was only faintly like her own—like a cloud that has changed. It was a face. It became a ball of yarn. It had drifted open. It had scattered.

I was never one single thing anyway, she thought. *Never my own. I was only loaned to myself.*

But the thing wasn't over yet. And in fact she didn't know for certain that it was ever going to be over. You only had other people's word for it that death was such-and-such. How do I know? she asked herself challengingly. Her anger had sobered her for a little while. Now she was again drunk. . . . *It was strange. It is strange. It may continue being strange.* She further thought, *I used to wish for death more than I do now. Because I didn't have anything at all. I changed when I got a roof of my own over me. And now? Do I have to go? I thought Marian loved me, but she already has a sister. And I thought Helen and Jerry would never desert me, but they've beat it. And now Pace has insulted me. They think I'm not going to make it.*

She went to the cupboard—she kept the bourbon bottle there; she drank less if each time she had to rise and open the cupboard door. And, as if she were being watched, she poured a drink and swallowed it.

The notion that in this emptiness someone saw her was connected with the other notion that she was being filmed from birth to death. That this was done for everyone. And afterward you could view your life. A hereafter movie.

Hattie wanted to see some of it now, and she sat down on the dogs'-paw cushions of her sofa and, with her knees far apart and a smile of yearning and of fright, she bent her round back, burned a cigarette at the corner of her mouth and saw—the Church of Saint Sulpice in Paris where her organ teacher used to bring her. It looked like country walls of stone, but rising high and leaning outward were towers. She was very young. She knew music. How she could ever have been so clever was beyond her. But she did know it. She could read all those notes. The sky was gray. After this she saw some entertaining things she liked to tell people about. She was a young wife. She was in Aix-les-Bains with her mother-in-law, and they played bridge in a mud bath with a British general and his aide. There were artificial waves in the swimming pool. She lost her bathing suit because it was a size too big. How did she get out? Ah, you got out of everything.

She saw her husband, James John Waggoner IV. They were snow-bound together in New Hampshire. "Jimmy, Jimmy, how can you fling a wife away?" she asked him. "Have you forgotten love? Did I drink too much—did I bore you?" He had married again and had two children. He had gotten tired of her. And though he was a vain man with nothing to be vain about—no looks, not too much intelligence, nothing but an old Philadelphia family—she had loved him. She too had been a snob about her Philadelphia connections. Give up the name of Waggoner? How could she? For this reason she had never married Wicks. "How dare you," she had said to Wicks, "come without a shave in a dirty shirt and muck on you, come and ask me to marry! If you want to propose, go and clean up first." But his dirt was only a pretext.

Trade Waggoner for Wicks? she asked herself again with a swing of her shoulders. She wouldn't think of it. Wicks was an excellent man. But he was a cowboy. Socially nothing. He couldn't even read. But she saw this on her film. They were in Athens Canyon, in a cratelike house, and she was reading aloud to him from *The Count of Monte Cristo*. He wouldn't let her stop. While walking to stretch her legs, she read, and he followed her about to catch each word. After all, he was very dear to her. Such a man! Now she saw him jump from his horse. They were living on the range, trapping coyotes. It was just the second gray of evening, cloudy, moments after the sun had gone down. There was an animal in the trap, and he went toward it to kill it. He wouldn't waste a bullet on the creatures but killed them with a kick, with his boot. And then Hattie saw that this coyote was all white—snarling teeth, white scruff. "Wicks, he's white! White as a polar bear. You're not going to kill him, are you?" The animal flattened to the ground. He snarled and cried. He couldn't pull away because of the heavy trap. And Wicks killed him. What else could he have done? The white beast lay dead. The dust of Wicks's boots hardly showed on its head and jaws. Blood ran from the muzzle.

AND NOW came something on Hattie's film she tried to shun. It was she herself who had killed her dog, Richie. Just as Rolfe and Pace had warned her, he was vicious, his brain was turned. She, because she was on the side of all dumb creatures, defended him when he bit the trashy woman Jacamares was living with. Perhaps if she had had Richie from a puppy he wouldn't have turned on her. When she got him he was already a year and a half old and she couldn't break him of his habits. But she thought that only she understood him. And Rolfe had warned her, "You'll be sued, do you know that? The dog will take out after somebody smarter than that Jacamares's woman, and you'll be in for it."

Hattie saw herself as she swayed her shoulders and said, "Nonsense."

But what fear she had felt when the dog went for her on the porch. Suddenly she could see, by his skull, by his eyes that he was evil. She screamed at him, "Richie!" And what had she done to him? He had lain under the gas range all day growling and wouldn't come out. She tried to urge him out with the broom, and he snatched it in his teeth. She pulled him out, and he left the stick and tore at her. Now, as the spectator of this, her eyes opened, beyond the pregnant curtain and the air-wave of marl dust, summer's snow, drifting over the water. "Oh, my God! Richie!" Her thigh was snatched by his jaws. His teeth went through her skirt. She felt she would fall. Would she go down? Then the dog would rush at her throat—then black night, bad-odored mouth, the blood pouring from her neck, from torn veins. Her heart shriveled as the teeth went into her thigh, and she couldn't delay another second but took her kindling hatchet from the nail, strengthened her grip on the smooth wood, and hit the dog. She saw the blow. She saw him die at once. And then in fear and shame she hid the body. And at night she buried him in the yard. Next day she accused Jacamares. On him she laid the blame for the disappearance of her dog.

She stood up; she spoke to herself in silence, as was her habit. *God, what shall I do? I have taken life. I have lied. I have borne false witness. I have stalled. And now what shall I do? Nobody will help me.*

And suddenly she made up her mind that she should go and do what she had been putting off for weeks, namely test herself with the car, and she slipped on her shoes and went outside. Lizards ran before her in the thirsty dust. She opened the hot, broad door of the car. She lifted her lame hand onto the wheel. Her right hand she reached far to the left and turned the wheel with all her might. Then she started the motor and tried to drive out of the yard. But she could not release the emergency brake with its rasplike rod. She reached with her good hand, the right, under the steering wheel and pressed her bosom on it and strained. No, she could not shift the gears and steer. She couldn't even reach down to the hand brake. The sweat broke out on her skin. Her efforts were too much. She was deeply wounded by the pain in her arm. The door of the car fell open again and she turned from the wheel and with her stiff legs hanging from the door she wept. What could she do now? And when she had wept over the ruin of her life she got out of the old car and went back to the house. She took the bourbon from the cupboard and picked up the ink bottle and a pad of paper and sat down to write her will.

"My Will," she wrote, and sobbed to herself.

Since the death of India she had numberless times asked the question, To Whom? Who will get this when I die? She had unconsciously put people to the test to find out whether they were worthy. It made her more severe than before.

Now she wrote, "I Harriet Simmons Waggoner, being of sound mind and not knowing what may be in store for me at the age of seventy-two (born 1885), living alone at Sego Desert Lake, instruct my lawyer, Harold Claiborne, Paiute County Court Building, to draw my last will and testament upon the following terms."

She sat perfectly still now to hear from within who would be the lucky one, who would inherit the yellow house. For which she had waited. Yes, waited for India's death, choking on her bread because she was a rich woman's servant and whipping girl. But who had done for her, Hattie, what she had done for India? And who, apart from India, had ever held out a hand to her? Kindness, yes. Here and there people had been kind. But the word in her head was not kindness, it was succor. And who had given her that? *Succor?* Only India. If at least, next best after succor, someone had given her a shake and said, "Stop stalling. Don't be such a slow, old, procrastinating sit-stiller." Again, it was only India who had done her good. She had offered her succor. "Het-tie!" said that drunken mask. "Do you know what sloth is? Demn you! poky old demned thing!"

But I was waiting, Hattie realized. *I was waiting, thinking, "Youth is terrible, frightening. I will wait it out. And men? Men are cruel and strong. They want things I haven't got to give."* There were no kids in me, thought Hattie. *Not that I wouldn't have loved them, but such my nature was. And who can blame me for having it? My nature?*

She drank from an old-fashioned glass. There was no orange in it, no ice, no bitters or sugar, only the stinging, clear bourbon.

So then, she continued, looking at the dry sun-stamped dust and the last freckled flowers of red wild peach, *to live with Angus and his wife? And to have to hear a chapter from the Bible before breakfast? Once more in the house—not of a stranger, perhaps, but not far from it either?* In other houses, in someone else's house, to wait for mealtimes was her lifelong punishment. She always felt it in the throat and stomach. And so she would again, and to the very end. However, she must think of someone to leave the house to.

And first of all she wanted to do right by her family. None of them had ever dreamed that she, Hattie, would ever have something to bequeath. Until a few years ago it had certainly looked as if she would die a pauper. So now she could keep her head up with the proudest of them. And, as this occurred to her, she actually lifted up her face with its broad nose and victorious eyes; if her hair had become shabby as onion roots, if, at the back, her head was round and bald as a newel post, what did that matter? Her heart experienced a childish glory, not yet tired of it after seventy-two years. She, too, had amounted to something. *I'll do some good by going,* she thought. *Now I believe I should leave it to, to* . . . She returned to the old point of struggle. She had decided many times and many times changed her mind. She tried to think, *Who would get the most out of this yellow house?* It was a tearing thing to go through. If it had not been the house but, instead, some brittle thing she could hold in her hand, then her last action would be to throw and smash it, and so the thing and she herself would be demolished together. But it was vain to think such thoughts. To whom should she leave it? Her brothers? Not they. Nephews? One was a submarine commander. The other was a bachelor in the State Department. Then began the roll call of cousins. Merton? He owned an estate in Connecticut. Anna? She had a face like a hot-water bottle. That left Joyce, the orphaned daughter of her cousin Wilfred. Joyce was the most likely heiress. Hattie had already written to her and had her out to the lake at Thanksgiving, two years ago. But this Joyce was another odd one; over thirty, good, yes, but placid, running to fat, a scholar—ten years in Eugene, Oregon, working for her degree. In Hattie's opinion this was only another form of sloth. Nevertheless, Joyce yet hoped to marry. Whom? Not Dr. Stroud. He wouldn't. And still Joyce had vague hope. Hattie knew how that could be. At least have a man she could argue with.

She was now more drunk than at any time since her accident. Again she filled her glass. *Have ye eyes and see not? Sleepers awake!*

Knees wide apart she sat in the twilight, thinking. Marian? Marian didn't need another house. Half Pint? She wouldn't know what to do with it. Brother Louis came up for consideration next. He was an old actor who had a church for the Indians at Athens Canyon. Hollywood stars of the silent days sent him their negligees; he altered them and wore them in the pulpit. The Indians loved his show. But when Billy Shawah blew his brains out after his two-week bender, they still tore his shack down and turned the boards inside out to get rid of his ghost. They had their old religion. No, not Brother Louis. He'd show movies in the yellow house to the tribe or make a nursery out of it for the Indian brats.

And now she began to consider Wicks. When last heard from he was south of Bishop, California, a handy man in a saloon off toward Death Valley. It wasn't she who heard from him but Pace. Herself, she hadn't actually seen Wicks since—how low she had sunk then!—she had kept the hamburger stand on Route 158. The little lunchroom had supported them both. Wicks hung around on the end stool, rolling cigarettes (she saw it on the film). Then there was a quarrel. Things had been going from bad to worse. He'd begun to grouse now about this and now about that. He beefed about the food, at last. She saw and heard him. "Hat," he said, "I'm good and tired of hamburger." "Well, what do you think I eat?" she said with that round, defiant movement of her shoulders which she herself recognized as characteristic (*me all over,* she thought). But he opened the cash register and took out thirty cents and crossed the street to the butcher's and brought back a steak. He threw it on the griddle. "Fry it," he said. She did, and watched him eat.

And when he was through she could bear her rage no longer. "Now," she said, "you've had your meat. Get out. Never come back." She kept a pistol under the counter. She picked it up, cocked it, pointed it at his heart. "If you ever come in that door again, I'll kill you," she said.

She saw it all. *I couldn't bear to fall so low,* she thought, *to be a slave to a shiftless cowboy.*

Wicks said, "Don't do that, Hat. Guess I went too far. You're right."

"You'll never have a chance to make it up," she cried. "Get out!"

On that cry he disappeared, and since then she had never seen him.

"Wicks, dear," she said. "Please! I'm sorry. Don't condemn me in your heart. Forgive me. I hurt myself in my evil. I always had a thick idiot head. I was born with a thick head."

Again she wept, for Wicks. She was too proud. A snob. Now they might have lived together in this house, old friends, simple and plain.

She thought, *He really was my good friend.*

But what would Wicks do with a house like this, alone, if he was alive and survived her? He was too wiry for soft beds or easy chairs.

And she was the one who had said stiffly to India, "I'm a Christian person. I do not bear a grudge."

Ah yes, she said to herself. *I have caught myself out too often. How long can this go on?* And she began to think, or try to think, of Joyce, her cousin's daughter. Joyce was like herself, a woman alone, getting on in years, clumsy. Probably never been laid. Too bad. She would have given much, now, to succor Joyce.

But it seemed to her now that that too, the succor, had been a story. First you heard the pure story. Then you heard the impure story. Both stories. She had paid out years, now to one shadow, now to another shadow.

Joyce would come here to the house. She had a little income and could manage. She would live as Hattie had lived, alone. Here she would rot, start to drink, maybe, and day after day read, day after day sleep. See how beautiful it was here? It burned you out. How empty! It turned you into ash.

How can I doom a younger person to the same life? asked Hattie. It's for somebody like me. When I was younger it wasn't right. But now it is, exactly. Only I fit in here. It was made for my old age, to spend my last years peacefully. If I hadn't let Jerry make me drunk that night—if I hadn't sneezed! Because of this arm, I'll have to live with Angus. My heart will break there away from my only home.

She was now very drunk, and she said to herself, *Take what God brings. He gives no gifts unmixed. He makes loans.*

She resumed her letter of instructions to lawyer Claiborne: "Upon the following terms," she wrote a second time. "Because I have suffered much. Because I only lately received what I have to give away, I can't bear it." The drunken blood was soaring to her head. But her hand was clear enough. She wrote, "It is too soon! Too soon! Because I do not find it in my heart to care for anyone as I would wish. Being cast off and lonely, and doing no harm where I am. Why should it be? This breaks my heart. In addition to everything else, why must I worry about this, which I must leave? I am tormented out of my mind. Even though by my own fault I have put myself into this position. And I am not ready to give up on this. No, not yet. And so I'll tell you what, I leave this property, land, house, garden, and water rights, to Hattie Simmons Waggoner. Me! I realize this is bad and wrong. Not possible. Yet it is the only thing I really wish to do, so may God have mercy on my soul."

How could that happen? She studied what she had written and finally she acknowledged that she was drunk. "I'm drunk," she said, "and don't know what I'm doing. I'll die, and end. Like India. Dead as that lilac bush."

Then she thought that there was a beginning and a middle.

She shrank from the last term. She began once more—a beginning. After that, there was the early middle, then middle middle, late middle middle, quite late middle. In fact the middle is all I know. The rest is just a rumor.

Only tonight I can't give the house away. I'm drunk and so I need it. And tomorrow, she promised herself, I'll think again. I'll work it out, for sure.

JAMES FETLER

The Dust
of Yuri Serafimovich

ALEXÁNDER ALEXANDROVICH KOLODNY,
one of San Francisco's oldest and least prosperous dealers in
used foreign books, weighed the old man's dog-eared volumes
unenthusiastically, lifting them out of the rain-soaked carton
with his left hand and giving them the one-eyed treatment.
Dreck! Rain was always bad, it mildewed the covers and caused
the pages to stick together, and now it had been raining without
interruption for three days, and no letup in sight. Typical San
Francisco winter. He felt the covers with the tips of his bony
fingers, like a safecracker, and sniffed the inside pages.
"Mold," he said, adjusting his glasses. He didn't want the
books, he could see that at once, there was no demand for
them—who wants nineteenth-century treatises on animals and
bugs—they would simply take up extra space.

"No mold," the old man objected. His beard was like steel
wool rusting in a kitchen sink. "A little damp, maybe, but no
mold." He pressed his bandaged thumb against a volume in
Russian on the wildfowl of the Ukraine. 1897. "I wouldn't be
parting with this if I didn't have to eat."

Kolodny stared at the books. The books were useless, but the old man was tired and obviously in need of some cash. That bandage needed changing.

The old man lit a cigarette and immediately his beard began steaming like a pile of wet leaves. He pulled out a study of the commercial fishing industry in the Black Sea. "Georgi Melezhny spent seven years gathering the data."

They continued the half-hearted haggling, and as they talked Kolodny kept his eyes on the old man and felt himself weakening. It was his cardinal fault, and he knew it—his wife had always pointed it out to him, and she was right. But on the other hand—an old countryman down on his luck. And that enormous, ancient coat, soaked from the rain.

"No one wants books on fish."

"There is much to be learned from a fish."

2

THE WATER KETTLE in the back room began whistling. Kolodny glared at the rain as it streaked across the plate glass window. "The kettle," he said, padding between the shelves like a monk in his cloister. "Come in here."

The old man followed him to the back room.

Kolodny flipped the switch on the hot plate. "Look here, I'll be truthful with you. The books are worthless, an albatross around my neck. I'm in no position—but I'm cooking some hot soup and tea."

"The soup I don't need. My books."

"Soup first."

They faced each other like antagonists. The old man's beard quivered. Finally he gave in.

"You play chess," he said, tapping the board with his cane. He glanced around. A typical widower's room—a bed and a table with a hot plate. An old Morris chair, frayed, as though cats had scratched on it over the years. A couple of wooden chairs, the legs reinforced with wire. A cupboard. Nothing more. "You're from the south," Kolodny observed, carefully wrapping a hot pad around the handle of the spoon.

"Odessa."

"I never liked it. I was robbed in Odessa. Thirty-six years ago."

"Everyone to his taste."

3

THE OLD MAN sucked up the soup noisily, wielding the spoon with his left hand as though he were digging a hole in a flowerpot. In his eagerness to sell the books he had forgotten his hunger. Now it came. A noodle stuck to his whiskers.

As they shared the simple meal—instant soup with black bread and tall glasses of very weak tea—the two countrymen talked. The old fellow's name was Yuri Vassilyvich Serafimovich, and he had come to the end of his savings, which he had been accumulating in small lumps over the years here and there as a seaman, a prospector, a veterinarian, a gardener in a Mexican convent. He had seen the world in his day, roaming about, examining the ways of wild creatures and men.

Always there had been animals in his life. Animals were important, they explained many facts of existence. He talked about the pets he had owned. "Parakeets," he sighed. "More than one. And, dear God—monkeys and drakes, and a trained rat, a rat who slept on the pillow with me. And how many cats I don't remember. Calico and long-haired. And when I worked in the convent I had an armadillo, *Dasypus novemcinctus,* and a deer which was shot by a hungry policeman. And birds. Birds who talked. Give me more tea. I'll tell you something. There are places I went where a man does not usually venture. Do you know about the island of cats? In the Irish Sea is a great reef, off the Isle of Man, where only cats live. Cats. I row out in a skiff. I row for a long time, and then there is a reef, like a sea serpent lying on its side. Over the years the cats have grown large and ferocious. I sit in the skiff, near the edge of the reef. In the bottom of the skiff is a leak. All day I bail water and study the cats. Then the sun sets, and the moon comes, and the cats creep down to the strand and fish with their claws. I watch the cats fish."

They drank their tea in silence.

Serafimovich leaned back and studied his wet moccasins. "Look at those clubs. With those two clubs I tramped through Sonora at the time of the worst peasant revolts, when whole villages looked like butchering shambles. In Yucatan I was captured by drug-chewing insurgents who left me head-down in a pit with my dead mule. And when I was very young, hardly out of my teens, I crept into the Potala in Lhasa disguised as a stone-mason. It's the truth. I froze my toes."

"And the convent?"

"Young nuns," he said mournfully. "To this day I have marks from their teeth."

Kolodny poured them more tea. Such a durable, fragile old man. Older than his seventy-four years. His coat smelled of tobacco and rain. And such a coat—a regular tent with a broken ridgepole about to collapse in a heap.

"Then how do you live?"

Serafimovich lit a fresh cigarette. "I live. But my money is gone."

"No income? No pension?"

No income, no pension. Serafimovich's explanation seemed curiously impersonal. A man who by habit scrutinizes himself with detachment. Always he had been on the move, forward, forward—the American Southwest, Siberia, New Zealand— and he had never stopped long enough to take out citizenship papers. According to his enigmatic reckoning, he was still, strictly speaking, a subject of Czar Nicholas II.

4

KOLODNY was amused.

No, no. He was still under the Imperial Flag. And without American citizenship he was ineligible for the elderly indigents' pension.

"You're in bad shape," Kolodny said.

"Pretty bad." His only solace these days was the zoo. Several times a week he visited the animals. Brought them *knäckebrod* and grapes. But now, with his back against the wall, he was selling the last of his beloved technical manuals. Flora and fauna. And when they went, there would be no more.

"What about your rent?"

"The rent is due. Overdue."

To Kolodny the solution seemed so obvious that he felt puzzled. Why hadn't the old man thought of it himself? "You must take steps. File for papers. It's the only way." Kolodny himself had been a naturalized citizen for over twenty-five years. "A simple operation: a brief interview, a few questions about the government. Very painless."

Serafimovich hitched up his eyebrows. "I am too old to learn, Alexander Alexandrovich. There are interrogations and inquisitions." The eyebrows came down. "I will die under the Imperial Flag." In his younger days his status as a citizen of the world had appealed to him. He had always equated national allegiances with cant—the last refuge of a scoundrel. "In my youth I espoused nihilism. Now I am too old. I cannot retain simple facts."

"But you remember your *Dasypus novemcinctus*."

"The *Dasypus* is different." He closed his eyes. "It is not the same thing."

"Your rent is already overdue?"

"Overdue. I told you."

"And the landlord?"

"Oriental Machiavelli." He seemed to be rocking himself very slightly. "I don't blame him. Everyone has to eat. He is threatening to change locks on the door."

"You are wasting your time at the zoo when you should be studying about the Congress."

"Perhaps."

"You have seen enough animals in your life."

"All my animals are in cages and pens nowadays." He kept rocking. "It can't be helped."

Kolodny picked up the soup bowls and brushed off the bread-board. Instead of a sink, there was only the basin in the closet. The toilet stood yellow and exposed in one corner of the small ante-room. "How much do you know about the laws of the land?"

"I know what I know, but my memory is dim."

"I have books." He scraped the bread crumbs into the toilet. "Who is Tip O'Neill?"

Serafimovich plucked the noodle from his beard and gazed at it with curiosity. "Tip O'Neill isn't important."

Kolodny seated himself on his bed. "Look here, Yuri Vassilyvich." He leaned forward and began rubbing his calves. The dampness always affected the joints, and often he kept his knees wrapped in flannel. "You are older than me, and we spring from the same soil. I'm not rich, you can see that, but I have a canvas cot and a sleeping bag packed away in the closet. When my son was a boy we went into the mountains together. Before you get your citizenship you must have instruction, and you need a small corner to sleep in. Bring your belongings. Let this room be your home. I will teach you how to pass the examination. And when you get your pension you will purchase a penthouse on Telegraph Hill."

"And live like a Turk. Give me a match, all my matches are damp." He lit his cigarette. "I am too old. I told you. Did you see the new ratel at the zoo?"

Kolodny watched Serafimovich as he packed his books back into the carton. "Think it over."

"*Mellivora capensis,*" Serafimovich grunted, pushing the door open with his shoulder. "Very much like a badger," and he was gone.

5

THE FOLLOWING DAY he was back, the whiskers steaming, the carton of books even soggier than before. "Machiavelli changed the lock," he belched, the cigarette still in his mouth. "Get the cot from the closet, I am bringing my things.

The books are my rent, but the Smirkin seal study I keep."

He tapped the Smirkin with the handle of his cane, as if to protect it from confiscation, flicked his tobacco ashes onto the warped plywood counter, and fast-stepped out like a mechanical dwarf. Kolodny blinked at him as he padded across the street in his flapping moccasins. An electric bus was humming toward him, horn honking. Serafimovich sidestepped the bus like a bullfighter who has learned holy indifference.

6

HE RETURNED with a suitcase lashed together with twine—the handle was missing—and went back again for a laundry-type bundle wrapped in butcher paper and Scotch tape, and a five-gallon rectangular tin, dented and bent.

He began unpacking the suitcase at once. Instead of clothing, it contained documents and drawings—sketches of curious rodents and birds, topographical atlases of Africa and the Arctic marked with arrows and X's, and long yellow sheets of mathematical computations.

"Good news," he announced as he dug into a pocket for thumbtacks and proceeded to tack his pictures and maps to the walls. "They are going to construct a new pit for the apes at the zoo. About time."

Kolodny said nothing. Africa on the wall wasn't part of the bargain. But then he softened. "You'll be a good mouser," he said, unfolding the cot. The cot brought back difficult memories: his young son feeding fig bars to coons, asking questions about Cassiopeia. "The rats chew on the books. You'll be cheaper to keep than a cat. Can you cook?"

"I like rats," Serafimovich said, checking the bandage on his thumb. He wiggled his thumb. "On the seas I knew plenty of rats. I have a way with animals."

So alone, Kolodny thought. Most men live for their sons; this one talks about rats. Like a man in a laboratory. Like a clock ticking all by itself.

7

THEY PLAYED chess that evening and talked about their youth. The old Russia, the land kept intact only in books. To Kolodny it was an album-world artificially tinted by his failing memory. He had left so long ago that he was unsure of his reminiscences—they were too familiar, too much like staged scenes with predictable dialogue and props. But to Serafimovich the old land was still fresh, the impressions were as varied and minute and distinct as the morning he had boarded the merchantman in Odessa. And Kolodny took note of the fact that the old man continued not only to speak but to think in his native tongue. There were roots which had never been yanked out, and this would have to be changed: the roots led to the Imperial Flag, just as his manuals kept him confined in an obsolete scientific world.

8

BUT THE CHESS, at any rate, was a comfort, and Serafimovich was a crafty, a deceptively cunning opponent: it was clear that he knew, as he pored over the board, flicking ashes on the pawns, what he was about. Chess gave Kolodny a temporary reprieve from his personal griefs and regrets.

Since the death of his wife seven years ago the business had gone steadily down. He was impractical by nature, too soft to conclude the hard bargains required in the trade. Roger, his one son and early delight, had established himself in the insurance game, and by inheriting his mother's shrewd aggressiveness, had prospered. Although they lived in the same city, and Roger was apparently committed to the life of a bachelor, Kolodny never saw him. Even his name he had altered to Coleman. Well.

And the chess also helped the dealer forget the interminable winter rain and the sagging shelves of mildewing books which no one seemed to require, at least not at this time of the year.

9

KOLODNY DUG around among his shelves the next morning, found a manual published by the Department of Justice, a simple text in spiral-notebook form which treated in systematic fashion the basic nature and function of the federal government, and they set to work.

It gave him a quiet pleasure to observe that Serafimovich had made himself completely at home. The laundry bundle, the suitcase and the tin were shoved neatly under the cot, and the old man rocked back and forth in the Morris chair and gazed with absorption at the sketches he had tacked to the walls.

And work it was—more than the dealer had anticipated. If not a tough nut, Serafimovich was at least a slippery kernel to crack. And another thing: either the old man was hard of hearing or he chose to play deaf at convenient moments, so that much of the lecture had to be delivered at the level of a shout. *The Congress of the United States . . . the House of Representatives . . . the branches of government.* Serafimovich listened intently—but to what? Was he chewing on his mustache to indicate his understanding, or was he conducting a private dialogue involving his rare fish and fowl? *The judiciary.* It was like yanking his whiskers out, one tobacco-stained hair at a time. And each time the dealer turned the page of the manual Serafimovich's eyebrows would suffer from tortuous convolutions.

IO

KOLODNY GAVE UP after an hour. "Tomorrow will be better," he suggested. "It's the first time."

Instead of replying, Serafimovich lit a cigarette, arose, browsed among the bookshelves, found an edition of John Muir's account of the Yosemite, and began reading it on the spot.

And so it went, in pretty much the same fashion, day after frustrating day. If not uncooperative, he was at least distant, aimed somehow in the wrong direction. Kolodny would lecture him, shouting instructions into his left ear, and in response he would volunteer little-known facts relative to mandrakes (*Mandragorae*) and Venus's-flytraps, lovely swamp plants which possessed leaves with double-hinged blades and an appetite for insects.

Of course Kolodny understood: his youthful commitment to nihilism had left him with an inner resistance to statutes and codes. But still. *Instead of playing ball,* he thought glumly, *we're duelling.*

Yet, paradoxically, whenever the dealer decided to call it quits, Serafimovich would wax childlike and make use of encouraging slogans. He would return stimulated from the zoo and insist that they must forge forward, they were almost on the verge, the Great Leap.

Very well. But nevertheless. Alexander Kolodny was a compassionate man, but business was truly wretched, and the winter rains didn't let up, and he was gradually losing his patience.

II

ONE GRAY AFTERNOON, as he was attempting vainly to interrogate Serafimovich on the Bill of Rights, he noticed that the old man was even more inattentive than usual. He was staring thoughtfully at the rectangular tin under his cot. Kolodny waited. Eyes sunken, almost turned inward and aimed at the brain, Serafimovich continued his meditations. The dealer slapped the manual shut and threw it to the floor.

Serafimovich awoke, startled. "So?"

Kolodny went to the front of the store and began wiping the counter.

"Proceed," Serafimovich said, picking up the manual and brushing it off. He opened it to the section they had covered the preceding week. "Forward!"

Kolodny came back, the dustcloth still in his hand. "What's in the tin?"

"What?"

"The box under the cot—what is it?"

"Nothing." He shrugged. "Go. Look."

Kolodny threw the cloth on the table and went down on his hands and knees. Cobwebs and dust balls. Serafimovich had left tea bags all over the floor, along with his butts. Kolodny pulled the tin out. He flicked off a spider which was scuttling across his wrist. Wedging the tin between his knees, he pried off the lid.

The tin was filled with black, powdery soil, so fine that it resembled dust. Just that. He looked more closely. He reached in and felt it between his fingers. Nothing. Just dust.

He looked at the old man.

"Put it away," Serafimovich said.

"What is it?"

"It doesn't concern you. I am weary," and he arose and limped out of the room.

12

BUT DURING SUPPER that night, after describing in great detail the progress that had been made on the pit for the apes, he changed his mind and asked the bookdealer to drag out the tin again.

Kolodny dragged out the tin. He pried off the lid.

"In this tin," Serafimovich said gravely, as though delivering his own funeral oration, "is our mother soil. This is our soil. You understand what I say, Alexander Alexandrovich. This soil I dug up from a frozen field near Murmansk when I was a young man. A young man. I have kept it, my friend, because this has been country and home. This soil. The soil from which our seed sprang."

He took the tin, balanced it on his lap, and inhaled the dust, as though human bones lay buried in it—bones of Father and Mamushka and girls he had loved. Bones of uncles in fur coats and comrades in school.

"I had been sailing, you know. On the *Catherine the*

Great—what a name for a freighter! One day we docked in Murmansk. High noon. Early spring. I stood on the wharf. I looked at the sledges and the horses, steaming, and the dock-hands tamping their boots in the snow. Soon we would be off again, Portugal, Argentina. How long would we be gone? No one knew. We went where the cargo was—if in hell, then to hell. And with the sun, and the snow, and the horses, I felt a desire to bring back to my cabin some part of the land where my seed was begun."

He rocked back and forth. "I started to walk through the snow. It was like broken glass, the snow. Dear God, the cold! I searched for a field. From a tailor's wife whose husband had recently perished I bought the tin—she had used it for tea—and borrowed a shovel. I never saw such a blunt shovel. And I began to dig. As I dug, the tailor's wife told me a long tale about how her husband had died. Some kind of disease of the blood. I kept digging. *God sees everything!* she wept, and I cried *Amen!* and kept digging. I had to dig deep before I found blackness. It was frozen, the earth, like a great shelf of stone, but finally I had hacked out several chunks. I hacked until I had enough for this tin."

He let the tin slide between his legs to the floor. "You understand me, Alexander Alexandrovich. From that day it has been with me, this dust. I carried it with me through four continents. A fact. Sometimes on my mule, sometimes strapped to my back. Poor old Pedro."

He exhaled. Where was that breath coming from?

"On certain afternoons, when I am tired and my memory is sharp, full of visions and smells of the past, I take off the cover and savor this soil, and I hold it against my stomach and ribs. Against my bowels. This is my home, after all. My nose understands this rare smell," and he frowned a fierce frown: for a moment the old man turned gargoyle. Then his face relaxed. "And the animals know."

"The animals know?"

"I communicate with them."

Kolodny bent over the tin. It smelled more like dust from an attic than earth from a cold Russian field, and there was also something of the sea in it, a faint trace of canvas and hemp.

Bad business, bad business. Obviously this was part of his problem. Too many knots tying him to the past. Dust and wild animals. It was surely bad business. He was clearly not ready to surrender the tin.

13

OF COURSE they weren't prepared—preparation for him meant tin-sniffing and spinning his yarns—but Kolodny had submitted all the documents and forms, along with a passport-type photo he had paid for himself (a deplorable shot, like a circus portrait of The World's Oldest Living Homo Sapiens), and the day of the examination came. They took the bus to the federal building on Sansome Street. Although they were late, Serafimovich seemed unbearably calm. Optimistic. "The Potala," he winked as they walked through the lobby.

The examiner's name was T. J. Hunter and his head was a neatly combed circle—a friction-free head which the Lord had designed for utility. Kolodny disliked him at once. He reminded him of Roger and his insurance policies. Clinical.

Serafimovich seated himself at the side of the desk and Kolodny took a chair against the beaver-board partition, under a photograph of the Justices of the Supreme Court.

"Back," Hunter droned, waving his ball-point pen at Kolodny. "Can't have you here. Back to the waiting room." A ventriloquist: his lips didn't move but the words came out anyway. He kept his tongue rolled up in the back of his nose. Serafimovich folded his hands. His beard quivered.

"The old man has bad ears," Kolodny said.

The examiner leaned back in his swivel chair, thoughtful and annoyed. His head was like a balloon with a pinprick. The gas was leaking out slowly.

"His hearing is bad," Kolodny insisted.

"Hard of hearing, are you?" Hunter asked.

Serafimovich crossed his legs and scowled at the bookdealer. "No."

14

IT WAS TOO HOT in the waiting room. Too many pregnant women, too many clerks wielding rubber stamps. The man sitting half-asleep in the back row looked too much like a CIA agent. Kolodny roamed through the halls with his hands in his pockets, read the bulletin boards, filled his mouth with warm water from the fountain, studied the faces of the clerks and the elevator operators, and stared out the window at San Francisco Bay, gray and rainswept below him. Over there, out of view behind the hill, was Clement Street and the shop. Today, perhaps, customers were waiting for him.

Not likely. Mount Tamalpais to the north rose up pale and unlovely, its haunches immersed in a mist which washed out depth and shade and left everything underexposed. He saw the ridge where he used to go hiking with Roger. His breath was steaming up the glass. He wiped it off.

And almost directly below him, slightly to the left, the financial district and the fancy aluminum building where Roger sat with his pushbutton phones.

Kolodny forced his eyes back to the mountain. There is also destruction in distance: either end of the telescope bruises and robs.

15

THEN HE HEARD Hunter's voice summoning him from the end of the hall. "Come in here," he demanded, his tongue in his nose. "I can't spend the whole morning on one deaf old man."

Kolodny went into the office and sat down.

"Hallo," Serafimovich said brightly, uncrossing his legs. "I am finished?"

Hunter didn't even look at him. He rubbed his eyes. "How many states in the Union?"

"Alabama—"

"How many houses in Congress?"

Serafimovich opened his mouth, then closed it. He looked at Kolodny. The bookdealer remained deadpan.

Hunter droned on. "How many branches in the government? What are the branches?"

"In the government," Kolodny shouted, mouthing his words into the old man's left ear, "how many *branches?*"

"High Court—"

Hunter waited, one shoe under the other.

"Legislature—senators." Pause. "Senators."

Hunter reversed his feet. "Checks and balances—what does that mean?"

"Checks and balances," Kolodny said.

"Checks and balances," Hunter repeated.

The beard quivered.

Hunter flipped the page of the examination booklet. "How many years does a President serve?"

Serafimovich sat up, then leaned forward. "Which one?"

Silence.

"What should I do with this old man?" Hunter asked. "He doesn't know what I'm talking about."

Serafimovich cleared his throat. "You permit me to smoke, brother?"

"Smoke," Hunter said. "You don't need my permission to smoke."

They looked at each other. Serafimovich blew smoke through his nose.

"He's pretty old," Kolodny suggested.

16

AS THEY STEPPED into the elevator Serafimovich fluffed out his whiskers. "Okay?"

Kolodny stared blankly at the emergency-exit instructions. "Fine."

"I passed?"

"No."

The eyebrows went to work.

"Button your coat. It's still raining."

"I am tired," he said. "I—," and he rapped his cane against the elevator wall. Down plunged the steel box, beneath streets and houses, and lower and lower. "We will try again," Serafimovich said, and the steel cage went deeper and yet farther down.

17

SO THEY PICKED up the pieces. Kolodny put the old man on a rigid schedule: when to eat, when to study, when to pay court to tigers and apes. He employed sundry threats. He resorted to bribery: promises of all the *pelmeni* he could eat. Serafimovich looked grave, twisted his beard between his fingers and responded as one might have expected. Kolodny brought up the geographical locations of the prairie states and Serafimovich plunged into a sermon on partridges. Gallinaceous fowl. "A *Perdix perdix* of the subspecies *Perdicinae*—a gray partridge I had painstakingly trained—and I would call to him, as though he were a regular seafowl: Hulloa there, Mishka, you foolish *Perdix*, how's the weather upstairs?"

"You will not get your papers," Kolodny assured him. "You will die under the Imperial Flag."

" . . . and a frigate bird who had followed our ship out of Newfoundland, a *Fregata aquila*. . . . "

And suddenly Kolodny felt the burden of his years on his shoulders and back. For one stone-cold moment he felt the death of his wife and the indifference of his son, and the rain kept on falling, and the business was going kaput.

He struggled to put on his raincoat. "Enough!" One sleeve had been pulled inside out. "I'm going for air. Watch the store."

Serafimovich glanced up. "What's the matter?"
"I don't know."
"Men must focus their eyes on essentials."

18

KOLODNY REGRETTED his temper at once, before he had reached Ninth Avenue. Had he offended the old man? Would he pack up and leave? But where would he go? Already he saw Serafimovich removing his maps from the walls, slipping the tacks into his pockets, packing his suitcase, wiping the cobwebs from the tin. He hurried back to the shop.

Dear God, he had done it. The shade was down and the CLOSED sign lay propped on the sill. Kolodny stared at the sign. He was cursed—a man destined to suffer a series of losses. Even the key was rebelling: it stuck in the lock.

19

BUT THERE he was, the old reprobate, lying on his cot, a book propped against his knees. Kolodny said nothing. He felt greatly relieved. What are manuals and flags? Serafimovich could stay with him, eat his soup *ad infinitum.* He wanted him to stay. And he made a decision: there would be no more lessons or interrogations.

"Still raining," Serafimovich observed, noting the puddle Kolodny was leaving on the floor.

"Still raining." He shook out his raincoat. "Let's have tea."

20

AND THE FOLLOWING DAY, as if in reaction to the book-dealer's new policy, the inexplicable card came. How to account for it? An administrative error? A clerical mistake?

It was no mistake. An official postcard, Department of Immigration and Naturalization, signed T. J. H. Kolodny was dumbfounded. He had misjudged this man Hunter. Hunter had bowels, after all, and a heart.

The card advised that Yuri V. Serafimovich had successfully passed the naturalization examination and would be sworn in at the Federal Courthouse on the twenty-first of the month, at 3 P.M., Judge Harry Neumann presiding.

21

ON THE DAY of the swearing in Kolodny arranged to close the shop early and meet Serafimovich at the New Manchuria for dinner. There are things men must celebrate. Already he had bought him a full pound of halvah—Serafimovich was childishly fond of halvah—and a carton of Camels. "First an early dinner," the bookdealer said, "then we'll go to the zoo. Since my boy graduated from high school I haven't been to the zoo."

"Good!" Serafimovich broke off a large chunk of halvah, leaving crumbs on his coat and the floor. He began shoving it into his beard. "I want to take a few notes. I told you about the new ratel, the rare *Mellivora capensis—*"

"For God's sake, don't plunge into lectures on ratels! You'll be late for the swearing in. The New Manchuria—you know where it is? Brush your coat."

"I know where it is, but we'll have to eat fast. They lock the zoo gates at five."

"Wait a minute. Five. No. Better go first to the zoo. Then we can take the whole night with our meal, and I'll order a bottle of kvass."

"I'm going," Serafimovich said. "The zoo first. I'll be there before you. Look for me. I'll be smoking your Camels in front of the ratel."

22

A CUSTOMER came in looking for Lazhechnikov's *House of Ice*. Kolodny knew he had it, but it was difficult to find. By the time he had ferreted out the volume, Serafimovich had departed, and Kolodny noticed that he had taken his tin with him. Incorrigible! Crumbs of halvah and a tin in a dignified courthouse!

23

BUSINESS was unaccountably brisk that afternoon, a group of language students from Berkeley, a good omen, but it meant that Kolodny was delayed.

Finally he was able to close up the shop. He took the streetcar to the zoo. Almost closing time, and the rain had given way to a dense fog which was blowing in from the ocean in large pockets, like great, heavy opera-house curtains.

Serafimovich wasn't at the ratel's cage, or anywhere else. Over the loudspeaker a voice announced that the zoo was closing. Where was he? Avoiding the watchmen and caretakers, who were whirring about in the fog on three-wheeled scooters, he slipped past the various animal shelters. He gave silent thanks for the fog and the poor visibility.

Yuri Vassilyvich. The fog kept rearranging itself around him. Kolodny tiptoed on, soles squeaking, past the oxen and ibex, the apes and the pronghorn, and then he discovered the old man.

Serafimovich was shuffling from compound to compound, from railing to railing, and each time he stopped he plunged his hand into the tin box and scattered the dust among the beasts. Kolodny kept his distance and peered through the curtains of fog. When Serafimovich stopped, Kolodny stopped. When he moved, the bookdealer went forward. Dust to the elephants, dust to the imprisoned cats. Like a planter the old man was sowing his dust.

CAROL BLY

Gunnar's
Sword

As she climbed the hill to the Home, Harriet White
felt the town falling away behind her. She usually despised the
town in a casual, peaceful way, the way adults sometimes de-
spise their parents' world once they've left it. The mind simply
remembers it as something unpleasant, but dead. Right now
she felt annoyed with the town in general because she had begun a quarrel with the Golden Age Auxiliary women about the
quilts they were making: they were using old chenille bed-
spreads for centers, since the center can never be seen, and
then doing elegant patchwork covers. The pastor had held the
quilts up at service and praised the ladies. These quilts, which
looked cosy but didn't keep out the cold, were then sent to
Lutheran World Relief. Harriet was irritated with these
women's ethics, which often seemed like little more than an
uneasy suspension of local pastors' remarks and the inchoate
strictures of their husbands in the VFW Lounge.

She had lived all her adult life with her husband and son on
their quarter section, where a half mile in every direction was
theirs: when she came to the Home, she had somehow to
shrink it all to the size of her room. Some people managed that

by stuffing all the furniture they could bring from their old houses into the tiny rooms of the Lutheran Home; Harriet managed it by working away at her pastimes with a fury. The crafts room was full of her output; she was like a factory; she turned out more sweaters and afghans than twenty residents together. But when it snowed, even during the tiresome snows of late March, she felt a settling inside her, as if her mind lowered and glided outward, like the surface of a lake. She would fetch her coat and overshoes and walk about the ordinary, dreamless town as if lost in thought on her knees, someone who has been dealt with cordially.

Harriet's neck was ropy and knotted, in the way of old people who have got thin. She forgave herself that. As a little girl, and later as a young woman, she had feared the degradation that age might bring. She remembered watching the hired girl, who had cared for her over weekends when her parents went to their club, pulling on her stockings. Above the knee, Harriet had seen the white meat of the thigh swelling and she had sworn, I shall never let my legs look like that! And later she had sworn, I shall never let my chin sag like that! Or, I shall never lower myself to *that!* Now, as she swung fairly easily up the hill, she thought she was less discontented with her body, and self, than she had been at any time earlier. She was eighty-two, but she kept a jaunty air, some of which was gratitude when her right ankle didn't act up. She climbed firmly, noting how soundless the cold air was, except for traffic in the town below. The elm treetops were broomy and vague; the smoke from the Home power plant piped slowly straight up. She hoped it would snow.

ON THE UPPER SIDEWALK at last, she saw Arne, the Home's driver and man of all work, helping Mr. Solstad, the mortician, wheel a casket out of the east entrance. Harriet paused, partly for the flag that lay over the coffin, and she knew it was the body of Mr. Ole Morstad whose funeral was to be down at the church that afternoon. She was not sorry that he was dead; he had been taken up to the infirmary floor on third more than three years ago. Then, rather than now, they had recognized his death; her roommate, LaVonne Morstad, had cried and Harriet had held her shoulder and hand. "He will never come back down into second!" cried Vonnie then. And so he hadn't.

Arne and Mr. Solstad eased the casket off its wheeled cart into the hearse. Then Arne came over to Harriet, with his workingman's sidewise walk, blowing on his hands. He smiled at her. "Morning, missus," he said respectfully, as he always did. Residents who were very feeble or not very alert he tended to call by their Christian names. "Will you be wanting a ride down to the services this afternoon, Mrs. White?"

"I'll walk, Arne—it isn't so cold!"

"Not for you maybe," he said admiringly. "But some of 'em, they wouldn't go if they had to walk."

"I bet you won't be taking down storm windows today after all," Harriet said, remembering an announcement over the public-address system that morning.

"Feels like snow," he said, swinging his head northwest, where the tiny cars ran along on the cold gray highway. "Weather don't seem to scare you none though."

They both paused as the hearse drove by them carefully—and then they gave each other that odd farm-people's signal, as they parted. It was a slight wave with the right hand—half like a staff officer's from his jeep; half like a pastor's benediction. Harriet went in.

She avoided the reception entrance, with the residents sitting about looking hot and faint, and the few children inevitably hanging around the TV sets instead of going up to the grandparents they'd been sent to visit. She marched straight off to the back, where the crafts room was, and had the good luck to find Marge Larson, the therapist, there. The room was full of half-finished products at this end—but at the other end, divided by a

Sears Roebuck room divider, was the "shop" where the finished hot pads, napkin holders, aprons were on sale. The Golden Age Auxiliary members came by regularly and bought. Harriet's work was known because it was fair isle knitting, in western Minnesota called Norwegian knitting. Not everyone could do it. Harriet also helped Marge with other people's unfinished work, or work that needed to be taken out and remade, which she kept quiet about.

Together they discussed some of the projects lying around on tables. Some weren't any good. An old man was in the room, too, but it was Orrin Bjorning who could not hear and could not work. He sat utterly still, and the dull light came in off the snow so that the skin on his forehead and cheeks looked like a hood—as if a monk sat there frozen—instead of like a face. He insisted on spending whole mornings in the crafts room, his fingers bent around a piece of 1 x 1. He never stirred. When the PA system announced dinner time, he would shake himself and slowly leave, never speaking.

Harriet and Marge walked around the room, touching and lifting Orlon, felt, acrylic, cotton. Harriet promised to return in the afternoon, and work a little on that Mrs. Steensen's rug. Mrs. Steensen had started braiding. Marge often placed new lots of nicely stripped wool in the woman's lap and Mrs. Steensen always looked up and said energetically, "Yes—good, thanks then, Marge!" in her Scandinavian accent. "*Ja*—I've been needing just such a blue—now I can get on with my rug!" And then all morning her hands made little plucking gestures at the rags in her lap. Marge and Harriet together worked up two or three feet of the braid from time to time and Mrs. Steensen seemed not to notice. "Rug's coming along pretty good!" she would shout, when Marge came by.

AT TEN Harriet left. She still had her coat to hang up, and she had to write a short speech. Later she would have to help

Vonnie Morstad dress for the funeral.

But she stopped at the second-floor landing because Mr. Helmstetter and Kermit Steensen were sitting by the elevators.

"Thank you very much for that little rabbit favor, missus," Helmstetter said. "I gave it to my granddaughter—the one they called Kristi. Kristi is for Christine, that's her aunt on the other side, then Ann for the middle name. I suppose it's for someone. She was very pleased."

"*Ja*, I suppose you told her you made it, huh," Kermit said, one of the Home wits.

Helmstetter blushed. "She wouldn't have believed that, I guess. Where you going in such a rush?" he said to Harriet. "You're always rushing. Chasing. This way, that way. Such a busy lady."

"Busier'n Jacqueline Kennedy," Kermit said.

Harriet sat down beside them and they all faced the aluminum elevator doors. "I can sit down a moment."

"Work'll keep," Helmstetter said.

"Work don't run away," Kermit Steensen said in a witty tone: again they all laughed, all of them more heartily than they felt like, but they all felt pretty cheerful for a second. Harriet rose to the occasion.

"Well, how's 'Edge of Night' coming?" Harriet asked them. She knew that they all listened to television drama serials during afternoon coffee in the coffee room. In the morning the sun didn't come into the coffee room, so it was empty save for the candy-stripers' carts and a slight odor of dentures. In the afternoon, however, the lace curtains were transformed and a light fell on the people as they were served their "lunch"—the western Minnesota word for the midafternoon snack. Sometimes the sun was so gorgeous that they had to squint to make out the dove-pale images on the TV set. Helmstetter and Steensen and a couple of other men—and nearly all the second floor women—kept track of the dramas. From time to time, Harriet asked them about them.

"We don't watch that anymore," Kermit told her. "'Splendor of Our Days' is what we're watching now."

"This young fellow has got an incurable disease and he is trying not to tell his girl about it, but she knows. She wants to talk it over with him so she can help him."

"Oh, that isn't the point!" Kermit said sharply. "The point is he doesn't want her to find out he's scared to die. He wants to keep on laughing and joking right up to the end. She belongs to the country club that his folks want to get into."

"There's an old Viking story like that," Harriet put in. "Do you remember that old legend about how the Vikings believed you must make a joke before you died, in order to show Death you were better than he is?"

Letting the *Lutheran Herald* sag on his knees, Helmstetter said courteously, "How'd that hang together then?"

Harriet said, "There was a particular young Viking and he and his friends had a grudge against a man named Gunnar. So one day they decided they would put a ladder up to the loft where Gunnar slept, while he was away, then they'd hide in there and then kill him when he came in at night. So the friends helped the young fellow put up the ladder, and up he went, with his knife between his teeth. Just as he was heaving himself over the windowsill, however, Gunnar, who happened not to be away after all, leapt off his straw bed and ran his sword right through the young Viking. The Viking fell off the ladder backward, and of course his friends raced over to where he lay, with the blood coursing out of his chest.

"'Oh—Gunnar is at home, then?' they asked with astonishment.

"'Well, now' the young man said as he died, 'I don't know if Gunnar is home but his sword is.'"

Helmstetter and Steensen hesitated: they weren't sure they got the point of the story, yet they felt moved. "Pretty good, pretty good," they both murmured. There was a polite pause, and then Kermit Steensen fidgeted and brightened and said,

"Not to change the subject, you see this girl belongs to the country club, but the boyfriend isn't interested at all, but all the time his parents are anxious for him to belong and they keep throwing him together with this girl."

"But she's really interested in that other fellow—the doctor fellow!" cried Helmstetter with a laugh.

"She isn't either!" said Steensen. "That was all over weeks ago. In fact they've dropped him; you don't see him anymore."

"I seen him on there just yesterday!"

"You see lots of things!" Helmstetter said.

Harriet rose after a moment, and said, "Are you going to be in the dining room at eleven?"

"What for then?" Both men were very anxious not to be forgetful of any part of the Home schedule.

"We're having coffee in honor of Marge Larson, you know the woman who helps us with crafts? It's her birthday. We'd do it this afternoon but there's the Morstad funeral."

"Oh, *ja*, then," the men said. When Harriet left, they fingered the church magazines on their knees in a distracted sort of way, and Kermit began deliberately snapping over the pages.

HARRIET looked forward to getting to her room. She not only had two books going at the same time but she also had one small bit of knitting—a patterned complicated sweater for little Christopher. She had not used a pattern, but had counted the stitches there were to be across the shoulders, at front and back, and then, using the same number of squares on light-blue-inked graph paper, she had made up her own pattern. She blocked in the colors with crayons, trying different combinations. It was immensely satisfying, because she not only had the problem of what colors and shapes would look well in wool, but also, she wanted, if possible, to make up a pattern that would work in the different colors in any one row at least as often as every fifth stitch. If a row were to have blue and white, for example, she made sure the blue yarn was used at least as often as once in five—or the white, conversely. This way she prevented "carrying" yarn for more than an inch in the back. Long, carried yarn tended to get caught in buttons and baby fingers. Harriet laughed at herself for her love of knitting—you are simple-minded, she told herself—yet it sustained her in a way that would have surprised her years before. For example, during the meals—as in most institutions meals were a weak side of life at the Home—she could keep cheerful and even hold up a sort of one-handed conversation, by reminding herself that the orderly, beautiful knitting lay waiting upstairs. Sometimes the thought of her knitting even came to her during Larry's visits. I do hope, she told herself, I won't get so my own son is overshadowed by a pair of worsted mittens. She felt certain that the best defense of one's personality, against everything—senility mostly, and worse, later—was one's humor. And hers was intact. Or at least, so people assured her.

"You have a wonderful sense of humor, Mother," Larry had told her on one of his visits from Edina. "When did you develop it? Was it when you married Dad and went into farming?"

She opened her top bureau drawer to take out the lined paper to write the speech for Marge on, and found Larry's last letter. "I'm hoping to get out to Jacob over the weekend, hopefully Saturday," he wrote. Ghastly usage, Harriet thought affectionately. "I'll call Saturday around noon if I do. Are you having a cold horrible March? The city is a mess—mud and melting snow. I don't know why we Minnesotans complain about winter, spring is what's horrible. See you soon. Love from us all, a kiss from that wonderful little Christopher—Larry." Harriet read it over again, and then laid it under her notebook.

She began work on the speech. "We are gathered here this morning in honor of Marge's birthday," she began. "But it seems to me it would make a lot more sense if she were gathered here in honor of *our* birthdays—we've had so many more of them." She sat back, staring at the smudgy storm window that Arne had not removed. "What drivel," she thought, glancing at her speech again. She crossed it out. Even first-rate jokes didn't work particularly well at the Home—and second-rate jokes went very badly. She visualized the dining room—the bleached foreheads, held motionless over the plates full of desserts, the stately, plastic flowers. She bent to the job again, forcing herself not to hope that Larry might offer her a ride out into the country to look at the farm. She worked away at the speech, finished, shortened it, and had just thought to check the time when Vonnie came in.

The young girl volunteers called candy-stripers had put curlers in Vonnie's hair for her. On the first floor was a shampooing room, where once a week a few members of the Jacob Lutheran Church—the Golden Age Auxiliary—laid their heavy coats on the steel-tubing chairs, and washed and set the hair of any of the women who cared to come down. In between those Tuesday afternoons, the candy-stripers would sometimes do it. The residents preferred the services of the Golden Age women, most of whom were in their fifties and could remember how hair "should be done nice"—meaning, with bobby pins screwed to the head, dried hard, and then brushed and combed, leaving discernible curls. The young girls, on the other hand, believed in either back-combed hair—or more recently, in simply straight "undone" hair. Vonnie came into the room scowling, and Harriet supposed she wasn't pleased with the way the candy-stripers had done her.

"Shall we lay out our clothes for this afternoon?" Harriet said, closing her notebook.

Vonnie grasped the arms of her rocking chair, got ready, and then jammed herself down in it. "You lay out *your* clothes!"

"Can I help?" Harriet said gently.

"I can lay out my own clothes; I can get into my own clothes. Next thing you'll want to rinse my teeth!"

"Going to the dining room for the birthday coffee for Marge?" Harriet said after a pause.

"To hear your speech you mean?" snapped Vonnie. Her cheeks shook.

"Vonnie!"

"Oh, *ja,* Vonnie! Don't Vonnie me!" cried the woman. "I am sick of you doing everything like you were better than everyone else. Speech for Marge! Why couldn't we of got a printed card like everyone wanted? A nice printed card, with a nice picture, a photo of some roses, on nice paper with a nice poem on it, they got hundreds now, at either one of the drugstores—you're always going on them walks, you could of walked to the drugstore and you could have got it and you could of read it aloud to us, and then we would have the cake and it would be real nice. But oh no, you got to do some fancy thing no one ever thought of—oh, *ja,* it had to be something—a speech!"

"Ridiculous," Harriet said. "A woman like Marge gets a hundred cards like that a year. The idea is to do something more personal."

"Whose idea? Everyone else thought a card would be real nice!"

Vonnie turned around and faced Harriet—the day's full light on her stretched forehead. "And I got something else to say to you also! My knitting! You can just keep to your own and leave my work alone! When I want your help with my work, I'll ask you for it."

"Oh, Vonnie," Harriet said, "all we did was take out back to the row where the increasing was supposed to start, and do the increasing every second row—and then you take over again from there."

"Don't you have any of your own to do? Why don't you do your own increasing and your own decreasing and leave mine be."

They both stood up and stiffly began taking fresh stockings, their better shoes, their dark print dresses out of their closets. If they dressed now, they wouldn't be caught dressing later when LaVonne's relations began coming in to pick her up to go down to the church. They had a half hour before the birthday coffee for Marge.

When they both were dressed, there was a pause. There was a problem they simply had to solve, Vonnie's hair. Harriet finally took the lead. "Vonnie," she said as efficiently and impersonally as she could, "let's get your curlers out now—because now's when we've got time to get it combed out before LeRoy and Mervin come."

The widow grumbled, but let herself down in her chair, with her eyes pointed coldly into the mirror. "I don't want it brushed out too much. I don't like the way that one candy-striper girl does it. No sense of how hair should be done."

"The one called Mary?" Harriet asked. Standing behind Vonnie, she began gently taking out curlers.

"*Ja*. Now that other one's a real nice girl. Friend of the Helmstetters. My Mervin married a Helmstetter." Slowly the curlers came off—LaVonne Morstad kept one trembling wrist raised, to receive them one by one from Harriet. Talking to each other in the mirror, the two women pulled together again, a little.

THE CHAPLAIN'S VOICE now came over the PA system: his voice was rusty and idealistic. In his Scandinavian accent, he said: "If everyone will please come straight down to the dining room, we will be having a coffee hour in honor of Mrs. Marge Larson. *Vil De vaer så snill å komme til spisesalen; vi skal ha kaffee . . .* " continuing in Norwegian. He did not give his announcement in German, for in the Jacob area most of the German-Americans were Catholics. There were only a dozen or so in the Lutheran Home.

Harriet left Vonnie muttering over the funeral programs. The widow had the conviction something had been printed incorrectly, and she kept running her big finger across the lines again, pronouncing the names, the thou's and thee's, in a hoarse whisper.

Harriet found Marge and Arne dragging the PA system

hookup over to the standing mike, near the diabetic table. Now the younger residents came in briskly, glancing out at the snow-lit window, nodding to one another. The more aged people followed, looking like the wooden carvings of Settesdal valley and the Jotenheim. Over the shuffling slippers, the stooped backs were immobile; you were aware of the folds and creases of sleeves, the velvety skin coating elbows that looked sore, the huge blocky ankles of the old, like knots of marble. Harriet listened, a little nervous as always before she addressed a group, aware of rayon rubbing, now chair legs being dragged out. Finally everyone was seated—even old Orrin Bjorning sat gazing at his right hand cupped over his left. Harriet was delighted to find Kermit Steensen and some of the other men sitting where she could see them; if you had just a face or two responding, you could carry the others.

"Harriet," Marge said, "would you read off the birthday list for this month? We were going to do it for Golden Age this afternoon, but since most of them will be down at the funeral, we thought we'd better do it this morning."

Harriet flattened the typed yellow sheet over her clipboard, rapidly checking the names for those she might not pronounce right. Three were crossed through—she recognized the names of two men who had died in the past few weeks, and of a woman whose relatives had moved her to the Dawson Nursing Home. Mr. Ole Morstad's name was still on. "Shan't I pencil through this?" Harriet asked, pointing.

"Oh my goodness—thanks!" cried Marge, leaning across Harriet to run her ball-point through it. "I'm glad you caught that!"

They stood together, planning the next few minutes—odd, Harriet thought, this stupid fifteen-minute affair, a two-minute speech for a birthday, and yet it had all the trappings of the hundreds of meetings she had presided over. It had also the old lilt to it—the sense that she herself was exciting, someone who could bring off things, someone to be relied on; if little difficulties arose, she could back and fill. She was a leader. Color came up into her face and she knew it.

As Arne knelt at her feet tinkering with the extension cord, Harriet thought, I used to believe that as I got old I'd feel closer to people of all sorts of backgrounds. I thought there was some great common denominator we'd all sink to—and I'd feel *more* affectionate toward clumsy, or unexperienced people. But it hasn't worked out. I don't! I am perfectly resigned to being among people who never read or reflect on anything but I don't feel close. And less than ever can I understand how they can bear life with one another. She looked out, now, over the whole dining room because Arne was through, and her birthday list, touching the mike, gave a hoarse rattle, showing the current was on.

"Good morning!" she said, remembering not to duck to the mike. "We are gathered together this morning in honor of someone who means a great deal to every one of us." She went on, faces turned toward her. Quietly, at the edges of the room, the kitchen staff with their red wrists carried in coffee urns and set down plates of dessert. Harriet noticed with the speed of eight years' residency that the dessert was sawed slices of angel food with Wilderness Cherry Pie filling and Cool Whip on it. She was aware of Marge herself, modestly perched on a chair at the diabetic table. When the speech was over, and the gift received, Marge would be off again—flying around doing the dozens of chores she somehow accomplished during a day—pushing a wheelchair to the shampoo room, helping a church women's group plan their surprises for the infirmary trays, even helping to tip the vats of skinned potatoes in the kitchen. Harriet mentioned some of these tasks so graciously done—and she heard the warmth fill in her voice. It had its effect, too. She had the people's attention: the moment she saw that, she felt still another warmth in her voice: the warmth of success. So she wound up with some lilt, made Marge stand, handed over the gift, excused the roomful of people from singing "Happy Birthday" because she knew they hated it—the sound of their awful voices—and she read the birthday list, after which everyone clapped. Then she said to Marge, "We all say, bless you, Marge," and retreated from the microphone.

Harriet settled herself in a folding chair by the maid's serving stand, to hear Marge's thanks but Siegert, the head nurse, was bending over her shoulder: "It's your son, Mrs. White. He's waiting for you in your room. I said you'd come up, but surely you can stay and have your coffee . . . "

"No, no!" cried Harriet. "I'm coming! Larry! No, I don't want any coffee! Thanks, Mrs. Siegert!"

The nurse smiled. "Tell you what, I'll bring up some of the dessert for both of you—and some coffee, how's that?"

"How nice you are," Harriet cried, and hurried out.

She wanted to go the fastest way, which is to say up the staircase, but then she would be short of breath when she arrived and then Larry would worry. So she pressed the stupid bell and waited for the poky elevator to sink all the way down from the infirmary on third.

SHE FOUND room 211 full of Morstad men. They were milling about in the tiny space between the bureaus, the two rocking chairs, the beds—in heavy dark overcoats flung open in the hot air of the Home. They were shaking hands, in turns, and then prowling about the room, trying not to bump into one another or the radiator. Vonnie herself stood rummaging in the top drawer of her bureau. Her rocking chair kept rocking as one man or another struck it with his ankles. Harriet paused a moment, daunted by the crowd, and then entered, and shook hands with each person separately. They were in their good clothes. "I think I ought to know yer face . . . Mervin Morstad's my name. My brother LeRoy, Mrs. White. He's from the Cities—over in Edina. Well I guess you know our mother all right." (Sociable laughter.) " . . . Deepest sympathy." "Oh, thank you now.... Yes, he was. He sure was—a blessing in a way, if you get how I mean.... Here—Mother, never mind—it don't matter...."

But Vonnie was furious. "Don't matter! I'll say it does. Look, right there, in print, and we paid for it, too!"

Both her sons, Mervin and LeRoy, huge men with gleaming, round cheeks, tipped their gigantic shoulders like circling airplanes over the card she held. She handed it to Mervin, and he read aloud: "Olai Vikssen Morstad. Born 14th April, 1886. Entered into Eternal Rest, 9th March 1971. 84 Years 1 Month 6 Days!"

"Well, it ought to be five days, shouldn't it?" Vonnie shouted.

"Oh, Mom, it doesn't matter," the son called LeRoy said.

"Oh doesn't it! Well, people will just sit through the services, you know what people are, and they'll count that up and they'll see just as sure as anything someone didn't add straight. There'll be talk."

"Come on, Mama," Mervin said. "Here's your coat ... hat." Harriet found and gave him Vonnie's black bag, her gloves. "Come on, Mama," Mervin said, helping her. "They've got a real nice dinner down at the church—and Corrine's are all there already and they want to visit with you. And Mahlin's—all except Virgil, he's away at school yet—" And gently he went on, listing the various relations who had come for the old man's funeral, and now were being served a hot luncheon by one of the church circles. The big men followed poor Vonnie out of the room—Mervin taking her arm in the doorway. LeRoy hung back a minute and said civilly, "I know what you done for our ma, Mrs. White. All these years. She wouldn't get by near as good without you being so good to stay by. So thank you then!" A final view of his huge blushing face.

"Oh, Larry!" Harriet cried. "It's so good to see you!" For her son was there; all that while, he'd been waiting in that crowded room, quietly sitting on the edge of her bed near the far wall, glancing through her books.

They hovered a moment, hugging each other, in the middle of the room; "Mama," he said delighted, like a boy: "Look what I brought!"

There was a huge bundle of what looked like used clothing on her bed.

"You can hold it if you're good!" Larry laughed. He picked up the clumsy package unwinding some of the clothes.

Harriet darted over without a word. Trembling, she undid the rest of some old padded jacket the baby was wrapped in, loosened his knit blanket—not without noticing through her tears, though, that this was one she had knitted. She carried Christopher to her rocking chair, and sat down. For a moment baby and great-grandmother made tiny struggles to get sorted. Harriet had to get her good foot, the left, which never gave her trouble even recently, onto the ground, to use for pushing to make the chair rock. The baby had to move his tiny shoulders as though scratching an itch, but in actuality, finding where and how this set of arms would hold him. He didn't pay much attention to what he saw out of his eyes: he saw only the dull whitish light off the snow, smeary and without warmth. What he felt in his shoulders, behind the small of his back, under his knees, was the very soul of whoever was holding him; it streamed into the baby from all those places. The baby stilled, paying attention to it, deciding, using shoulder blades, back-bone, and legs to make the decision whether or not the energy entering was safe and good. Everything now told him it was, so in the next second, he let each part of his body loosen into those hands, and let his feet be propped on that lap, then let his chest be lifted and pressed to that breast and shoulder—his colorless rather inexpressive eyes went slatted half-shut. He made a little offering of his own; he let his cheek lean on that old, trustworthy cheek, and then with a final wiggle, he gave himself up to being held. All she ever said to him was, "Christopher, precious!" but that was nothing to him—that was just noise.

Larry had stood up and gone over to the doorway; someone

was conferring with him. He returned with a tray with two cups of coffee on it, and a plate with some white cake with the inevitable Wilderness Cherry filling on it. "That was your head nurse—Mrs. Siegert, isn't it?" he asked, proudly keeping track of the Home staff.

He sat down on Vonnie's rocking chair, with the tray; he shoved Vonnie's Bible over. The lace bureau cloth immediately caught in one corner of it and wrinkled up, and the program for Ole Morstad's funeral, a paper rabbit candy basket, and a tube of Chapstick fell on the floor.

Larry, sipping his coffee, told his day's news. It hadn't been a bad drive out from Edina, although Evelyn had sworn he would run into snow. One hundred and fifty miles with very few icy patches this time—not like last year at this time! "Met some of your menfolk here, in the hallway, on the way up," he added conversationally. "I told them who I was and they said, 'Oh sure we know your mother! She's a real alert, real nice lady!' "

"I'm a regular Miss Jacob Lutheran Home!" Harriet said.

They both laughed, and he told her Evelyn sent her love. He told her about bringing Janice, his oldest son's daughter, out to see her folks in Boyd, and how he begged the baby away from her on condition he wrap him up well.

"What farm business did you come about?" Harriet said, meaning to ask intelligent questions although in truth she was only holding the baby.

"Oh that—" Larry said, frowning. "Before I get to that, there's something we've been over before, Mother, and I want to say it all again."

"Yes—all right!" She laughed at him ironically, mainly because it felt so marvelous holding the baby. His little eyes were half-open, but she held him so close, up to her cheek, that the eye against her cheek was of course out of focus, and therefore only a dark blur: she thought, I shall never forget that look of a baby's eye when you hold him too close to see—the dark, blurry, soft fur-bunch of his eye!

"You know that Evelyn and I have plenty of room, Mama. We want you, Mama. This is OK"—he gave a kind of wave at the tray of Marge Larson's birthday cake and Vonnie's mirror—"but, Mama, we want something different for you."

"You're right," Harriet said gently, "we *have* been over this before. You know how touched I am you feel that way, Larry. You and Evelyn."

She imagined again their house in Edina. It was one of a Cape Cod development—white, but with the green black shutters hung behind, rather than hinged on top of, the outside woodwork, and therefore straight-away visibly fake. But they had some marvelous rooms in it: a kind of library with a wood-burning fireplace and a Viss rug with a light blue pattern, and the dining room. The other rooms had somehow soaked up the builder's ideas, and they all seemed to wail, Edina! Help! Evelyn had done what she could, but the built-in hi-fi cabinet in its fake Early American paneling suffocated the walls.

This wasn't why Harriet didn't go to live with them but she conjured up the picture anyway.

"I know perfectly well you moved in here because that was the right thing for Dad," Larry was saying. "That was *then,* Mama. True he would have been a burden to us—you never said that, but we knew that's what you thought. Anyway it's all different now, and I want you to reconsider. Very carefully."

"There's still your dad to think of, you know," Harriet remarked.

Larry put down his cake. "I don't know if that's true or not," he said. "I mean I don't know if that's the right thinking for you or us to be doing at all. I can't think it would make any difference—and meantime I've got a mother 150 miles away from me that I'd like to have living with me if you don't mind." He spoke a little feverishly—which Harriet understood as slight insincerity on his part.

"I don't know how to thank you," she said. She squinted hard into the baby's sleeping shoulders. His woolly sweater and the upper lip of his blanket she felt clearly on her eyelids. "I expect I could thank you by knitting baby blanket number 234 for Christopher here?"

They both laughed a little but Larry let the laugh fall and quickly took up his point again. "And Evelyn feels the same way, too, Mama."

Harriet was thinking as fast as she could. She had to think: why was Larry feverish? He must be talking excitedly because he didn't really feel so enthusiastic about her moving in with them as he wished to show. Or, that he felt enthusiastic about it now, but that the offer really—very deep within him—was good only so long as his mother was sprightly, alert, a little witty, and so forth. And that he was not giving her the profoundly felt invitation—which would be an invitation to live with him and Evelyn when she might be incontinent, irritable, afraid, or even demented. And perhaps she, like Einar, would have a bad stroke.

As Harriet went through this in her mind, being as systematic about it as she could, she felt this last was the real explanation of Larry's nervousness. It reassured her in her refusal to live with them: even if she should choose not to consider Einar, going to live with her son would mean having to make this adjustment to the Home later—to this one or some other less familiar one she'd have less energy to face it with than she had now.

Having thought this through to the end, she gained her poise. She said kindly, "I know Evelyn feels that way. And I know you do, too—both of you—well, you're marvelous children. I'm going to stay put, I think though. You know I thank you very much."

"Well, there's another reason, Mama," Larry said.

Harriet looked up, still feeling the new sense of control from having thought through the whole thing.

"You see, Mama, I've actually sold the farm. That's one reason I am out here this weekend."

She felt damaged. This piece of news was like an actual

danger to her body. The trouble with being at the end of life, Harriet thought, was that body and mind get too close together: that is, when the mind takes a blow—such as from Larry's selling the farm—the body takes the blow as well. You feel the thing physically. Other times, she had noticed it worked in reverse. When she had originally tripped over Orrin Bjorning's bird-feeding station he left on the floor of the crafts room—a good five years ago now—not only had she hurt her right ankle and toe, but she had felt a kind of damage to her soul. Tears of hurt feelings had come, she remembered. Senility, she suspected, arrived the day you forgot to laugh at these incidents.

Rapidly she now went over Larry's actual words. If he hadn't literally sold the farm, she might convince him not to. But she thought she could still hear his voice saying he had already done it.

He hadn't asked her. She didn't expect to be begged for advice, but it would have been lovely, really lovely, if he had let her in on the various stages of the dealing. He could have told her, I'm beginning to consider offers on the farm, Mama. Or, Well, Mama, two of the buyer prospects look pretty good.

No doubt he had sensed that she would try to talk him out of it! In any case, she gathered herself carefully, meaning to have nothing of the wounded about her.

"You ought to sell the farm, my dear," she said smoothly. "You can't manage a piece of real estate properly unless you're right there, available, when things come up—and goodness knows, it doesn't look as if you and Evelyn are ever going to farm—and certainly Janice and Bob aren't moving in that direction. And I can't really think any of you would want to *retire* to the farm. No, that was probably a good thing!"

Larry gave her a sharp look but she gave away nothing—he surely saw only half old-woman-being-sensible, half great-grandmother-holding-the-baby.

"I don't want you to get around me this time, Mama," Larry said. "I want you to come live with us. We have all that room now. And time. And there'd be congenial people for you to meet. We're not country club people you know! Look, Mama—you've spent your whole life out here!"

The loudspeaker made its electric whine, and the pastor's hoarse, nasal voice came on with the table prayer. *"I Jesu navn, går vi til bords, å spise og drikke pa ditt ord. . . . "* It was dinner time at the Home—and the only sound on the second floor was the soft rub of nurses' shoes, as they moved about their duties.

"Let's go to lunch!" Larry said, standing. "Which one of the marvelous French restaurants of Jacob, Minnesota, shall we take in today? McGregor's Cafe or the Royal?"

"Neither for me," Harriet said. "Give me ten more minutes, dear—and then you go because I've got to go to that funeral this afternoon—and I just had cake and coffee. I don't want more now."

O N A S C A F F O L D outside, Arne was manhandling a large screen frame. Apparently he had decided to start with the taking down of the storm windows after all. Both Harriet and Larry watched him a moment, in the way people who have done any job many times can't help pausing to watch someone else tackle it. They nearly felt the weight in their hands of the storm window coming off—they knew which snapholders had been loosened first; they knew the instant the weight of the glass and wood dropped into the vault of Arne's palm.

"You don't feel bad about the farm then?" Larry said, still looking out the window. Arne's shadow kept sliding back and forth in the room.

"No, dear. It was a good idea. Probably, you should have done it ages ago."

"You used to like it when we drove out there and checked out the old place," he said. "You'll miss that."

"Nonsense. There're hundreds of places I enjoy driving past."

"If you won't come to lunch, Mama, I've got to take that baby back to his mother, I'm afraid. You're sure you won't come?"

Christopher had wet through his clothing a little; his blanketed bottom was moist and warm, but Harriet, whose arm had ached the past half hour, couldn't bear to part with him. This moist, hot weight seemed like a part of her—she dreaded handing him over. She dreaded it. Yet, a minute later, when Larry carefully reached down, she managed a social smile up. Suddenly her breasts and lap were cool. She felt abominable, never to nurse or hold a baby again. Her heart turned really black; she felt her whole body was like a cold andiron.

Larry promised to write, to repeat the invitation. They kissed and he left, saying he'd go see Dad on the way out.

Harriet waited until from down the hall she heard the elevator doors open, close, then she hurried out herself.

"Oh, *ja!* there she goes!" cried Helmstetter, sitting in his usual place at the landing. So everyone was up from dinner already.

Now there were four other men taking up all the chairs there, or she'd have joined him. They all looked especially fragile and pale because they had now put on their good suits; the corrugated necks were so thin, they touched their white collars only at the ribby cords. They were all ready for the funeral.

The two candy-stripers were approaching the elevators from the new wing; glasses and pitcher tinkled like little bells on their cart.

"Hullo, Mrs. White!" they both said.

"Hello—DeAnn . . . Mary."

"Oh my," the one called DeAnn said, cocking her head at the men sitting about, "aren't we dressed up all fine and nice! Everybody looking so nice!"

"They're going to a funeral," cried the other candy-striper.

DeAnn swung the light cart about. Mary had to step back, so it could enter the elevator when the doors opened. "Well, they all look real nice," DeAnn sang. She pointed her arm at full-length to press the elevator button, and turned her head, with the faultless, groomed hair, to the men. "Mr. Morstad was a real fine man," she sang to them. "And he looked real nice, too, for the services."

"I didn't think he did!" said Mary in a low tone to Harriet, dodging close to make room for the head nurse, Mrs. Siegert, who came up to wait beside them. Looking younger than fourteen and very exposed, Mary seemed to gather her bravery and she blurted out, "I didn't think he looked very nice! He looked so tiny and brown and . . . " Her voice faded in terror, for the head nurse, as well as DeAnn, who no doubt despised her, and the four old men in the lounge chairs, now were staring at her.

"And dead," Harriet said, helping. "I agree. But then, the funeral had to be the fourth day instead of the third so the relatives could get here—that's why." Harriet brought out her best, sensible tone: "I remember on the first day he looked rather like himself—only asleep. The second day he began to look diminished, somehow. I remember thinking, that face wants to *leave*. The face is begging us to let it go—like a guest on the porch trying to get away from an officious host. . . . Then, yesterday, I remember—I happened into the chapel coming from my walk, and he looked simply like a dead man—he'd simply lost his distinction. It wasn't that he wasn't preserved or anything like that—but just that he had got generalized—he had become a sampling of death."

The candy-striper's hands came together. "Oh yes!" she cried. "Yes—exactly—that's how he was!" Still the elevator hadn't come down; the light showed it was on three; and they could hear metal scraping and men drawling instructions on the floor above.

The young candy-striper whispered, leaning over the cart toward Harriet, "I even noticed a tear under his eyelashes, Mrs. White."

"Oh for goodness' sake!" the head nurse snapped.

"That happens," Harriet said. "I know what that racket is,"

she said to Mrs. Siegert. "I bet Arne's stuffing storm windows into that elevator—"

They had still to wait, half-listening to the scraping noises upstairs as something was fitted into or out of the elevator.

"You girls hold back with that cart," Mrs. Siegert said, when the elevator came. "Let Mrs. White get in first." But when the tall metal doors had slid open, no one could get in, for the elevator was full of men and a stretcher—Arne, now in his good dress, and Mr. Solstad, the mortician, both men standing soldierly beside a stretcher cart. The significant mounds and hollows under the white sheet told the mind *A body is lying there,* but such an observation was only academic. Harriet couldn't seriously believe in a human being under there. "We'll be done with the elevator in a moment," Arne said. The doors closed again. Harriet, Mrs. Siegert, and DeAnn watched the first floor light come on, and they all had to listen to the elevator door springs downstairs, being struck open twice. Harriet unwillingly imagined the body on its tray being nudged and guided out.

Harriet and Mrs. Siegert walked down the third floor new wing. The infirmary rooms ran along the north side, so they were walking along in direct light from the tall windows facing south. In the middle of the corridor Ardyce, a very, very old person who had been incontinent for over a year stood urinating on the rubber runner. Feeling the hot liquid course over her great ankles, she had begun to cry. Her bony, caving body gave this shriek like some poor sort of violin.

Mrs. Siegert was not an easily likable nurse but she had her strong side; swiftly she got to Ardyce and had the limp elbow and said, "Don't cry, honey—I'll take you. We'll get cleaned up OK—don't cry"; they wobbled together to the old woman's room.

Two younger nurses were guiding a white-curtained screen out of number 307 on little metal wheels. "Oh . . . it was Mr. Kjerle?" Harriet asked.

One of the nurses bent to wipe up the urine from the corrugated rubber mat, and in a moment all was quiet again. Only mysterious breathing came from some room or other, and a cough like small twigs rubbing from some other room.

Harriet put her head into 307. She had meant to do whatever it is we intend in a place where someone has just died. She meant to give some honor or to wish him luck flying off the earth; she meant to help to lift him far off the curvature of the earth by evening. She wasn't clear about it but she felt somehow obligated. She crept into the room, if only to sense his possible presence. In any case, Harriet had expected the room to be empty. Everyone knew Mr. Kjerle's relatives never came to visit—only a retired piano teacher from two miles west of Jacob used to stop in sometimes. The piano teacher's visits weren't much. He really only prowled aimlessly about the infirmary room, not really visiting the old man, at least not keeping up a conversation. Whenever Harriet was up on the infirmary floor, he would waylay her, talk to her eagerly; sometimes, leaning in the doorway of 307, he would tell her it was cruel the way some of the residents never got any visitors.

Harriet was brought up short to see a woman sitting at the bare little desk under the window. She sat so still and wrote with such concentration, that in the indifferent northern light, she looked positively spooky. She wore an elegant knit dress of dark lavender—for a second Harriet felt pleased as if for a glimpse of the *grand monde*. Harriet received three impressions in rapid order: first, that this elegant figure writing was the spirit of the dead man; second, that it was some beautiful creature of society set here like a statue, just to give pleasure, and third—and she smiled with simple happiness at this—that it was the doctor.

Dr. Iversen didn't wear her medical jacket; like the other two doctors in Jacob, she avoided looking like a physician when she went to the Home. If you carried a medical bag, the old people snatched at you, telling of new sets of aches or about old prescriptions that didn't help anymore. Right now she had been called to the Home to "pronounce," that is, to legalize, a death.

She had been sitting quietly, therefore, making out the certification.

"Hullo," she said courteously, as she saw an inmate pause in the doorway. Then, with the instant calculation, the mental sorting of people that she exercised every day in her job, she added, "Mrs. White. Hullo, Mrs. White."

"How are you?" Harriet said, coming in, shyly. "I'm sorry, I didn't know anyone was in here."

"No, of course not," the doctor said. She had not quite finished, but without showing any haste, she quickly picked up the sheet placing the printed side that read Minnesota Department of Health, Section of Vital Statistics, inward, against her hip. She rose. "How is that painful foot of yours anyway?" she asked.

"It isn't very painful," Harriet told her, gratified to be asked. "When it is, I take those gigantic tablets of yours anyway, and can't tell left foot from right!"

"Most of them," the doctor said, "wouldn't admit that a prescription ever did any good. I wouldn't dare ask how their foot is."

"By most of them I gather you mean most *old* people." Harriet laughed. "Don't talk so quickly! I shall be like that someday—and so will you. In fact, it's too bad you're so much younger—we could sit in our rocking chairs and tell each other what ached, and neither one of us would pay the slightest bit of attention to the other one. In fact, maybe you'll be worse. You'll be tired of listening to other people complain."

"No change, I suppose?" the doctor inquired, nodding toward the wall between the room they were in, number 307, and the next, 308.

"I haven't been in today—I'm just going now," Harriet said.

"It is hard, isn't it?"

"Yes—and I feel so sorry for him," Harriet added, not having planned to say anything like that.

ROOM 308, like 307, faced north, the cold light seeming simply to stand outside. There was the same little window desk, whose purpose was simply to be a piece of furniture for a sickroom. There was a high bureau, on which stood favors sent up from the public school children. At Christmas there had been paper reindeer with sleighs made of egg carton sections. Now there was an Easter bunny, stapled to a bit of egg carton, in which one or two of the hard candies that must have filled it remained. Harriet supposed the staff took a candy now and then, just as they gradually were taking the bureau space. In the top drawer were the clothes Einar had worn when they brought him up. But in the other drawers were odds and ends, a few more added right along, a small plastic bag of curlers, some lip moisturizing cream, two magazines read by the candy-striper who spoon-fed patients, half a box of tissues. More and more that had nothing to do with Einar seemed to sift into the room; his small influence, like a little scattering of pebbles, was being buried lightly under other influences.

Harriet spent a second by the desk, her eyes on the fields plowed black and to the north, and the semis moving like little blocks on U.S. 75. Then she straightened and went back over to the bed.

"Hello, dear," she said. She pulled the white-painted rocker over and sat down to talk to him. On the good days he gave a sound, as well as he could, to recognize her; on the other days, no particular sign. Today—nothing; so she settled to talk to him. "A little news for you, Einar," she said. "Larry's selling the farm—probably a very good idea," she went on. "And considering the condition of the buildings, he did very well I think. There's no doubt that was the right idea, selling the farm."

She paused. She pulled herself together and said, "There's no doubt that was the right idea, selling the farm."

She took another pause—pulled herself together again. "I gave him the go-ahead on that. . . . " She was trying to remember other things to tell; she remembered in the crook of her elbow, with the palm of her hand, the feeling of Christopher in her arms, but the memory was still too personal. In fact, it was not yet a memory, but still part of herself and therefore couldn't be told. "I gave another speech this morning," she went on cheerfully. "Anyway"—she smiled—"the speech went off all right. About the only other news is I've fairly well planned little Christopher's sweater now, so I'll start the knitting of it soon. Oh yes—and the men said to give you their best. That Helmstetter whose first name I never can remember—and Kermit—they both said to greet you. They were telling me about television. They don't watch 'Edge of Night' anymore, they said. They watch something called 'Splendor of Our Days.' It sounds dumber than the other one, but I expect if you kept track of it all the time, it would begin to seem real—you'd begin to care what happened to those people. . . . But those television characters don't seem like real people at all—and you know, they never show *where* the people are—they're always in a room somewhere—you never see a real place that counts, like a farm or anything like it—it's as if none of them had any place to belong to. Did I tell you, Larry sold the farm, Einar? Yes—very good idea, too!" She talked to him some more, and then rose saying, "I'll be back at five again to help you with your dinner, dear," and she went out.

She had spoken truthfully to the doctor in saying her right foot was not painful. When she finally got outside with her hat and scarf and gloves, she swung along well, and drew deep breaths of the cold burdened air. It definitely was going to snow. She lightly dropped down the hill to the traffic circle, noticing all the cars and the hearse parked in the church lot. She turned west on 11th Street and was still moving freshly and gladly when she came to U.S. 75, with the closed Dairy Queen building and Waltham's Flower Shoppe.

When she turned north, on the right-hand shoulder of the highway, the wind struck her forehead. It wasn't bitter, but it was colder than she had hoped for. She turned away from it, long enough to pull her scarf up about her neck better, and now the buildings of the town, even the hasty gimcrackery of the Dairy Queen, looked protective and familiar. Well, I don't have to walk all the way to the farm on the ugliest day of spring, she told herself wryly, but she turned into the wind again, bending her head. Under her feet the dozens of pebbles on the road's shoulder underfoot looked shrunken and abandoned. She tried to set up her walking motion into a kind of automation, the way she and Einar and Larry had done for years and years when they were tired from the farmwork. At first you grew tired, then you grew so tired you felt you might cry, and then, by not feeling any pity for any part of your body, by not weakening those parts, that is, with pity, you actually exacted from them more character; once the ankles, back, shoulders, wrists, learnt to expect no mercy of you, they began to work as if automated. Then you weren't exhausted anymore, and you could sift fertilizers, or lift alfalfa, or shovel to an auger for hours and hours, until, with their headlights glowing like tiny search beams, coming out of the fields as if out of the sky itself, the tractors came home with the men who had been hired—and everyone could quit. Thus the tiredness could be held back until you all leaned over the salmon hot dish, and reached for the bread.

Harriet did the same thing now, looking up only once really—taking in a field of corn that someone hadn't gotten plowed, or even disked down at all. It'd do it good to snow a little. She thought of the scenery critically. So she was delighted like a child when the first flakes blew at her, around three-thirty.

IT TOOK HER another two hours to get to Haglund's Crossroads, and a half hour to the farm from there. This last half hour was the township road running east, however, so the steady snow, that had been hurting her forehead, now struck only her left cheek, and she took her second wind cheerfully.

When she reached the corner of her farm, she felt surprised: her old land, not ten feet from her now, across the ditch past the telephone company marker, looked just like all the fields she had been walking past. When she had sat on the porch in the hot evenings, all the dozens of years she and Einar had had the place, she certainly never would have thought those particular sights—Elsie Johnson's barn with the louver-window towers, Vogel's run, the Streges' line of cottonwoods to the south— would lose their distinction. When Larry had taken her out for rides, she always knew the place. Yet now, this late afternoon, she felt no particular recognition.

"Well, but the house will make the difference—when I can see the house," she said. Because the driveway lay another quarter of a mile to the east, she decided to cut across the plowing instead. She paused and then went down into the ditch, some pebbles falling into her boots, and then slowly up, and began working along the headlands of the field. Her forehead was tight and silky now with cold, and the skin gave an unpleasant sensation of not being close to her head. Harriet moved carefully, not just because she was exhausted, but because it was borne in on her that she was a very old woman and she would make a fool of herself if she fainted out here in the middle of nowhere, with night coming on.

The plowing was coarse, and from her height—as she imagined herself an airplane passing over it—it became a chain of harsh, tumbled mountains, with peaks turning floury but the smooth sides, scoured by the shares, still gleaming black. At last the farmhouse, or at least some dark, square, blessedly man-made shape, stood out 100 yards ahead. Its lightless windows, broken, its tumbledown porch seemed friendly and very memorable. It had been a marvelous idea to come—marvelous!

Harriet's fingers, particularly on the right hand, were starting to freeze, but she put them in her coat pocket and went forward quickly. She also planned ahead, using her common sense: she would stay in the house or around it, but not for more than half an hour. She wasn't a fool; it would be difficult to explain why she'd come, but if she left soon and got home she might not even be missed.

The rough plowing ended; she stepped into the spineless pigeon grass, and emptied her boot. The snow stopped, but enough was down so the farmyard, with the L-shaped old house on it, rose a pale, glowing mound. Harriet went happily up.

The front door was half-ruined and stood open. She decided that it would be depressing inside the house so she sat down gratefully on the edge of the porch, feeling sorry for its beautifully milled railing posts wrecked and lying in the snow. She crossed her hands in her lap — a trick she had had all her life — in order to think deliberately, and get things right.

Immediately her mind and body seemed to have opposing wishes. Her mind wanted to go over favorite memories — it wanted to swoon, to graze, to be languid, and to rove over things that are delicious, such as her old loves. Her own mother and father, for example, whom she visualized dancing in their club, or drinking with faces yellow from the firelight at home. The mind wanted to go over how she loved them although she had despised their shallow, rich, greedy life; how much she loved her parents and would like to know what they were thinking now . . . It wasn't a new line of thought but her mind wanted so very much to go over it again. But her body, or her soul, whichever it was, was thoroughly excited and seemed to be urging, something very strange is about to happen! It was alerted like an animal — it refused to let her dream along the old intelligent reflections — it wanted to get the scent of something, it seemed to send fingers out beyond the broken porch. Oh — she thought, holding these two parts as well as she could — it is definitely something spiritual, something about to happen! And not from inside me! All these years I assumed it was all inside me — but apparently it isn't! — and I am afraid! In any case, it was in the outer circle of darkness now, rising over the Haglund Road maybe; anyway it lay outside the farm, and was lifting and falling, coming in closer, without any excitement of its own, simply waiting, not crouching nor threatening—something calm, but mortally large. She needed to invite it, Harriet felt, if it was to come in any closer.

THEN A THIRD thing happened: headlights were moving along the snowy road to the south, going east the way Harriet had come, and then going past the place where she had turned up through the field. Now the invisible car presented its red taillights for a moment but then, in the next, the headlights swung left and were quartering on Harriet. So they knew she was gone and had figured she might do just this—walk up here; and they were coming, to save her from the cold and dark. Her hand, particularly the fingers, hurt enough; she nearly leapt forward gratefully.

Wait a moment, she thought, sensibly: there are three different things I can do. I can still run behind the house—it isn't too late—they would call about a little here and there, but they wouldn't think of the old chicken house we had used for lawn mowers. Then, whatever that part of her was that wanted to invite the huge mortal thing outside, would have a little more time to do it in. But no, Harriet thought intelligently, they would see her footsteps in the snow and she would be tracked like an animal, and she would never recover her pride—not ever, after that. Now the headlights were fully turned in her direction, and as soon as the car tipped up to make the rise, the lights would flood over her, as the lights of all their visitors always had, blinding anyone on the porch. It was going to be unpleasant, whatever happened; but she tried very hard to think of some little speech to give that would not let them think she was old and out of her wits—something to pass it off lightly—but how? For she didn't feel she had any light touch at the moment at all; more and more, her soul was being engaged by the gigantic, mortal thing waiting in its wide arc outside; one minute it

seemed to offer to go away, and leave her with her ordinary life
in her hands again: this she couldn't bear, not now that she'd
once seen it. She had a taste for it now. The next minute, however, she found she was still too mortal, too frightened by far,
and she would agree to marry any sort of dullness rather than to
join whatever that was. She couldn't toss off anything with a
laugh now. If she herself were so deadly serious, how could she
hope to make whoever was driving up in this car take the whole
thing lightly?

Now the headlights were brilliant on her, so she had to look
down at the wrecked railing and posts, that lay like a ladder
thrown down in the snow. The headlights came no closer: the
car must have stopped, and she heard the incredible confidence
of an American automobile engine idling in neutral. Doors
clicked open and shut—men were tramping in the darkness behind the headlights—someone in a low tone could be heard
saying, "It's her all right!" Another voice—"You all wait. I'll go
up!" Then a gigantic black profile of someone came at her,
shielding her from the beams.

"Hi, Mama," the man said.

In a flash Harriet was angry at this grown Larry—a shallow
thing he seemed, no matter that he was her son, no matter he
was being dear and dignified and not talking at her, helping her
step over the smashed banister in the snow. But she thought,
how different he is from the baby he was, with the dark, blurry
eyes so close to her face, for now he was only a grown
son—predictable, and wrapped around with his health and
sense.

Other people sat in the car. As Harriet got into the front seat,
she saw all their faces in the light from the car's ceiling—Arne,
it was; Larry; Siegert, the head nurse; some other nurse she had
seen but didn't know—and she felt comforted, partly, by this
lighted little circle. Outside the car, in a much wider circle, the
mortal presence still wafted lightly. Harriet felt very definitely
that it was offering to lap forward toward her again; she felt she

could rally it and offer to go out with it, like something bobbing on lumpy, stale seawater in the darkness; she felt it wouldn't take her quickly, it would lap forward and receive her, but for a while it would let her look back to the tiny car, with the tiny circle of human beings; but they were all she knew, so she fled into the front seat, and let herself be walled up with Arne's shoulders on one side, moving as he went into reverse, and Larry's great shoulder on the other side. And from the back seat came low, special voices—the nurses talking to each other professionally. Harriet hoped she had not lost individuality from their viewpoint: now she was a woman who wandered off from the Home and had to be brought back at a good deal of inconvenience, and on such a busy day. She must be very careful to be light and sociable. "So good of you all," she murmured. "It was very cold."

She was very grateful for losing the sensation of God being close—or perhaps she had made up in her mind the whole impression of something in the darkness. In any case it didn't matter. She hadn't the slightest curiosity to think it over, for something much worse occupied her. Squeezed between these kind men, with the car heater blowing hot breath into her face, and with her eyes full of the dancing needles and blue tiny fires on the dashboard, she was sharply aware that she wasn't safe with these protectors. Her hand was in great pain now, from the freezing: but suppose *all* of her were in pain, and suppose death did come, and not some death she chose to conjure up and call upon, but plainly death himself, the real one—she would flash down like silk between these men, past the glittering dashboard without leaving the slightest impression, the way the pebbles in the road were blown off by the speeding car. I'm simply not going to be able to do anything about it, she thought with surprise.

They were driving rapidly down the Haglund Road—she felt the millions of pebbles of gravel that had always lain there, unwrapped, which no one pays any attention to, all the millions of things that lie about unbound to the millions of other things. With a tremendous burst of humility and joy Harriet thought:

what a tremendous lot I have failed to think through! Yet I always thought I thought through things so well!

FROM A MILE and a half north, the Jacob Lutheran Home suddenly stood up, with its three stories of lighted windows. It was difficult to visualize the shuffling heels moving about near bureaus, or to believe in the cartful of magazines parked idle for the night in the coffee room. The Home looked at least like a mighty office complex where far-reaching decisions are made that affect common people without their even knowing it. It was difficult to believe in Einar up there, lying lightly gowned in white, scarcely touching, like a bit of string, as he had lain for fourteen months. Harriet thought, And I shall lie up there, too, and from month to month, because I will no doubt get less amusing and I will get more frightened, there will be fewer and fewer visitors, even this huge man next to me, Larry, my son, will come much less often, and perhaps my death will rock forward and backward on its heels waiting a long time, and I shall be so diminished by the time it comes even the staff won't feel anything personal. There will be none of the old recognition . . .

Now they were approaching the confident little town.

Harriet was very surprised to find that she hadn't spent eighty-two years in love with all there is, and tiny things like pebbles, which were in some strange way her equal: pebbles were her equal; she was astounded she had missed it! Now she needed every possible second, even if it were to be spent in a daze. How could she ever have said, "It is cruel that so-and-so's life drags on like this!" or, "It is a blessing that death came to so-and-so!" Or, "I certainly hope I shall go quickly when I go"—as if it were a question of being fastidious.

The heat of the car did not help her frozen hand. The pain was frightful—but her thoughts seemed so much more frightful to her that she deliberately gave in to the pain. From the back seat came kind voices: "Soon there, Harriet . . . " and "You're not the only one to go out walking, you know," and "We all do it, Harriet . . . " And in the front seat, her son's shoulder jerked a little next to hers and he stared ahead, silently, through the windshield.

When they were up in room 211, the doctor examined her fingers carefully. "We'll have you knitting again—it won't be long," she said. "She can have something to help her sleep," she said pointedly to the head nurse, who paused in the doorway.

Larry sat on Mrs. Ole Morstad's bed, with his knees spread, his hat thrown up on the pillow. He was turning over Harriet's alarm clock, and he looked very tense and bored. Harriet, too, felt very strained and bored.

"If you would *please* reconsider, Mama," Larry was saying—still asking her to go live with him. A second ago her heart had leapt—but only for a second. She would love to leave this fate! She would love to go to him! Again she imagined his house, the flowery rug with its wide edge of sky blue that looked like a cool, ancient summer all the time, and the marvelous tone of the Vivaldi on his record machine; Janice would come on weekends, perhaps, and bring the baby, and Harriet would rock with the baby, and look at all the woolen yellow flowers in the rug.

Larry was making the offer, but she heard a new apprehension in his voice. I am a very old woman apparently, she told herself, and I've wandered off in a snowstorm, but I'm not going to add this to my other sins. As she turned him down, she smiled quite genuinely, because the pill she'd been given was taking effect—her hand no longer hurt—and everything looked peaceful and colorless. From time to time, the upper echelon of the staff and residents looked in and greeted her—even Marge Larson, the therapist, stopped a moment, Kermit Steensen nodded from the hall—the candy-stripers had long since gone home or she knew Mary would have greeted her.

Tomorrow morning, word would have got around the whole community, and the simpler, the very aged, or the less acquainted people would take to hobbling by room number 211. They would want to have a look at someone who had stirred them all by getting a notion to go back home. Their flagged expressions didn't suggest that actually their hearts were rather aflutter by this Harriet White's doings—the way the hearts of young women feel roused, and unstable, and prescient, when the first of their friends is going to marry.

II

A Theory
of Knowledge

A SHADOW moved silently through the grass. Professor Weber looked up from his work, startled, and saw a child approaching him.

"Yes? Who are . . . ?

The boy was four or five years old, a stranger. He was barefoot; there were innumerable reddened marks on his feet and legs; his short pants were ripped and filthy, and his shirt was partly unbuttoned. Professor Weber stared. Should he know whose child this was? The boy carried himself oddly, as if one side of his body were higher than the other. He was unusually quiet, timid, not like Professor Weber's grandsons, who ran anywhere they liked around the old farm, noisily, in robust good health, whenever his married daughter came to visit. "Yes? Hello? Are you a neighbor of mine?" Professor Weber said. He smiled; he did not want to frighten the boy.

The boy smiled shyly and came no closer.

It was a shock—seeing the boy's teeth. They were greenish, that thin, near-transparent look of poverty, ill health, malnutrition. The boy had wild curly hair, blue-black as an Indian's; his face was thin, too pale for this time of year, but Professor Weber thought him strangely beautiful—the eyes especially, large dark eyes that seemed entirely pupil. And so intense! The boy licked his lips. His mouth moved in a kind of convulsion, shaping words that could not be given sound. Professor Weber stared, pitying; his own lips moved in sympathy with the boy's. *Hel- Hel- Hello.* It cost the child some effort to pronounce this word.

"Can you tell me your name?" Professor Weber asked softly. "Where do you live?"

The boy was older than he had appeared at first. Professor Weber judged him to be seven or eight years old, severely un- dernourished. His eyes were so dark, so intense!—the intensity of his gaze deepened by an obscure shame, a despair that was al- most adult. He reminded Professor Weber of a misshapen, dwarfish man who had lived in a hut beyond the village dump- ing ground in Katauga . . . but that had been many years ago, a half-century or more.

"Have we met, little boy? I'm notoriously forgetful about names, faces . . . you'll have to forgive me if. . . . "

Embarrassed at such attention, the boy squatted in the grass and pretended an interest in something there—it was Professor Weber's journal, which must have slipped from his lap. Had he dozed off again? And where was his pen?—he was holding his pen, clutching it tightly. The boy turned pages slowly, frown- ing. A convulsive tic began at the corner of his mouth and worked gradually up into his cheek, as if the effort needed for concentration on Professor Weber's writing was painful. His lips moved soundlessly, shaping ghost-words. But of course the tight, slanted handwriting would have been too difficult for him, even if he could read; it was doubtful that he could read. "You wouldn't be interested in that, I'm afraid. Just jottings . . . labored whims . . . propositions that float of their own accord and lead nowhere. You wouldn't be interested in Reuben Weber's theory of knowledge, little boy; no one else is. Could you hand my book here, please?" The boy did not seem to hear. He was imitating or perhaps mocking the effort of reading: his head bowed, his chin creasing towards his chest, his child's forehead furrowed like an old man's. Professor Weber thought suddenly: What if he rips the pages? What if he runs off with it maliciously? The child must have wandered over from a neighboring farm. Probably the Brydons'. But Professor Weber had not known they had a grandson. Had their son married? The child did not resemble anyone in the area; but of course Professor Weber knew few people, he had kept to himself all along, it was his daughter Maude who took an interest in local news and had a fair number of acquaintances in the area. . . . Professor Weber's legs were thin as sticks, but the muscles of his calves and thighs had tensed like those of a much younger man, preparing to get him to his feet if necessary. "Little boy, could you hand that to me? This lap-desk is so awkward to set down, and this blanket. . . . "

"Go away, please!" someone called, behind him.

It was his daughter Maude, down from the house.

The boy lifted his head; but not quickly; rather slowly, as if he had not heard the words, had only sensed someone else's presence. At once his dark eyes widened with fear. Professor Weber was sorry his daughter had discovered them, after all; the boy was a sweet, docile child, obviously not malicious. "He isn't harming anything," Professor Weber said curtly. "He doesn't seem to be . . . isn't any. . . . Just a little visit. . . . "

"Please go home, little boy," Maude said. She spoke calmly and flatly, as she sometimes spoke to Professor Weber himself. "Can't you hear? Can't you understand? I said. . . . "

The boy straightened cautiously, as if he were afraid of being struck. He began to scratch at himself—his neck, his shoulders, his ribs. The dark eyes, fixed upon Maude, were now narrowed.

"I believe he came from that direction, from the creek," Professor Weber said, embarrassed. His voice was kindly; he wanted the boy to look at him again, as if this were a social occasion of some kind, swerving into error. It required the human element, an intelligent restoration of balance. "He evidently cut

himself on the bushes, or fell on the rocks—do you see his legs?
I don't think it's anything serious, he isn't crying, but perhaps
we could . . . it might be a good idea to wash him and. . . . "

"Do you want me to tell your parents on you?" Maude asked
the child.

He turned and ran away.

They watched him until he was out of sight—across the
creek, through a field of wild shrubs and saplings. He seemed to
be headed in the direction of the Brydon farm.

Professor Weber was drained by the excitement but wanted
very much to talk. "Did the Brydon boy marry, after all? Is that
his son? . . . and I didn't know about it until now? Could it be
possible that. . . . "

"The Brydons have been gone for years," Maude said flatly.
"You know that." She stooped to pick up his journal. And his
pen, too, which had just fallen into the grass. "*That* certainly
isn't any Brydon—did you see him scratching himself? Lice.
That's the kind of people living there now and I don't want
anything to do with them. Nobody does. The things people say
about that family, the woman especially. . . . " She broke off,
sighing angrily. "Imagine, a child with lice! Letting him go like
that, running wild!"

"But who are they?" Professor Weber asked. He was confused; as always, his daughter seemed to know far more than he
did; the variety of things she knew, and the emotional dis-
charges they allowed her, seemed remarkable. He was contemptuous of the gossip she repeated—yet he wanted very much
to know about the boy. "He didn't seem. . . . I really don't think
he has lice. . . . Who told you that? What kind of people are his
parents?"

"Never mind," Maude said. "I won't let him bother you
again. . . . The sun has moved behind that tree, hasn't it? Are
you still warm enough?"

Professor Weber was staring down toward the creek, at the
tangle of trees, saplings, and bushes. A marvelous thick-bodied

white willow—three enormous poplars in a row—birds fluttering in their leaves. He could not see the creek from here, but he could make out its sound; he was very happy here, no matter what people might whisper about him, and he did not want to be moved. He had not exactly heard his daughter's question. "Yes, yes," he said firmly. "Yes. That's so."

JUNE, 1893. No: it was 1897. Professor Weber kept mixing those dates together, and he did not know why. There was nothing important about 1893 that he could recall. His wife had died a few years earlier. . . . No, there was nothing special about that date. The perplexing, humiliating tricks of the mind. . . . He had spent the greater part of his life trying to cut through obscurity, murkiness, the self-indulgent metaphysics of the past. *Of laws logically contingent the most universal are of such a kind that they must be true provided every form by which logical necessity must be thought of a given subject is also a form of its real being. If this be "metaphysical" necessity we may divide laws logically contingent into laws metaphysically necessary and laws metaphysically contingent.* But his hands trembled, it was so difficult to write, to keep pace with his thoughts. They sped forward, youthful as always, darting ahead into sub-propositions, into qualifications, refinements, hypothetical objections put forth by his enemies . . . his thoughts seemed, at times, not his at all, but the brilliant, tireless, relentless thoughts of a stranger. And his hands trembled, unable to keep pace. He had to steady one hand with the other. He bit his lower lip with the effort, impatient at how long it took him to scribble into his journal a thought that had sprung fully matured into his mind: *Humanism was feeble in its mental powers . . . incapable of subtlety. The acceptance of nominalist beliefs has poisoned all of Western thinking. As if a reality that has no representation could be other than one without relation and quality. . . .*

He had waited so long for summer. Winter here, in the

foothills of the Chautauqua Mountains, was interminable . . .
spring was unpredictable, heartbreaking for an old man who
craved the open air, release at last from the stuffy rooms of the
house and from his absurd dependency upon the wood-burning
stove in the kitchen. From time to time he had been actually
frightened at the prospect of a chilly spring. Why had he come
here to this dismal place? Several miles north of the small town
of Rockland, on the Alder River . . . a full day's drive to a decent
library, at the seminary in Albany; and of course that library was
always disappointing. Twelve years ago, was it, since his retirement? His "retirement"? Everyone had urged him not to move
away from Philadelphia, even his enemies had hypocritically
urged him to reconsider his decision; there were vague airy in-
sincere promises . . . the possibility of lecturing, tutoring, independent work with advanced post-doctoral students who required more logic and mathematics. James Emmett Morgan
had said . . . Charles Lewes had said . . . But he had moved
away just the same.

And he did not regret it, really. The foothills were
beautiful—the poplars, willows, blue spruce, elms surrounding
his house—the many birds, including pine grosbeaks and dark-
headed juncos—the fragrance of open air, solitude—freedom at
last to compose his book on the foundations of human
knowledge—freedom to sit in the sun for hours, brooding,
dozing. He half hoped the curly-haired boy would appear again,
to interrupt his work. Though he had lived in the old farmhouse
for years now, he knew no one in the neighborhood; he could
count the number of times he had bothered to go into Rockland. . . . Insignificant, the affairs of most men. Monstrous eco-
nomic snarls, shortsighted passions, the ignorance of which
Socrates spoke with a good humor perhaps ill-advised. So no
one came to interrupt him; it had been years now since he'd
really talked with anyone, argued with anyone about matters of
importance; he half hoped the neighbor boy might. . . . But
Maude said they were no better than gypsies. She said it was a

"scandal," the things that went on . . . as bad as living on the outskirts of Rockland itself, where there was a paper mill and mill-workers' hovels . . . unspeakable crimes that went ignored. But the child had seemed to Professor Weber remarkably well-behaved, especially in contrast with his own grandsons.

WHAT WAS that sound?—high pitched vibrating racket? Ah, the flicker in that big poplar. Professor Weber strained to listen.

No, he did not regret his move. Not once had he indicated to anyone, in his correspondence, that he regretted it—or any decision of his life. He was stubborn, flamboyant as in his prime, immensely certain of himself. He *knew* what was right; he had an instinct for the truth. The stone farmhouse with the rotting roof, originally build in 1749, the three acres of land, the several decaying outbuildings his grandchildren played in when they came . . . these were pleasant, agreeable things, hardly a mistake. What had been needed so sorely, his defenders told him, was a single work, a work that set forth his system; had he had time, while teaching, to bring together the thousands of pages of notes, sketches, hypothetical problems . . . the essence of "Weber's Epistemology" . . . he and his disciples could hold their own against the outrageously popular William James and the equally insupportable ideas that were coming in from Germany, like an infection Anglo-Saxons seemed eager to catch every half-century or so. Had he the time. . . . Had he the energy. . . . What he kept secret from everyone, even his closest colleagues, was the perplexing fact that ideas stormed his brain with such violence that he was capable even at the best of times of doing no more than jotting down five or six pages of continuous discovery. If only he were content with being superficial like James! . . . but that was unfair, he supposed, since James had written several very perceptive and kindly letters to him, and had even arranged for a lecture series . . . unfair, unfair . . . his thinking was muddled because of the tranquility of this place,

the seductive qualities of . . . Was William James still alive?
Were Lewes and Wrightson still alive? Why had it never been
offered him, that position at Harvard everyone knew he deserved . . . ? The jealousy of his colleagues at Rochester he could
well understand; the jealousy of his colleagues at Philadelphia
had been quite a surprise. That they should gossip behind his
back . . . refer to him in the presence of graduate students and
young faculty as a crank . . . laugh and jeer and ridicule his ora-
torical method of teaching. . . . Or had he imagined it? Bursting
into the Common Room, hearing laughter, had he misinter-
preted the silence, the guilty looks, the uneasy smiles? Of course
he had always intimidated them. Always. His attacks upon their
complacency, upon their beloved "areas of specialization," his
pronouncement that all philosophical speculation must flow
through the rigorously narrow channel of logic and linguistic
analysis—he had intimidated them all! He had frightened them
all!

"Father. *Father.*"

Maude was speaking. He awoke: was astonished to see that it
was no longer daylight, that he was in the old leather chair by
the fireplace, a book on his lap. What day was this? Where was
the little boy? He checked the book—yes, it was Euclid—so he
did remember something of what was going on. He had been
dictating to Maude and she had allowed him to fall asleep, as
usual. Now she was asking him, in the kind of impertinent tone
one hears in the nursery or the sickroom, if he was all right?
"You seemed to be having a nightmare . . . you were twitching
all over . . . talking in your sleep. . . . "

"Leave me alone," he said. " . . . persecuting me. All of
you."

"Father, did you have a nightmare?"

"It was because I frightened them . . . outraged them, wasn't
it," he muttered. It seemed to him obvious that an injustice had
been committed against him; a series of injustices had been
committed, in fact; and why was Maude staring at him so un-

comprehendingly? "What I must live to establish, when I finish the book I'm doing, is a science of a newer sort . . . a Science of the Unique . . . a respect for . . . awareness of. . . . Let the Hegelians rage, let the Platonists . . . let them band against me. . . . It wasn't fair, you know. I was never taken seriously . . . I had anticipated in the fifties the methodology of 'pragmatism' . . . if not the term, that despicable misleading term! . . . they could not forgive me that I valued Truth over social pieties and religious nonsense . . . that my first marriage was . . . was not . . . did not prove stable. . . . Cowards, all of them."

"Yes, Father," Maude said.

"Is not belief 'that upon which a man is prepared to act'?—and is not anything man will not *act* upon likely to be fraudulent belief—hypocrisy—lies—sheer rubbish? And so, because I valued my search for Truth over—over—"

"Yes."

"Philosophy must be cleansed, harshly. Without mercy. Are you writing this down, dear? Or am I speaking too fast? . . . Philosophy must be cleansed . . . purified . . . must keep aloof of the myriad sordid political skirmishes of the day . . . must keep aloof of the historical world altogether. And the church in any form. That goes without saying. . . . Without saying. What is dead will sink, what is vital and living will rise to the surface. The future . . . the future. . . . "

"Yes, Father?" Maude said flatly.

But for a moment he could not think: could not even seem to comprehend the meaning of that term.

Future. *Future?*

TIME ITSELF had betrayed him.

"I was born before my time, you see. A premature birth. Graduated from Harvard at the age of eighteen, my Master's at twenty . . . considered abrasive and insolent simply because . . .

because others resented my youth. Did I tell you that as early as the fifties I had formulated the concept of 'pragmatism' . . . without using that word, of course . . . but the methodology, the . . . the aura of . . . the reliance upon phenomenological procedure. . . . According to my notes it was in 1859. No longer young then, no longer a rebellious 'upstart' . . . thirty-nine years old, in fact . . . yet no one listened to me. No one."

AH, BUT IT was dangerous, to allow his body such nervous excitement! He knew very well that it was dangerous; he had no need for an ignorant backwoods general practitioner to tell him . . . a man with tobacco-stained hands and teeth . . . a medical degree from a school probably unrecognized in the East. He had no need for his wife or Maude or Clara or. . . . His heartbeat accelerated until his entire body seemed to rock. His face grew heated, flushed. His muscles twitched with the need to act, to break free of these idiotic restraints . . . to assert himself as his will demanded he must. But time had betrayed him. Time: an abstract term, a mere condition of the human mind . . . a condition dependent upon perception, grammar, the logical assumption of . . . of finitude. Time had betrayed him, had leaped from the early decade of his young manhood to this decade of exile . . . had confused every issue . . . splashing him with blobs of color, emotion, noise, tears . . . that hideous time when, after his first stroke, he had had to watch a scrawny stray cat systematically torture a chipmunk out in the yard . . . fifteen minutes of it . . . *fifteen minutes* . . . and Maude hadn't heard his cries, his shouts of anger and despair. Time had rushed him along, too hurriedly for him to organize his thoughts, set down an outline for *A Theory of Human Knowledge* . . . he had been a rather fashionably dressed young man with a full blond beard, a penetrating voice, a frame that had been solid, muscular . . . rather short legs, and slightly bowed, but of undeniable strength. And purpose. He had been too young for his elders to take seriously; now he was too old for anyone to take seriously. His elders: enemies. They were dead now. He did not want revenge on them. Truly, he did not want to hurt them. He wanted only justice. Recognition. Acceptance of his ideas. He did not ask to be loved or even liked, but simply tolerated. Was it too much to ask? . . . Incredible, that he, Reuben, his father's most promising son, a boy who had absorbed all there was to know of mathematical theory before the age of thirteen, was now so altered that his own mirrored face repulsed him!

" . . . but you must draw your ideas together, Professor Weber. You must construct a system, Professor Weber. Your ideas will be lost . . . will be misunderstood . . . will be appropriated by lesser men or by your enemies. You must compose a rebuttal to Professor Madison's shameless neo-nominalism. You must compose a letter explaining your own actions in regard to your absence from the university community for those years. You must withdraw from this atmosphere . . . purify your thoughts . . . draw your ideas together before it is too late."

He began to laugh.

He opened his eyes: the boy was laughing with him.

It was July now. The boy had visited only twice, but they were on quite friendly, comfortable terms. Professor Weber wrote in his journal, or fussed and sighed with his notes, or called the boy's attention to certain birds' songs—the flicker, some cardinals, some warblers—while the boy usually sat in the grass, silently, listening with great concentration. He did not speak; even trying to speak was too much of an effort. But from time to time he laughed, which delighted Professor Weber. He had not tried hard enough, as a teacher, to be amusing . . . witty . . . playful. He would have liked, perhaps, to have been more entertaining. A robust lecturer, yes, but too driven by a sense of urgent points to be made during a lecture period, too nervously abrupt. . . . It pleased him when the boy laughed. "Yes, that's right," he said. "That's the proper judgment."

The boy's eyes were immense. Gypsy blood, perhaps. But no, that was Maude's nonsense. . . . Too pale to have gypsy blood. Looked more like the child of a mill-worker or one of those luckless children Professor Weber had seen occasionally, in Boston, sickly pale, staggering with weariness, workers at one of the factories along the river. A pity, a pity. The young blond-bearded man walking along so quickly, lost in abstract thought, and the scrawny pale children, unnaturally quiet for children . . . an adult or two, probably their parents or an older brother or sister, herding them along. A pity. Couldn't something be . . . ? But he would forget them in a few minutes; would forget whatever had been upsetting him. "People haven't anything to do out here except gossip," Professor Weber told the boy, shaking his head. "My own daughter is one of the worst offenders. I don't listen any longer, I press my hands over my ears and refuse to listen! . . . But you evidently don't go to school? You can't read? A pity, a pity. Why don't they send you to school? . . . Perhaps I could teach you. If we could work out some way of. . . . Of course without offending your. . . . "

He was staring at the boy's forehead. The skin was discolored near his left temple, as if he had banged his head against something. A very pale violet-orange. As Professor Weber spoke, the boy stared and smiled and then half closed his eyes, basking in the sun. Marvelous, this peace. The two of them. Maude did not like the child but would not dare interrupt. No need to talk, of course. The wind in the poplars . . . the cicadas . . . the sun. July now; midsummer. A pile of notes on Professor Weber's lap, an outline in faded ink that he had discovered the evening before . . . which would save him the labor of writing an outline . . . hadn't known he had already gotten so far with *A Theory of Human Knowledge* or *Knowing*, as it was to be tentatively called . . . really, the outline was excellent; it would do. "Platonic Realism: must be defended against its own excesses. The extremities of Realism touch Nominalism itself. How could Plato not know . . . ? How could he fail to see . . . ? A tragedy, that Plato never consolidated his system but presented it piecemeal . . . gave in to the performer in Socrates. . . . No," Professor Weber said suddenly, "it's really too late. Plato is lost, he can't be resuscitated. Shameless. That he could allow one of his characters to tease us by saying *Not-being is a sort of being*. . . . Spinoza. You will fall under his spell, like children. Adulthood cannot be approached except by way of the . . . the mastery of . . . submitting of oneself to. . . . Discipline, rigor, tautological propositions . . . language . . . beauty. Ah, what beauty! It cannot be denied. But he lacked humanity, he lacked a sense of terror. As for Kant. . . . Why are you startled? Why are you no longer taking notes? I suppose you will report me to the dean of the college, who imagines himself a Kantian! . . . without possessing even the rudiments (I know: I have quizzed him personally) of a mind. As for Emerson. . . . It was an insult, and yet I nearly accepted. 1869. 1870. Reuben Weber to follow Emerson's lecture series: a disciplined philosopher to follow a scatterbrain! No evidence of mental powers at all. Baffling, that he should be so shameless, arrogant. And yet successful. Cambridge infected with it . . . monstrosity, parody . . . fragments of ideas from Hegel, Schelling, Plotinus, even from Boehm; and from the East, of course. The unsightly pantheism of the East. Undifferentiated. Evil. And now offered to the New World. What an insult!" Professor Weber laughed.

The convulsive twisting of his mouth woke him.

A woman was dragging the boy away, screaming at him.

No. He opened his eyes and the boy was still there, lying in the grass at his feet, asleep.

WHY, MATTHEW and Tim are grown up," Maude said slowly. "Matthew is at West Point and Tim is. . . . You know that. Whyever are you saying such things?"

"I thought they might . . . might like to come visit," Professor Weber said in an agony of shame. "Boys, farms, the country . . . playmates . . . that sort of thing. They used to like the big hay barn so much."

"They're grown up now and you know it."

"Why do you persecute me?" Professor Weber whispered, bringing his hands to his face. "Why do you lead me into traps, and laugh at me?"

ONE HUMID AFTERNOON, when the sky had suddenly darkened over, Professor Weber heard quite clearly the boy's screams.

They were beating him over there. Abusing him.

He knew, he knew. Maude would not tell him what the neighborhood rumor was—said it was none of his concern. The boy was not "right in his head." He was sickly, he was always dirty. Those people . . . ! No better than gypsies. Trash that had moved out of Rockland. Had probably been forced to move. The man drank. The woman drank. They were no good, were only renting the old Brydon place, would probably be moving out once cold weather set in . . . so there was no need to get involved with them. Or even to talk about them.

"Maude, help me! Maude!"

He got to his feet unaided. He was on his feet. But his legs were so weak; there was a sensation of tingling, harsh fleshless vibration; he knew he was going to fall.

"Maude—"

SHE DENIED hearing the screams.

"I don't hear anything," she said.

To prove it, she went down to the creek—to the very edge of their property. He watched her: watched her stand with one hand cupped to her ear, in a pretense of listening.

"No, I don't hear anything," she told him flatly, looking into his eyes. He saw a middle-aged woman, stout, graying, her hair wispy, her expression a curious blend of insolence and melancholy. " . . . Now we'd better get you back to the house; it looks like a thunderstorm. . . . "

"There—do you hear it?"

But it was only a jay.

THERE ARE an infinite number of logics, of structures into which sense experience can be put; there are an infinite number of mathematical systems and geometries. We have no reason to believe that only one system is valid for Nature, since Nature is infinite. When our myopic systems intrude upon Nature, Nature takes revenge simply by retreating. We reach out—but the object of our inquiry eludes us. Philosophy falters because it must use words. Philosophy is words. Still, it is noble, it points to the reality beyond itself, reverently, if it cannot chart the wonders of a multi-dimensional universe but must remain in the three-dimensional, it can at least . . . it can at least. . . .

Early August. But the starlings and red-winged blackbirds were already flocking . . . ! It must be some mistake. Early August according to the calendar. Hot, humid, shadowless days. Still summer, surely. And yet certain species were already flocking. . . . Professor Weber mentioned it to Maude and she said that she'd seen quite a number on her way to town, in a burnt-out field. Yes, they seemed to be flocking early this year. But certainly they knew what they were doing.

It frightened Professor Weber, and rather angered him, the birds' perverse behavior.

When the boy came to visit that week, ascending the hill shyly as always, furtively, not responding to Professor Weber's enthusiastic greeting . . . when the boy came to visit . . . when he came to sit in the grass a few yards away, wiping at his nose, sniffing, Professor Weber complained to him about the birds; it did not seem quite right. Then he heard his voice complaining about the trickery of time, which philosophy had not adequately explored. It was subjective, of course: the worst kind of idealism. And yet. . . . During his absence from teaching, his self-imposed retreat from both teaching and marriage (ah, how they had persecuted him afterward!), as a man still young in his ideas, he had seemed to slip into another dimension of time: working as a ship-loader in New Orleans, later working on a freighter on the West Coast . . . one year in a lumbering camp in Alberta, Canada. . . . Ah, he had experienced a different sort of time. He had gazed back upon his earlier self and upon his colleagues and saw them sluggish-slow, elephantine, trapped by their own theories of numbers and knowledge and love and God. But his intellect had not surrendered. It had struggled, had fought bitterly. Nominalism would not triumph. The sleazy sordid Sophistic relativism of the Republic would not triumph over *him*. . . . And it did not. Even while he worked with his hands, a laboring man among laboring men, his mind had held itself detached, it had continued to operate with the same rigor and purity as before . . . though now he felt himself strengthened with an additional wisdom. He had slipped out of the dimension of language and had entered the dimension of brute reality, in which time is so ruthless a tyrant. And he had gazed back upon his earlier life—upon what he had imagined to be all of life—and found it anemic, self-deceiving, and vain. Still, he had not rejected it. He had assimilated it into himself, had somehow grown into it once again, from another direction, no longer his father's son or his professors' most promising student, but Reuben Weber, and no other. Physical labor had come to seem, during the last weeks of his obligation to the lumbering company, as phantasmal as any idea or proposition. And gradually he had come to see that ultimately only the mental processes were real, since only the mental processes activated and recorded the other processes. . . . "I don't mind dying," he whispered to the boy. The boy slept, breathing noisily through his mouth. There was a raspy, hoarse sound to his breathing. "But I must tell people what I have discovered. Before I die, I must consolidate these notes . . . these thousands of. . . . Otherwise. . . . They will shake their heads and say, *He failed, he was only a crank. Look at the unreadable mess he has bequeathed! Fifty-five years of brooding . . . fifty-five years of notes . . . into the fire with them, hurry, before we're infected with his madness!* They will laugh at me, I know. They will pass the cruelest judgment on me. They have no mercy, no mercy. I don't mind dying, if only. . . . " He stared at the sleeping boy. Hideous irony, that his salvation lay in the twentieth century, that the child—the child would live into that century—wouldn't he?—one of them must! His salvation lay in the future, for only future logicians and philosophers could begin to comprehend his work; and yet that future would exclude him. It would vindicate him, redeem him, bless him—and yet exclude him. "Little boy, are you ill? You shouldn't sleep so long . . . your mother will be angry with you, she'll wonder where you are . . . she'll come get you and be very, very angry. . . . Little boy?"

No one visited him now: no one wrote. He had been careless about writing to people, even to Professor James, who had been so kind and had meant well, hadn't intended to be so patronizing. No one visited, and the boy came so infrequently, limping up the hill from the creek . . . shy, smiling guiltily, fearful. He must call Maude. The boy might be ill; his breath sounded so labored. And he must insist that Maude notify the authorities. He would insist. He would write a letter himself if she refused to tell the sheriff. He would. . . . "Lewes. Charles Lewes," he said suddenly, just remembering. The boy opened his eyes groggily. "Yes, it was Charles Lewes—my last visitor. I don't suppose it mattered, the favor he did. . . . Or perhaps he never did it, how could I know?"

The boy was awake now. In a moment he would leave.

" . . . must have been eight years ago, at least," Professor Weber said sadly. "If only I could teach you to read! That would be so very, very rewarding.... But you don't come close enough, do you?... shy and frightened as a wild animal... as if I would hurt you.... Yes, you'd better hurry home; it's late. Can you come visit tomorrow? Tomorrow?... I want to tell you about Professor Hockings, Myron Hockings ... that wonderful old man.... Will you come back tomorrow?"

The boy looked over his shoulder, hurrying away.

" ... wonderful, brave old man.... A head of white hair, snow white. At least eighty years old and still teaching, though it was, I believe, his last year of teaching. And so gentle! ... I barged into his office and for two hours I told him the implications of Holub's work on numbers theory ... how it totally superseded his own work.... A young man no more than twenty-one at the time and yet I saw in a flash all that Holub was up to, the most extraordinary demolition work since Hume!... and it totally, totally superseded Professor Hockings' own work in the field. An incredible intellect, Holub. Professor Hockings as well. So much learning, so much... and courage as well... nobility ... that he argued with me dispassionately for two hours and then, at last comprehending the superior strategy of Holub ... that he should do no more than close his eyes for a moment or two... and then whisper *I see*. Only that: *I see*. That he had been eighty years old and had dedicated the last twenty years of his life to ... to a spirited but wrong-headed defense of.... And the genuine nobility with which he admitted defeat, finally, holding no resentment against me for having been so impertinent or against Holub for having ... having superseded him. Eighty years old, a renowned teacher, so patient with young argumentative men like me, so very kindly, though intense discussions obviously exhausted him, his hands would tremble and his eyelids flutter.... "

The jays were squawking. Probably a squirrel. They were unusually active at this time of day: very late afternoon.

Professor Hockings was dead, was he? Probably. Yes, certainly. He had lived a long, full life, eminently respectable, perhaps rather cagey in terms of Harvard and Boston society: had endured somehow one of the usual marriages to one of the usual well-bred young ladies. Odd, that Professor Weber should remember that gentleman so clearly, as if it were only a few weeks ago that their exciting conversation had taken place; as if many years had not intervened . . . decades . . . in fact, more than half a century, incredible though it was. He was now seventy-seven years old, had been twenty-one at the time, just beginning to assemble various theories, hypotheses, "flexible foundations" as he came to call them, and of course numerous notebooks and journals, none of which he had ever really rejected, though as time went on he realized that his continually developing and continually skeptical intellect had long moved beyond the scribblings of his youth. Remarkable, the restless movements of the human intellect! Not to be contained within the sober, somber, all-too-proper restraints of a mere article for *Journal of Metaphysics* or *Monist* or . . . what was that other periodical, the one edited by James Morgan . . . in which Professor Weber's first, iconoclastic, and rather famous little piece had appeared, "Recent Fallacies in Epistemological Methodologies" . . . ? Ah yes: *Transactions of the American Hegelian Society*. Well, nothing could restrain the intellect. That was a triumph, of a kind, was it not? In one sense he had failed, had not even managed to put anything together between hard covers, anything to be set defiantly on the shelf beside the others . . . but in another sense he had . . . someone had . . . *it* had triumphed, however improbably, however difficult it would be to explain to any of his enemies or jealous, spiteful colleagues or even to his sympathetic associates . . . or . . . or to anyone who cared to know. "Difficult to explain," he whispered, watching where the boy had gone. "Impossible. They would say I had gone insane or had become senile, they would dismiss whatever wisdom I had to offer, thinking it was simply that of a deluded old man who had never quite succeeded in . . . in . . . doing whatever it was . . . Maude? Maude?" He managed to get to his feet, had even taken several steps down toward the creek, walking slowly, his arms outstretched like a sleepwalker's, before she came running to him.

"What are you doing? Why are you behaving like this?— Why are you becoming so childish, Father!"

THERE IT came again—that isolated, piercing cry.

There was no mistaking it.

He called for Maude, but she failed to come. He shouted for her, banged on the floor of his bedroom with a shoe, and still she refused to come. "I know what's happening ... I can hear ... I'm not deaf, I'm not a deluded old man. ... " Finally his daughter did come: anxious, drawn, her face thickened with something very like terror. She told him it was very late, after 2 A.M. He had been screaming in his sleep again. A bad dream. Would he like a sleeping draught, would he like the window closed? She closed the window before he could reply. " ... nightmares," she murmured. " ... you must be working too hard during the day, straining yourself. ... "

"I don't want that window closed," he said feebly.

OWLS in the distance. Loons. The gathering force of the wind, as summer retreated. Noises of nighttime, so very different from those of the day—haunting, teasing, undifferentiated. Mysterious. Why were the peepers—the frogs—so noisy one night, and silent the next? Why did a single cricket take up residence just outside Professor Weber's bedroom window, so that its solitary singing became something irritating and rather monstrous? Professor Weber loved the crickets *en masse.* But this cricket kept him awake. ... And yet, a day or two later, the cricket was gone and the night should have been harmonious again, why was it so turbulent and frightful?

He wrote a letter to the local authorities, explaining his suspicions as briefly as possible. *Have reason to believe that a child is being mistreated. Demand that you send investigators.* Maude promised to mail the letter; afterward, she claimed she had mailed it. It was late August now and autumnal, actually cold in the evenings, not always pleasant during the day. Days passed quickly. Daylight was abbreviated, unpredictable. "Why doesn't he come over again?" Professor Weber asked. "How long has it been since . . . ?" He lay awake, listening. There were owls, loons, occasional dogs' cries and, well before dawn, the cries of roosters that must have been miles away. He could not sleep and no longer wanted to sleep. Thoughts raced and jammed together in his skull: colliding and then ricocheting away. *What if. . . . If only. . . . Have reason to believe. . . . Demand. . . .*

Then, one night, he could stand it no longer.

He rose and dressed as quietly as possible; he stood trembling before the door of his closet for some time, worrying that it would creak when he opened it, but finally he did open it, and the sight of the clothes inside somehow strengthened him, they were his, his own and he would not need Maude to take them from the hangers and help him dress. Quiet, quiet. He found himself at the door to his room; he listened for some time, hearing only the ticking of a clock, and in the distance the usual night noises and, at irregular intervals, that peculiar human cry his daughter had refused to acknowledge. He heard it. He knew. . . . There it was again, there. It was unmistakable and he could not deny it though his entire body trembled with fear and with a sense of . . . a sense of intelligent awareness that . . . that he was perhaps making a mistake: the parents would yell at him, would demand that he go away, would possibly punish the child even more cruelly than before. Those welts on his bare, thin legs! The discoloration on his forehead and upper arm! "Here, stop, what are you doing, you don't know what you're doing, you don't know the pain you are inflicting, you can't possibly know how it hurts, what agony he is suffering. . . . "

He rehearsed his speech as he made his way along the darkened corridor... to the kitchen, to the back door... and, breathing hard, pausing to get his bearings after every five or six steps, outside into the moonlit night, onto the dew-wet lawn. Quiet. Must be quiet. He was walking bent over, as if fearful of straightening. A curious shuffling walk, an old man's walk. Descending the hill, however, he discovered that it was not necessary—such caution—he could breathe better by straightening his back—bringing arms out at his sides, like a sleepwalker.

At the bottom of the hill, the creek.

Ah, he had forgotten how shallow it was in late summer. So there was no real difficulty in making his way across: he was able to cross without getting his feet very wet, inching along a ridge of gravel and rock. Then the creek bank. Fortunately there were bushes, he seized branches in both hands and hauled himself up, heart pounding but triumphant. Now it was necessary to rest for a while; he forced himself to rest, to be prudent. "I hear you, I hear you," he whispered. The child's cries were louder now. He had to resist the temptation to run to the house and shout at them with all the authority of his position. *Stop! You are criminals and I have come to free your child—I will take him back home with me—*

But the child was not in the house at all. There would be no confrontation with the parents at all.

When he finally got to the end of the lane, and in sight of the old Brydon farmhouse—distressingly decayed, even by moonlight—it was obvious that the cries and moans were coming from one of the outbuildings. He whispered, "I hear you, I hear you," and crossed the grassy open space as quickly as possible. His legs ached; his entire body was rocking with the effort of his heart; but his thoughts were surprisingly calm, and in a sense he did not seem to be thinking at all. His mind, the consciousness with which he had been so familiar, had become wonderfully calm... clear... a liquid purity he had never before experienced, as if another person or another aspect of his own being had taken over. They had locked the child in an old shed or rabbit hutch, evidently. He seized the wooden handle of the door—was surprised that it wasn't locked, after all—"Are you in here? What has happened?" he said aloud. "Are you—?"

The boy was there, on the floor.

He had been tied to a weight of some kind, or perhaps it was an old farm implement; bound cruelly and tightly with leather straps; and they had even wound a rag around his mouth, which had come loose. He was sobbing. He saw Professor Weber and his eyes widened in amazement. His mouth opened, soundless. In the moonlight Professor Weber could see the welts and bleeding scratches on the child's bare chest, beneath the straps. "I'll untie you, it's all right, everything is all right," Professor Weber whispered. He was agitated, even terrified. Such trembling. . . . But he hid his alarm, he didn't want the boy to see. In another minute or two, in another minute, as soon as he caught his breath. . . .

He needed something to cut the straps with. A knife—a pair of scissors—

The boy was whimpering.

What if the parents came—?

Isn't my love enough, Professor Weber thought, why isn't it enough, no one understands me!—kneeling beside the boy, tugging wildly at the straps. He too was whimpering. His breath had become shallow and ragged. What if the parents came! All he needed was a knife or a pair of scissors or a file, something sharp enough to cut through these ugly straps—if only he had known before leaving the house, if only he had guessed what he would encounter—

"What have they done to you? Why—?"

His fingers were bleeding. His thumbnail was broken close to the flesh. The surprise of pain—! But then, miraculously, one of the straps broke. He worked his fingers desperately under another and tugged at it, panting. "Here. It's weak. It's rotten. I think I can get it. . . . Ah: there you are. It's going to be all right now, you're going to be all right now, those horrible people won't hurt you any longer. . . . "

The boy was staring up at him. His face was swollen, hardly a child's face now, puffy and bruised; his lips were twitching as he tried to speak. Luminous, his poor skin. So pale. And his eyes so dark. Professor Weber touched his cheek to comfort him—"No need to speak! You're safe with me!"—and suddenly the last strap broke—the ordeal was over.

The boy laughed in delight.

"You see—? It's over. I've saved you," Professor Weber said.

They laughed quietly together, so that no one else could hear.

Dreamers in a Dead Language

THE OLD are modest, said Phillip. They tend not to outlive one another.

That's witty, said Faith, but the more you think about it the less it means.

Phillip went to another table where he repeated it at once. Faith thought a certain amount of intransigence was nice in almost any lover, she said oh well, OK . . . .

Now why at that lively time of life, which is so full of standing up and lying down, *why* were they thinking and speaking sentences about the old.

Because Faith's father, one of the resident poets of The Children of Judea, Home for the Golden Ages, Coney Island Branch, had written still another song. This amazed nearly everyone in the Green Coq, that self-mocking tavern full of artists, entrepreneurs, and working women. In those years, much like these, amazing poems and grizzly tales were coming from the third grade, from the first grade in fact, where the children of many of the drinkers and talkers were learning creativity. But the old! This is very interesting, said some. This is too much, said others. The entrepreneurs said, not at all—watch it—it's a trend.

Jack, Faith's oldest friend, never far, but usually distant, said, I know what Phillip means. He means the old are modest. They tend not to outlive each other by too much. Right Phil?

Well, said Phillip, you're right, but the mystery's gone.

In Faith's kitchen, later that night, Phillip read the poem aloud. His voice had a timbre which reminded her of evening, maybe nighttime. She had often thought of the way wide air lives and moves in a man's chest. Then it's strummed into shape by the short-stringed voice box to become a wonderful secondary sexual characteristic.

Your voice reminds me of evening too, said Phillip.

This is the poem he read:

> There is no rest for me since love departed
> no sleep since I reached the bottom of the sea
> and the end of this woman, my wife.
> My lungs are full of water. I cannot breathe.
> Still I long to go sailing in spring among realities.
> There is a young girl who waits in a special time and
>   place
> to love me to be my friend and lie beside me all through
>   the night.

Who's the girl? Phillip asked.

Why my mother of course.

You're sweet, Faith.

Of course, it's my mother Phil. My mother, young.

I think it's a different girl entirely.

No, said Faith. It has to be my mother.

But Faith, it doesn't matter who it is. What an old man writes poems about doesn't really matter.

Well, good-bye, said Faith. I've known you one day too long already.

OK. Change of subject, smile, he said. I really am *crazy* about old people. Always have been. When Anita and I broke up, it was those great Sundays playing chess with her dad that I missed most. They don't talk to me you know. People take everything personally. I don't, he said. Listen, I'd love to meet your daddy *and* your mom. Maybe I'll go with you tomorrow.

We don't say mom we don't say daddy. We say mama and papa, when in a hurry we say pa and ma.

I do too, said Phillip. I just forgot myself. How about I go with you tomorrow. Damn it, I don't sleep. I'll be up all night. I can't stop cooking. My head. It's like a percolator. Pop! pop! Maybe it's my age, prime of life you know. Didn't I hear that the father of your children if you don't mind my mentioning it, is doing a middleman dance around your papa.

How about a nice cup of sleepy time tea.

Come on Faith, I asked you something.

Yes.

Well, I could do better than he ever dreams of doing. I know—on good terms—more people. Who's that jerk know? Four old maids in advertising, three Seventh Avenue models, two fairies in TV, one literary dyke . . .

Phillip . . .

I'm telling you something. My best friend is Ezra Kalmback. He made a fortune in the great American Craft and Hobby business—he can teach a four-year-old kid how to make an ancient Greek artifact. He's got a system and the equipment. That's how he supports his other side, the ethnic, you know. They publish these poor old dreamers in one dead language—or another. Hey! How's that! A title for your papa. Dreamer in a Dead Language. Give me a pen. I got to write it down. OK Faith I give you that title free of charge, even if you decide to leave me out.

Leave you out of what? she asked. Stop walking up and down. This room is too small. You'll wake the kids up. Phil why does your voice get so squeaky when you talk business. It goes higher and higher. Right now you're above High C.

He had been thinking printing costs and percentage. He

couldn't drop his answer more than half an octave. That's because I was once a pure-thinking English major—but alas, I was forced by bad management, the thoughtless begetting of children and the vengeance of alimony into low practicality.

Faith bowed her head. She hated the idea of giving up the longed-for night in which sleep, sex and affection would take their happy turns. What will I do she thought. How can you talk like that to me Phillip? Vengeance . . . you really stink Phil. Me. Anita's old friend. Are you dumb? She didn't want to hit him. Instead her eyes filled with tears.

What'd I do now? he asked. Oh I know what I did. I know exactly.

What poet did you think was so great when you were pure?

Milton, he said. He was surprised. He hadn't known till asked, that he was lonesome for all that Latin moralizing. You know Faith, Milton was of the party of the devil, he said. I don't think I am. Maybe it's because I have to make a living.

I like two poems, said Faith, and except for my father's stuff that's all I like. This was not necessarily true, but she was still thinking with her strict offended face. I like, Hail to thee blithe spirit, bird thou never wert, and I like, Oh what can ail thee knight at arms alone and palely loitering. And that's all.

Now listen Phillip if you ever see my folks, if I ever bring you out there, don't mention Anita Franklin—my parents were crazy about her, they thought she'd be a Ph.D. medical doctor. Don't let on you were the guy who dumped her. In fact, she said sadly, don't even tell me about it again.

FAITH'S FATHER had been waiting at the gate for about half an hour. He wasn't bored. He had been discussing the slogan Black is Beautiful with Chuck Johnson the gatekeeper. Who thought it up Chuck?

I couldn't tell you Mr. Darwin. It just settled on the street one day, there it was.

It's brilliant, said Mr. Darwin. If we could've thought that one up, it would've saved a lot of noses believe me. You know what I'm talking about?

Then he smiled. Faithy! Richard! Anthony! You said you'd come and you came. Oh oh I'm not sarcastic—it's only a fact. I'm happy. Chuck you remember my youngest girl? Faithy this is Chuck in charge of coming and going. Richard! Anthony! say hello to Chuck. Faithy, look at me, he said.

What a place! said Richard.

A castle! said Tonto.

You are nice to see your Grandpa, said Chuck. I bet he been nice to you in his day.

Don't mention day. By me it's morning. Right, Faith? I'm first starting out.

Starting out where? asked Faith. She was sorry so much would have to happen before the true and friendly visit.

To tell you the truth, I was talking to Ricardo, the other day.

That's what I thought, what kind of junk did he fill you up with?

Faith in the first place don't talk about their father in front of the boys. Do me the favor. It's a rotten game. Second, probably you and Ricardo got the wrong chemistry.

Chemistry? The famous scientist. Is that his idea? How's his chemistry with you? Huh?

Well, he talks.

Is daddy here? asked Richard.

Who cares? said Tonto looking at his mother's face. We don't care much, do we Faith?

No no, said Faith. Daddy isn't here. He just spoke to Grandpa, remember I told you about Grandpa writing that poetry. Well, daddy likes it.

That's a little better, Mr. Darwin said.

I wish you luck Pa, but you ought to talk to a few other people. I could ask someone else, Ricardo is a smart operator I know. What's he planning for you?

Well, Faithy two possibilities. The first a little volume, put out in beautiful vellum, maybe something like vellum you know Poems from the Golden Age . . . You like that?

Ugh! said Faith.

Is this a hospital? asked Richard.

The other thing is like this Faithy, I got dozens of songs, you want to call them songs. You could call them songs or poems whatever, I don't know. Well, he had a good idea, to put out a book also with some other people here—a series—if not a book. Keller for instance is no slouch when it comes to poetry, but he's more like an epic poet, you know . . . When Israel was a youth, then I loved . . . it's a first line, it goes on a hundred pages at least. Madame Nazdarova, our editor from *A Bessere Zeit*—did you meet her?—she listens like a disease. She's a natural editor. It goes in her ear one day. In a week you see it without complications, no mistakes, on paper.

You're some guy pa, said Faith. Worry and tenderness brought her brows together.

Don't wrinkle up so much he said.

Oh shit! said Faith.

Is this a hospital? asked Richard.

They were walking toward a wall of wheelchairs that rested in the autumn sun. Off to the right under a greatleaf linden a gathering of furious arguers were leaning—every one of them—on aluminum walkers.

Like a design, said Mr. Darwin. A beautiful sight.

Well, *is* this a hospital? Richard asked.

It looks like a hospital I bet sonny. Is that it?

A little bit, grandpa.

A lot, be honest. Honesty, my grandson, is *one* of the best policies.

Richard laughed. Only one, huh, grandpa.

See, Faithy, he gets the joke. Oh, you darling kid. What a sense of humor! Mr. Darwin hoped for the joy of a grandson with a sense of humor. Listen to him laugh, he said to a lady volunteer who had come to read very loud to the deaf.

I have a sense of humor too, grandpa, said Tonto.

Sure sonny, why not. Your mother was a constant entertainment to us. She could take jokes right out of the air for your grandma and me and your aunt and uncle. She had us in stitches, your mother.

She mostly laughs for company now, said Tonto, like if Phillip comes.

Oh, he's so melodramatic, said Faith, pulling Tonto's ear. What a lie . . .

We got to fix that up, Anthony. Your mama's a beautiful girl. She should be happy. Let's think up a good joke to tell her. He thought for about twelve seconds. Well OK. I got it. Listen:

There's an old Jew. He's in Germany. It's maybe '39, '40. He comes around to the Tourist office. He looks at the globe. They got a globe there. He says, Listen, I got to get out of here. Where you suggest, Herr agent, I should go? The agency man also looks at the globe. The Jewish man says, Hey, how about here? He points to America. Oh, says the agency man, sorry, no, they got finished up with their quota. Ts, says the Jewish man, so how about here? He points to France. Last train left already for there, too bad, too bad. Nu, then to Russia? Sorry, absolutely nobody they let in there at the present time. A few more places . . . the answer is always, port is closed. They got already too many, we got no boats. . . . So finally the poor Jew, he's thinking he can't go anywhere on the globe, also he can't stay where he is, he says *oi*, he says *ach!* he pushes the globe away, disgusted. But he got hope. He says, So this one is used up, Herr agent. Listen—you got another one?

Oh, said Faith, what a terrible thing. What's funny about that? I hate that joke.

I get it, I get it, said Richard. Another globe. There is no other globe. Only one globe, mommy, see? He had no place to go. On account of that old Hitler. Grandpa, tell it to me again. So I can tell my class.

I don't think it's so funny either, said Tonto.

Pa, is Hegel-Shtein with Mama? I don't know if I can take her today. She's too much.

Faith, who knows? You're not the only one. Who can stand her? One person, your mama, the saint. That's who. I'll tell you what—let the boys come with me. I'll give them a quick rundown on the place. You go upstairs. I'll show them wonderful sights.

Well, OK . . . . will you go with grandpa boys?

Sure, said Tonto. Where'll you be?

With grandma.

If I need to see you about anything, said Richard, could I?

Sure, sonny boys, said Mr. Darwin. Any time you need your mama say the word one, two, three you got her. OK? Faith, the elevator is over there by that entrance.

Christ I know where the elevator is.

Once, not paying attention, rising in the gloom of her troubles the elevator door had opened and she'd seen it—the sixth floor ward.

Sure—the incurables, her father had said. Then to comfort her, Would you believe it Faithy? Just like the world, the injustice. Even here, some of us start on the top. The rest of us got to work our way up.

Ha ha said Faith.

It's only true, he said.

He explained that incurable did not mean near death necessarily, it meant in most cases, just too far from living. There were in fact, thirty-year-old people in the ward, with healthy hearts and satisfactory lungs. But they lay flat or curved by pain, or they were tied with shawls into wheelchairs. Here and there an old or middle-aged parent came every day to change the sheets or sing nursery rhymes to her broken child.

The third floor however, had some of the characteristics of a hotel, that is—there were corridors, rugs and doors, and Faith's mother's door was, as always, wide open. Near the window using up light and the curly shadow of hanging plants, Mrs.

Hegel-Shtein was wide awake, all smiles and speedy looks, knitting needles and elbows jabbing the air. Faith kissed her cheek for the awful sake of her mother's kindness. Then she sat beside her mother to talk and be friends.

Naturally, the very first thing her mother said was: The boys? She looked as though she'd cry.

No no Ma, I brought them, they're with Pa a little.

I was afraid for a minute. . . . This gives us a chance. . . . So Faithy tell me the truth. How is it? A little better? The job helps?

The job . . . ugh. I'm buying a new typewriter Ma. I want to work at home. It's a big investment you know like going into business.

Faith! Her mother turned to her. Why should you go into business? You could be a social worker for the city. You're very good-hearted, you always worried about the next fellow. You should be a teacher, you could be off in the summer. You could get a counsellor job, the children would go to camp.

Oh Ma . . . oh damn it! . . . said Faith. She looked at Mrs. Hegel-Shtein who, for a solid minute, had not been listening because she was counting stitches.

What could I do, Faithy? You said eleven o'clock. Now it's one. Am I right?

I guess so said Faith. There was no way to talk. She leaned her head down on her mother's shoulder. She was much taller and it was hard to do. Though awkward, it was necessary. Her mother took her hand—pressed it to her cheek. Then she said, Ach! what I know about this hand . . . the way it used to eat applesauce, it didn't think a spoon was necessary. A very backward hand.

Oh boy, cute, said Mrs. Hegel-Shtein.

Mrs. Darwin turned the hand over, patted it, then dropped it. My goodness! Faithy. Faithy, how come you have a boil on the wrist. Don't you wash?

Ma, of course I wash. I don't know. Maybe it's from worry, anyway it's not a boil.

Please don't tell me worry. You went to college. Keep your

hands clean. You took biology. I remember. So wash.

Ma. For god's sakes. I know when to wash.

Mrs. Hegel-Shtein dropped her knitting. Mrs. Darwin, I don't like to interfere, only it so happens your little kiddie is right. Boils on the wrist is the least from worry. It's a scientific fact. Worries what start long ago don't come to an end. You didn't realize. Only go in and out, in and out the heart a couple hundred times something like gas. I can see you don't believe me. Stubborn Celia Darwin. Sickness comes from trouble. Cysts, I got all over inside me since the depression. Where the doctor could put a hand, Cyst! he hollered. Gallbladder I have since Archie married a fool. Slow blood, I got that when Mr. Shtein died. Varicose veins, with *hemorrhoids* and a crooked neck I got when Mr. Shtein got social security and retired. For him that time nervousness from the future come to an end. For me it first began. You know what is responsibility? To keep a sick old man alive. Everything like the last supper before they put the man in the electric chair. Turkey. Pot roast. Stuffed *kishkas, kugels* all kinds, soups without an end. Oi, Faithy, from this I got arthritis and rheumatism from top to bottom. Boils on the wrist is only the beginning.

What you mean is, Faith said, what you mean is—life has made you sick.

If that's what I mean, that's what I mean.

Now, said Mr. Darwin who was on his way to the roof garden with the boys. He had passed the room, stopped to listen, he had a comment to make. He repeated: Now! then continued, that's what I got against modern times. It so happens you're in the swim, Mrs. H. Psychosomatic is everything nowadays. You don't have a cold that you say, I caught it on the job from Mr. Hirsh. No siree, you got your cold nowadays from your wife whose health is perfect, she just doesn't think you're so handsome. It might turn out that to her you were always a mutt. Usually then you get hay fever for life. Every August is the anniversary of don't remind me.

All right, said Mrs. Darwin, the whole conversation is too much. My own health doesn't take every lopsided idea you got in your head, Sid. Meanwhile, wash up a little bit extra anyway, Faith, all right? A favor.

OK, Ma, OK, said Faith.

What about me? said Mr. Darwin, when will I talk to my girl. Faithy come take a little walk.

I hardly sat down with Mama yet.

Go with him, her mother said. He can't sit. Mr. Pins and Needles. Tell her, Sid, she has to be more sensible.

She's a mother. She doesn't have the choice.

Please don't tell me what to tell her, Celia. Faithy, come. Boys stay here, talk to your grandma. Talk to her friend.

Why not, boys. Mrs. Hegel-Shtein smiled and invited them. Look it in the face: old age! Here it comes, ready or not. The boys looked, then moved close together, their elbows touching.

Faith tried to turn back to the children, but her father held her hand hard. Faithy, pay no attention. Let Mama take care. She'll make it a joke. She has presents for them. Come! We'll find a nice tree next to a bench. One thing this place got is trees and benches. Also every bench is not just a bench—it's a dedicated bench. It has a name.

From the side garden door he showed her. That bench there, my favorite, is named *Jerome* (Jerry) *Katzoff,* six years old. It's a terrible thing to die young. Still it saves a lot of time. Get it? That wonderful circular bench there all around that elm tree (it should live to be old) is a famous bench named *Sidney Hillman.* So you see we got benches. What we do *not* have here, what I am suffering from daily, is not enough first class books. Plenty of best sellers, but first class literature? . . . I bet you're surprised. I wrote the manager a letter. Dear Goldstein, I said. Dear Goldstein. Are we or are we not the People of the Book. I admit by law we're a little nonsectarian, but by and large we are here living mostly People of the Book. Book means mostly to you Bible, Talmud, etc. probably. To me, and to my generation, idealists all, book means BOOKS. Get me? Goldstein, how about putting a little from Jewish Philanthropies into keeping up the reputation for another fifty years. You could do it single-handed, adding very little to the budget. Wake up, brother, while I still got my wits.

That reminds me, another thing, Faithy. I have to tell you a fact. People's brains, I notice, are disappearing all around me. Every day.

Sit down a minute. It's pressing on me. Last one to go is Eliezer Heligman. One day I'm pointing out to him how the seeds, the regular germinating seeds of Stalinist anti-Semitism, existed not only in clockwork, Russian pogrom mentality, but also in the everyday attitude of even Mensheviks to Zionism. He gives me a big fight, very serious, profound, fundamental. If I weren't so sure I was right, I would have thought I was wrong. A couple of days later I pass him, under this tree resting on this exact bench. I sit down also. He's with Mrs. Grund, a lady well-known to be in her second, maybe third, childhood at least.

She's crying. Crying. I don't interfere. Heligman is saying, Madam Grund, you're crying. Why?

My mother died, she says.

Ts, he says.

Died. Died. I was four years old and my mother died.

Ts, he says.

Then my father got me a stepmother.

Oi, says Heligman. It's hard to live with a stepmother. It's terrible. Four years old to lose a mother.

I can't stand it, she says. All day. No one to talk to. She don't care for me, that stepmother. She got her own girl. A girl like me needs a mother.

Oi, says Heligman, a mother, a mother. A girl surely needs a mother.

But not me, I ain't got one. A stepmother I got, no mother.

Oi, says Heligman.

Where will I get a mother from? Never.

Ach, says Heligman. Don't worry, Madam Grund, darling,

don't worry. Time passes. You'll be healthy, you'll grow up, you'll see. Soon, you'll get married, you'll have children, you'll be happy.

Heligman, *oi*, Heligman, I say, what the hell are you talking about?

Oh, how do you do, he says to me, a passing total stranger, Madam Grund here, he says, is alone in the world, a girl four years old, she lost her mother. (Tears are in his disappearing face.) But I told her, she wouldn't cry forever, she'll get married, she'll have children, her time will come, her time will come.

How do you do yourself, Heligman, I say. In fact, good-bye, my dear friend, my best enemy, Heligman, forever good-bye.

Oh Pa! Pa! Faith jumped up. I can't stand your being here.

Really? Who says *I* can stand it?

Then silence.

He picked up a leaf. Here you got it. Gate to Heaven. Iolanthus. They walked in a wide circle in the little garden. They came to another bench: Dedicated to Theodore Herzl Who Saw the Light if Not the Land/in Memory of Mr. and Mrs. Johannes Mayer 1958. They sat close to one another.

Faith put her hand on her father's knee. Papa darling, she said.

Mr. Darwin felt the freedom of committed love. I have to tell the truth. Faith, it's like this. It wasn't on the phone. Ricardo came to visit us. I didn't want to talk in front of the boys. Me and your mother. She was in a state of shock from looking at him. She sent us out for coffee. I never realized he was such an interesting young man.

He's not so young, said Faith. She moved away from him—but not more than half an inch.

To me, he is, said Mr. Darwin. Young. Young is just not old. What's to argue. What you know, *you* know. What I know, *I* know.

Huh! said Faith. Listen, did you know he hasn't come to see the kids. Also he owes me a chunk of dough.

Aha! Money! Maybe he's ashamed. He doesn't have money.

He's a man. He's probably ashamed. Ach Faith, I'm sorry I told you anything. On the subject of Ricardo, you're demented.

Demented? Boy oh boy, I'm demented. That's nice. You have a kind word from Ricardo and I'm demented.

Calm down, Faithy, please. Can't you lead a more peaceful life? Maybe you call some of this business down on yourself. That's a terrible neighborhood. I wish you'd move.

Move? Where? With what? What are you talking about?

Let's not start that again. I have more to say. Serious things, my dear girl, compared to which Ricardo is a triviality. I have made a certain decision. Your mother isn't in agreement with me. The fact is I don't want to be in this place any more. I made up my mind. Your mother likes it. She thinks she's in a nice quiet kibbutz only luckily Jordan is not on one side and Egypt is not on the other. She sits. She knits. She reads to the blind. She gives a course in what you call needlepoint. She organized the women. They have a history club, Don't Forget the Past. That's the real name, if you can believe it.

Pa, what are you leading up to?

Leading. I'm leading up the facts of the case. What you said is right. This: I don't want to be here, I told you already. If I don't want to be here, I have to go away. If I go away, I leave mama. If I leave mama, well, that's terrible. But, Faith, I can't live here any more. Impossible. It's not my life. I don't feel old. I never did. I was only sorry for your mother—we were close companions. She wasn't so well, to bother with the housework like she used to. Her operation changed her ... well, you weren't in on that trouble. You were already leading your private life ... well, to her it's like the Grand Hotel here, only full of *landsmen*. She doesn't see Hegel-Shtein, a bitter, sour lady. She sees a colorful matriarch, full of life. She doesn't see the Bissel twins, eighty-four years old, tragic, childish, stinking from urine. She sees wonderful! A whole lifetime together, brothers! She doesn't see, *ach!* Faithy, she plain doesn't see!

So?

So Ricardo himself remarked the other day, You certainly haven't the appearance of an old man, in and out, up and down the hill, full of ideas. It's true. . . . Trotsky pointed out, the biggest surprise that comes to a man is old age. OK. That's what I mean, I don't feel it. Surprise. Isn't that interesting that he had so much to say on every subject. Years ago I didn't have the right appreciation of him. Thrown out the front door of history, sneaks in the window to sit in the living room, excuse me, I mean I do not feel old. Do NOT. In any respect. You understand me, Faith?

Faith hoped he didn't really mean what she understood him to mean.

Oh yeah, she said. I guess. You feel active and healthy. That's what you mean?

Much more, much more. He sighed. How can I explain it to you, my dear girl. Well, this way. I have certainly got to get away from here. This is the end. This is the last station. Right?

Well, right . . .

The last. If it were possible, the way I feel suddenly toward life, I would divorce your mother.

Pa! . . . Faith said. Pa, now you're teasing me.

You, the last person to tease, a person who suffered so much from changes. No. I would divorce your mother. That would be honest.

Oh, Pa, you wouldn't really, though. I mean you wouldn't.

I wouldn't leave her in the lurch, of course, but the main reason—I won't, he said. Faith, you know why I won't. You must of forgot. Because we were never married.

Never married?

Never married. I think if you live together so many years it's almost equally legal as if the Rabbi himself lassoed you together with June roses. Still the problem is thorny like the rose itself. If you never got married, how can you get divorced?

Pa, I've got to get this straight. You are planning to leave Mama.

No, no, no. I plan to go away from here. If she comes, good, although life will be different. If she doesn't, then it must be good-bye.

Never married, Faith repeated to herself. Oh . . . well, how come?

Don't forget, Faithy, we were a different cut from you. We were idealists.

Oh, *you* were idealists . . . Faith said. She stood up, walking around the bench that honored Theodore Herzl. Mr. Darwin watched her. Then she sat down again and filled his innocent ear with the real and ordinary world.

Well, Pa, you know I have three lovers right this minute. I don't know which one I'll choose to finally marry.

What? Faith.

Well, Pa, I'm just like you, an idealist. The whole world is getting more idealistic all the time. It's so idealistic. People want only the best, only perfection.

You're making fun.

Fun? What fun? Why did Ricardo get out? It's clear: an idealist. For him somewhere, something perfect existed. So I say. That's right. Me too. Me too. Somewhere for me perfection is flowering. Which of my three lovers do you think I ought to settle for, a high class idealist like me. *I* don't know.

Faith. Three men, you sleep with three men. I don't believe this.

Sure. In only one week. How about that?

Faithy. Faith. How could you do a thing like that. My God, how? Don't tell your mother. I will never tell her. Never.

Why, what's so terrible, Pa. Just what?

Tell me. He spoke quietly. What for? Why you do such things for them? You have no money, this is it. Yes, he said to himself, the girl has no money.

What are you talking about?

. . . Money.

Oh sure, they pay me all right. How'd you guess? They pay me with a couple of hours of their valuable time. They tell me their troubles and why they're divorced and separated and they let me make dinner once in a while. They play ball with the boys in Central Park on Sundays. Oh sure, Pa, I'm paid up to here.

It's not that I have no money, he insisted. You have only to ask me. Faith, every year you are more mixed up than before. What did your mother and me do? We only tried our best.

It sure looks like your best was lousy, said Faith. I want to get the boys. I want to get out of here. I want to get away now.

Distracted, and feeling pains in her jaw, in her right side, in the small infection on her wrist, she ran into the Admitting Parlor past the library that was dark, and the busy arts and crafts studio. Without a glance, she rushed by magnificent, purple-haired, blacklace-shawled Madam Elena Nazdarova who sat at the door of the Periodical Department editing the prize-winning institutional journal *A Bessere Zeit*. Madam Nazdarova saw Mr. Darwin, breathless, chasing Faith, and called, "*Ai*, Darwin . . . no love poems this month? How can I go to press?"

Don't joke me, don't joke me, Mr. Darwin said, hurrying to catch Faith. Faith, he cried, you go too fast.

So. Oh boy! Faith said, stopping short on the first floor landing to face him. You're a young man, I thought. You and Ricardo ought to get a nice East Side pad with a separate entrance so you can entertain separate girls.

Don't judge the world by yourself. Ricardo had his trouble with you. I'm beginning to see the light. Once before I suggested psychiatric help. Charlie is someone with important contacts in the medical profession.

Don't mention Charlie to me. Just don't. I want to get the boys. I want to go now. I want to get out of here.

Don't tell your mother why I run after you like a fool on the stairs. She had a sister who was also a bum. She'll look at you and she'll know. She'll know.

Don't follow me, Faith yelled.

Lower your voice, Mr. Darwin said between his teeth. Have pride, do you hear me?

Go away, Faith whispered, obedient and frantic.

Don't tell your mother.

Shut up! Faith whispered.

THE BOYS are down playing Ping-Pong with Mrs. Reis. She kindly invited them. Faith, what is it, you look black, her mother said.

Breathless, Mr. Darwin gasped, Crazy, crazy like Sylvia, your crazy sister.

Oh her, Mrs. Darwin laughed, but took Faith's hand and pressed it to her cheek. What's the trouble, Faith? Oh yes, you are something like Sylvie. A temper. Oh, she had life to her. My poor Syl, she had zest. She died in front of the television set. She didn't miss a trick.

Oh, Ma, who cares what happened to Sylvie?

What exactly is the matter with you?

A cheerful man's face appeared high in the doorway. Is this the Darwin residence?

Oh, Phil, Faith said. What a time!

What's this? Which one is this? Mr. Darwin shouted.

Phillip leaned into the small room. His face was shy and determined, which made him look as though he might leave at any moment. I'm a friend of Faith's he said. My name is Mazzano. I really came to talk to Mr. Darwin about his work. There are lots of possibilities.

You heard something about me, Mr. Darwin asked. From who?

Faithy, get out the nice china, her mother said.

What? asked Faith.

What do you mean what? What, she repeated, the girl says what.

I'm getting out of here Faith said. I'm going to get the boys and I'm getting out.

Let her go, Mr. Darwin said.

Phillip suddenly noticed her. What shall I do? he asked. What do you want me to do?

Talk to him, I don't care. That's what you want to do. Talk. Right? She thought, this is probably a comedy, this crummy afternoon. Why?

Phillip said, Mr. Darwin, your songs are beautiful.

Good-bye, said Faith.

Hey wait a minute, Faith. Please.

No she said.

ON THE BEACH, the old Brighton Beach of her childhood, she showed the boys the secret hideout under the boardwalk, where she had saved the scavenged soda pop bottles. Were they three cents or a nickel? I can't remember she said. This was my territory. I had to fight for it. But a boy named Eddie helped me.

Mommy, why do they live there. Do they have to? Can't they get a real apartment. How come?

I think it's a nice place, said Tonto.

Oh shut up you jerk, said Richard.

Hey boys, look at the ocean. You know you had a great-grandfather who lived way up north on the Baltic Sea, and you know what, he used to skate, for miles and miles and miles along the shore with a frozen herring in his pocket.

Tonto couldn't believe such a fact. He fell over backwards into the sand. A frozen herring! He must of been a crazy nut.

Really Ma? said Richard. Did you know him, he asked.

No Richie, I didn't. They say he tried to come. There was no boat. It was too late. That's why I never laugh at that story Grandpa tells.

Why does Grandpa laugh?

Oh Richie stop for godsakes.

Tonto, having hit the sand hard, couldn't bear to get up. He had begun to build a castle. Faith sat beside him on the cool sand. Richard walked down to the foamy edge of the water to look past the small harbor waves, far far out as far as the sky. Then he came back. His little mouth was tight and his eyes worried. Mom you have to get them out of there. It's your mother and father. It's your responsibility.

Come on Richard, they like it. Why is everything my responsibility, every goddamn thing?

It just is, said Richard. Faith looked up and down the beach. She wanted to scream Help!

Had she been born ten, fifteen years later she might have done so, screamed and screamed.

Instead, tears made their usual protective lenses for the safe observation of misery.

So bury me, she said, lying flat as a corpse under the October sun.

Tonto immediately began piling sand around her ankles. Stop that! Richard screamed. Just stop that you stupid jerk. Mom I was only joking.

Faith sat up. Goddam it Richard, what's the matter with you? Everything's such a big deal. I was only joking too. I mean bury me only up to here, like this under my arms, you know, so I can give you a good whack every now and then when you're too fresh.

Oh ma . . . said Richard, his heart eased in one long sigh. He dropped to his knees beside Tonto, and giving her lots of room for wiggling and whacking, the two boys began to cover most of her with sand.

The World
of Apples

ASA BASCOMB, the old laureate, wandered around his
work house or study—he had never been able to settle on a
name for a house where one wrote poetry—swatting hornets
with a copy of *La Stampa* and wondering why he had never been
given the Nobel Prize. He had received nearly every other sign
of renown. In a trunk in the corner there were medals, citations,
wreaths, sheaves, ribbons, and badges. The stove that heated
his study had been given to him by the Oslo P.E.N. Club, his
desk was a gift from the Kiev Writer's Union, and the study itself had been built by an international association of his admirers. The presidents of both Italy and the United States had
wired their congratulations on the day he was presented with
the key to the place. Why no Nobel Prize? Swat, swat. The
study was a barny, raftered building with a large northern
window that looked off to the Abruzzi. He would sooner have
had a much smaller place with smaller windows but he had not
been consulted. There seemed to be some clash between the
altitude of the mountains and the disciplines of verse. At the
time of which I'm writing he was eighty-two years old and lived
in a villa below the hill town of Monte Carbone, south of Rome.

He had strong, thick white hair that hung in a lock over his forehead. Two or more cowlicks at the crown were usually disorderly and erect. He wet them down with soap for formal receptions, but they were never supine for more than an hour or two and were usually up in the air again by the time champagne was poured. It was very much a part of the impression he left. As one remembers a man for a long nose, a smile, birthmark, or scar, one remembered Bascomb for his unruly cowlicks. He was known vaguely as the Cézanne of poets. There was some linear preciseness to his work that might be thought to resemble Cézanne but the vision that underlies Cézanne's paintings was not his. This mistaken comparison might have arisen because the title of his most popular work was *The World of Apples*—poetry in which his admirers found the pungency, diversity, color, and nostalgia of the apples of the northern New England he had not seen for forty years.

Why had he—provincial and famous for his simplicity—chosen to leave Vermont for Italy? Had it been the choice of his beloved Amelia, dead these ten years? She had made many of their decisions. Was he, the son of a farmer, so naïve that he thought living abroad might bring some color to his stern beginnings? Or had it been simply a practical matter, an evasion of the publicity that would, in his own country, have been an annoyance? Admirers found him in Monte Carbone, they came almost daily, but they came in modest numbers. He was photographed once or twice a year for *Match* or *Epoca*—usually on his birthday—but he was in general able to lead a quieter life than would have been possible in the United States. Walking down Fifth Avenue on his last visit home he had been stopped by strangers and asked to autograph scraps of paper. On the streets of Rome no one knew or cared who he was and this was as he wanted it.

Monte Carbone was a Saracen town, built on the summit of a loaf-shaped butte of sullen granite. At the top of the town were three pure and voluminous springs whose water fell in pools or conduits down the sides of the mountain. His villa was below the town and he had in his garden many fountains, fed by the springs on the summit. The noise of falling water was loud and unmusical—a clapping or clattering sound. The water was stinging cold, even in midsummer, and he kept his gin, wine, and vermouth in a pool on the terrace. He worked in his study in the mornings, took a siesta after lunch, and then climbed the stairs to the village.

The tufa and pepperoni and the bitter colors of the lichen that takes root in the walls and roofs are no part of the consciousness of an American, even if he had lived for years, as Bascomb had, surrounded by this bitterness. The climb up the stairs winded him. He stopped again and again to catch his breath. Everyone spoke to him. *Salve, maestro, salve!* When he saw the bricked-up transept of the twelfth-century church he always mumbled the date to himself as if he were explaining the beauties of the place to some companion. The beauties of the place were various and gloomy. He would always be a stranger there, but his strange-ness seemed to him to be some metaphor involving time as if, climbing the strange stairs past the strange walls, he climbed through hours, months, years, and decades. In the piazza he had a glass of wine and got his mail. On any day he received more mail than the entire population of the village. There were letters from admirers, propositions to lecture, read, or simply show his face, and he seemed to be on the invitation list of every honorary society in the Western world excepting, of course, that society formed by the past winners of the Nobel Prize. His mail was kept in a sack, and if it was too heavy for him to carry, Antonio, the *postina*'s son, would walk back with him to the villa. He worked over his mail until five or six. Two or three times a week some pilgrims would find their way to the villa and if he liked their looks he would give them a drink while he autographed their copy of *The World of Apples*. They almost never brought his other books, although he had published a dozen. Two or three evenings a week he played backgammon with Carbone, the local padrone. They both thought that the other cheated and neither of them would leave the board during a game, even if their bladders were killing them. He slept soundly.

Of the four poets with whom Bascomb was customarily grouped one had shot himself, one had drowned himself, one had hanged himself, and the fourth had died of delirium tremens. Bascomb had known them all, loved most of them, and had nursed two of them when they were ill, but the broad implication that he had, by choosing to write poetry, chosen to destroy himself was something he rebelled against vigorously. He knew the temptations of suicide as he knew the temptations of every other form of sinfulness and he carefully kept out of the villa all firearms, suitable lengths of rope, poisons, and sleeping pills. He had seen in Z—the closest of the four—some inalienable link between his prodigious imagination and his prodigious gifts for self-destruction, but Bascomb in his stubborn, countrified way was determined to break or ignore this link—to overthrow Marsyas and Orpheus. Poetry was a lasting glory and he was determined that the final act of a poet's life should not—as had been the case with Z—be played out in a dirty room with twenty-three empty gin bottles. Since he could not deny the connection between brilliance and tragedy he seemed determined to bludgeon it.

Bascomb believed, as Cocteau once said, that the writing of poetry was the exploitation of a substrata of memory that was imperfectly understood. His work seemed to be an act of recollection. He did not, as he worked, charge his memory with any practical tasks but it was definitely his memory that was called into play—his memory of sensation, landscapes, faces, and the immense vocabulary of his own language. He could spend a month or longer on a short poem but discipline and industry were not the words to describe his work. He did not seem to choose his words at all but to recall them from the billions of sounds that he had heard since he first understood speech.

Depending on his memory, then, as he did, to give his life use-fulness he sometimes wondered if his memory were not failing. Talking with friends and admirers he took great pains not to repeat himself. Waking at two or three in the morning to hear the unmusical clatter of his fountains he would grill himself for an hour on names and dates. Who was Lord Cardigan's adversary at Balaklava? It took a minute for the name of Lord Lucan to struggle up through the murk but it finally appeared. He conjugated the remote past of the verb *esse*, counted to fifty in Russian, recited poems by Donne, Eliot, Thomas, and Wordsworth, described the events of the Risorgimento beginning with the riots in Milan in 1812 up through the coronation of Vittorio Emanuele, listed the ages of prehistory, the number of kilometers in a mile, the planets of the solar system, and the speed of light. There was a definite retard in the responsiveness of his memory but he remained adequate, he thought. The only impairment was anxiety. He had seen time destroy so much that he wondered if an old man's memory could have more strength and longevity than an oak; but the pin oak he had planted on the terrace thirty years ago was dying and he could still remember in detail the cut and color of the dress his beloved Amelia had been wearing when they first met. He taxed his memory to find its way through cities. He imagined walking from the railroad station in Indianapolis to the memorial fountain, from the Hotel Europe in Leningrad to the Winter Palace, from the Eden-Roma up through Trastevere to San Pietro in Montori. Frail, doubting his faculties, it was the solitariness of this inquisition that made it a struggle.

His memory seemed to wake him one night or morning, asking him to produce the first name of Lord Byron. He could not. He decided to disassociate himself momentarily from his memory and surprise it in possession of Lord Byron's name but when he returned, warily, to this receptacle it was still empty. Sidney? Percy? James? He got out of bed—it was cold—put on some shoes and an overcoat and climbed up the stairs through the garden to his study. He seized a copy of *Manfred* but the author was listed simply as Lord Byron. The same was true of *Childe Harold*. He finally discovered, in the encyclopedia, that his lordship was named George. He granted himself a partial excuse for this lapse of memory and returned to his warm bed. Like most old men he had begun a furtive glossary of food that seemed to put lead in his pencil. Fresh trout. Black olives. Young lamb roasted with thyme. Wild mushrooms, bear, venison, and rabbit. On the other side of the ledger were all frozen foods, cultivated greens, overcooked pasta, and canned soups.

In the spring a Scandinavian admirer wrote, asking if he might have the honor of taking Bascomb for a day's trip among the hill towns. Bascomb, who had no car of his own at the time, was delighted to accept. The Scandinavian was a pleasant young man and they set off happily for Monte Felici. In the fourteenth and fifteenth centuries the springs that supplied the town with water had gone dry and the population had moved halfway down the mountain. All that remained of the abandoned town on the summit were two churches or cathedrals of uncommon splendor. Bascomb loved these. They stood in fields of flowering weeds, their wall paintings still brilliant, their façades decorated with griffins, swans, and lions with the faces and parts of men and women, skewered dragons, winged serpents, and other marvels of metamorphoses. These vast and fanciful houses of God reminded Bascomb of the boundlessness of the human imagination and he felt lighthearted and enthusiastic. From Monte Felici they went on to San Georgio, where there were some painted tombs and a little Roman theater. They stopped in a grove below the town to have a picnic. Bascomb went into the woods to relieve himself and stumbled on a couple who were making love. They had not bothered to undress and the only flesh visible was the stranger's hairy backside. *Tanti, scusi,* mumbled Bascomb and he retreated to another part of the forest but when he rejoined the

Scandinavian he was uneasy. The struggling couple seemed to have dimmed his memories of the cathedrals. When he returned to his villa some nuns from a Roman convent were waiting for him to autograph their copies of *The World of Apples*. He did this and asked his housekeeper, Maria, to give them some wine. They paid him the usual compliments—he had created a universe that seemed to welcome man; he had divined the voice of moral beauty in a rain wind—but all that he could think of was the stranger's back. It seemed to have more zeal and meaning than his celebrated search for truth. It seemed to dominate all that he had seen that day—the castles, clouds, cathedrals, mountains, and fields of flowers. When the nuns left he looked up to the mountains to raise his spirits but the mountains looked then like the breasts of women. His mind had become unclean. He seemed to step aside from its recalcitrance and watch the course it took. In the distance he heard a train whistle and what would his wayward mind make of this? The excitements of travel, the *prix fixe* in the dining car, the sort of wine they served on trains? It all seemed innocent enough until he caught his mind sneaking away from the dining car to the venereal stalls of the Wagon-Lit and thence into gross obscenity. He thought he knew what he needed and he spoke to Maria after dinner. She was always happy to accommodate him, although he always insisted that she take a bath. This, with the dishes, involved some delays but when she left him he definitely felt better but he definitely was not cured.

In the night his dreams were obscene and he woke several times trying to shake off this venereal pall or torpor. Things were no better in the light of morning. Obscenity—gross obscenity—seemed to be the only fact in life that possessed color and cheer. After breakfast he climbed up to his study and sat at his desk. The welcoming universe, the rain wind that sounded through the world of apples had vanished. Filth was his destiny, his best self, and he began with relish a long ballad called The Fart That Saved Athens. He finished the ballad that morning and burned it in the stove that had been given to him by the Oslo P.E.N. The ballad was, or had been until he burned it, an exhaustive and revolting exercise in scatology, and going down the stairs to his terrace he felt genuinely remorseful. He spent the afternoon writing a disgusting confession called The Favorite of Tiberio. Two admirers—a young married couple—came at five to praise him. They had met on a train, each of them carrying a copy of his *Apples*. They had fallen in love along the lines of the pure and ardent love he described. Thinking of his day's work, Bascomb hung his head.

On the next day he wrote The Confessions of a Public School Headmaster. He burned the manuscript at noon. As he came sadly down the stairs onto his terrace he found there fourteen students from the University of Rome who, as soon as he appeared, began to chant "The Orchards of Heaven"—the opening sonnet in *The World of Apples*. He shivered. His eyes filled with tears. He asked Maria to bring them some wine while he autographed their copies. They then lined up to shake his impure hand and returned to a bus in the field that had brought them out from Rome. He glanced at the mountains that had no cheering power—looked up at the meaningless blue sky. Where was the strength of decency? Had it any reality at all? Was the gross bestiality that obsessed him a sovereign truth? The most harrowing aspect of obscenity, he was to discover before the end of the week, was its boorishness. While he tackled his indecent projects with ardor he finished them with boredom and shame. The pornographer's course seems inflexible and he found himself repeating that tedious body of work that is circulated by the immature and the obsessed. He wrote The Confessions of a Lady's Maid, The Baseball Player's Honeymoon, and A Night in the Park. At the end of ten days he was at the bottom of the pornographer's barrel; he was writing dirty limericks. He wrote sixty of these and burned them. The next morning he took a bus to Rome.

He checked in at the Minerva where he always stayed and

telephoned a long list of friends, but he knew that to arrive un-
announced in a large city is to be friendless, and no one was
home. He wandered around the streets and, stepping into a
public toilet, found himself face to face with a male whore, dis-
playing his wares. He stared at the man with the naïveté or the
retard of someone very old. The man's face was idiotic—doped,
drugged, and ugly—and yet, standing in his unsavory orisons,
he seemed to old Bascomb angelic, armed with a flaming sword
that might conquer banality and smash the glass of custom. He
hurried away. It was getting dark and that hellish eruption of
traffic noise that rings off the walls of Rome at dusk was rising to
its climax. He wandered into an art gallery on the Via Sistina
where the painter or photographer—he was both—seemed to
be suffering from the same infection as Bascomb, only in a more
acute form. Back in the streets he wondered if there was a uni-
versality to this venereal dusk that had settled over his spirit.
Had the world, as well as he, lost its way? He passed a concert
hall where a program of songs was advertised and thinking that
music might cleanse the thoughts of his heart he bought a ticket
and went in. The concert was poorly attended. When the ac-
companist appeared, only a third of the seats were taken. Then
the soprano came on, a splendid ash blonde in a crimson dress,
and while she sang *Die Liebhaber der Brücken* old Bascomb began the disgusting and unfortunate habit of imagining that he
was disrobing her. Hooks and eyes, he wondered? A zipper?
While she sang *Die Feldspar* and went on to *Le temps des lilas et
le temps des roses ne reviendra plus* he settled for a zipper and imagined unfastening her dress at the back and lifting it gently off
her shoulders. He got her slip over her head while she sang
L'Amore Nascondere and undid the hooks and eyes of her bras-
siere during *Les Rêves de Pierrot*. His reverie was suspended
when she stepped into the wings to gargle but as soon as she returned to the piano he got to work on her garter belt and all that
it contained. When she took her bow at the intermission he applauded uproariously but not for her knowledge of music or the

gifts of her voice. Then shame, limpid and pitiless as any pas-
sion, seemed to encompass him and he left the concert hall for
the Minerva but his seizure was not over. He sat at his desk in
the hotel and wrote a sonnet to the legendary Pope Joan. Tech-
nically it was an improvement over the limericks he had been
writing but there was no moral improvement. In the morning he
took the bus back to Monte Carbone and received some grateful
admirers on his terrace. The next day he climbed to his study,
wrote a few limericks and then took some Petronius and Juvenal
from the shelves to see what had been accomplished before him
in this field of endeavor.

Here were candid and innocent accounts of sexual merri-
ment. There was nowhere that sense of wickedness he experienced when he burned his work in the stove each afternoon.
Was it simply that his world was that much older, its social re-
sponsibilities that much more grueling, and that lewdness was
the only answer to an increase of anxiety? What was it that he
had lost? It seemed then to be a sense of pride, an aureole of
lightness and valor, a kind of crown. He seemed to hold the
crown up to scrutiny and what did he find? Was it merely some
ancient fear of Daddy's razor strap and Mummy's scowl, some
childish subservience to the bullying world? He well knew his
instincts to be rowdy, abundant, and indiscreet and had he allowed the world and all its tongues to impose upon him some
structure of transparent values for the convenience of a conser-
vative economy, an established church, and a bellicose army
and navy? He seemed to hold the crown, hold it up into the
light, it seemed made of light and what it seemed to mean was
the genuine and tonic taste of exaltation and grief. The
limericks he had just completed were innocent, factual, and
merry. They were also obscene, but when had the facts of life
become obscene and what were the realities of this virtue he so
painfully stripped from himself each morning? They seemed to
be the realities of anxiety and love: Amelia standing in the
diagonal beam of light, the stormy night his son was born, the

day his daughter married. One could disparage them as homely but they were the best he knew of life—anxiety and love—and worlds away from the limerick on his desk that began: "There was a young consul named Caesar/Who had an enormous fissure." He burned his limerick in the stove and went down the stairs.

The next day was the worst. He simply wrote F--k again and again covering six or seven sheets of paper. He put this into the stove at noon. At lunch Maria burned her finger, swore lengthily, and then said: "I should visit the sacred angel of Monte Giordano." "What is the sacred angel?" he asked. "The angel can cleanse the thoughts of a man's heart," said Maria. "He is in the old church at Monte Giordano. He is made of olive wood from the Mount of Olives and was carved by one of the saints himself. If you make a pilgrimage he will cleanse your thoughts." All Bascomb knew of pilgrimages was that you walked and for some reason carried a seashell. When Maria went up to take a siesta he looked among Amelia's relics and found a seashell. The angel would expect a present, he guessed, and from the box in his study he chose the gold medal the Soviet Government had given him on Lermontov's Jubilee. He did not wake Maria or leave her a note. This seemed to be a conspicuous piece of senility. He had never before been, as the old often are, mischievously elusive, and he should have told Maria where he was going but he didn't. He started down through the vineyards to the main road at the bottom of the valley.

As he approached the river a little Fiat drew off the main road and parked among some trees. A man, his wife, and three carefully dressed daughters got out of the car and Bascomb stopped to watch them when he saw that the man carried a shotgun. What was he going to do? Commit murder? Suicide? Was Bascomb about to see some human sacrifice? He sat down, concealed by the deep grass, and watched. The mother and the three girls were very excited. The father seemed to be enjoying complete sovereignty. They spoke a dialect and Bascomb understood almost nothing they said. The man took the shotgun from its case and put a single shell in the chamber. Then he arranged his wife and three daughters in a line and put their hands over their ears. They were squealing. When this was all arranged he stood with his back to them, aimed his gun at the sky, and fired. The three children applauded and exclaimed over the loudness of the noise and the bravery of their dear father. The father returned the gun to its case, they all got back into the Fiat and drove, Bascomb supposed, back to their apartment in Rome.

Bascomb stretched out in the grass and fell asleep. He dreamed that he was back in his own country. What he saw was an old Ford truck with four flat tires, standing in a field of buttercups. A child wearing a paper crown and a bath towel for a mantle hurried around the corner of a white house. An old man took a bone from a paper bag and handed it to a stray dog. Autumn leaves smoldered in a bathtub with lion's feet. Thunder woke him, distant, shaped, he thought, like a gourd. He got down to the main road where he was joined by a dog. The dog was trembling and he wondered if it was sick, rabid, dangerous, and then he saw that the dog was afraid of thunder. Each peal put the beast into a paroxysm of trembling and Bascomb stroked his head. He had never known an animal to be afraid of nature. Then the wind picked up the branches of the trees and he lifted his old nose to smell the rain, minutes before it fell. It was the smell of damp country churches, the spare rooms of old houses, earth closets, bathing suits put out to dry—so keen an odor of joy that he sniffed noisily. He did not, in spite of these transports, lose sight of his practical need for shelter. Beside the road was a little hut for bus travelers and he and the frightened dog stepped into this. The walls were covered with that sort of uncleanliness from which he hoped to flee and he stepped out again. Up the road was a farmhouse—one of those schizophrenic improvisations one sees so often in Italy. It seemed to have been bombed, spatch-cocked, and put together, not at random but as a deliberate assault on logic. On one side there was a wooden lean-to where an old man sat. Bascomb asked him for the kindness of his shelter and the old man invited him in.

The old man seemed to be about Bascomb's age but he seemed to Bascomb enviably untroubled. His smile was gentle and his face was clear. He had obviously never been harried by the wish to write a dirty limerick. He would never be forced to make a pilgrimage with a seashell in his pocket. He held a book in his lap—a stamp album—and the lean-to was filled with potted plants. He did not ask his soul to clap hands and sing, and yet he seemed to have reached an organic peace of mind that Bascomb coveted. Should Bascomb have collected stamps and potted plants? Anyhow, it was too late. Then the rain came, thunder shook the earth, the dog whined and trembled, and Bascomb caressed him. The storm passed in a few minutes and Bascomb thanked his host and started up the road.

He had a nice stride for someone so old and he walked, like all the rest of us, in some memory of prowess—love or football, Amelia or a good dropkick—but after a mile or two he realized that he would not reach Monte Giordano until long after dark and when a car stopped and offered him a ride to the village he accepted it, hoping that this would not put a crimp in his cure. It was still light when he reached Monte Giordano. The village was about the same size as his own with the same tufa walls and bitter lichen. The old church stood in the center of the square but the door was locked. He asked for the priest and found him in a vineyard, burning prunings. He explained that he wanted to make an offering to the sainted angel and showed the priest his golden medal. The priest wanted to know if it was true gold and Bascomb then regretted his choice. Why hadn't he chosen the medal given him by the French Government or the medal from Oxford? The Russians had not hallmarked the gold and he had no way of proving its worth. Then the priest noticed that the citation was written in the Russian alphabet. Not only was it false gold; it was Communist gold and not a fitting present for the sacred angel. At that moment the clouds parted and a single ray of light came into the vineyard, lighting the medal. It was a sign. The priest drew a cross in the air and they started back to the church.

It was an old, small, poor country church. The angel was in a chapel on the left, which the priest lighted. The image, buried in jewelry, stood in an iron cage with a padlocked door. The priest opened this and Bascomb placed his Lermontov medal at the angel's feet. Then he got to his knees and said loudly: "God bless Walt Whitman. God bless Hart Crane. God bless Dylan Thomas. God bless William Faulkner, Scott Fitzgerald, and especially Ernest Hemingway." The priest locked up the sacred relic and they left the church together. There was a café on the square where he got some supper and rented a bed. This was a strange engine of brass with brass angels at the four corners, but they seemed to possess some brassy blessedness since he dreamed of peace and woke in the middle of the night finding in himself that radiance he had known when he was younger. Something seemed to shine in his mind and limbs and lights and vitals and he fell asleep again and slept until morning.

ON THE NEXT DAY, walking down from Monte Giordano to the main road, he heard the trumpeting of a waterfall. He went into the woods to find this. It was a natural fall, a shelf of rock and a curtain of green water, and it reminded him of a fall at the edge of the farm in Vermont where he had been raised. He had gone there one Sunday afternoon when he was a boy and sat on a hill above the pool. While he was there he saw an old man, with hair as thick and white as his was now, come through the woods. He had watched the old man unlace his shoes and undress himself with the haste of a lover. First he had wet his hands and arms and shoulders and then he had stepped into the torrent, bellowing with joy. He had then dried himself with his underpants, dressed, and gone back into the woods and it was not until he disappeared that Bascomb had realized that the old man was his father.

Now he did what his father had done—unlaced his shoes, tore at the buttons of his shirt and knowing that a mossy stone or the force of the water could be the end of him he stepped naked into the torrent, bellowing like his father. He could stand the cold for only a minute but when he stepped away from the water he seemed at last to be himself. He went on down to the main road where he was picked up by some mounted police, since Maria had sounded the alarm and the whole province was looking for the maestro. His return to Monte Carbone was triumphant and in the morning he began a long poem on the inalienable dignity of light and air that, while it would not get him the Nobel Prize, would grace the last months of his life.

BERNARD MALAMUD

In Retirement

HE HAD LATELY taken to studying his old Greek grammar of fifty years ago. He read in Bullfinch and wanted to reread the *Odyssey* in Greek. His life had changed. He slept less these days and in the morning got up to stare at the sky over Gramercy Park. He watched the clouds until they took on shapes he could reflect on. He liked strange, haunted vessels and he liked to watch mythological birds and animals. He had noticed that if he contemplated these forms in the clouds, could keep his mind on them for a while there might be a diminution of his morning depression. Dr. Morris was sixty-six, a physician, retired for two years. He had shut down his practice in Queens and moved to Manhattan. He had retired himself after a heart attack, not too serious but serious enough. It was his first attack and he hoped his last, though in the end he hoped to go quickly. His wife was dead and his daughter lived in Scotland. He wrote her twice a month and heard from her twice a month. And though he had a few friends he visited, and kept up with medical journals, and liked museums and theater, generally he contended with loneliness. And he was concerned about the future; the future was old age possessed.

After a light breakfast he would dress warmly and go out for a walk around the Square. That was the easy part of the walk. He took this walk even when it was very cold, or nasty rainy, or had snowed several inches and he had to proceed very slowly. After the Square he crossed the street and went down Irving Place, a tall figure with a cape and cane, and picked up his *Times*. If the weather was not too bad he continued on to Fourteenth Street, around to Park Avenue South, up Park and along East Twentieth back to the narrow, tall, white stone apartment building he lived in. Rarely, lately, had he gone in another direction, though when on the long walk, he stopped at least once on the way, perhaps in front of a mid-block store, perhaps at a street corner, and asked himself where else he might go. This was the difficult part of the walk. What was difficult was that it made no difference where he went. He now wished he had not retired. He had become more conscious of his age since his retirement, although sixty-six was not eighty. Still it was old. He experienced moments of anguish.

One morning after his rectangular long walk in the rain, Dr. Morris found a letter on the rubber mat under the line of mailboxes in the lobby. It was a narrow, deep lobby with false green marble columns and several bulky chairs where few people ever sat. Dr. Morris had seen a young woman with long hair, in a white raincoat and maroon shoulder bag, carrying a cellophane bubble umbrella, hurry down the vestibule steps and leave the house as he was about to enter. In fact he held the door open for her and got a breath of her bold perfume. He did not remember seeing her before and felt a momentary confusion as to who she might be. He later imagined her taking the letter out of her box, reading it hastily, then stuffing it into the maroon cloth purse she carried over her shoulder; but she had stuffed in the envelope and not the letter. That had fallen to the floor. He imagined this as he bent to retrieve it. It was a folded sheet of heavy white writing paper, written on in black in a masculine hand. The doctor unfolded and glanced at it without making out the salutation or any of its contents. He would have to put on his reading glasses, and he thought Flaherty, the doorman and elevator man, might see him if the elevator should suddenly descend. Of course Flaherty might think the doctor was reading his own mail, except that he never read it, such as it was, in the lobby. He did not want the man thinking he was reading someone else's letter. He also thought of handing him the letter and describing the young woman who had dropped it. Perhaps he could return it to her? But for some reason not at once clear to him the doctor slipped it into his pocket to take upstairs to read. His arm began to tremble and he felt his heart racing at a rate that bothered him.

After the doctor had got his own mail out of the box—nothing more than the few circulars he held in his hand—Flaherty took him up to the fifteenth floor. Flaherty spelled the night man at 8 a.m. and was himself relieved at 4 p.m. He was a slender man of sixty with sparse white hair on his half-bald head, who had lost part of his jaw under the left ear after two bone operations. He would be out for a few months; then return, the lower part of the left side of his face caved in; still it was not a bad face to look at. Although the doorman never spoke about his ailment, the doctor knew he was not done with cancer of the jaw, but of course he kept this to himself; and he sensed when the man was concealing pain.

This morning, though preoccupied, he asked, "How is it going, Mr. Flaherty?"

"Not too tough."

"Not a bad day." He said this, thinking not of the rain but of the letter in his pocket.

"Fine and dandy," Flaherty quipped. On the whole he moved and talked animatedly and was careful to align the elevator with the floor before letting passengers off. Sometimes the doctor wished he could say more to him than he did; but not this morning.

He stood by the large double window of his living room overlooking the Square, in the dull rainy-day February light, in pleasurable excitement reading the letter he had found, the kind he had anticipated it might be. It was a letter written by a father to his daughter, addressed to "Dear Evelyn." What it expressed after an irresolute start was the father's dissatisfaction with his daughter's way of life. And it ended with an exhortatory paragraph of advice: "You have slept around long enough. I don't understand what you get out of that type of behavior any more. I think you have tried everything there is to try. You claim you are a serious person but let men use you for what they can get. There is no true payoff to you unless it is very temporary, and the real payoff to them is that they have got themselves an easy lay. I know how they think about this and how they talk about it in the lavatory the next day. Now I want to urge you once and for all that you ought to be more serious about your life. You have experimented long enough. I honestly and sincerely and urgently advise you to look around for a man of steady habits and good character who will marry you and treat you like the person I believe you want to be. I don't want to think of you any more as a drifting semi-prostitute. Please follow this advice, the age of twenty-nine is no longer sixteen." The letter was signed, "Your Father," and under his signature, another sentence, in neat small handwriting, was appended: "Your sex life fills me full of fear." "Mother."

The doctor put the letter away in a drawer. His excitement had left him and he felt ashamed of having read it. He was sympathetic to the father and at the same time sympathetic to the young woman, though perhaps less so to her. After a while he tried to study his Greek grammar but could not concentrate. The letter remained in his mind like a billboard sign as he was reading *The Times* and he was conscious of it throughout the day, as though it had aroused in him some sort of expectation he could not define. Sentences from it would replay themselves in his thoughts. He reveried the young woman as he had imagined her after reading what the father had written, and as the woman—was she Evelyn?—he had seen coming out of the house. He could not be certain the letter was hers. Perhaps it was not; still he thought of the letter as though belonging to her, the woman he had held the door for, whose perfume still lingered in his senses. That night thoughts of her kept him from falling asleep. "I'm too old for this nonsense." He got up to read and was able to concentrate, but when his head lay once more on the pillow, a long freight train of thoughts of her rumbled by drawn by a black locomotive. He pictured Evelyn, the drifting semi-prostitute, in bed with various lovers, engaged in various acts of sex. Once she lay alone, erotically naked in bed, her maroon cloth purse drawn close to her nude body. He also thought of her as an ordinary girl with many fewer lovers than her father seemed to think. This was probably closer to the truth. He wondered if he could be useful to her in some way. He then felt a fright he could not explain but managed to dispel it by promising himself to burn the letter in the morning. The freight train, with its many cars, disappeared in the foggy distance. When the doctor awoke at 10 a.m. on a sunny winter's morning, there was no sense, light or heavy, of his usual depression.

But he did not burn the letter. He reread it several times during the day, each time returning it to his desk drawer and locking it there. Then he unlocked the drawer to read it again. As the day passed he was aware of an unappeased insistent hunger in himself. He recalled memories, experienced intense longing, desires he had not felt in years. The doctor was worried, alarmed by this change in him, this disturbance. He tried to blot the letter out of his mind but could not. Yet he would still not burn it, as though if he did he had shut the door on certain possibilities in his life, other ways to go, whatever that might mean. He was astonished—even thought of it as affronted, that this should be happening to him at his age. He had seen it in others, in former patients, but had not expected it in himself. The hunger he felt, a hunger for pleasure, disruption of habit, renewal of feeling, yet a fear of it, continued to grow in him like a dead tree come to life and spreading its branches. He felt as though he were hungry for exotic experience, which, if he were to have it, might make him forever ravenously hungry. He did not want that to happen to him. He recalled mythological figures: Sisyphus, Midas, who for one reason or another had been eternally cursed. He thought of Tithonus, his youth gone, become a grasshopper living forever. The doctor felt he was caught in an overwhelming emotion, a fearful dark wind.

When Flaherty left for the day at 4 p.m. and Silvio, who had tight curly black hair, was on duty, Dr. Morris came down and sat in the lobby, pretending to read his newspaper. As soon as the elevator ascended he approached the letter boxes and quickly scanned the name plates for an Evelyn, whoever she might be. He found no Evelyns though there was an E. Gordon and an E. Cummings. He suspected one of them might be she. He knew that single women often preferred not to reveal their first names in order to keep cranks at a distance, conceal themselves from potential annoyers. He casually asked Silvio if Miss Gordon or Miss Cummings was named Evelyn, but Silvio said he didn't know although probably Mr. Flaherty would because he distributed the mail. "Too many peoples in this house," Silvio shrugged. Embarrassed, the doctor remarked he was just curious, a lame remark but all he could think of. He went out for an aimless short walk and when he returned said nothing more to Silvio. They rode silently up in the elevator, the doctor standing tall, almost stiff. That night he again slept badly. When he fell deeply asleep a moment his dreams were erotic. He woke with desire mixed with repulsion and lay quietly mourning himself. He felt powerless to be other than he was.

He was up before five and though he tried to kill time was uselessly in the lobby before seven. He felt he must find out, settle in his mind, who she was. In the lobby, Richard, the night man who had brought him down, returned to a pornographic paperback he was reading; the mail, as Dr. Morris knew, hadn't come. He knew it would not arrive until shortly after eight but hadn't the patience to wait in his apartment. So he left the building, bought *The Times* on Irving Place, continued on his walk, and because it was a pleasant morning, not too cold, sat on a bench in Union Square Park. He stared at the paper but could not read it. He watched some sparrows pecking at dead grass. He was an old man, true enough; but he had lived long enough to know that age often meant little in man-woman relationships. He was still vigorous and bodies are bodies. He was back in the lobby at eight-thirty, an act of great restraint. Flaherty had received the mail sack and was alphabetizing the first-class letters on the long large table before distributing them into the boxes. He did not look well today. He moved slowly. His misshapen face was gray; the mouth slack, one heard his breathing; his eyes harbored pain.

"Nothin for you yet," he said to the doctor without looking up.

"I'll wait this morning," said Dr. Morris. "I ought to be hearing from my daughter."

"Nothin yet but you might hit the lucky number in this last bundle." He removed the string.

As he was alphabetizing the last bundle of letters the elevator buzzed and Flaherty had to go up for a call.

The doctor pretended to be absorbed in his *Times*. When he heard the elevator door shut he sat momentarily still, then went to the table and hastily rifled through the C pile of letters. E. Cummings was Ernest Cummings. He shuffled through the G's, watching the metal arrow as it showed the elevator beginning to descend. In the G pile there were two letters addressed to Evelyn Gordon. One was from her mother. The other, also handwritten, was from a Lee Bradley. Almost against his will the doctor removed this letter and slipped it into his suit pocket. His body was sweaty hot. This is an aberration, he thought. He was sitting in the chair turning the page of his newspaper when the elevator door opened.

"Nothin at all for you," Flaherty said after a moment.

"Thank you," said Dr. Morris. "I think I'll go up now."

In his apartment the doctor, conscious of his whisperous breathing, placed the letter on the kitchen table and sat looking at it, waiting for a tea kettle of water to boil. The kettle whistled as it boiled but still he sat with the unopened letter before him. For a while he sat there with dulled thoughts. Soon he fantasied what the letter said. He fantasied Lee Bradley describing the sexual pleasure he had had with Evelyn Gordon, and telling her what else they might try. He fantasied the lovers' acts they engaged in. Then though he audibly told himself not to, he steamed open the flap of the envelope. His hands trembled as he held the letter. He had to place it down flat on the table so he could read it. His heart beat heavily in anticipation of what he might read. But to his surprise the letter was a bore, an egoistic account of some stupid business deal this Bradley was concocting. Only the last sentences came surprisingly to life. "Be in your bed when I get there tonight. Be wearing only your white panties. I don't like to waste time once we are together." The doctor didn't know whom he was more disgusted with, this fool or himself. In truth, himself. Slipping the sheet of paper into the envelope, he resealed it with a thin layer of paste he had rubbed carefully on the flap with his fingertip. Later in the day he tucked the letter into his inside pocket and pressed the elevator button for Silvio. The doctor left the building and soon returned with a copy of the afternoon *Post* he seemed to be involved with until Silvio had to take up two women who had come into the lobby; then the doctor thrust the letter into Evelyn Gordon's box and went out for a breath of air.

He was sitting near the table in the lobby when the young woman he had held the door open for came in shortly after 6 p.m. He was aware of her cool perfume almost at once. Silvio was not around at that moment; he had gone down to the basement to eat a sandwich. She inserted a small key into Evelyn Gordon's mailbox and stood before the open box, smoking, as she read Bradley's letter. She was wearing a light-blue pants suit with a brown knit sweater-coat. Her tail of black hair was tied with a brown silk scarf. Her face, though a little heavy, was pretty, her intense eyes blue, the lids lightly eye-shadowed. Her body, he thought, was finely proportioned. She had not noticed him but he was more than half in love with her.

He observed her many mornings. He would come down later now, at nine, and spend some time going through the medical circulars he had got out of his box, sitting on a thronelike wooden chair near a tall unlit lamp in the rear of the lobby. He would watch people as they left for work or shopping in the morning. Evelyn appeared at about half-past nine and stood smoking in front of her box, absorbed in the morning's mail. When spring came she wore brightly colored skirts with pastel blouses, or light slim pants suits. Sometimes she wore very short minidresses. Her figure was exquisite. She received many letters and read most of them with apparent pleasure, some with what seemed suppressed excitement. A few she gave a short shrift to, scanned these quickly and stuffed them into her bag. He imagined they were from her father, or mother. He thought that most of her letters came from lovers, past and present, and he felt a curious anguish that there was none from him in her box. He would write to her.

He thought it through carefully. Some women needed an older man; it stabilized their lives. Sometimes a difference of as many as thirty or even thirty-five years offered no serious disadvantages, granted differences in metabolism, energy. There would of course be less sex, but there would be sex. His would go on for a long time; he knew that from the experience of friends and former patients, not to speak of medical literature. A younger woman inspired an older man to remain virile. And despite the heart incident his health was good, in some ways better than before. A girl like Evelyn, probably at odds with herself, could benefit from a steadying relationship with an older man, someone who would respect and love her and help her to respect and love herself more than she perhaps presently did; who would demand less from her in certain ways than some young men awash in their egoism; who would awake in her a stronger sense of well-being, and if things went quite well, perhaps even love for one particular man.

"I am a retired physician, a widower," he wrote to Evelyn Gordon. "I write to you with some hesitation and circumspec-tion, although needless to say with high regard, because I am old enough to be your father. I have observed you often in this building and sometimes as we passed by each other in nearby streets, and I have grown to admire you deeply. I wonder if you will permit me to make your acquaintance? I wonder if you would care to have dinner with me and perhaps enjoy a film or performance of a play? My intentions, as used to be said when I was a young man, are 'ancient and honorable.' I do not think my company will disappoint you. If you are so inclined—so kind, certainly—to consider this request tolerantly, I will be obliged if you will place a note to that effect in my mailbox. I am respectfully yours, Simon Morris, M.D."

He did not go down to mail his letter at once. He thought he would keep it to the last moment. Then he had a fright about it that woke him out of momentary deep sleep. He dreamed he had written and sealed the letter and then remembered he had appended another sentence: "Be wearing only your white panties." When he woke he wanted to tear open the envelope to see whether he had included Bradley's remark. But when he was thoroughly waked up, in his senses, he knew he had not. He bathed and shaved early and for a while observed the cloud formations out the window. None of them interested him. At close to nine Dr. Morris descended to the lobby. He would wait till Flaherty answered a buzz, and when he was gone, drop his letter into her box; but Flaherty that morning seemed to have no calls to answer. The doctor had forgotten it was Saturday. He did not know it was till he got his *Times* and sat with it in the lobby, pretending to be waiting for the mail delivery. The mail sack arrived late on Saturdays. At last he heard a prolonged buzz, and Flaherty, who had been on his knees polishing the brass door knob, got up on one foot, then rose on both legs and walked slowly to the elevator. His asymmetric face was gray. Shortly before ten o'clock the doctor slipped his letter into Evelyn Gordon's mailbox. He decided to withdraw to his apartment but then thought he would rather wait where he usually waited while she collected her mail. She had never noticed him there.

The mail sack was dropped in the vestibule at ten-after, and Flaherty alphabetized the first bundle before he had to respond to another call. The doctor read his paper in the dark rear of the lobby because he was not really reading it. He was anticipating Evelyn's coming. He had on a new green suit, blue striped shirt, and a pink tie. He was wearing a new hat. He waited in anticipation and love.

When the elevator door opened Evelyn walked out in an elegant slit black skirt, sandals, her hair tied with a red scarf. A sharp-featured man with puffed sideburns and carefully combed medium-long hair, in a turn-of-the-century haircut, followed her out of the elevator. He was shorter than she by half a head. Flaherty handed her two letters, which she dropped into the black patent-leather pouch she was carrying. The doctor thought—hoped—she would walk past the mailboxes without stopping; but she saw the white of his letter through the slot and stopped to remove it. She tore open the envelope, pulled out the single sheet of handwritten paper, and read it with immediate intense concentration. The doctor raised his newspaper to his eyes, though he could still watch over the top of it. He watched in fear.

How mad I was not to anticipate she might come down with a man.

When she had finished reading the letter, she handed it to her companion—possibly Bradley—who read it, grinned broadly, and said something inaudible when he handed it back to her.

Evelyn Gordon quietly ripped the letter into small bits, and turning, flung the pieces in the doctor's direction. The fragments came at him like a blast of wind-driven snow. He thought he would sit forever on his wooden throne in the swirling snow.

The old doctor sat lifelessly in his chair, the floor around him littered with his torn-up letter.

Flaherty swept it up with his little broom into a metal container. He handed the doctor a thin envelope stamped with foreign stamps.

"Here's a letter from your daughter just came."

The doctor, trying to stand without moving, pressed the bridge of his nose. He wiped his eyes with his fingers.

"There's no setting old age aside," he said after a while.

"Not in some ways," said Flaherty.

"Or death."

"It moves up on you."

The doctor tried to say something kind to him but could not.

Flaherty took him up to the fifteenth floor in his elevator.

WARREN ADLER

The Angel
of Mercy

THEY CALLED her "the Angel of Mercy," and there was no mistaking the sarcasm. They observed her on her daily rounds, a bent-over snip of a woman, with piano legs that made one wonder how she was able to get around in the first place, matted gray hair over which she wore a yellow bandana, and a faded old-fashioned black dress, a little shiny with use. She wore sensible but quite ugly laced shoes, a necklace, obviously a piece of Yemenite jewelry that someone might have brought her from Israel, and she always carried her pocketbook, a heavy brown thing, by the handle so that it hung down to her knees.

Even her closest neighbor on the ground-floor row of condominiums had never been inside of her place, seeing it only from the outside, as the woman opened or closed her door. She had caught sight of a rather overstuffed but threadbare couch and an upholstered chair with stiff doilies pinned to its backrest and arms. While she never really got close enough, the neighbor had the impression, just the impression, that the place smelled a trifle unclean, musty and old. But this could have been the impression that the woman herself gave. It was hard to tell how she might have looked as a girl, or even a middle-aged woman, since old age had shaped and gnarled her so completely. The Florida sun had tanned her deeply lined face like muddy-colored brier, and only the fact that she smeared a deep-red lipstick too generously on her cracked lips and put two circles of rouge on her cheeks provided evidence of a still-lingering feminine vanity.

It was unfortunate that she gave such an impression, since she hardly thought of herself as eccentric, and the sick and infirm that she visited daily, sometimes five or six in a day, actually began to look forward to her visits. They, too, had formed bad first impressions and were always surprised when she first showed up, wondering, after seeing her ancient face, whether she was the harbinger of death. This, in itself, was neither strange nor morbid, since in a community like Sunset Village death was an ever-present specter, actually a friend who seemed to be watching everyone from some balcony in the heavens, observing all the aged Jews and trying to decide who goes next.

Maybe it was something genetic, something buried in the Jewish psyche, the thing that gave the world so many Jewish comedians, but, at least here in Sunset Village, death was treated somewhat as a joke, a kind of embarrassment, like a cuckolded husband in a French farce. That was probably why a sick person, lying supine in his bed gasping for air, could actually smile when he saw this little bent-over woman appear and draw out of her huge pocketbook a cellophane-wrapped bag of candies tied with a tiny red ribbon.

"Well, it's all over now," a patient would say when she had gone, "the Angel of Mercy has arrived." But when she came again and the patient had still survived, she was treated with somewhat more respect and might be offered tea and cakes, which she rarely refused.

"You feel better, Mr. Brodsky?" she would ask, parting her overred lips in an odd grin.

"I feel wonderful, Mrs. Klugerman. I'm already in the undertaker's cash-flow projections." Mr. Brodsky had been an accountant and the Angel of Mercy assumed that this might be a joke and smiled more broadly.

"Why should you make them rich?" she would say. Such a remark would provide the patient with a key to the Angel of Mercy's character and would, despite his first impression, find himself cheered.

Sometimes a healthy spouse or child or other relative would be annoyed at the woman's constant visits.

"She's a ghoul. I understand she spends her entire day visiting the sick."

"So what's wrong with that?" the patient would say.

"Ghoulish, that's all."

"She annoys you?"

"It's weird."

"If you're flat on your back it's not so weird."

In a place like Sunset Village, with most of the population well over sixty and growing older, the sickbed activity was, if the term could be applied in connection with Yetta Klugerman, frenetic. There she would go, ploddingly along, utilizing the little open-air trailer bus to get around, visiting her wards. She never left the premises of Sunset Village. This meant that she could choose from three types of patients: the not-very-sick, the post-operative, and the terminal.

The odd thing about her visits was, from the patients' point of view, that she revealed very little about herself and her history. This was odd in Sunset Village, since everyone at that stage in life had a history. She was friendly, humorous, gentle, even loving, but when she left there was never any completed picture about her—as though she were an apparition.

A bedded yenta with little to do but sponge up gossip from her visitors could summon up a good head of outrage during a visit by Yetta Klugerman.

"You lived in New York?" the yenta would say.

"Yes."

"Brooklyn?"

"No."

"The Bronx?"

"You're looking so much better, Mrs. Rabinowitz. The hip is healing?"

"I get occasionally a gnawing pain, but the doctor said it is to be expected." There would be a pause as the patient surveyed Yetta Klugerman's kindly face.

"In Manhattan?"

"Actually, we lived all over," Yetta would say and smile benignly.

They would sit for a few moments, contemplating each other, the overrouged lips poised in a half-smile.

"Your husband died?"

"I'm sure you'll be up and around in a few days, Mrs. Rabinowitz. You'll see how easy it is to use the walker."

"I'll be a walking wounded, like an old lady, ready for the home."

"You'd be surprised how many people have had your problem. They use the walker for a few weeks, then all of a sudden, they're recovered. Believe me, it's not so bad. You should see some of the cases I've visited."

The yenta would be torn between trying to discover more intimate details about Mrs. Klugerman and learning about her visitations. In the end, the stories of the other sick people won out. Nothing seemed more compelling to a bedridden patient than the ailments and mental attitude of people in the same boat.

"Mr. Schwartz lost a leg from diabetes," Mrs. Klugerman would say.

"Oh my God."

"His attitude is getting better. They'll give him an artificial leg and a cane and he'll be able to get around. Look, it's better than Mrs. Silverman."

"She has cancer?" The patient's face would tighten, revealing the impending fear of the answer.

Mrs. Klugerman would nod her head. "She has a very marvelous attitude. She said she had a full life, a lot of children and grandchildren and her husband is alive to take care of her."

"She has pain?"

"They give her something for it. Really, it's not so bad."

"You must see a lot of people who are dying, Mrs. Klugerman."

"One way or another we're all going to go in the same direction."

"Better tomorrow than today."

"You'll be dancing, Mrs. Rabinowitz. You'll see. I give you less than a month."

"You think I can do a cha-cha-cha with a pin in my hip?"

"You should see them."

"Next week I'll go on the dance floor with my walker."

Because the people who became sick were older, both the recovery period or the lingering with some terminal disease was longer and Mrs. Klugerman sometimes would stretch her visits over many months. She became something of a legend. Most of the time, she learned about a sick person from the patients she visited. Other times, people would simply call her to provide her with the information and request a visit. It was one of the inevitable consequences of living in Sunset Village that if you were sick, sooner or later you would get a visit from Mrs. Klugerman.

It became somewhat of a local joke around the card tables, or the pool. Someone would complain of an ache or a pain.

"Better watch out. You'll soon be ready for the Angel of Mercy."

"Who?"

"Mrs. Klugerman."

"God forbid."

But if Mrs. Klugerman knew about these jokes, she said nothing. The initial visit always created somewhat of a stir. First, there was a shock of seeing the little bent woman at the

door clutching her huge pocketbook and drawing out a little cellophane bag of candies. A son or a daughter or a sister or
brother, usually someone who had flown down to act as nurse,
would scurry back to the sickbed.

"You know a Mrs. Klugerman?"

"Yetta Klugerman?"

"I didn't ask her first name."

"A little old lady with piano legs?"

"The same."

"She has candy?"

"That's her."

"She's the Angel of Mercy."

"The what?"

"It's a local joke."

In the end they let her come in, since it was well known that
she would be persistent in her efforts. Some had tried to bar her
way, but her tenacity usually won out. Besides, there was a suspicion, particularly in the minds of those who had been sick,
that somehow she had had something to do with their recovery.
Naturally the people who had died might have had a different
story.

"Laugh all you want," a former patient might tell a skeptic.
"She was there maybe four five times a week. More than my so-
called friends." At this point the patient, male or female, might
glare at his or her companion, who might melt with guilt. "And
I'm here to tell about it."

"You might have been here just the same."

"That's the one thing I can't be sure about."

So Yetta Klugerman became welcome wherever there was a
sick person. It was well known, too, that she never went to fu-
nerals, which gave some added encouragement to those
patients sufficiently uncertain about their prospects. Max
Shinsky was a case in point.

He returned from the Poinsettia Beach Memorial Hospital,
after his third heart attack, convinced that his faulty ticker could

hardly withstand even the slightest activity. He would lie in his bed in the bedroom of his condominium depressed and frightened that each move would be his last. Mrs. Shinsky was a woman of great courage and energy whose loquaciousness was a legend in itself. Compulsively, every day, when she was not attending to Max, she would sit next to the telephone and call a long list of friends to whom she would outline the minutest details of Max's illness. There seemed to be an element of salesmanship about these calls, as if she was trying to sell her friends on the proposition that her troubles far exceeded those of anyone else.

"You think you got troubles, Sadie," she would say when the innocent at the other end of the phone tried to make a cause for her own misfortunes.

"I've got troubles," Mrs. Shinsky said. "What you got is aches and pains. I've got *tsooris.*"

When Mrs. Klugerman arrived on the scene with her little cellophane candy bags, her presence was an added confirmation of Mrs. Shinsky's monumental misfortunes.

"I've got Mrs. Klugerman visiting my Max—daily," she told her friends on the phone.

"That's trouble," her friends would agree. "On a daily basis? That's trouble."

Mrs. Klugerman would arrive first thing in the morning, a sign in itself, since it had come to be assumed that the first visitation of the day was reserved for the patient who was least likely to make it to sundown, a fact that did not improve Max Shinsky's spirits.

"You had a good night, Mr. Shinsky," Mrs. Klugerman would say, her overrouged mouth ludicrous in the bright morning sunlight that came streaming into the room.

"Lousy," Max would say, his hands crossed and clasped over his stomach.

"That's to be expected, Mr. Shinsky," Mrs. Klugerman would reply. "It gets worse before it gets better."

"From your mouth to God's ears."

"I know what I'm talking about."

When she had left, Max would shift in his bed and Mrs. Shinsky would bring him a cup of tea.

"She has to come so early?" he would ask.

"Look, I could tell her not to come," Mrs. Shinsky would reply.

"Do I have to be the first one? When she walks in the room, I begin to hear the angels singing."

"For you it wouldn't be angels, Max," Mrs. Shinsky would say, trying to cheer him up.

He would look up at the ceiling and raise his hand. "You gave me her for fifty years. You were so good to me."

"You're making a big deal about Mrs. Klugerman," Mrs. Shinsky would say, straightening the bed. "At least she visits."

One day, Mrs. Klugerman did not arrive first thing in the morning. Max looked at the clock which showed it was past eleven and the sun was high in the sky and threw different shadows in the room. Despite himself, he felt the beginnings of his own anxiety.

"How come Mrs. Klugerman didn't come?" he finally said, when the clock read noon.

"I can't understand it."

"You think she's sick herself?"

"Mrs. Klugerman? How can the Angel of Mercy be sick?"

"I'm worried about her."

"Worry about yourself."

Finally, just after noon, Mrs. Klugerman arrived. She moved slowly into the bedroom and sat down by the bed. Max Shinsky felt relieved.

"I'm surprised you didn't come earlier," he said, searching her wrinkled face, the features composed under the smudged and hopeless make-up.

"First I went to Mr. Haber, then Mrs. Klopman, then Mr. Katz. They all just came home from the hospital."

He was tempted to ask about their condition, but a sense of fear tightened his throat.

"You look better," Mrs. Klugerman said suddenly.

"Then I wish I felt like I looked."

"He's a real *kvetch*," Mrs. Shinsky volunteered.

"When people tell me I look better, it's time to worry," he said.

She stood for a while watching him, smiling thinly, benignly. He had never paid much attention to her before, except as an odd joke, something to be endured. Now she appeared differently, a puzzle. Why did she do this? he wondered. Was she a little bit touched in the head—as everyone seemed to imply?

"You must be very busy, Mrs. Klugerman," he said suddenly, looking about him. "In this place. All of us *alte cockers.*" He knew he was leading up to something. He wanted to know why she did it. "I appreciate it," he said, wondering if that was what he really meant.

When she had left, he discovered that his depression had dissipated.

"You think I should go outside and sit?" he asked his wife, who secretly marveled at his sudden change of attitude.

"Mrs. Klugerman made you better?" She felt a sudden elation within herself. Was such a thing possible? When she telephoned her friends that day, she felt the hollowness of her own insistence on the extent of her troubles. Could Max be really getting better?

The fact was that Max did, indeed, show signs of getting better and despite his own lingering fears about his condition, he was able to take walks about the house and had begun to sit outside in the morning sun. Mrs. Klugerman's visits came toward evening now. He was no longer in bed, but sitting in the living room when she arrived.

"I'm not coming tomorrow, Mr. Shinsky," Mrs. Klugerman said.

"You're not?" He felt his heart lurch, but there was no pain.

"You're not sick anymore, Mr. Shinsky." It seemed a confirmation of his new-found strength.

After a while she got up and he walked her to the door, holding out his hand, which she grasped. He felt the parchmentlike skin and the hand's strength that belied the little bent body and the piano legs. As he watched her, she seemed to walk directly into the blood-red sunset, a tiny figure disappearing.

She is more than what she says she is, he thought, wondering if it would seem childish to articulate his feelings, especially to his wife. But as he grew in physical strength, he pondered the riddle of Mrs. Klugerman. Occasionally on his daily walks he would see her from a distance and would wave, but she did not seem to notice. Perhaps her eyes were failing, or had she forgotten who he was?

But the idea that she was somehow responsible for his recovery persisted in his mind and, although he resisted giving it expression, he could not subdue its power. He wanted to know more about Mrs. Klugerman and began to ask questions of others who had been sick and who had received her visits.

"She has no permanent friends?" he might ask, casually, hoping his curiosity would not seem blatant.

"Nobody knows."

"Has anyone ever seen her place, been inside?"

"I never heard of any."

"And you say you were very sick?"

"Like a dog."

"She came early in the morning?"

"At first. Then later and later."

"And the last time?"

"At the end of the day. Like I was being released from her custody."

"You felt that too?"

It was as if the idea of her strange power was floating through the soft tropical air, hovering near the surface of the minds of all those who had been sick and visited by Mrs. Klugerman. Not that the jokes did not continue—but only among those who had not been sick. The healthy ones actually laughed as they saw her plodding along on her daily rounds, clutching her pocketbook filled with cellophane bags full of candy.

"There goes the Angel of Mercy."

"Who?"

"Oh, the local ghoul."

But Max Shinsky continued to wonder and ask questions. Once he even rang Mrs. Klugerman's bell, but no one had answered. The Venetian blinds had been drawn and he could not see inside her condominium, although he knew from the way it was situated that it was the smallest one they had built at Sunset Village. Finally he began to follow Mrs. Klugerman around, always at a distance, dallying about innocently while she made her daily visits, amazed at her energy. He was convinced, after a series of confrontations, that she had forgotten who he was.

"Where do you go on those walks, Max?" his wife would ask.

At first he had ignored her questioning, but one day he responded directly: "I'm following Mrs. Klugerman around."

"You keep doing that you'll have her visiting you again." She lifted her arm and made a circular motion with her finger at her temple.

"I wouldn't dare repeat what I'm finding out to anyone but you." He felt the chill along his spine and goose pimples pop out on his flesh. "She's not just Mrs. Klugerman."

Mrs. Shinsky squinted into her husband's eyes, sighing, convinced that her troubles were multiplying again. Heart, I can understand, she thought. But the mind—God forbid.

"It sounds crazy, right?"

"Right."

"Then how come some of the terrible sick cases she visits, people they have given up, like me, suddenly recover?"

"Not everyone she visits recovers," Mrs. Shinsky said.

"That's right," he said. "It is as if she chooses who will live and who will die."

Mrs. Shinsky stood up, her lips trembling with anger and disbelief. "Now I got a nut on my hands," she said.

"You're not going to say anything about this?" he asked, ignoring her outburst. She was a peppery woman, and he had been prepared for her reaction.

"Believe me," she cried, "I'm not as crazy as my husband."

At that point he decided to refrain from airing his suspicions. Especially now, when they were, at least in his own mind, confirmed beyond a shadow of a doubt.

Sometimes he would make discreet inquiries about patients Mrs. Klugerman had been visiting.

"She was so sick I thought she would never see the light of day."

"And now?" he would ask.

"It's a miracle."

Which was a word he had refused to voice, especially to himself. Whenever he saw or heard about a new sick patient that Mrs. Klugerman was visiting he wondered: Will she choose to make that person live? Or die?

Finally he found he could not keep on following her on her daily rounds. Instead, he took to hanging around the court in which her condominium was located, sitting on a bench and observing her door, waiting for her return. Occasionally he would engage a neighbor in conversation. They were all very pleasant, very polite, even talkative, but what he learned could be put into a thimble.

"You know Mrs. Klugerman?"

"I say hello."

"She has no friends?"

"I never see anybody come to her place."

"Children?"

"I don't know."

"How old?"

"Mister, in Sunset Village that's the one question you don't ask."

"When I was sick she visited me."

"That's her business."

"A business?"

"I don't mean a business business."

He learned nothing, but, nevertheless sat watching her door and the windows with the drawn blinds to which she rarely returned except, surely, to sleep. But by then he was long gone.

One night he awakened with a start and turned to his wife, who was a light sleeper and woke the minute he moved.

"How did she know I was sick?"

"Who?"

"Mrs. Klugerman."

"Mrs. Klugerman again?"

"Did you send for her?"

Mrs. Shinsky shrugged. "Why would I send for her?"

"Then how did she know?"

"How does she know anything?"

In the morning he called the Poinsettia Beach Memorial Hospital, but no one on the staff had ever heard of her. If this was so, how then was she able to know the discharge date of each Sunset Village patient? He remembered that he himself had not known when he would go home until the morning of his discharge. And she had arrived almost immediately upon his return.

He wanted to confide in his wife again, to reiterate his suspicions, but he dared not. It wasn't only fear of ridicule, he decided. She'd already rejected the idea of it. He imagined that he might hear her as she busily called her friends on the telephone, voice lowered, conspiratorial, as she was when she had something to impart about him and his illness.

"Max thinks Mrs. Klugerman is really an Angel from Heaven."

"You're kidding."

"He really believes it."

"Are you going to see a doctor?"

"I'm afraid if I mentioned it, he would have another heart attack."

As a result, he became more secretive, more inhibited about his confidences, more cunning in his subterfuges. At times, walking in the bright sunlight, breathing in the heavy tropical scents of the planted shrubbery, he mocked himself for his childish suspicions. It did not seem possible in this peaceful sunlit world, where everything was clearly defined. But at night, observing the mystery of the stars, a canopy for the universe, he felt the pull of other forces. The literal observations dissipated. There was more, much more, out there than met the eye and could be logically explained. Sometimes, sitting outside near the rear screened-in porch, looking upward into the eternity of the twinkling sky, he felt a strange elation, as if someone had entrusted him with knowledge that he could not define or articulate. At these moments, too, he might argue with himself, or, more precisely, two parts of himself would debate the question.

I'm a reasonable man, one part of him could testify. A practical man. A shoe salesman, after all, must be particularly practical. As a boy I went to *shul.* I was *bar mitzvahed* and, today, if I am not overly religious it doesn't mean that I don't think there is a God. I accept that—even if I don't indulge in heavy intellectual activities on the subject. I am not superstitious. I don't believe in ghosts. I don't get frightened at horror movies. And I am convinced that the supernatural is ridiculous. And yet—

How come I lived? How come Mrs. Klugerman knew when I got home from the hospital? How come she knew exactly when to stop coming first thing in the morning? How come nobody knows anything about her early life? How come I am thinking what I am thinking?

Sometimes his more practical side would win out, and he would go for days without giving Mrs. Klugerman much thought, spending his time by the pool or going to the clubhouse at night to watch the entertainment.

But the idea always hung over his mind like a morning mist, and when he heard of a death, read about it, or felt an occasional twinge in his chest, it reminded him of his own mortality, and he would believe absolutely in the miraculous force possessed by Mrs. Klugerman.

Sometimes, after a particularly disturbing night of doubt and debate with his more practical self, he would rise early and rush to find a vantage point near Mrs. Klugerman's condominium, and post himself there to await her exit. At precisely seven he would see her open the door and leave—a tiny bent woman plodding along the neatly trimmed path while the dew still glistened on the tips of the grass. Her eyes were always slightly lowered, and if she saw him, she never acknowledged it.

As the months wore on, and his less practical self became more ascendant, his morning assignations increased until it became a kind of ritual in his life.

"Where do you go every morning?" his wife would ask.

"I love the mornings," he would respond. "Walking in them refreshes me."

His wife would shrug and turn her back to him as he sat on the bed putting on his shoes and socks.

It was only natural in a ritual so precise and rhythmical that the least disruption could become a major source of anxiety. It had, of course, been the moment he most dreaded: when Mrs. Klugerman would prove to him her vulnerability, her mortality, evidence of which he feared as much as death itself.

When she did not leave her condominium precisely at seven one morning, he knew that the moment of truth had indeed arrived. He had, of course, shaken his watch to be sure of the time, reassuring himself by the position of the sun that the hour had come and gone. But even then he could think of many reasons for some delay, since even in his wildest musings he had invested the Angel of Mercy with human raiment. Whatever she was, she was still encased in a decrepit body, one in which the aging joints and muscles might interfere with the plans of the spirit, her spirit. He gave such a possibility the benefit of his growing doubt. As the morning wore on and the sun's heat became a hardship, he moved to the feeble shade of a palm tree. The morning progressed. People moved past him, eying him curiously as he leaned against the back of the bench concentrating on his vigil. As always, nothing stirred behind the drawn Venetian blinds. And while he was tempted to ring her buzzer, he concluded that she might have left before he arrived. Perhaps an emergency case had intervened, he thought, leaving his post by the palm tree after being convinced of this assumption by his more practical self.

But when he arrived earlier the next morning, and still Mrs. Klugerman did not appear, he began to lose faith in that assumption. Finally he gathered the courage to ring her buzzer. There was no response, nor could he see anything through the drawn blinds.

When he returned to his own condominium, he decided to enlist the aid of his wife, who, through her network of yentas, could be relied upon to ferret out all sorts of surreptitious information.

"I think Mrs. Klugerman is sick," he said casually, feeling the tension build in his chest and throat.

"That's funny," his wife replied.

"Funny?"

"Mrs. Zuckerman had a gall bladder and Mrs. Klugerman was paying her visits. Then two days ago she stopped coming."

"Stopped completely?"

"Mrs. Zuckerman decided that she was getting better."

"Was she?"

"Not really. I think the gall bladder was just a *boobimeister.* I think she's sicker than that."

"Something is definitely wrong with Mrs. Klugerman," he said aloud. He could feel the panic grip him and a cold sweat begin to drip down his back and under his arms.

"You're pale as a ghost, Max," his wife said with some concern. "Do you feel okay?"

"I'm worried about Mrs. Klugerman."

Perhaps it was his paleness and the look of anxiety on his face, but Max Shinsky's wife swung into action on the telephone to investigate the disappearance of Yetta Klugerman.

"You're right, Max," she said later. "Nobody has seen her."

Later that day he went back to Mrs. Klugerman's condominium and rang the buzzer for a long time. He also banged on the door, despite the fact that he could clearly hear the sound of the buzzer. Then he called out her name in ever-increasing crescendos.

"Mrs. Klugerman! Mrs. Klugerman!"

A door opened beside him. It was Mrs. Klugerman's neighbor, someone he had talked to earlier.

"I don't think she's home. I haven't heard a sound," she said.

"You think we should call the management?" he asked.

"Maybe she went away."

"Where?"

"To visit. How should I know?"

"All of a sudden?

"I think maybe we should call the management," Max said and quickly walked to the end of the court and took the little trailer to the management office. A woman with harlequin glasses on a chain and blue-gray hair smiled at him, showing slightly yellow teeth.

"You got a record of Mrs. Klugerman leaving?" he asked, giving her the name and address of the Angel of Mercy.

"You're the third person today that has asked," she said. "No, we haven't heard anything."

"Then I think you had better open her place."

"I'll have to talk to Mr. Katz."

"Of course," he said, wanting to add "and hurry," but he lacked the courage. He was now afraid of what he might find behind her closed door. He watched the woman with the blue-gray hair dial the phone and speak to someone on the other end.

"Yes, of course. I'll go myself." She nodded into the phone, then hung up.

"I knew he'd approve," she said.

"This happens often?" he asked as he climbed beside her into the Sunset Village station wagon.

"When you have this many old people and lots of them living alone, you have to expect it." She seemed indifferent, looking at him through faded blue eyes, the harlequin glasses hanging over her thin chest.

"Found one last week," she said, gunning the motor and then accelerating out of the parking lot. "Had been dead for three weeks. It was actually the odor that prompted our going in there." He felt his stomach turn. "Actually it's a tremendous complication in terms of the estate. Sometimes we can't find the children or any heirs. It makes it rather difficult, considering the condominium fees." He sensed her feeling of superiority over him. Old *shiksa,* he thought contemptuously.

She parked the car in front of Mrs. Klugerman's condominium and searched in her pocketbook for a ring of keys. Then perching her glasses on her nose, she observed the numbers on the keys, singled one out, knocked and waited, then inserted the key in the lock. Max felt his heart beating. Could he explain to anyone what he was feeling? The door opened and the woman flicked a switch, lighting up the interior.

The odor was heavy, but it was the familiar one of musty dampness. The bedroom was sparsely furnished, a narrow sagging bed with an embroidered foreign-looking bedspread. In the living room was an upholstered chair, with starched doilies pinned to the backrest and arms, and a little formica table. There were no pictures on the walls, no books, no television set, no radio, no photographs. There was a battered unpainted chest, a few sparse articles of clothing, but no visible make-up tubes or vials, or medicines. In the closet there was, however, a large cardboard box filled with little cellophane bags of candy. In the kitchen, the refrigerator was empty. There was no sign of food and the shelves of the cabinets contained only a few chipped dishes and cups.

"Well, that's a relief," the woman said, after he had inspected the premises. "She's probably gone on a trip. It's quite obvious that she's not living here now."

"Yes," he said, "that's quite obvious." But he dared not explore the thought further. He needed time, he told himself.

The woman went through the door before him and as he moved the door back, he unlatched the lock in the doorknob. He closed the door after him and fiddled with it to illustrate that he was checking it.

"Make sure it's locked," the woman said as she got into her car.

"I'll walk," he said, waving her on, watching her drive to the main road. When she had turned the corner, he opened the door of the condominium again and slipped into the darkened living room. He did not turn on the lights. Sitting down on the chair, he put his head back and let his eyes become accustomed to the darkness. He sat there for a long time, calm, not frightened.

"Mrs. Klugerman," he whispered, listening. "Mrs. Klugerman," he repeated, feeling the first faint bursts of elation. "I know you're here, Mrs. Klugerman." He sat there for a long time, until he could see through the thin strips of the closed blinds that darkness had come. Then he got up from the chair, walked to the door, and let himself out.

"Thank you, Mrs. Klugerman," he said as he closed the door. He was certain that she had heard his voice.

DANIEL MENAKER

The Three-Mile Hill Is Five Miles Long

O N SATURDAY at around noon, Dave and Anne left the ski slopes at Butternut Basin and drove back to Uncle Sol's farmhouse, where they were staying, for lunch. Dave said he didn't want to pay seventy-five cents at the ski lodge for a hamburger that looked to him as thin as a buzz-saw blade. Anne said that she had known that Dave would say that; he had said it the first time he had brought her to Uncle Sol's, a month ago. So she had made a lunch to take with them before they left the city Friday evening for the Berkshires. She had packed it in with the rest of the groceries for the weekend, and it was now sitting in Uncle Sol's refrigerator.

"What's in it?" Dave said.

"All your favorites," Anne said.

"What are my favorites?" Dave said.

"Peanut butter and jelly on Wonder Bread, Canada Dry Ginger Ale, Pepperidge Farm Milanos, and Cracker Barrel cheese—sharp," Anne said.

With his ski gear on, Dave could barely squeeze in and out of the driver's seat of his car. At the top of the driveway at Uncle Sol's, he heaved his legs out of the car and then popped the rest of his body out from under the steering wheel, feeling like a cartoon character. The rigid plastic ski boots he was wearing made his footing uncertain on the icy driveway, and as he tried to stand, he slipped and fell. He wasn't hurt, but he lay there anyway, staring at the cold, bright-blue February sky and at the black tree branches stacked with snow. When he and Anne were driving up the Taconic, the night before, the stars were out. The snow must have started after they went to sleep. When they woke up, a bright sun was shining and the Berkshires were dazzling with three or four inches of new snow. Dave found it disturbing that so great a change—the transformation of an entire countryside—had taken place while he was asleep.

Dave still did not get up. He lay there watching his breath form frost clouds, and he listened to the pulse pumping in his ears, steady and strong, as if it would go on forever. He heard the door to the farmhouse close. She'll go into the kitchen and take off her parka, he thought. She'll wash her hands, and as she washes her hands, she'll look out at the driveway to see what has happened to me. She won't be able to see me lying here, so she'll come out to look for me. She'll be slightly worried, but she'll also suspect that I'm just playing another trick on her. She'll find me here, ask if I'm O.K., and when she knows that I am, she'll wait for me to get up. "Come on," she'll say, "it's freezing out here."

He heard the door to the farmhouse close again. After a few seconds, Anne appeared around the front of the car. Dave smiled up at her.

"Did you hurt yourself?" she said.

"No," Dave said. "I'm just lyin' here, groovin' on the ice vibrations and the basic basicness of the cosmos. Can you dig it?"

"Come on, get up," Anne said.

"Aren't you going to say it's freezing out here?"

"It's not bad in the sun. But I'm starving. Come on."

The door to Uncle Sol's house opened directly into the dining room, which had large windows at the far end and cherry-wood paneling and a long mahogany table in the center. To the left was the kitchen, and to the right the living room, and, beyond that, Uncle Sol's bedroom. Five more bedrooms were upstairs. The original building had been erected in the seventeen-nineties, and as it and the land changed hands over the years, it grew, as if, Dave thought, it were alive. Like many other New England farmhouses, it now resembled a telescope set down horizontally on the ground, with the smallest section in the rear and the largest fronting the road.

Dave sat on one of the dining room chairs struggling to get his boots off. He stopped for a moment and looked around. The house was quiet. Uncle Sol had left for Mexico to nurse his sinuses a few days before, so Dave and Anne had the place to themselves. Dave looked at the floor and noticed for the first time that its boards were not of uniform width. Centuries, he thought; you could almost say that this house had existed for centuries.

"Somebody stole our lunch," Anne shouted from the kitchen.

"Who?" Dave said.

" 'Who?' " Anne said. "What do you mean 'Who?' "

"Well, where is it?" Dave said.

"I'm telling you it's gone. Somebody must have taken it. I put it in a separate bag in the refrigerator, and the bag is gone."

"You shouldn't put peanut butter stuff in the refrigerator," Dave said. "It gets rigid." He had finally gotten his boots off, and he went into the kitchen.

"It was right there," Anne said. She was standing next to the open refrigerator, gesturing toward it like Betty Furness.

"Hello," said a reedy and tremulous voice behind them.

They both jumped a little and turned around. Standing in the doorway between the kitchen and the dining room was a short, stocky man wearing brown corduroy pants, a soiled plaid shirt, an ancient pea jacket, and a blue baseball cap with the New York Mets' insignia on it. In his hand was an empty ginger ale bottle. He had blue eyes, a prominent hook nose, and large ears. He looked like Dave transformed from thirty-three to eighty-three.

"Uncle Nick!" Dave said. "I thought you were in New York. You startled us."

"Hello, Robert," the old man said, smiling pleasantly. "I was upstairs taking a nap."

"I'm Dave—your nephew," Dave said.

"Why are you shouting?" Anne said.

"He's almost deaf," Dave said softly. "I'm Dave," he shouted again. "Bob is your brother—my father."

"Oh, yes," the old man said. "David." He looked at Anne. "You are the young woman from the South."

Anne smiled. "What is he talking about?" she whispered to Dave.

"No, Nick," Dave yelled. "That was someone else. This is Anne Springer."

"Pleased to meet you, Anne," said Uncle Nick.

"Uncle Nick, did you eat our lunch that was in the bag in the refrigerator?" Dave boomed.

The old man said, "I have sold a book for seventy-two million dollars. I am already working on a second one. They say they will give me more for the second one. The one they have already bought is about my son's psychoanalysis. I paid fifty thousand dollars for my son's psychoanalysis." He came into the kitchen a few steps and put the ginger ale bottle in the kitchen sink.

"Uncle Nick," Dave said, "are you staying at the Chicken House?"

The old man went back and stood in the doorway. "Yes," he said.

"But you have no heat, I thought."

"Heat, but no hot water. I've been walking up here to use the water."

"Where's your car?"

"They took my license away."

"How did you get up here?"

"I came up from the city last week. I took a bus and then a taxi out from town."

Dave closed the refrigerator and walked over to where Uncle Nick stood. "Let me drive you back to the Chicken House," he said, putting his hand on the old man's shoulder.

"I have to get the camp ready," Uncle Nick said. "A lot of work needs to be done. I've got all the counselors lined up, and my wife, Ruth, is recruiting boys in New York."

"I THOUGHT you told me that your Aunt Ruth was dead," Anne said to Dave when he got back from the Chicken House.

"She is," Dave said. "She died ten years ago. The Boys Camp has been closed ever since." He paused. "Listen, let's drive into Great Barrington and go to McDonald's."

"O.K.," Anne said. "If you really prefer shredded compressed something to buzz-saw blades."

They put on their coats and went outside.

Dave backed the car out of the driveway. They drove for a mile or so in silence, and then Anne said, "Why does he live in a chicken house?"

"*The* Chicken House," Dave said. "After Aunt Ruth died, Nick couldn't handle the camp by himself. He sold their house but kept the land and the camp. He renovated part of an old chicken house and moved in there. He also has an apartment in New York. I thought he was there." He paused. "Don't ask me," he said. "I don't know."

Dave slowed the car to make a left turn on to Route 23. They started down the long hill that leads into Great Barrington.

"The Three-Mile Hill is five miles long, doo-dah, doo-dah," Dave sang, to the tune of "Camptown Races."

"What is that," Anne said.

"A family ditty about this hill," Dave said. "When Uncle Sol sings it, he always says, 'Doo-dah, singee doo-dah.' "

"I don't understand your family," Anne said.

"Neither do I."

"Tell me what you know," Anne said.

"Someday," Dave said.

They drove past Butternut Basin.

"The slopes," Dave said. "Did you see how beautiful it was at the top today?"

"But who takes care of him?" Anne said.

"He had an operation last summer, for varicose veins. His mind hasn't been right since then, Uncle Sol told me. Nobody takes care of him, I guess. Who knows? Perhaps he is fiercely independent. With seventy-two million dollars, he can certainly afford to be."

"Don't make fun of him," Anne said.

"Listen," Dave said, "when I drove him to the Chicken House, he made me guess how much his shoes cost. It turned out he bought them at a thrift shop and they cost a quarter. In the very next breath, as they say, he told me he had made them himself—out of doeskin."

"Why do you try to make all this into a joke?" Anne said.

"Who's laughing?" Dave said.

Dave turned into the McDonald's parking lot. "The golden arches," he said. "An oasis of sanity." He parked and turned off the motor. "Don't get out yet," he said. "Listen, it's just that the whole thing makes me feel a little on the precarious side."

"I could tell that," Anne said. She put her hand on his shoulder and leaned over and kissed his cheek.

THEY SKIED again in the afternoon until the lifts shut down, at five. At the end, Dave took one of his gloves off and put it in the inside pocket of his parka. He and Anne skied over to the main chair lift, where the operator had just started turning people away. The lift was still running, however, so that the last people aboard could get to the top. Dave told the operator that he had lost one of his gloves, and couldn't he please go up to look for it. The operator said O.K. Anne decided she was too tired for another run, and said that she would wait for Dave in the car.

After Dave got off the lift, he put on his other glove. Then he turned left and skied slowly down a gentle, narrow trail that went across the top of a ridge and fed into the slope he wanted. He was alone, and everything was still. Below and in the distance, he could see small towns and clusters of houses, and tiny, bright-colored automobiles that scooted like bugs along roads that looked like thin, gray scars. The hills were white, and the pines stood up from them like green armies. Closer by, he heard a mountain stream rushing. An owl hooted. Crepuscular, Dave thought.

He started down the slope. He pretended that he was a soldier in the Finnish ski troops during the Second World War. He was on his way to rescue a wounded comrade lying at the foot of the mountain. If he didn't get there fast, the Russians would cut him off, which would spell certain death for both of them. He skied much faster than he did ordinarily, and took some dangerous risks. When he reached a large mogul that he usually avoided, he went directly over it and flew for a few yards in the air. He slapped his skis down on the snow harder and louder than he needed to when he landed, and he bent his knees more than was necessary to cushion the impact.

Then the trail bent and the parking lot appeared below. Dave came to a stop. It was unlikely, he reflected, that the Russians would have arrived in a fleet of Volvos.

WHEN DAVE AND ANNE got back to Uncle Sol's, Dave searched the house. "He's not here," he reported to Anne, who was lighting the fire in the living room fireplace. "But what if he comes back?"

"What if he does?"

"To use the water," Dave said.

"Just forget about him," Anne said. "Listen, will you cook? I want to take a shower."

"I would be glad to," Dave said. "Provided my grandfather hasn't come back from the grave and stolen our supper."

They ate in front of the fire while watching what Anne called "the programs"—Mary Tyler Moore and Bob Newhart—on the TV set that Dave had taken out of Uncle Sol's bedroom. Dave rated all the jokes. "*That*'s funny," he would say, or "Average," or "Fair," or "Weak, very weak." Anne kept telling him, "Hush. Keep still."

" 'Hush. Keep still,' " Dave said. "Nobody says that anymore."

As it got later, Dave felt more and more relaxed. He and Anne had nearly finished a bottle of wine that Dave had found in Uncle Sol's room behind the TV. He cleared away the dishes. He came back to the living room, put a log on the fire, and sat down next to Anne on the couch. Bob Newhart was trying to convince his wife that flying was nothing to be afraid of.

"Let's do something," Dave said.

"I don't know if I can resist you when you are so romantic," Anne said.

"Come on," Dave said.

"I want to watch the programs," Anne said.

"Why doesn't Suzanne Pleshette do something about her hair?" Dave said. "It's a question that is now on the lips of many Americans."

Anne laughed and put her head on his shoulder.

Dave heard the front door open.

"Oh, dear," Anne said. "Listen, just try to ignore him."

Uncle Nick appeared in the doorway between the dining room and the living room. His baseball cap was on backward. "Hello," he said. "I need to take a bath."

"Go ahead," Dave shouted.

The old man stood in the doorway for a minute or so, looking at the fire and the television and Dave and Anne as if, Dave thought, he were a tourist. Then he crossed in front of them and went into the small bathroom between the living room and Uncle Sol's bedroom. They heard the water start to run in the bathtub.

"Why couldn't he have gone upstairs?" Dave said.

"It won't take long," Anne said. "Finish the wine."

After a few minutes, the water stopped running. A few minutes later, mumbling sounds started coming out of the bathroom. Then the old man started shouting. "Give me back that money!" he yelled. "I did not give you ten dollars, I lent it to you. You won't get away with this! You owe me ten dollars."

"Jesus," Dave said.

"Robert," the old man yelled. "Come in here and help me. This man is trying to steal my ten dollars."

Dave got up and went into the bathroom. The old man sat in the bathtub gripping the wooden rim that went around the top.

"Nick, you must have gone to sleep and had a dream," Dave said.

"What?" the old man said.

"I'm Dave—your nephew. Everything is O.K. You must have dozed off in the water. Nobody took any money."

"David," the old man said. "I thought he stole ten dollars from me." He pointed toward his pea jacket, which was hanging on top of the rest of his clothes on a towel rack.

"Nobody's in here but you and me," Dave said. "Why don't you dry off and get dressed." He looked at his uncle, who had now calmed down. His body was very white in the tub, but he seemed in remarkably good shape. Only his face looked old. Tears came to Dave's eyes. "You get dressed," Dave said. "I'll be right outside." He went back out into the living room.

"Jesus," he said to Anne. "He thought his coat was a person."

"He'll be gone soon," Anne said, "and he won't be back tonight." She took Dave's arm. "Sit down," she said.

After a short time, the bathroom door opened. Uncle Nick stood in the doorway, fully dressed except for his cap, which he held in his hands.

"I'm very sorry," he said. "I can't imagine what came over me."

Dave felt a great sense of relief. "Don't worry about it, Uncle Nick," he said. "I told you: You were just dreaming."

"I simply didn't realize that he was colored," the old man said. "If I had seen that he was colored, I would have let him keep the ten dollars. I don't care about money."

IT STARTED to snow that night when they were half-way down the Taconic. The flakes were big and ragged, and looked to Dave like flakes of paint scraped from an immense ceiling. The snow reduced his visibility, so he had to slow the car down.

"I told you we should have waited till tomorrow to drive home," Anne said. "The skiing would have been fantastic tomorrow, and the driving is dangerous tonight."

"If he had gone back to the Chicken House, if he hadn't fallen asleep in that chair, I would have stayed."

"Why couldn't we just go to bed and pay him no attention?"

"You know, he always claimed to be a Marxist. He was embarrassed about how successful the camp was. At the end, he had a hundred and fifty rich Jewish boys from New York at about fifteen hundred dollars a throw. Along with a few token blacks. When I was a kid, I used to hear him say things like 'Every cent goes back into the land,' and 'Ruth and I live on thirty-three hundred dollars a year.'"

"He would have just slept there," Anne said.

"Listen," Dave said, "if we had gone to sleep, what if he started shouting again downstairs? What if he went chasing thieves through our bedroom? No thanks."

"I think he liked our company."

"Oh, I'm sure plenty of people will be dropping in on him."

"There you go again," Anne said.

"Listen," Dave said, "I don't like things creeping up on me when I'm not looking."

III

FRANK O'CONNOR

Old-Age Pensioners

ON FRIDAY evening as I went up the sea road for
my evening walk I heard the row blowing up at the other side of
the big ash-tree, near the jetty. I was sorry for the sergeant, a
decent poor man. When a foreign government imposed a cruel
law, providing for the upkeep of all old people over seventy, it
never gave a thought to the policeman who would have to deal
with the consequences. You see, our post office was the only
one within miles. That meant that each week we had to endure
a procession of old-age pensioners from Caheragh, the lonely,
rocky promontory to the west of us, inhabited—so I am told—
by a strange race of people, alleged to be descendants of a
Portuguese crew who were driven ashore there in days gone by.
That I couldn't swear to; in fact, I never could see trace or
tidings of any foreign blood in Caheragh, but I was never one
for contradicting the wisdom of my ancestors. But government
departments have no wisdom, ancestral or any other kind, so
the Caheraghs drew their pensions with us, and the contact
with what we considered civilization being an event in their
lonesome lives, they usually brought their families to help in
drinking them. That was what upset us. To see a foreigner
drunk in our village on what we rightly considered our money
was more than some of us could stand.

So Friday, as I say, was the sergeant's busy day. He had a young guard called Coleman to assist him, but Coleman had troubles of his own. He was a poet, poor fellow, and desperately in love with a publican's daughter in Coole. The girl was incapable of making up her mind about him, though her father wanted her to settle down; he told her all young men had a tendency to write poetry up to a certain age, and that even himself had done it a few times until her mother knocked it out of him. But her view was that poetry, like drink, was a thing you couldn't have knocked out of you, and that the holy all of it would be that Coleman would ruin the business on her. Every week we used to study the *Coole Times,* looking for another poem, either a heart-broken "Lines to D———," saying that Coleman would never see her more, or a "Song." "Song" always meant they were after making it up. The sergeant had them all cut out and pasted in an album; he thought young Coleman was lost in the police.

When I was coming home the row was still on, and I went inside the wall to have a look. There were two Caheraghs: Mike Mountain and his son, Patch. Mike was as lean as a rake, a gaunt old man with mad blue eyes. Patch was an upstanding fellow but drunk to God and the world. The man who was standing up for the honour of the village was Flurry Riordan, another old-age pensioner. Flurry, as you'd expect from a bachelor of that great age, was quarrelsome and scurrilous. Fifteen years before, when he was sick and thought himself dying, the only thing troubling his mind was that a brother he had quarreled with would profit by his death, and a neighbour had come to his cottage one morning to find Flurry fast asleep with his will written in burnt stick on the white-washed wall over his bed.

The sergeant, a big, powerful man with a pasty face and deep pouches under his eyes, gave me a nod as I came in.

"Where's Guard Coleman from you?" I asked.

"Over in Coole with the damsel," he replied.

Apparently the row was about a Caheragh boat that had

beaten one of our boats in the previous year's regatta. You'd think a thing like that would have been forgotten, but a bachelor of seventy-six has a long memory for grievances. Sitting on the wall overlooking the jetty, shadowed by the boughs of the ash, Flurry asked with a sneer, with such wonderful sailors in Caheragh wasn't it a marvel that they couldn't sail past the Head—an unmistakable reference to the supposed Portuguese origin of the clan. Patch replied that whatever the Caheragh people sailed it wasn't bum-boats, meaning, I suppose, the pleasure boat in which Flurry took summer visitors about the bay.

"What sailors were there ever in Caheragh?" snarled Flurry. "If they had men against them instead of who they had they wouldn't get off so easy."

"Begor, 'tis a pity you weren't rowing yourself, Flurry," said the sergeant gravely. "I'd say you could still show them a few things."

"Ten years ago I might," said Flurry bitterly, because the sergeant had touched on another very sore subject; his being dropped from the regatta crews, a thing he put down entirely to the brother's intrigues.

"Why then, indeed," said the sergeant, "I'd back you still against a man half your age. Why don't you and Patch have a race now and settle it?"

"I'll race him," shouted Patch with the greatest enthusiasm, rushing for his own boat. "I'll show him."

"My boat is being mended," said Flurry shortly.

"You could borrow Sullivan's," said the sergeant.

Flurry only looked at the ground and spat. Either he wasn't feeling energetic or the responsibility was too much for him. It would darken his last days to be beaten by a Caheragh. Patch sat in his shirt-sleeves in the boat, resting his reeling head on his oars. For a few minutes it looked as if he was out for the evening. Then he suddenly raised his face to the sky and let out the wild Caheragh war-whoop, which sounded like all the seagulls in

Ireland practising unison-shrieking. The effect on Flurry was magical. At that insulting sound he leaped from the wall with an oath, pulled off his coat, and rushed to the slip to another boat. The sergeant, clumsy and heavy-footed, followed, and the pair of them sculled away to where Sullivan's boat was moored. Patch followed them with his eyes.

"What's wrong with you, you old coward?" he yelled. "Row your own boat, you old sod, you!"

"Never mind," said Mike Mountain from the top of the slip. "You'll beat him, boat or no boat. . . . He'll beat him, ladies and gentlemen," he said confidently to the little crowd that had gathered. "Ah, Jase, he's a great man in a boat."

"I'm a good man on a long course," Patch shouted modestly, his eyes searching each of us in turn. "I'm slow getting into my stroke."

"At his age I was the same," confided his father. "A great bleddy man in a boat. Of course, I can't do it now—eighty-one; drawing on for it. I haven't the same energy."

"Are you ready, you old coward?" shrieked Patch to Flurry who was fumbling savagely in the bottom of Sullivan's boat for the rowlocks.

"Shut up, you foreign importation!" snarled Flurry.

He found the rowlocks and pulled the boat round in a couple of neat strokes; then hung on his oars till the sergeant got out. For seventy-six he was still a lively man.

"Ye know the race now?" said the sergeant. "To the island and back."

"Round the island, sergeant," said Mike Mountain plaintively. "Patch is like me; he's slow to start."

"Very good, very good," said the sergeant. "Round the island it is, Flurry. Are ye ready now, both of ye?"

"Ready," grunted Flurry.

"Yahee!" shrieked Patch again, brandishing an oar over his head like a drumstick.

"Mind yourself now, Patch!" said the sergeant who seemed

to be torn between his duty as an officer of the peace and his duty as umpire. "Go!—ye whoors," he added under his breath so that only a few of us heard him.

They did their best. It is hard enough for a man with a drop in to go straight even when he's facing his object, but it is too much altogether to expect him to do it backwards. Flurry made for the *Red Devil*, the doctor's sailing boat, and Patch, who seemed to be fascinated by the very appearance of Flurry, made for him, and the two of them got there almost simultaneously. At one moment it looked as if it would be a case of drowning, at the next of manslaughter. There was a splash, a thud, and a shout, and I saw Flurry raise his oar as if to lay out Patch. But the presence of the sergeant probably made him self-conscious, for instead he used it to push off Patch's boat.

"God Almighty!" cried Mike Mountain with an air of desperation, "did ye ever see such a pair of misfortunate bosthoons? Round the island, God blast ye!"

But Patch, who seemed to have an absolute fixation on Flurry, interpreted this as a command to go round him, and, seeing that Flurry wasn't at all sure what direction he was going in, this wasn't as easy as it looked. He put up one really grand spurt, and had just established himself successfully across Flurry's bow when it hit him and sent him spinning like a top, knocking one oar clean out of his hand. Sullivan's old boat was no good for racing, but it was grand for anything in the nature of tank warfare, and as Flurry had by this time got into his stroke, it would have taken an Atlantic liner to stop him. Patch screamed with rage, and then managed to retrieve his oar and follow. The shock seemed to have given him new energy.

Only gradually was the sergeant's strategy beginning to reveal itself to me. The problem was to get the Caheraghs out of the village without a fight, and Flurry and Patch were spoiling for one. Anything that would exhaust the pair of them would make his job easier. It is not a method recommended in Police Regulations, but it has the distinct advantage of leaving no unseemly aftermath of summonses and cross-summonses which, if neglected, may in time turn into a regular vendetta. As a spectacle it really wasn't much. Darkness had breathed on the mirror of the water. A bonfire on the island set a pendulum reflection swinging lazily to and fro, darkening the bay at either side of it. There was a milky light over the hill of Croghan; the moon was rising.

The sergeant came up to me with his hand over his mouth and his big head a little on one side, a way he had of indicating to the world that he was speaking aside.

"I see by the paper how they're after making it up again," he whispered anxiously. "Isn't she a changeable little divil?"

It took me a moment or two to realize that he was referring to Coleman and the publican's daughter; I always forget that he looks on me as a fellow-artist of Coleman's.

"Poets prefer them like that," I said.

"Is that so?" he exclaimed in surprise. "Well, everyone to his own taste." Then he scanned the bay thoughtfully and started suddenly. "Who the hell is that?" he asked.

Into the pillar of smoky light from the bonfire a boat had come, and it took us a little while to identify it. It was Patch's, and there was Patch himself pulling leisurely to shore. He had given up the impossible task of going round Flurry. Some of the crowd began to shout derisively at him but he ignored them. Then Mike Mountain took off his bowler hat and addressed us in heart-broken tones.

"Stone him!" he besought us. "For Christ's sake, ladies and gentlemen, stone him! He's no son of mine, only a walking mockery of man."

He began to dance on the edge of the slip and shout insults at Patch who had slowed up and showed no inclination to meet him.

"What the hell do you mean by it?" shouted Mike. "You said you'd race the man and you didn't. You shamed me before everyone. What sort of misfortunate old furniture are you?"

"But he fouled me," Patch yelled indignantly. "He fouled me twice."

"He couldn't foul what was foul before," said his father. "I'm eighty-one, but I'm a better man than you. By God, I am."

A few moments later Flurry's boat hove into view.

"Mike Mountain," he shouted over his shoulder in a sobbing voice, "have you any grandsons you'd send out against me now? Where are the great Caheragh sailors now, I'd like to know?"

"Here's one of them," roared Mike, tearing at the lapels of his coat. "Here's a sailor if you want one. I'm only a feeble old man, but I'm a better man in a boat than either of ye. Will you race me, Flurry? Will you race me now, I say?"

"I'll race you to hell and back," panted Flurry contemptuously.

Mike excitedly peeled off his coat and tossed it to me. Then he took off his vest and hurled it at the sergeant. Finally he opened his braces, and, grabbing his bowler hat, he made a flying leap into his own boat and tried to seize the oars from Patch.

"'Tisn't fair," shouted Patch, wrestling with him. "He fouled me twice."

"Gimme them oars and less of your talk," snarled his father.

"I don't care," screamed Patch. "I'll leave no man lower my spirit."

"Get out of that boat or I'll have to deal with you officially," said the sergeant sternly. "Flurry," he added, "wouldn't you take a rest?"

"Is it to beat a Caheragh?" snarled Flurry viciously as he brought Sullivan's boat round again.

Again the sergeant gave the word and the two boats set off. This time there were no mistakes. The two old men were rowing magnificently, but it was almost impossible to see what happened then. A party of small boys jumped into another boat and set out after them.

"A pity we can't see it," I said to the sergeant.

"It might be as well," he grunted gloomily. "The less witnesses the better. The end of it will be a coroner's inquest, and I'll lose my bleddy job."

Beneath us on the slip, Patch, leaning against the slimy wall, seemed to have fallen asleep. The sergeant looked down at him greedily.

"And 'tis only dawning on me that the whole bleddy lot of them ought to be in the lock-up," he muttered.

"Sergeant," I said, "you ought to be in the diplomatic service."

He brought his right hand up to shield his mouth, and with his left elbow he gave me an agonizing dig in the ribs that nearly knocked me.

"Whisht, you divil you! Whisht, whisht, whisht!" he said.

The pendulum of firelight, growing a deeper red, swayed with the gentle motion of an old clock, and from the bay we could hear the excited voices of the boatful of boys, cheering on the two old men.

" 'Tis Mike," said someone, staring out into the darkness.

" 'Tisn't," said a child's voice. " 'Tis Flurry. I sees his blue smock."

It was Flurry. We were all a little disappointed. I will say for our people that whatever quarrel they may have with the Portuguese, in sport they have a really international outlook. When old Mike pulled in a few moments later he got a rousing cheer. The first to congratulate him was Flurry.

"Mike," he shouted as he tied up Sullivan's boat, "you're a better man than your son."

"You fouled me," shouted Patch.

In response to the cheer Mike rose in the rocking boat. He stood in the bow and then, recollecting his manners, took off his hat. As he removed his hand from his trousers, they fell about his scraggy knees, but he failed to perceive that.

"Ladies and gentlemen," he said pantingly, " 'twasn't a bad race. An old man didn't wet the blade of an oar these twelve months, 'twasn't a bad race at all."

"Begod, Mike," said Flurry, holding out his hand from the slip, "you were a good man in your day."

"I was, Flurry, said Mike, taking his hand and staring up affectionately at him. "I was a powerful man in my day, my old friend, and you were a powerful man yourself."

It was obvious that there was going to be no fight. The crowd began to disperse in an outburst of chatter and laughter. Mike turned to us again, but only the sergeant and myself were listening to him. His voice had lost its carrying power.

"Ladies and gentlemen," he cried, "for an old man that saw such hard days, 'tis no small thing. If ye knew what me and my like endured ye'd say the same. Ye never knew them, and with the help of the Almighty God ye never will. Cruel times they were, but they're all forgotten. No one remembers them, no one tells ye, the troubles of the poor man in the days gone by. Many's the wet day I rowed from dawn to dark, ladies and gentlemen; many's the bitter winter night I spent, ditching and draining, dragging down the sharp stones for my little cabin by starlight and moonlight. If ye knew it all, ye'd say I was a great man. But 'tis all forgotten, all, all, forgotten!"

Old Mike's voice had risen into a wail of the utmost poignancy. The excitement and applause had worked him up, and all the past was rising in him as in a dying man. But there was no one to hear him. The crowd drifted away up the road. Patch tossed the old man's clothes into the boat, and, sober enough now, stepped in and pushed off in silence, but his father still stood in the bow, his bowler hat in his hand, his white shirt flapping about his naked legs.

We watched him till he was out of sight, but even then I could hear his voice bursting out in sharp cries of self-pity like a voice from the dead. All the loneliness of the world was in it. A flashlight glow outlined a crest of rock at the left-hand side of the case histories, draws up reports, works toward the solution of one of the most tragic situations we face in modern society."

"Which is?"

"That should have been made obvious by the title of the organization, Mr. Treadwell. Gerontology is the study of old age and the problems concerning it. Do not confuse it with geriatrics, please. Geriatrics is concerned with the diseases of old age. Gerontology deals with old age as the problem itself."

"I'll try to keep that in mind," Mr. Treadwell said impatiently. "Meanwhile, I suppose, a small donation is in order? Five dollars, say?"

"No, no, Mr. Treadwell, not a penny, not a red cent. I quite understand that this is the traditional way of dealing with various philanthropic organizations, but the Society for Gerontology works in a different way entirely. Our objective is to help you with your problem first. Only then would we feel we have the right to make any claim on you."

"Fine," said Mr. Treadwell more amiably. "That leaves us all even. I have no problem, so you get no donation. Unless you'd rather reconsider?"

"Reconsider?" said Bunce in a pained voice. "It is you, Mr. Treadwell, and not I who must reconsider. Some of the most pitiful cases the Society deals with are those of people who have long refused to recognize or admit their problem. I have worked months on your case, Mr. Treadwell. I never dreamed you would fall into that category."

Mr. Treadwell took a deep breath. "Would you mind telling me just what you mean by that nonsense about working on my case? I was never a case for any damned society or organization in the book!"

It was the work of a moment for Bunce to whip open his portfolio and extract several sheets of paper from it.

"If you will bear with me," he said, "I should like to sum up the gist of these reports. You are forty-seven years old and in excellent health. You own a home in East Sconsett, Long Island, on which there are nine years of mortgage payments still due, and you also own a late-model car on which eighteen monthly payments are yet to be made. However, due to an excellent salary you are in prosperous circumstances. Am I correct?"

"As correct as the credit agency which gave you that report," said Mr. Treadwell.

Bunce chose to overlook this. "We will now come to the point. You have been happily married for twenty-three years, and have one daughter who was married last year and now lives with her husband in Chicago. Upon her departure from your home your father-in-law, a widower and somewhat crotchety gentleman, moved into the house and now resides with you and your wife."

Bunce's voice dropped to a low, impressive note. "He's seventy-two years old, and, outside of a touch of bursitis in his right shoulder, admits to exceptional health for his age. He has stated on several occasions that he hopes to live another twenty years, and according to actuarial statistics which my Society has on file *he has every chance of achieving this.* Now do you understand, Mr. Treadwell?"

It took a long time for the answer to come. "Yes," said Mr. Treadwell at last, almost in a whisper. "Now I understand."

"Good," said Bunce sympathetically. "Very good. The first step is always a hard one—the admission that there is a problem hovering over you, clouding every day that passes. Nor is there any need to ask why you make efforts to conceal it even from yourself. You wish to spare Mrs. Treadwell your unhappiness, don't you?"

Mr. Treadwell nodded.

"Would it make you feel better," asked Bunce, "if I told you that Mrs. Treadwell shared your own feelings? That she, too, feels her father's presence in her home as a burden which grows heavier each day?"

"But she can't!" said Mr. Treadwell in dismay. "She was the one who wanted him to live with us in the first place, after Sylvia got married, and we had a spare room. She pointed out how much he had done for us when we first got started, and how easy he was to get along with, and how little expense it would be—it was she who sold me on the idea. I can't believe she didn't mean it!"

"Of course, she meant it. She knew all the traditional emotions at the thought of her old father living alone somewhere, and offered all the traditional arguments on his behalf, and was sincere every moment. The trap she led you both into was the pitfall that awaits anyone who indulges in murky, sentimental thinking. Yes, indeed, I'm sometimes inclined to believe that Eve ate the apple just to make the serpent happy," said Bunce, and shook his head grimly at the thought.

"Poor Carol," groaned Mr. Treadwell. "If I had only known that she felt as miserable about this as I did—"

"Yes?" said Bunce. "What would you have done?"

Mr. Treadwell frowned. "I don't know. But there must have been something we could have figured out if we put our heads together."

"What?" Bunce asked. "Drive the man out of the house?"

"Oh, I don't mean exactly like that."

"What then?" persisted Bunce. "Send him to an institution? There are some extremely luxurious institutions for the purpose. You'd have to consider one of them, since he could not possibly be regarded as a charity case; nor, for that matter, could I imagine him taking kindly to the idea of going to a public institution."

"Who would?" said Mr. Treadwell. "And as for the expensive kind, well, I did look into the idea once, but when I found out what they'd cost I knew it was out. It would take a fortune."

"Perhaps," suggested Bunce, "he could be given an apartment of his own—a small, inexpensive place with someone to take care of him."

"As it happens, that's what he moved out of to come live with us. And on that business of someone taking care of him—you'd never believe what it costs. That is, even allowing we could find someone to suit him."

"Right!" Bunce said, and struck the desk sharply with his fist. "Right in every respect, Mr. Treadwell."

Mr. Treadwell looked at him angrily. "What do you mean—right? I had the idea you wanted to help me with this business, but you haven't come up with a thing yet. On top of that you make it sound as if we're making great progress."

"We are, Mr. Treadwell, we are. Although you weren't aware of it we have just completed the second step to your solution. The first step was the admission that there was a problem; the second step was the realization that no matter which way you turn there seems to be no logical or practical solution to the problem. In this way you are not only witnessing, you are actually participating in, the marvelous operation of The Blessington Method which, in the end, places the one possible solution squarely in your hands."

"The Blessington Method?"

"Forgive me," said Bunce. "In my enthusiasm I used a term not yet in scientific vogue. I must explain, therefore, that The Blessington Method is the term my co-workers at the Society for Gerontology have given to its course of procedure. It is so titled in honor of J. G. Blessington, the Society's founder, and one of the great men of our era. He has not achieved his proper acclaim yet, but he will. Mark my words, Mr. Treadwell, some day his name will resound louder than that of Malthus."

"Funny I never heard of him," reflected Mr. Treadwell. "Usually I keep up with the newspapers. And another thing," he added, eyeing Bunce narrowly, "we never did get around to clearing up just how you happened to list me as one of your cases, and how you managed to turn up so much about me."

Bunce laughed delightedly. "It does sound mysterious when you put it like that, doesn't it? Well, there's really no mystery to it at all. You see, Mr. Treadwell, the Society has hundreds of investigators scouting this great land of ours from coast to coast, although the public at large is not aware of this. It is against the rules of the Society for any employee to reveal that he is a professional investigator—he would immediately lose effectiveness.

"Nor do these investigators start off with some specific person as their subject. Their interest lies in *any* aged person who is willing to talk about himself, and you would be astonished at how garrulous most aged people are about their most intimate affairs. That is, of course, as long as they are among strangers.

"These subjects are met at random on park benches, in saloons, in libraries—in any place conducive to comfort and conversation. The investigator befriends the subjects, draws them out—seeks, especially, to learn all he can about the younger people on whom they are dependent."

"You mean," said Mr. Treadwell with growing interest, "the people who support them."

"No, no," said Bunce. "You are making the common error of equating *dependence* and *finances*. In many cases, of course, there is a financial dependence but that is a minor part of the picture. The important factor is that there is always an *emotional* dependence. Even where a physical distance may separate the older person from the younger, that emotional dependence is always present. It is like a current passing between them. The younger person by the mere realization that the aged exist is burdened by guilt and anger. It was his personal experience with this tragic dilemma of our times that led J. G. Blessington to his great work."

"In other words," said Mr. Treadwell, "you mean that even if the old man were not living with us, things would be just as bad for Carol and me?"

"You seem to doubt that, Mr. Treadwell. But tell me, what makes things bad for you now, to use your own phrase?"

Mr. Treadwell thought this over. "Well," he said, "I suppose it's just a case of having a third person around all the time. It gets on your nerves after a while."

"But your daughter lived as a third person in your home for over twenty years," pointed out Bunce. "Yet, I am sure you didn't have the same reaction to her."

"But that's different," Mr. Treadwell protested. "You can have fun with a kid, play with her, watch her growing up—"

"Stop right there!" said Bunce. "Now you are hitting the mark. All the years your daughter lived with you you could take pleasure in watching her grow, flower like an exciting plant, take form as an adult being. But the old man in your house can only wither and decline now, and watching that process casts a shadow on your life. Isn't that the case?"

"I suppose it is."

"In that case do you suppose it would make any difference if he lived elsewhere? Would you be any the less aware that he was withering and declining and looking wistfully in your direction from a distance?"

"Of course not. Carol probably wouldn't sleep half the night worrying about him, and I'd have him on my mind all the time because of her. That's perfectly natural, isn't it?"

"It is, indeed, and, I am pleased to say, your recognition of that completes the third step of The Blessington Method. You now realize that it is not the *presence* of the aged subject which creates the problem, but his *existence.*"

Mr. Treadwell pursed his lips thoughtfully. "I don't like the sound of that."

"Why not? It merely states the fact, doesn't it?"

"Maybe it does. But there's something about it that leaves a bad taste in the mouth. It's like saying that the only way Carol and I can have our troubles settled is by the old man's dying."

"Yes," Bunce said gravely, "it is like saying that."

"Well, I don't like it—not one bit. Thinking you'd like to see somebody dead can make you feel pretty mean, and as far as I know it's never killed anybody yet."

Bunce smiled. "Hasn't it?" he said gently.

He and Mr. Treadwell studied each other in silence. Then Mr. Treadwell pulled a handkerchief from his pocket with nerveless fingers and patted his forehead with it.

"You," he said with deliberation, "are either a lunatic or a practical joker. Either way, I'd like you to clear out of here. That's fair warning."

Bunce's face was all sympathetic concern. "Mr. Treadwell," he cried, "don't you realize you were on the verge of the fourth step? Don't you see how close you were to your solution?"

Mr. Treadwell pointed to the door. "Out—before I call the police."

The expression on Bunce's face changed from concern to disgust. "Oh, come, Mr. Treadwell, you don't believe anybody would pay attention to whatever garbled and incredible story you'd concoct out of this. Please think it over carefully before you do anything rash, now or later. If the exact nature of our talk were even mentioned, you would be the only one to suffer, believe me. Meanwhile, I'll leave you my card. Anytime you wish to call on me I will be ready to serve you."

"And why should I ever want to call on you?" demanded the white-faced Mr. Treadwell.

"There are various reasons," said Bunce, "but one above all." He gathered his belongings and moved to the door. "Consider, Mr. Treadwell: anyone who has mounted the first three steps of The Blessington Method inevitably mounts the fourth. You have made remarkable progress in a short time, Mr. Treadwell—you should be calling soon."

"I'll see you in hell first," said Mr. Treadwell.

Despite this parting shot, the time that followed was a bad one for Mr. Treadwell. The trouble was that having been introduced to The Blessington Method he couldn't seem to get it out of his mind. It incited thoughts that he had to keep thrusting away with an effort, and it certainly colored his relationship with his father-in-law in an unpleasant way.

Never before had the old man seemed so obtrusive, so much in the way, and so capable of always doing or saying the thing most calculated to stir annoyance. It especially outraged Mr. Treadwell to think of this intruder in his home babbling his private affairs to perfect strangers, eagerly spilling out details of his family life to paid investigators who were only out to make trouble. And, to Mr. Treadwell in his heated state of mind, the fact that the investigators could not be identified as such did not serve as any excuse.

Within a very few days Mr. Treadwell, who prided himself on being a sane and level-headed businessman, had to admit he was in a bad way. He began to see evidences of a fantastic conspiracy on every hand. He could visualize hundreds—no, thousands—of Bunces swarming into offices just like his all over the country. He could feel cold sweat starting on his forehead at the thought.

But, he told himself, the whole thing was *too* fantastic. He could prove this to himself by merely reviewing his discussion with Bunce, and so he did, dozens of times. After all, it was no more than an objective look at a social problem. Had anything been said that a *really* intelligent man would shy away from? Not at all. If he had drawn some shocking inferences, it was because the ideas were already in his mind looking for an outlet.

On the other hand—

It was with a vast relief that Mr. Treadwell finally decided to pay a visit to the Society for Gerontology. He knew what he would find there: a dingy room or two, a couple of underpaid clerical workers, the musty odor of a piddling charity operation—all of which would restore matters to their proper perspective again. He went so strongly imbued with this picture that he almost walked past the gigantic glass and aluminum tower which was the address of the Society, rode its softly humming elevator in confusion, and emerged in the anteroom of the Main Office in a daze.

And it was still in a daze that he was ushered through a vast and seemingly endless labyrinth of rooms by a sleek, long-legged young woman, and saw, as he passed, hosts of other young women, no less sleek and long-legged, multitudes of brisk, square-shouldered young men, rows of streamlined machinery clicking and chuckling in electronic glee, mountains of stainless-steel card indexes, and, over all, the bland reflection of modern indirect lighting on plastic and metal—until finally he was led into the presence of Bunce himself, and the door closed behind him.

"Impressive, isn't it?" said Bunce, obviously relishing the sight of Mr. Treadwell's stupefaction.

"Impressive?" croaked Mr. Treadwell hoarsely. "Why, I've never seen anything like it. It's a ten-million-dollar outfit!"

"And why not? Science is working day and night like some Frankenstein, Mr. Treadwell, to increase longevity past all sane limits. There are fourteen million people over sixty-five in this country right now. In twenty years their number will be increased to twenty-one million. Beyond that no one can even estimate what the figures will rise to!

"But the one bright note is that each of these aged people is surrounded by many young donors or potential donors to our Society. As the tide rises higher, we, too, flourish and grow stronger to withstand it."

Mr. Treadwell felt a chill of horror penetrate him. "Then it's true, isn't it?"

"I beg your pardon?"

"This Blessington Method you're always talking about," said Mr. Treadwell wildly. "The whole idea is just to settle things by getting rid of old people!"

"Right!" said Bunce. "That is the exact idea. And not even J. G. Blessington himself ever phrased it better. You have a way with words, Mr. Treadwell. I always admire a man who can come to the point without sentimental twaddle."

"But you can't get away with it!" said Mr. Treadwell incredulously. "You don't really believe you can get away with it, do you?"

Bunce gestured toward the expanses beyond the closed doors. "Isn't that sufficient evidence of the Society's success?"

"But all those people out there! Do they realize what's going on?"

"Like all well-trained personnel, Mr. Treadwell," said Bunce reproachfully, "they know only their own duties. What you and I are discussing here happens to be upper echelon."

Mr. Treadwell's shoulders drooped. "It's impossible," he said weakly. "It can't work."

"Come, come," Bunce said not unkindly, "you mustn't let yourself be overwhelmed. I imagine that what disturbs you most is what J. G. Blessington sometimes referred to as the Safety Factor. But look at it this way, Mr. Treadwell: isn't it perfectly natural for old people to die? Well, our Society guarantees that the deaths will appear natural. Investigations are rare—not one has ever caused us any trouble.

"More than that, you would be impressed by many of the names on our list of donors. People powerful in the political world as well as the financial world have been flocking to us. One and all, they could give glowing testimonials as to our efficiency. And remember that such important people make the Society for Gerontology invulnerable, no matter at what point it may be attacked, Mr. Treadwell. And such invulnerability extends to every single one of our sponsors, including you, should you choose to place your problem in our hands."

"But I don't have the right," Mr. Treadwell protested despairingly. "Even if I wanted to, who am I to settle things this way for anybody?"

"Aha." Bunce leaned forward intently. "But you do want to settle things?"

"Not this way."

"Can you suggest any other way?"

Mr. Treadwell was silent.

"You see," Bunce said with satisfaction, "the Society for Gerontology offers the one practical answer to the problem. Do you still reject it, Mr. Treadwell?"

"I can't see it," Mr. Treadwell said stubbornly. "It's just not right."

"Are you sure of that?"

"Of course I am!" snapped Mr. Treadwell. "Are you going to tell me that it's right and proper to go around killing people just because they're old?"

"I am telling you that very thing, Mr. Treadwell, and I ask you to look at it this way. We are living today in a world of progress, a world of producers and consumers, all doing their best to improve our common lot. The old are neither producers nor consumers, so they are only barriers to our continued progress.

"If we want to take a brief, sentimental look into the pastoral haze of yesterday we may find that once they did serve a function. While the young were out tilling the fields, the old could tend to the household. But even that function is gone today. We have a hundred better devices for tending the household, and they come far cheaper. Can you dispute that?"

"I don't know," Mr. Treadwell said doggedly. "You're arguing that people are machines, and I don't go along with that at all."

"Good heavens," said Bunce, "don't tell me that you see them as anything else! Of course, we are machines, Mr. Treadwell, all of us. Unique and wonderful machines, I grant, but machines nevertheless. Why, look at the world around you. It is a vast organism made up of replaceable parts, all striving to produce and consume, produce and consume until worn out. Should one permit the worn-out part to remain where it is? Of course not! It must be cast aside so that the organism will not be made inefficient. It is the whole organism that counts, Mr. Treadwell, not any of its individual parts. Can't you understand that?"

"I don't know," said Mr. Treadwell uncertainly. "I've never thought of it that way. It's hard to take in all at once."

"I realize that, Mr. Treadwell, but it is part of The Blessington Method that the sponsor fully appreciate the great value of his contribution in all ways—not only as it benefits him, but also in the way it benefits the entire social organism. In signing a pledge to our Society a man is truly performing the most noble act of his life."

"Pledge?" said Mr. Treadwell. "What kind of pledge?"

Bunce removed a printed form from a drawer of his desk and laid it out carefully for Mr. Treadwell's inspection. Mr. Treadwell read it and sat up sharply.

"Why, this says that I'm promising to pay you two thousand dollars in a month from now. You never said anything about that kind of money!"

"There has never been any occasion to raise the subject before this," Bunce replied. "But for some time now a committee of the Society has been examining your financial standing, and it reports that you can pay this sum without stress or strain."

"What do you mean, stress or strain?" Mr. Treadwell retorted. "Two thousand dollars is a lot of money, no matter how you look at it."

Bunce shrugged. "Every pledge is arranged in terms of the sponsor's ability to pay, Mr. Treadwell. Remember, what may seem expensive to you would certainly seem cheap to many other sponsors I have dealt with."

"And what do I get for this?"

"Within one month after you sign the pledge, the affair of your father-in-law will be disposed of. Immediately after that you will be expected to pay the pledge in full. Your name is then enrolled on our list of sponsors, and that is all there is to it."

"I don't like the idea of my name being enrolled on anything."

"I can appreciate that," said Bunce. "But may I remind you that a donation to a charitable organization such as the Society for Gerontology is tax-deductible?"

Mr. Treadwell's fingers rested lightly on the pledge. "Now just for the sake of argument," he said, "suppose someone signs one of these things and then doesn't pay up. I guess you know that a pledge like this isn't collectible under the law, don't you?"

"Yes," Bunce smiled, "and I know that a great many organizations cannot redeem pledges made to them in apparently good faith. But the Society for Gerontology has never met that difficulty. We avoid it by reminding all sponsors that the young, if they are careless, may die as unexpectedly as the old . . . No, no," he said, steadying the paper, "just your signature at the bottom will do."

WHEN MR. TREADWELL'S father-in-law was found drowned off the foot of East Sconsett pier three weeks later (the old man fished from the pier regularly although he had often been told by various local authorities that the fishing was poor there), the event was duly entered into the East Sconsett records as Death By Accidental Submersion, and Mr. Treadwell himself made the arrangements for an exceptionally elaborate funeral. And it was at the funeral that Mr. Treadwell first had the Thought. It was a fleeting and unpleasant thought just disturbing enough to make him miss a step as he entered the church. In all the confusion of the moment, however, it was not too difficult to put aside.

A few days later, when he was back at his familiar desk, the Thought suddenly returned. This time it was not to be put aside so easily. It grew steadily larger and larger in his mind, until his waking hours were terrifyingly full of it, and his sleep a series of shuddering nightmares.

There was only one man who could clear up the matter for him, he knew; so he appeared at the offices of the Society for Gerontology burning with anxiety to have Bunce do so. He was hardly aware of handing over his check to Bunce and pocketing the receipt.

"There's something that's been worrying me," said Mr. Treadwell, coming straight to the point.

"Yes?"

"Well, do you remember telling me how many old people there would be around in twenty years?"

"Of course."

Mr. Treadwell loosened his collar to ease the constriction

around his throat. "But don't you see? I'm going to be one of them!"

Bunce nodded. "If you take reasonably good care of yourself there's no reason why you shouldn't be," he pointed out.

"You don't get the idea," Mr. Treadwell said urgently. "I'll be in a spot then where I'll have to worry all the time about someone from this Society coming in and giving my daughter or my son-in-law ideas! That's a terrible thing to have to worry about all the rest of your life."

Bunce shook his head slowly. "You can't mean that, Mr. Treadwell."

"And why can't I?"

"Why? Well, think of your daughter, Mr. Treadwell. Are you thinking of her?"

"Yes."

"Do you see her as the lovely child who poured out her love to you in exchange for yours? The fine young woman who has just stepped over the threshold of marriage, but is always eager to visit you, eager to let you know the affection she feels for you?"

"I know that."

"And can you see in your mind's eye that manly young fellow who is her husband? Can you feel the warmth of his handclasp as he greets you? Do you know his gratitude for the financial help you give him regularly?"

"I suppose so."

"Now, honestly, Mr. Treadwell, can you imagine either of these affectionate and devoted youngsters doing a single thing—the slightest thing—to harm you?"

The constriction around Mr. Treadwell's throat miraculously eased; the chill around his heart departed.

"No," he said with conviction, "I can't."

"Splendid," said Bunce. He leaned far back in his chair and smiled with a kindly wisdom. "Hold on to that thought, Mr. Treadwell. Cherish it and keep it close at all times. It will be a solace and comfort to the very end."

JOHN SAYLES

At the Anarchists' Convention

SOPHIE CALLS to ask am I going to the Anarchists' Convention this year. The year before last I'm missing because Brickman, may he rest in peace, was on the committee and we were feuding. I think about the Soviet dissidents, but there was always something so it's hard to say. Then last year he was just cooling in the grave and it would have looked bad.

"There's Leo Gold," they would have said, "come to gloat over Brickman."

So I tell Sophie maybe, depending on my hip. Rainy days it's torture, there isn't a position it doesn't throb. Rainy days and election nights.

But Sophie won't hear no, she's still got the iron, Sophie. Knows I won't be caught dead on the Senior Shuttle so she arranges a cab and says, "But Leo, don't you want to see *me?*"

Been using that one for over fifty years.

Worked again.

We used to have it at the New Yorker hotel before the Korean and his Jesus children moved in. You see them on the streets peddling flowers, big smiles, cheeks glowing like Hitler Youth. High on the Opiate of the People. Used to be the New Yorker had its dopers, its musicians, its sad sacks and marginal types. We felt at home there.

So this year the committee books us with the chain that our religious friends from Utah own, their showpiece there on Central Park South. Which kicks off the annual difficulties.

"That's the bunch killed Joe Hill," comes the cry.

"Not to mention their monkey business with Howard Hughes and his will—"

"And what about their stand on blacks and Indians?"

Personally, I think we should have it where we did the year the doormen were on strike, should rent the Union Hall in Brooklyn. But who listens to me?

So right off the bat there's Pinkstaff working up a petition and Weiss organizing a countercommittee. Always with the factions and splinter groups those two, whatever drove man to split the atom is the engine that rules their lives. Not divide and conquer but divide and subdivide.

First thing in the lobby we've got Weiss passing a handout on Brigham Young and the Mountain Meadows Massacre.

"Leo Gold! I thought you were dead!"

"It's a matter of days. You never learned to spell, Weiss."

"What, spelling?"

I point to the handout. "Who's this Norman? 'Norman Hierarchy,' 'Norman Elders.' And all this capitalization, it's cheap theatrics."

Weiss has to put on his glasses. "That's not spelling," he says, "that's typing. Spelling I'm fine, but these new machines—my granddaughter bought an electric."

"It's nice she lets you use it."

"She doesn't know. I sneak when she's at school."

Next there's the placard in the lobby—WELCOME ANARCHISTS—and the caricature of Bakunin, complete with sizzling bomb in hand. That Gross can still hold a pen is such a miracle we have to indulge his alleged sense of humor every year. A malicious man, Gross, like all cartoonists. Grinning, watching the hotel lackeys stew in their little brown uniforms, wondering is it a joke or not. Personally, I think it's in bad taste, the bomb-throwing bit. It's the enemy's job to ridicule, not ours. But who asks me?

THEY'VE SET us loose in something called the Elizabethan Room and it's a sorry sight. A half-hundred old crackpots tiptoeing across the carpet, wondering how they got past the velvet ropes and into the exhibit. That old fascination with the enemy's lair, they fit like fresh *kishke* on a silk sheet. Some woman I don't know is pinning everyone with name tags. Immediately the ashtrays are full of them, pins bent by palsied fingers. Name tags at the Anarchists' Convention?

Pearl is here, and Bill Kinney in a fog and Lou Randolph and Pinkstaff and Fine and Diamond tottering around flashing his new store-boughts at everyone. Personally, wearing dentures I would try to keep my mouth shut. But then I always did.

"Leo, we thought we'd lost you," they say.

"Not a word, it's two years."

"Thought you went just after Brickman, rest his soul."

"So you haven't quit yet, Leo."

I tell them it's a matter of hours and look for Sophie. She's by Baker, the committee chairman this year. Always the committee chairman, he's the only one with such a streak of masochism. Sophie's by Baker and there's no sign of her Mr. Gillis.

There's another one makes the hip act up. Two or three times I've seen the man since he set up housekeeping with Sophie, and every time I'm in pain. Like an allergy, only bone deep. It's not just he's CP from the word go—we all had our fling with the Party, and they have their point of view. But Gillis is the sort that didn't hop off of Joe Stalin's bandwagon till after it nose-dived into the sewer. The deal with Berlin wasn't enough for Gillis, or the purges, no, nor any of the other tidbits that started coming out from reliable sources. Not till the Party announced officially that Joe was off the sainted list did Gillis catch a whiff. And him with Sophie now.

Maybe he's a good cook.

She lights up when she sees me. That smile, after all these years, that smile and my knees are water. She hasn't gone the Mother Jones route, Sophie, no shawls and spectacles, she's nobody's granny on a candy box. She's thin, a strong thin, not like Diamond, and her eyes, they still stop your breath from across the room. Always there was such a crowd, such a crowd around Sophie. And always she made each one think *he* was at the head of the line.

"Leo, you came! I was afraid you'd be shy again." She hugs me, and tells Baker that I'm like a brother.

Sophie who always rallied us after a beating, who bound our wounds, who built our pride back up from shambles and never faltered a step. The iron she had! In Portland they're shaving her head, but no wig for Sophie, she wore it like a badge. And the fire! Toe to toe with a fat Biloxi deputy, head to head with a Hoboken wharf boss, starting a near riot from her soapbox in Columbus Circle, but shaping it, turning it, stampeding all that anger and energy in the right direction.

Still the iron, still the fire, and still it's Leo you're like a brother.

Baker is smiling his little pained smile, looking for someone to apologize to, Blum is telling jokes, Vic Lewis has an aluminum walker after his stroke, and old Mrs. Axelrod, who knew Emma Goldman from the Garment Workers, is dozing in her chair. Somebody must be in charge of bringing the old woman, with her mind the way it is, because she never misses. She's our museum piece, our link to the past.

Not that the rest of us qualify for the New Left.

Bud Odum is in one corner trying to work up a sing-along. Fifteen years younger than most here, a celebrity, still with the denim open at the chest and the Greek sailor cap. The voice is shot though. With Harriet Foote and the old Lieber joining they sound like the look-for-the-Union-label folks on television. Determined but slightly off-key. The younger kids aren't so big on Bud anymore, and the hootenanny generation is grown, with other fish to fry.

Kids, the room is crawling with little Barnard girls and their tape recorders, pestering people for "oral history." A pair camp by Mrs. Axelrod, clicking on whenever she starts awake and mutters some Yiddish. Sophie, who speaks, says she's raving about the harness-eyes breaking and shackles bouncing on the floor, some shirt-factory tangle in her mind. Gems, they think they're getting, oral-history gems.

There are starting to be Rebeccas again, the little Barnard girls, and Sarahs and Esthers, after decades of Carol, Sally, and Debbie. The one who tapes me is a Raisele, which was my mother's name.

"We're trying to preserve it," she says with a sweet smile for an old man.

"What, Yiddish? I don't speak."

"No," she says. "Anarchism. The memories of anarchism. Now that it's served its dialectical purpose."

"You're a determinist."

She gives me a look. They think we never opened a book. I don't tell her I've written a few, it wouldn't make an impression. If it isn't on tape or film it doesn't register. Put my name in the computer, you'll draw a blank.

"Raisele," I say. "That's a pretty name."

"I learned it from an exchange student. I used to be Jody."

DINNER IS CALLED and there's confusion, there's jostling, everyone wants near the platform. The ears aren't what they used to be. There is a seating plan, with place cards set out, but nobody looks. Place cards at the Anarchists' Convention? I manage to squeeze in next to Sophie.

First on the agenda is fruit cup, then speeches, then dinner, then more speeches. Carmen Marcovicci wants us to go get our own fruit cup. It makes her uneasy, she says, being waited on. People want, they should get up and get it themselves.

A couple minutes of mumble-grumble, then someone points out that we'd be putting the two hotel lackeys in charge of the meal out of a job. It's agreed, they'll serve. You could always reason with Carmen.

Then Harriet Foote questions the grapes in the fruit cup. The boycott is over, we tell her, grapes are fine. In fact grapes were always fine, it was the labor situation that was no good, not the *fruit.*

"Well I'm not eating *mine,* " she says, blood pressure climbing toward the danger point, "it would be disloyal."

The Wrath of the People. That's what Brickman used to call it in his articles, in his harangues, in his three-hour walking diatribes. Harriet still has it, and Carmen and Weiss and Sophie and Bill Kinney on his clear days and Brickman had it to the end. It's a wonderful quality, but when you're over seventy and haven't eaten since breakfast it has its drawbacks.

Baker speaks first, apologizing for the site and the hour and the weather and the Hundred Years' War. He congratulates the long travelers—Odum from L.A., Kinney from Montana, Pappas from Chicago, Mrs. Axelrod all the way from Yonkers. He apologizes that our next scheduled speaker, Mikey Dolan, won't be with us. He apologizes for not having time to prepare a eulogy, but it was so sudden.

More mumble-grumble, this being the first we've heard about Mikey. Sophie is crying, but she's not the sort you offer your shoulder to or reach for the Kleenex. *If steel had tears,* Brickman used to say. They had their battles, Brickman and Sophie, those two years together—'37 and '38. Neither of them known as a compromiser, both with healthy throwing arms, once a month there's a knock and it's Sophie come to borrow more plates. I worked for money at the movie house, I always had plates.

The worst was when you wouldn't see either of them for a

week. Phil Rapf was living below them then and you'd see him in Washington Square, eight o'clock in the morning. Phil who'd sleep through the Revolution itself if it came before noon.

"I can't take it," he'd say. "They're at it already. In the morning, in the noontime, at night. At least when they're fighting the plaster doesn't fall."

Less than two years it lasted. But of all of them, before and after, it was Brickman left his mark on her. That hurts.

Bud Odum is up next, his Wisconsin accent creeping toward Oklahoma, twanging on about "good red-blooded American men and women" and I get a terrible feeling he's going to break into "The Ballad of Bob La Follette" when war breaks out at the far end of the table. In the initial shuffle Allie Zaitz was sitting down next to Fritz Groh and it's fifteen minutes before the shock of recognition. Allie has lost all his hair from the X ray treatments, and Fritz never had any. More than ever they're looking like twins.

"*You*," says Allie, "you from the Dockworkers!"

"And you from that yellow rag. They haven't put you away from civilized people?"

"They let *you* in here? You an *an*archist?"

"In the fullest definition of the word. Which you wouldn't know. What was that coloring book you wrote for?"

At the top of their voices, in the manner of old Lefties. What, old, in the manner we've always had, damn the decibels and full speed ahead. Baker would apologize but he's not near enough to the microphone, and Bud Odum is just laughing. There's still something genuine about the boy, even if he does get all weepy when you mention Eleanor Roosevelt.

"Who let this crank in here? We've been infiltrated!"

"Point of order! Point of order!"

What Allie is thinking with point of order I don't know, but the lady from the name tags gets them separated, gives each a Barnard girl to record their spewings about the other. Something Fritz said at a meeting, something Allie wrote about it, centuries ago. We don't forget.

Bud gets going again and it seems that last year they weren't prepared with Brickman's eulogy, so Bud will do the honors now. I feel eyes swiveling, a little muttered chorus of "Leo-leoleo" goes through the room. Sophie knew, of course, and conned me into what she thought would be good for me. Once again.

First Bud goes into what a fighter Brickman was, tells how he took on Union City, New Jersey, single-handed, about the time he organized an entire truckload of scabs with one speech, turning them around right under the company's nose. He can still rouse an audience, Bud, even with the pipes gone, and soon they're popping up around the table with memories. Little Pappas, who we never thought would survive the beating he took one May Day scuffle, little one-eyed, broken-nosed Pappas stands and tells of Brickman saving the mimeograph machine when they burned our office on Twenty-seventh Street. And Sam Karnes, ghost pale, like the years in prison bleached even his blood, is standing, shaky, with the word on Brickman's last days. Tubes running out of him, fluids dripping into him, still Brickman agitates with the hospital orderlies, organizes with the cleaning staff. Then Sophie takes the floor, talking about spirit, how Brickman had it, how Brickman was it, spirit of our cause, more spirit sometimes than judgment, and again I feel the eyes, hear the "Leoleoleo," and there I am on my feet.

"We had our troubles," I say, "Brickman and I. But always I knew his heart was in the right place."

Applause, tears, and I sit down. It's a sentimental moment. Of course, it isn't true. If Brickman had a heart it was a well-kept secret. He was a machine, an express train flying the black flag. But it's a sentimental moment, the words come out.

Everybody is making nice then, the old friendly juices flowing, and Baker has to bring up business. A master of tact, a genius of timing. A vote—do we elect next year's committee before dinner or after?

"Why spoil dinner?" says one camp.

"Nobody will be left awake after," says the other. "Let's get it out of the way."

THEY ALWAYS started small, the rifts. A title, a phrase, a point of procedure. The Chicago Fire began with a spark.

It pulls the scab off, the old animosities, the bickerings, come back to the surface. One whole section of the table splits off into a violent debate over the merits of syndicalism, another forms a faction for elections *during* dinner, Weiss wrestles Baker for the microphone, and Sophie shakes her head sadly.

"Why, why, why? Always they argue," she says, "always they fight."

I could answer, I devoted half of one of my studies to it, but who asks?

While the argument heats another little girl comes over with used-to-be-Jody.

"She says you're Leo Gold."

"I confess."

"*The* Leo Gold?"

"There's another?"

"I read *Anarchism and the Will to Love.*"

My one turkey, and she's read it. "So you're the one."

"I didn't realize you were still alive."

"It's a matter of seconds."

I'm feeling low. Veins are standing out in temples, old hearts straining, distemper epidemic. And the sound, familiar, but with a new, futile edge.

I've never been detached enough to recognize the sound so exactly before. It's a raw-throated sound, a grating, insistent sound, a sound born out of all the insults swallowed, the battles lost, out of all the smothered dreams and desires. Three thousand collective years of frustration in the room, turning inward, a cancer of frustration. It's the sound of parents brawling with each other because they can't feed their kids, the sound of prisoners preying on each other because the guards are out of reach, the sound of a terribly deep despair. No quiet desperation for us, not while we have a voice left. Over an hour it lasts, the sniping, the shouting, the accusations and countercharges. I want to eat. I want to go home. I want to cry.

And then the hotel manager walks in.

Brown blazer, twenty-dollar haircut, and a smile from here to the Odessa Steps. A huddle at the platform. Baker and Mr. Manager bowing and scraping at each other, Bud Odum looking grim, Weiss turning colors. Sophie and I go up, followed by half the congregation. Nobody trusts to hear it secondhand. I can sense the sweat breaking under that blazer when he sees us coming, toothless, gnarled, suspicious by habit. Ringing around him, the Anarchists' Convention.

"A terrible mistake," he says.

"All my fault," he says.

"I'm awfully sorry," he says, "but you'll have to move."

Seems the Rotary Club, the Rotary Club from Sioux Falls, had booked this room *before* us. Someone misread the calendar. They're out in the lobby, eyeballing Bakunin, impatient, full of gin and boosterism.

"We have a nice room, a smaller room" coos the manager, "We can set you up there in a jiffy. Much less drafty than this room, I'm sure the older folks would feel more comfortable."

"I think it stinks," says Rosenthal, every year the committee treasurer. "We paid cash, the room is ours."

Rosenthal doesn't believe in checks. "The less the Wall Street boys handle your money," he says, "the cleaner it is." Who better to be treasurer than a man who thinks gold is filth?

"That must be it," says Sophie to the manager. "You've got your cash from us, money in the bank, you don't have to worry. The Rotary, they can cancel a check, so you're scared. And

maybe there's a little extra on the side they give you, a little folding green to clear out the riffraff?"

Sophie has him blushing, but he's going to the wire anyhow.
Like Frick in the Homestead Strike, shot, stomped, and
stabbed by Alexander Berkman, they patch him up and he fin-
ishes his day at the office. A gold star from Carnegie. Capital-
ism's finest hour.

"You'll have to move," says the manager, dreams of corpo-
rate glory in his eyes, the smile hanging onto his face by its fingernails, "it's the only way."

"Never," says Weiss.

"Out of the question," says Sophie.

"Fuck off," says Pappas.

Pappas saw his father lynched. Pappas did three hard ones in
Leavenworth. Pappas lost an eye, a lung, and his profile to a
mob in Chicago. He says it with conviction.

"Pardon?" A note of warning from Mr. Manager.

"He said to fuck off," says Fritz Groh.

"You heard him," echoes Allie Zaitz.

"If you people won't cooperate," huffs the manager, conde-
scension rolling down like a thick mist, "I'll have to call in the
police."

It zings through the room like the twinge of a single nerve.

"Police! They're sending the police!" cries Pinkstaff.

"Go limp!" cries Vic Lewis, knuckles white with excitement
on his walker. "Make 'em drag us out!"

"Mind the shuttles, mind the shuttles!" cries old Mrs. Axelrod in Yiddish, sitting straight up in her chair.

Allie Zaitz is on the phone to a newspaper friend, the Barnard
girls are taping everything in sight, Sophie is organizing us into
squads, and only Baker holding Weiss bodily allows Mr. Manager to escape the room in one piece. We're the Anarchists'
Convention!

Nobody bickers, nobody stalls or debates or splinters. We
manage to turn the long table around by the door as a kind of

barricade, stack the chairs together in a second line of defense, and crate Mrs. Axelrod back out of harm's way. I stay close by Sophie, and once, lugging the table, she turns and gives me that smile. Like a shot of adrenaline, I feel fifty again. Sophie, Sophie, it was always so good just to be at your side!

And when the manager returns with his two befuddled street cops to find us standing together, arms linked, the lame held up out of their wheelchairs, the deaf joining from memory as Bud Odum leads us in "We Shall Not Be Moved," my hand in Sophie's, sweaty-palmed at her touch like the old days, I look at him in his brown blazer and think *Brickman,* I think, *my God if Brickman was here we'd show this bastard the Wrath of the People!*

IV

V. S. PRITCHETT

Tea with
Mrs. Bittell

SHE LIKED to say it was "inconvenient," on the general ground that a lady should appear to complain beautifully when doing a kindness to someone outside her own class; lately she had been keeping an afternoon for a rather "quaint" person, a young man called Sidney, one of a red-jacketed ballet who hopped about at the busy tea counter in Murgatroyd and Foot's. He often chatted with her to annoy the foreign tourists who pushed and shouted at his counter. She discovered that he came on Sundays to her own church. Such a lonely person he was, sitting in his raincoat among the furs and black suits and in such a sad situation: his father had been in the hospital for years now—a coal miner—he had that dreadful thing miners get. It was so *good* that the young man came to church with a friend, another young man from the tea counter, and waking up from her snooze during the service, she often frowned with pleasure. She would say to her atheistical sister, "The younger generation are hungry for Faith." The second young man stopped coming after a month or two, and only Sidney was left. She astounded him by asking him to tea.

Mrs. Bittell was sitting in her flat in the expensive block

nearly opposite the church, among the wrongs and relics of her seventy years, when Sidney first came.

"Deliveries round the corner, second door," the doorman said.

"I'm a friend of Mrs. Bittell's," said Sidney.

The doorman's chestload of medals flashed. "Why didn't you say you were a friend?" he said, looking Sidney up and down. "Seventh floor."

"A very disagreeable man," said Mrs. Bittell when Sidney told her this, his wounded chin raised. She was a puddingy woman, reposing on a big sleepy belly; her hair was white and she had innocent blue eyes. She wore, as usual, a loosely knitted pink jersey, low in the neck, a heather-mixture skirt, flat-heeled shoes, and was very short. Her family had been army people and at first she thought Sidney rather civilian in a disappointing way when he was not wearing the red jacket he wore in the shop, as she led him across the wide old-fashioned paneled hall of her flat into the full light of her large drawing room, which, in addition to her furniture and pictures, owned a large part of the London sky where the clouds prospered: one looked down on the tops of three embassies and across to the creamy stucco of a long square.

Sidney sat looking at the distances between her sofas, her satiny chairs and other fine things. She remembered he had been so startled when she invited him to tea that he must be quite outside the concept of "invitations." Indeed, he had gone first of all to one of the large windows and searched the rooftops until he found the building where he and his family distantly lived. It was a high-rise block, a mile away, howling like cats, he told her, with the tenants' radios and television sets and children.

"We don't have anything to do with the neighbors," he said complacently. "Talk to the people next door, next thing they unscrew your front door or saw it off when you go out, and pinch the TV."

He turned his head slowly to Mrs. Bittell. He was a slow-talking young man, nearly handsome in a doleful way, and Mrs. Bittell liked this; she was slow and melancholy herself. He gave a droll laugh when he spoke of doors being sawn off and took a mild pride in the fact.

He also added something about the nearest roofs. "I can't stand slate," he said. "Slate is killing my father. The mine did it."

Mrs. Bittell murmured in her social way that, oh dear, she thought he had been a *coal* miner.

"No," he said. "Slate."

He spoke in short sentences between disconcerting pauses. "Dad took me down when I left school."

"You worked there?" said Mrs. Bittell

"No," he said fastidiously. "Slate mines are cold. I don't like the cold."

There was a long pause.

"The deeper you go, the colder it gets," he said.

Mrs. Bittell said her sister Dolly had had the same impression of the catacombs outside Rome, even though wearing a coat.

"I've heard of them," he said.

From his account of the mine it seemed to her that he was describing the block of flats in which he was sitting with her, but upside down, under the earth. Yet the mine also seemed like a buried church with aisles, galleries and side chapels, but in darkness and shaken by the noise of drilling holes for the sticks of dynamite and by the explosions in which the echoes pealed from cavern to cavern. The men worked with a stump of lighted candle on the peaks of their caps.

"Surely, Sidney, that is very dangerous, I've been told," said Mrs. Bittell. "Not lamps?"

"No gas in the slate mines," he said. But Sidney fell into a state of meditation. "Splinters," he said. "A splinter drops from the roof and goes clean through your skull. You have to wear a helmet. Dad never wore a helmet."

"Oh dear, how thoughtless," said Mrs. Bittell.

"No. A splinter never got him."

Sidney had a taste for horrors which he displayed as part of his family's limited capital. "The dust got him," said Sidney. "He wouldn't wear a mask.

"So I went to work in 'the grocery.' "

Mrs. Bittell was offering him a second cup of tea from her silver teapot. She held the cup above the slop basin.

"I forget, d'you like to keep your remains?"

He thought about this; a funeral appeared to her to be passing through his mind.

"I always keep mine," she said.

"It's okay, Mrs. Bittell," he said.

She was trying to think of a tactful way of saying the accent was on the second syllable of her name.

After that, talk became much easier. His long face still mooned but he warmed, although they got at cross purposes when she thought he was talking about the church when he was talking about the shop. He said he enjoyed the smell of furs, scent—they were like the smell of provisions. He looked at her piano and said, "Do you play it?"

Mrs. Bittell had a wide peaceful white forehead with fine lines on it, her eyes were delicately childlike and her voice was graceful, but now the peacefulness vanished. Her face became square and stubborn, and because his pauses were so long she was tempted to fill them with troubles and horrors of her own: her late husband's atrocious behavior—he had once hit her with a bedside lamp—the selfishness of her daughters, who had made such "hopeless" marriages; the suspicions of her trustees, her income not a quarter of what it used to be; the wicked rise of taxes. Her wrongs settled like a migraine in fortified lumps on her forehead. But she did say to Sidney when he mentioned her piano that once one has got used to the big wrongs of life, little ones wake up, with their mean little teeth.

There had been a new wrong in her life in the last few

months. The Misses Pattison on the floor below, she told him, the judge on the floor above, a Scottish "banker person," the general across the landing, had complained about her playing the piano. Several tenants had sent notes protesting: the landlord and even a solicitor had been dragged in to remind her of Clause 15 in her agreement about the hours when the playing of musical instruments were permitted. She had stonewalled, argued and evaded, tried tears, saying they were depriving an old lady of the only pleasure she had left in life. But she had had to give in: she was allowed to play between two and four in the afternoon. Even the doorman had turned against her. She supposed, she said, Sidney had seen, in the entrance hall to the flats, the board with a sliding slot indicating whether tenants were "In" or "Out." She was sure, she told Sidney, that the doorman changed her slot to "Out" when she was "In," and to "In" when she was "Out."

Sidney came to life when she said this; he exclaimed that the slot said "Out" when he had arrived. Mrs. Bittell had always loved a suspicion and she was impressed to find someone who shared one with her.

Before Sidney came to tea, on all his visits—Wednesday being his day off—Mrs. Bittell sat at her piano, a little distant from it because of her bold stomach, making one more attempt at a bit of Debussy. The notes came slowly from her fingers, for she was not one to vary her pace through life, and with occasional vehemence when she was uncertain. Biting her lips, she tried a little Chopin, but that went too fast, so she moved at last to one of those Hebridean songs she had known since she was a girl of fourteen. Now the fine lines on her forehead cleared and softened, her look became faraway and serene, her eyes became heavenly and she felt herself to be gliding like a lonely bird over the rocky Atlantic shore at Cranach, her grandmother's great house. She was back in her childhood, keeping her father's boat straight in the sea-loch as he stood up and cast his line. She remembered chiefly his moustache like a burn. As the song began to fall away to its end she ventured to sing faintly, her voice coming out strong with longing as she lingered over the last line.

"Sad am I without thee!"

Who was "thee"? Certainly not her father with his shout of "Keep your oars straight, girl"; certainly not her husband, who had helped himself to her money for years and left her contemptuously and gone to live only a mile away across the Park to play bridge with his military friends, and die. Certainly not a lover, though she had once thought the best man at her wedding rather attractive. Not the baby she had lost, or the daughters, who had made such unsuitable marriages. Sometimes she thought of "thee" as a girl—the self that had mysteriously slipped away when she was rushed into her marriage.

The buzzer sounded at the door. "Thee," of course, was not Sidney.

He took off his raincoat, folded it carefully and put it on the chest in the dim hall. They were on closer terms now.

"I heard you playing when I was coming up in the lift," he said.

"Oh dear!" she said.

"Not to worry, Mrs. Bittell. They can't touch you. It's five to four: you've got another five minutes."

And he dawdled to allow her to dash back and get the last ounce of her rights.

He was at ease in the room now.

"Now tell me, how is your father today?" she said.

"The same," he said. "Round at the hospital. He goes three days a week. The doctors think the world of him; he's very popular." He added lazily, "X rays. He must have had a hundred."

"The family depends on you," she said.

"Oh no," he said. "There was a sickness benefit; the pension; the grant; he's an important case." Sidney seemed to regard the illness as a profession, an investment.

"What a worry for your mother—but you have a sister,

haven't you? How old is she? Has she got a job?"

Sidney looked wounded at the suggestion. He was careful to let the peculiarity of his family sink in. "Seventeen," he said. "She sits on the sofa, sucking her thumb, like a baby, and looking at television. She's Mother's pet. They all sit looking at it. Dad too," he said.

This pleased him as he sat thinking about it and he laughed. "Mother goes out," he said, "and always comes back with a special offer she sees on the commercials or something from Bingo.

"That," he added, studying the spaces between things in Mrs. Bittell's flat, in which the well-mannered chairs and tables kept their distance from one another, "is why we're so crowded in our place. You can't cross the room."

Mrs. Bittell said, politely evading comparison, "You have long legs."

"Yes," said Sidney, shaking his head. "Jennifer says, 'You're always on about my legs, what about yours?'"

Sidney offered this information in a bemused way. Suddenly he woke up out of his own life and asked, "Who is that gentleman over there?"

She was relieved to see he was looking at one of three portraits on the wall.

"Oh," she said solemnly, "I thought you meant someone had got into the flat."

"No, hanging on the wall," he said.

"Oh, that's just the old Judge. We call him the Judge—the red robe and the fur collar. It was from my mother's family," said Mrs. Bittell in a deprecating way. She had caught Sidney's taste for horrors: "I fear not a very nice man. They say he sentenced his own son to death."

"Oh," Sidney nodded. "History."

"I suppose it is," said Mrs. Bittell. "I like the next one to it, the boy in blue satin with his little sword—the Little Count. I don't know whether he was really a Little Count."

"Is he the one that was sentenced to death?" said Sidney.

"Oh no," said Mrs. Bittell protectively. "The Little Count was the father of the Judge." She had her own pride in her family's crimes.

"Are you interested in pictures?" She got up and he followed her to look more closely.

"Antique," he said. "They must be valuable."

"So they say, but there is such a lot of that sort of thing about," she said.

He gazed a long time at the Little Count and again at the Judge. He gave a sigh. "*The Battle of Waterloo* was on television last night. Did you see it?"

"I'm afraid not," Mrs. Bittell apologized. "I haven't a television. I believe the Misses Pattison have. I can hear it at night." Her wrongs woke up indignantly. "I don't know why they should complain of my piano."

Sidney ignored this. "Do you think the Duke of Wellington was sincere?" he said.

"They say he was very witty," said Mrs. Bittell.

"But do you think he was sincere?"

"Sincere?" said Mrs. Bittell. She was lost. "I've never thought of that," she said.

She saw he was struggling with a moral question, but what was it? She felt one of those violent sensations that swept through her nowadays since her quarrels about the piano. Did Sidney, who was older than she had at first thought, more than thirty, his dark hair receding, did Sidney feel too that sincerity, honesty, consideration, were wearing thin in modern life?

"I know what you mean," said Mrs. Bittell, who did not. She compared Sidney with her ancestors and even with the Duke of Wellington. Sidney was reaching towards the Light; she could not say her forebears had ever done so. She had known the family pictures all her life as furniture: they represented the boredom of centuries, of now meaningless anger. When her husband left her she had seen herself as a woman ruined by generations of reckless plunderers of land, putting down rebellions, fighting wars, gambling and drinking away their money, building big houses, losing their land to lawyers and farmers, grabbing the money of their wives and quarreling with their children. She saw herself with unassuming pride as the victim of history. Even in the Mansions—her rising anger told her—her own class had betrayed her.

She calmed herself by showing him a photograph of a boy of ten. "My only grandson," she said. "Of course he's grown up now. Rupert."

"I've got a friend called Rupert," Sidney said.

"Really. Such a nice name," said Mrs. Bittell, putting the photograph down.

"He used to work at Murgatroyd's," he said, suddenly eager. "You must have seen him—tall, fair moustache. He left."

"I don't remember," she said. "But wait—didn't you bring him to the church?"

"That's it," said Sidney. "He brought me. You don't often meet a man who has had an education. Every Sunday we used to go to a different church—St. Paul's, Westminster Abbey. He knew about antiques too. Lunchtime and Saturdays we used to go to the National Gallery. He could see *into* pictures. If he was here now," he said, surveying her pictures and her furniture, "he'd have valued everything. It was very interesting."

"Very," said Mrs. Bittell.

"I was in the National Gallery this morning," he said. "It's my day off. I had the idea I might find him there. I've been everywhere we went. Holborn Baths too, we used to go swimming."

"And did you find him?" said Mrs. Bittell.

"No," said Sidney, looking aloof. "I don't know where he is. He walked out of the shop last August; not a word."

He paused in the midst of his mystery.

"He left the place where he lived. I went round, but he'd gone. The landlady didn't know. No address. Not a word."

"Too extraordinary," said Mrs. Bittell.

"I mean, you'd think a friend wouldn't go like that. I thought he was sincerely my friend." Sidney gazed at her for an answer. "After three years," he said.

He aged as he gazed. He sat there as if he were the last of a series of Sidneys who was now quite austerely alone, challenging her with a slight smile on his mouth, to see the distinction of his case.

"Oh, but there *must* be an explanation, Sidney," said Mrs. Bittell.

She had an inspiration. "Was he married? I mean—or was he going to get married?"

Sidney looked at her disparagingly. "Rupert would never marry," he said. "I know that. It was ruin, he always said; you were better alone."

"If it's the wrong person," said Mrs. Bittell, nodding, "but in the Kingdom of Heaven there is neither marriage nor giving in marriage," she said. "As the Bible says." The tune of "Sad Am I Without Thee," went through her head. Her words brought her to the point of confidence, but she did not give in to it.

Sidney considered her. He held his hurt face high. "There was an American who used to come into Murgatroyd's. He was from the Bahamas," he said. "Or somewhere."

"Ah, the Bahamas!" said Mrs. Bittell. "Then perhaps that's where your friend went? My husband's best man went to live in the Bahamas. Have you inquired? Business may have taken him to the Bahamas."

Sidney's pale long face swelled and his mouth collapsed with agonized movements. Mrs. Bittell was embarrassed to see tears on his face.

"I can't bear it, Mrs. Bittell." A loud howl like a dog's howling at the moon came out of him. He was sobbing.

"Oh, Sidney, what is it?" said Mrs. Bittell, moving from her chair to the sofa where he sat.

The cry took her back years to a painful scene in Aldershot when a subaltern in her husband's regiment had suddenly sobbed like this about some wretched girl. He had actually cried on her shoulder. Sidney suddenly did this: his head was on her bosom, weeping. His dark hair had a peculiar smell, just like the subaltern's smell. She patted Sidney on the head, but she was thinking, I mustn't tell my sister Dolly about this, or my daughters. It would be terrible if her grandson suddenly came; he often dropped in.

"I am sure you'll hear from him," she was saying.

"I loved him," Sidney wept.

"Love is never lost. In the Kingdom of Heaven, love is never lost, Sidney dear," said Mrs. Bittell. "I know how you feel. I have been through it too." She was thinking of her children.

He sat back away from her. He seemed to be saying that whatever she had been through, it was nothing to what he had been through. She also saw that in some kind of craven way he was worshipping her. And even while she felt compassion, she felt disturbed. Why had it never occurred to her, in her miserable troubles with her husband, long ago over and for which her own family blamed her, that there had been no "other woman"?

"We must turn to God," she said, though she knew that years ago she had done nothing of the sort, that outrage had possessed her.

"We must pray," she said. "The Kingdom of Heaven is within us, Sidney." And she declared, "There is no separation for the children of God."

Sidney looked around the room and then back to her, immovable in his gloom.

"We must not cling to our sorrows," she said, for he looked vain of his, but he nodded in a vacant fashion. She smiled beautifully, for she felt that there was some hope in that nod. As he got up to go Sidney changed too. He walked with her into the dim hall, at home in her company now. As he picked up his raincoat he saw himself reflected in the glass of a very large old picture, the full-length portrait of a girl, it seemed, though scarcely visible except for the face.

"Who is that?" he said.

"Oh, just a family thing. It used to be at Cranach. I'll switch on the light."

There was an overshadowing tree with leaves like hundreds of chattering tongues, a little stream in the foreground and a large grey mossy boulder. On it a sad, naked, wooden-looking nymph was sitting, the skin yellowed by time. In one corner of the picture was a little cupid aiming an arrow at her.

Sidney gaped. "Is that you?" he said.

Questions took a long time sinking into Mrs. Bittell's head, which was clouded by kindness and manners and a pride in her relics. She herself had not "seen" the picture for years. It was glazed and was hardly more than a mirror in which she could give a last look at her hat before she went out. She was not surprised by Sidney's remark.

"It doesn't really belong to me, it's really my sister's, but she doesn't like it so I put it there."

Sidney tried to cover his mistake. "That is what I meant. Your sister," he said.

"Oh no," said Mrs. Bittell, waking up. "It's Psyche, the goddess, the nymph, I believe. The Greek legend, Psyche—the soul. I really must get one of those lights they fix to frames. It's so hard to know what to do with big pictures, don't you find? Do you like it?

"It's supposed to be by—Lely, is it?" said Mrs. Bittell nervously. "My husband said it was probably only a copy. My daughter tells me I ought to get it cleaned and hang it in the drawing room, where one can see it more clearly."

The idea appeared to shock Sidney. "I've never seen one like that in a house before. In a gallery. Not in a house," he said censoriously.

"I mean," said Sidney. "The man who painted it, was he sincere?"

Mrs. Bittell was baffled again by the word and murmured politely. Her mind moved as slowly as her feet as she opened the door for him to leave and said, "You must call me Zuilmah, Sidney dear. Remember I will pray for you and Rupert. Ring for the lift," she said.

"I'll go down the stairs," said Sidney. He was bewildered.

S H E W E N T to the bathroom after he had left and saw from the window the top of the distant block of flats where he lived. Now that the evening was coming on, the block was a tall panel of electric light, standing up in the sky. A thought struck her: How absurd to say it's a portrait of Dolly—no resemblance at all.

She flushed the toilet.

For Mrs. Bittell, Psyche was part of her furniture. She had not really looked at it since she was a girl at Cranach. Then she remembered that she and Dolly used to giggle and say it was Miss Potter, their governess, with nothing on. Mrs. Bittell had long stopped noticing that Psyche was naked, and if she had been asked, would have said that the figure was wearing one of those gauzy scarves that pictures of nymphs wore in books. She had never even thought of naked statues as being naked. Men, she supposed, might think they were—they were so animal.

It came to her that Sidney was a man.

"How embarrassing," she said. She imagined she had seen a hot, reddish cloud in Sidney's eyes. He had gaped, mouth open, at the picture, and his mouth looked angry and wet. She had once or twice seen her wretched husband looking at the picture, mouth open in the same way, though (as she remembered) he was short of money and said, "We'd get a tidy price for it at Christie's," and they had their lifelong quarrel. He was always itching to sell her things to pay his debts.

"You can't sell it, it's Dolly's," she had said to him.

"Your bloody sister," he said.

Now Mrs. Bittell's peaceful face changed into a lump of fear. Sidney slipped into her husband's place and became dangerous. He had had an empty, staring expression when he looked at that body. And he had thought it was she herself! Things she had read in the papers rushed into her mind, tales of men breaking into houses and attacking women, grappling with them, murdering them. Sidney had cried on her shoulder. He had touched her hand. His was hot. The scene became transformed. She saw the struggle. She would scream—she looked at her table with a lamp on it—yes, she would hit him with a lamp. That was what her husband had used on her.

Mrs. Bittell sat on the sofa opposite to the one Sidney and she had sat on and looked at the squashed cushions, her heart thumping. Slowly the panic quietened.

"How foolish," she said.

She recovered and went to her piano. She played three or four notes secretively and sulkily, and the illicit sound restored her.

Of course—Psyche was the soul, a "thee," the thee of her dead baby, herself as a young girl before she married, a loss, a sadness. And Sidney too had a "thee." He must have been thinking of Rupert, poor young man.

I must pray. I must not let the Devil get hold of me, she thought. Sidney and Rupert are children of God made in His image and likeness.

And she closed her papery eyelids and prayed and pleasantly dropped off to sleep in the middle of the prayer.

FOR TWO WEEKS Sidney did not come to the church, then he reappeared and came to the flat again.

"I've been worrying about you," she said.

Sidney had changed. She noticed, once he had got out of the dim hall into her drawing room, that his hair was different. It was combed forward and he looked younger, leaner. She did not say anything; perhaps her prayers had been answered.

"I've been worrying about you," she said again. "Have you any news?"

"I made up my mind and packed the job in," he said. He looked careless and grand.

"Sidney! From Murgatroyd's. Was that wise? Why did you do that?" Mrs. Bittell was shocked.

"Undercurrents," he said.

Mrs. Bittell could understand that. There were undercurrents in the Mansions. There were even undercurrents at the church.

"No consideration," he said lazily.

Mrs. Bittell could understand that, too. Why was her youngest daughter so critical of her? Why did young people push past her in bus queues?

"What are you going to do?" she said.

"I'm in no hurry," he said. "I might go back to Reception Hotels."

"Is that better?" she said.

"Could be," he said.

"That is where I first met him—Rupert—hotel." He was offhand, cool, disdainful.

"Do sit down and tell me," she said.

He sat down. "It's all this stealing that goes on I can't stand. It's not the customers—it's the staff. Food, clocks, rugs—anything. Six Persian rugs last week. You can see it being wheeled off to Delivery and loaded onto vans in the bay. Tell the management, they don't want to know. Insured. Rupert couldn't stand it. I think that's why he left."

"We live in a terrible world," said Mrs. Bittell.

"Bomb in that restaurant yesterday—did you read it in the paper? A woman had her hand blown off," he said.

"How horrible," said Mrs. Bittell. His new haircut made it seem more horrible. "Did they catch the men?"

"Tell the police, they don't want to know," said Sidney.

One of those sudden rages which seized her flared up and made her heart thump; her stomach swelled and her sweet face became ugly. Rage was lifting her into the air. Once more all her wrongs came back to her. She felt herself to be united with him: he was no longer the "quaint" young man. He was human and alone, as she was. And then her rage declined. No, she mustn't give in to anger; one had to face evil. A sentence from one of the vicar's sermons came back to her: she loved the way he said it. "The darkest hour precedes the dawn." This was a dark hour for the world and for Sidney.

"When everything is dark, Sidney dear," she said, "we must pour in more love. We must open the floodgates." She was swimming in the growing exaltation of one who had sent out a message. She looked at his doubting face.

A vulgar buzzer went at the door which startled her.

"Oh dear," said Mrs. Bittell. "Now, who can that be? I hope it is not someone awkward."

How often in her life she had expected a prayer to be miraculously answered when she opened her eyes.

Sidney and she looked at each other. Then her face became stubborn. "How irritating," she said. "I'm losing my memory. It's Mr. Ferney. I'd forgotten him. He's a friend of my sister's and we've drunk all the tea. How silly of me."

"Shall I go to the door?" said Sidney possessively.

"No, I'll go. He's retired," she called back as she went. "Stay here. Would you do me a great kindness and put the kettle on? Wait—it's probably the doorman."

Mr. Ferney was at the door. Mr. Ferney was a meaty middle-aged man with two reproachful chins and a loud flourishing voice.

"Dear Zuilmah," he bawled. "Always the same. Like your Psyche, with a lily in your hand, waiting for Cupid's arrow. Am I late?"

"We didn't wait for you," said Mrs. Bittell.

Since he had retired Mr. Ferney's profession was having tea with ladies. He was on the verge of a belated search for a wife.

"You don't know Mr. Taplow, a dear friend," said Mrs. Bittell.

Mrs. Bittell went to make more tea.

"Tiplow," said Mr. Ferney. "Somerset Tiplows?"

"Taplow," said Sidney.

"Taplow, Tiplow, all Somerset names. Tiplawn, too. People

couldn't spell in the past. You'll find Ferns, Fennys, de la Fresne and of course Ferness. I tell Mrs. Bittell that she was a Battle," he confided in a loud voice. "Bataille."

"What are you talking about?" said Mrs. Bittell, returning with her silver teapot.

"Your horrible family, my dear," said Mr. Ferney. "The rogues' gallery—that awful fellow." He pointed to the Judge.

"Mr. Taplow and I were talking about that the other day, weren't we, Sidney? Sidney was saying that History is coming back, wasn't that it? Tell Mr. Ferney."

"History always comes back. I can't afford it, can you?" said Mr. Ferney.

Sidney's face became swollen on one side and he said, "I'll be going, then. I've got to get Father," to Mrs. Bittell.

"Must you? Oh dear. Of course you must," said Mrs. Bittell. "Mr. Taplow's father is in the hospital."

"Nothing serious, I hope."

"I'm afraid it is," said Mrs. Bittell.

"Such a tiresome man, I'm so sorry," she murmured as she took Sidney to the door. "Remember, Sidney dear, what I said. Open the floodgates. Don't forget to come to church on Sunday.

And seeing his unhappy look, she gave him a light kiss.

Sidney was shocked by the kiss.

"WHO IS THAT? What's he mean by 'then'? I've seen him somewhere. It'll come back to me . . . Treplawn," said Mr. Ferney.

"He used to work at Murgatroyd and Foot's," said Mrs. Bittell. "Terrible stories he's been telling me. I'm trying to help him."

"Oh, I see," said Mr. Ferney, relieved, and passed his cup. "What's he after? You do slave for people. I wish you'd slave for me."

THIEVES IN MURGATROYD and Foot's, a shop known all over the world for generations! The building itself became a long flaunting wrong and, for her, London changed overnight. Even the gardens in the squares became suspect to her. The doors of pillared terraces looked dubious, embassies were white sepulchres, the cars outside hotels carried loads of criminals away. Walking in her quiet way, in the past she had floated sedately above curiosity, merely noticing that the young rushed. But now she saw that the city had become a swarming bazaar: swarms of foreigners of all colors—Arabs, Indians, Chinese, Japanese, and all people jabbering languages she had never heard—came in phalanxes down the pavements, their eyes avid for loot. If she paused because she heard an English voice, she was pushed and trodden on, more than once laughed at. In the once quiet streets, such as the one in which her sister lived, there were empty bottles of whisky and brandy rolling in the gardens.

She noticed these things now because for three weeks Sidney had not been to church and when she was out walking she was looking at all the faces thinking she might see him. He had disappeared in the flood.

Yet the more impossible it was for her to know where he was or what he was doing or why he did not come, the calmer she became; inevitably the divine will would be manifested and, indeed, she went so far as to stop praying; in a modest way the sensation was exalting.

At church she gave up looking for Sidney in the congregation when the hymns were sung—she was too short to see far when she was sitting. It must have been on the fifth Sunday, as she stood up for the second hymn and heard the mouths of the well-dressed congregation shouting forth, that she noticed two men across the aisle who were holding their hymnbooks high and not singing. Sidney—and who was the other man? She hardly remembered him—it *must* be Rupert!

Mrs. Bittell stopped singing and said loudly, almost shouted "No" to the will of God. She flopped into her seat and her umbrella went to the floor. The church seemed to roll like a ship; the altar shot up into the air. The powerful odor of the fur coat of the woman in front of her was suffocating. The miracle had occurred. Rupert had returned. Sidney was standing beside him. Prayer had been answered: it has swept Rupert back across the Atlantic. All the old prayers of her life that had never been answered became like rubbish. A real miracle had been granted to her.

Flustered, she got to her feet and started singing the last verse and looked across the aisle. The two young men had heard her umbrella fall and now they were both singing, and singing at her, at least Rupert's mouth was open but Sidney was half hidden, and Rupert's teeth flashed. She nodded curtly; she had only one desire: to go at once across the aisle in anger and say, "Why didn't you tell Sidney you were going away? Why didn't you write? If he is sincerely your friend?"

When the service was over, they were ahead of her in the crowded aisle, but she found Sidney waiting for her on the pavement and Rupert a few yards away.

"He's back," said Sidney, beckoning to Rupert, who stood politely aside. For a moment the young man still looked unlike a real man but more like some photograph of a man.

"What did I tell you, Sidney?" she said as Rupert came nearer.

Sidney stood back, gazing up at the hero, his eyes begging her to admire.

"I remember you, Mrs. Bittell," Rupert said.

"What a time it has been," she said.

"What a time," he said.

"Our bus," said Sidney.

"You must tell me everything. Come to tea," she pleaded. "Monday? I don't want to lose you again."

They looked at each other and glanced at the bus and agreed. How flat she felt, but as they ran for the bus they turned back to wave—how delightful to see a miracle running.

MRS. BITTELL went beautifully and as if empowered to the door. There stood Sidney, so proud that he looked as if he would fall headfirst into the hall; behind him, stiffly controlled, stood Rupert, the answered prayer, perhaps rightly wearing dark glasses as if, as yet, shy of the spiritual life. She forgot to close the door and Rupert politely shut it for her.

"It gives a click," she called back to him.

"It clicked," he said.

Sidney went eagerly forward. They stood in the drawing room.

"The Judge!" said Sidney, pointing to the picture. Rupert ignored this and looked round the room.

"Now," said Mrs. Bittell playfully, "where is your sunburn?"

"He has been ill," said Sidney. "He's only just out of the hospital."

"I picked up one of those bugs," said Rupert.

"Oh dear. I hope it was not serious," said Mrs. Bittell.

"Two months," said Sidney dramatically. What an emotional young man he was!

It was disappointing not to see the miracle in perfect health. His voice was hoarse, he brought a smell of cigarettes with him and he had lost weight, so that his cocoa-colored suit was loose on him. His thin face seemed to have a frost on it, and when he took his dark glasses off, he was obliged to narrow his eyes because of the light in the room. The thinness of the face made his mouth and lips too wide. There was grey in his hair. She noticed this because she had never been sure which of the young men at the tea counter he was. He sat so stiff and still, and despite his illness, his bones looked too heavy for the chair. He picked up one of the cups on the tea table and looked at the mark as Mrs. Bittell went off to get her silver teapot.

"Now tell us all about the Bahamas," said Mrs. Bittell as she came back, and out came her story that her husband's best man at their wedding had been ADC to the Governor, whose name she could not remember; it was a long time ago, of course.

"Who is Governor now?"

The question made Rupert smile thoughtfully. "McWhirter," he said at last. "He's retired, though—not very popular—the new man came after I left."

"I must ask my sister. She'll tell us," said Mrs. Bittell.

This was disappointing. And Rupert's account of the Bahamas was bewildering. No Government House, no beaches, no palm trees. All Victorians, he said. Full of English stuff left by early settlers. Harmoniums everywhere, he said, grandfather's clocks. Fox-hunting pictures.

Sidney said enthusiastically that Rupert was "in antiques."

Mrs. Bittell recovered. "There used to be Bittells in sugar—though I believe that was in Jamaica." She spoke disdainfully, admitting—to put Rupert at ease—the shames that can occur in all families. She moved nearer home. "You must be very thankful you left Murgatroyd's," she said, admiring him. "There were undercurrents, Sidney tells me."

Rupert said, "You could put it that way."

"It takes courage," she said and she meant this for Sidney, for it seemed to her that Rupert was a decisive man, one who had struck out on his own.

"You have interesting things," he said, nodding at her very fine bureau.

"Just old things from Cranach," said Mrs. Bittell and she led them across the room.

"These are large flats," he said. "You've got a museum."

"And there's the big picture in the hall," said Sidney, the excited familiar of the place. "Lily."

They went out into the hall and Rupert looked closely at the picture. "It could be a Lely," he said.

An educated man!

And then Rupert said something which was not really very tactful. "It would pay you to have this cleaned," he said. "Six by four," he said, guessing the measurements. "It needn't cost too much if you go to the right firm—Dolland's, say—they do a good job. I mean, it would bring it out."

"I do not think my sister would care for that," Mrs. Bittell said. "It has never been cleaned. You see, it's always been in the family. I believe it was always like that."

She did not think Rupert knew her well enough to make suggestions about the tastes of the Bittells. They did not like things "brought out." She certainly did not wish to do anything as "inconvenient" as that. It would be like asking Dolly to get herself "brought out."

"It's very suitable with the paneling," she said.

"That's true enough," said Rupert disparagingly.

And then Rupert made one more worrying remark about the picture. It was, she reported to her sister more than once afterwards, kindly meant, she was sure.

"That's interesting. There's one in the National Gallery like this, Sid." (He called Sidney "Sid"!) "See the cupid down there in the corner? See how he's holding his bow! He's going to miss. He won't get her in the heart. He'll catch her in the—er—leg," he said. And he indicated the probable course of the arrow. And he gave a short laugh.

Over the years Mrs. Bittell had not particularly noticed that Psyche had a leg. Surely it was quite wrong to believe that the soul had legs.

And she could not understand why Rupert laughed.

She said, in her social voice, as one asking for information, "I always understood Cupid was blind."

Rupert stopped his laugh and she was amazed to see him turn to Sidney and do a most disconcerting thing: he winked at Sidney. The answer to prayer had winked. Even Sidney, she saw, was shocked by this.

Soon after this they said goodbye.

The miracle had vanished. The flat was empty now. Rupert had come back. Sidney was happy. There was nothing for her to do. He did not come to church. His visits stopped.

"SAD AM I without thee"—whoever "thee" was—she sang on some days as she played her piano in the agreed hours. That last chord became more vehement. Mrs. Bittell put jealousy into the chord. Surely Sidney could spare her one afternoon? The hardest aspect of the case was that she had no one left to pray for, but she was stubborn in her sense of loss and she began to feel, as her jealousy grew, that wherever Sidney was, whatever he was doing, she could still pray for the freedom of his soul. Freedom, of course, from that very puzzling love of that strange young man who had, after all, not been sincere.

It was a prayer without urgency. It would come into her head at night when she saw the lights of the flats where Sidney lived, or when she was visiting her sister, or sitting on the train coming home from one of those trying visits to her daughter.

On one of her returns, on a Sunday too, when she had been obliged to miss her church, at six in the afternoon—she was expecting her grandson. She feared she was late. She got to her flat. She *was* late. The boy was there. His suitcase was in the hall, open, in his untidy way and—strange—his shoes beside it.

"Rupert darling," she called.

And when there was no answer, she called again. There was a strange smell in the flat. But then there were sounds; he must be in the bathroom. She went to the bathroom door and said quietly, "Rupert. It's Granny."

The door was open. He was not there. She went to her bedroom, where the door was half open, and there she saw a pair of stockinged feet and the cocoa-colored trousers of a man kneeling at a drawer beside her bed.

"What *are* you doing, Rupert?" she said. The man got halfway to his feet.

She saw the face of Sidney's Rupert. His dark glasses were on her bed with some of her jewelry. A long smile split his face for a moment as he stood up. He had a bracelet in his hand.

"Put that down," said Mrs. Bittell. And called calmly, as if to her grandson, "Rupert, there's a man in my bedroom."

And with that she pulled the bedroom door to and turned the key in the lock.

"I've locked him in," she called.

The man was wrenching at the door handle. Then she heard him open the window.

But now Mrs. Bittell had exhausted the words she could speak. She opened her mouth to scream, but no sound came. Lead seemed to fill her legs, her heart thundered in her ears; she saw through the doorway of the drawing room (miles away it seemed) the telephone. She began a slow trudge that seemed to take hours, as in a dream, while the man returned to hammering at the door, shouting, "I'll break your bloody neck, you silly old bitch."

She was stupefied enough to turn and hear the sentence out. She got to the drawing room, then to the hall, and what she saw there drove her back. Psyche was not there. The frame was empty. That sight drove her back, and giddily she went to her piano and banged away at the keys, defying the whole block of flats, banging as the man banged at the closed door. The telephone rang and rang, but still she banged and banged on the keys and then the man broke through the door and was coming at her, but in his stockinged feet; on the parquet at the edge of one of her rugs he skidded and fell flat on his back.

Mrs. Bittell saw this. She had often, in her quiet way, thought of what she would do if someone attacked her. She had always planned to speak gently and to ask them why they were so unhappy and had they forgotten they were children of God. But a terrible thing had happened. She had wet herself, like a child, all down her legs. Red with shame, as he rushed and fell and was trying to get up, she tipped the piano stool over as he jumped at her. He stumbled over it. And this was the moment she had often imagined. She became as strong as History; she picked up the brass table lamp and bashed him on the neck, the head, anywhere. Not once, but twice or three times. And then fell back and fainted.

That is how the doorman, the general from across the landing, the Misses Pattison and her grandson found her, as Rupert, bleeding in the head, was trying to put on his shoes in the hall and run for it.

"Tell Sidney to come," she was murmuring as they knelt beside her, and for a long time the telephone still went on ringing.

"A man called Sidney," said the doorman, answering it. "He's asking for her."

He turned to the crowd. "He says it's urgent."

No one replied.

With pomp the doorman returned to the telephone and said, "Mrs. Bittell is indisposed."

ARTURO VIVANTE

The Soft
Core

IT WAS SUPPERTIME. The bell had rung. Everyone was around the table except his father, nearly eighty. Sometimes he didn't hear the bell. So Giacomo went and knocked at his bedroom door.

No answer came. Going in, he found his father lying on the bed with his shoes on. His eyes were open, but they didn't seem to recognize Giacomo.

"Papa, dinner is ready."

"What? What is it?"

"Dinner," Giacomo said, without any hope now that he would come to it.

"Dinner," his father echoed feebly, making no effort to get up but rather trying to connect the word. Dinner where, when, his eyes seemed to be saying.

"You are not feeling well?"

"Yes, I'm well," he said, almost inaudibly. "I am well, but . . . you . . . you are . . . ?" His father could not quite place him.

"Giacomo. I am Giacomo," the son said.

His name seemed to make little or no impression on his father. Indeed, he seemed to have forgotten it already and to be groping for some point of reference, something familiar to sustain his mind, which was wavering without hold in space and time.

Quickly Giacomo stepped out of the room, through an anteroom, and opened the dining-room door. His wife, his sister, their children, and a guest were round the table eating, talking. He called his wife.

She rose and hurried over. "Is he all right?"

"No."

"Like last time?"

"No, no, not as bad."

They had in mind a time five or six months before, when Giacomo's sister had called from Rome for a phone number that their father had in his address book. Giacomo, then as now, had gone to call him in his room, and found him on his bed, unconscious, breathing thickly, and in a sort of spasm. A stroke, he thought. Thoroughly alarmed, he rushed back to the phone, hung up after a few hurried words of explanation, and called the doctor. In a few minutes, everyone in the house was round his father's bed. It seemed to Giacomo that the end had come. Its suddenness appalled him. He wasn't prepared for it. He had been so unfriendly to his father lately—almost rude. Why, only the day before, when his father had asked him to drive him into town, as he often did, Giacomo told him that he couldn't, that he was too busy, which wasn't really true. And other things came to mind—his curt replies to his father's questions, the long silences at table, and when there was some conversation, his father's being left out of it, ignored; his not laughing at his father's little jokes; not complimenting him on the fruit that came from trees he had planted, and for which he so much expected a word of praise when it was served at table. If Giacomo had only had some warning, to make up for his behavior—oh, he would have been his father's chauffeur, if he had known, talked with him about his books, his philosophy, his fruit trees, laughed at his jokes, listened keenly to the things he said and pretended it was the first time he heard him saying them. With a sense of anguish, he watched his father, unconscious, on the bed. He couldn't die just yet; he must talk again. The prospect that he mightn't—that he might live on paralyzed and speechless on that bed—was even worse.

They waited for the doctor. Yet, even before the doctor came, something might be done. He couldn't just wait and watch his father die in this awful, sunken state. To ease his breathing, Giacomo took out the dentures, which seemed to lock his father's mouth, and opened the window, because the radiator, going full steam, had made the room stiflingly hot. Then he hurried upstairs. In the drug cabinet, there were some phials of a relaxant—papaverine—that had once been prescribed for his father to help his circulation. Giacomo gave him two, by injection—a certain knowledge of medicine having remained from when he had studied it, and even practiced it, long ago—then waited for the effect. But even before the drug could possibly have had one, his father seemed to improve, to rise from his prostration. The breathing was easier. His limbs were slowly relaxing. It seemed that whatever had commanded them to stiffen was easing its hold, loosening up. His eyes began to look and not just gaze; the sounds coming from his mouth were not just moans but language, or the beginnings of it— monosyllables, bits with which words and phrases could be made. And the improvement was continuous. By the time the doctor arrived, he was moving his limbs and uttering words, though the words were disconnected. As the doctor examined him and prescribed treatment, his voice gained strength. He answered questions; he sat up; he even asked for food. An hour or two later, he was reading, making notes, pencil in hand and postcard on the page, in case he should want to underline a word or a sentence that had struck him. And he looked very sweet there on the bed in his pajamas, reading under the light, thin and ethereal, all involved in that spiritual form of exercise.

His body—the material aspect of it, his physique—which had been so much in the foreground and had so preoccupied them a few hours before, now seemed quite forgotten, back where it should be, something one is hardly aware of, that works better when one's mind is off it.

So his father had been given back to life, and Giacomo had another chance to be warm and friendly to him. At intervals that night, he slipped into the room to see how he was doing, or, if the light was out, afraid to wake him, listened outside with his ear to the door. Oh, this was easy enough to do, and it was easy to be solicitous the next day—ask how he was, and help him with the half-dozen drugs the doctor had prescribed, and with the diet. But when his father—well again, his usual self, full of the same old preoccupations and requests—resumed getting about and Giacomo heard his aged yet determined step coming toward his room, something in him stiffened as if in defense, and he waited for the door to open.

His father came in without a knock, as was his custom. "After all, cars now are pleasingly designed," he said in a slightly plaintive, slightly polemical voice, from just inside the doorway.

For a moment, Giacomo wondered what he was talking about. Then he remembered his father's arguing a few days before against an ordinance barring cars from the main street of the town. Giacomo had disagreed, and now his father was bringing the subject up again, bothered as always by anyone's disputing his viewpoint. "You like them?" Giacomo said.

"Well, they are certainly more pleasant to watch than were carriages drawn by panting, weary horses. Besides, people put up with much more disturbing things than cars without complaining."

His father had his own peculiar ideas about traffic, about where Giacomo should park his car, about driving—about practically everything, in fact. He insisted on the frequent use of the horn, and if the person driving didn't blow it and he thought there was danger of a collision, he would shout to let the other party know that the car he was riding in was coming. It was almost as irritating as his bringing up an old argument and wanting to prove his point though a long time had passed. For him an argument was never closed. He went on pondering over it, debating it in his mind. One saw him doing it—wandering in the garden, pausing, starting to walk again, a true peripatetic—and if some new thought came to him he didn't hesitate to let you know it, wherever you might be.

About this matter of the ordinance, in the end Giacomo just nodded. Appeased, his father asked him for a favor. It was a way of showing he was on good terms with him. "Are you going into town tomorrow afternoon?"

Giacomo never planned his days ahead if he could help it. "Well, yes, I can go in, if you like."

"Would you? I need to buy some brown paper to line the crates of cherries with."

The cherries weren't ripe yet.

"Ah, yes, yes, I'll take you," Giacomo said.

"At about three o'clock?"

"The shops, you know, don't open until four."

"Say at half past three."

It took ten minutes to drive into town.

"Ah, yes, yes, all right."

Two or three times the next day, his father would remind him of the trip, and at a few minutes past three be at his door, ready to go. Giacomo would prevent himself from making any comments, but the very effort not to make them would keep him silent. "You are so silent," his father would observe in the car. "What is it?"

"Nothing. I am sorry."

"You have such a long face."

It was the hardest thing for Giacomo to look cheerful when he wasn't. He had no more control over his face than over his mood, and felt there was no poorer dissembler in the world than he. "I'm sorry if I can't be gayer," he would reply.

Sometimes his father would come into his room to ask him for advice on where to send an article he had written. But it seemed to Giacomo that he was asking for advice only in order to discard it. "I would send it to Wyatt, if I were you," Giacomo would suggest. But his father had already made up his mind whom to send it to, and it wasn't to Wyatt.

Speaking of his works, his father would say to him, "It is a *new* philosophy."

"Yes," Giacomo would reply, and be quite unable to elaborate. It was a pity, because his father yearned for articulate assent and recognition. People found his work difficult; some said they couldn't understand it. Nothing irked him more than to hear this. "Even Sylvia," he would say, referring to a guest, a pretty girl with a ready smile and pleasant manner, "who I don't think is very widely read in philosophy, found it clear." He never doubted that praise was offered in earnest. And no praise seemed more important to him than that which came from girls, from pretty women. Then a blissful smile would light his face and linger in his eyes.

With the single-mindedness of someone who has devoted his whole life to a cause, he gave or sent his articles around. He was so surely entrenched in his ideas that nothing could budge him from them. Each problem, each concept he came on had to be thrashed out and made known. Intent on it, if he met you—no matter where—he might stop and, pronouncing each word as if he were grinding it out, say without preamble, "Creativity is an underived, active, original, powerfully present, intrinsic, self-sustaining principle—something that cannot be resolved or broken up into preëxistent, predetermined data, and that is fraught with a negative possibility."

Giacomo would nod. He had been brought up to the tune of phrases such as these, had grown up with them, and though he had only begun to understand them he had finished by believing in them. At any rate, he was convinced there was a good measure of truth in what his father said. And yet he couldn't make it his own. "Negative possibility," "*causa sui,*" "psychic reality," "primal active"—these terms perplexed him. He knew they were full of meaning for his father, but he couldn't grasp it; it eluded him. They weren't in his language, and he looked on them with the detachment of one who looks on instruments he can never use.

The extraordinary importance his father gave his work! One had the feeling that nothing—not his wife, not his children—mattered to him quite so much as the vindication of certain principles. He probably saw his family, house, fruit trees, and philosophy as a whole—he had a unified view of everything—and felt that one could never damage the other; he probably even thought that his work was the key, the solution, to a host of problems, financial ones not excluded. Since he didn't teach and lived isolated in the country, to advance his views he tirelessly went to the post office to send off his manuscripts and books, as well as reprints of his articles, which he ordered by the hundreds. He sent them assiduously, and impatiently he waited for acknowledgments and answers that often failed to come.

It was all very admirable, but Giacomo couldn't really admire it. He was more inclined to admire his mother, who painted and often hid her paintings in a cupboard. He thought of some of the landscapes she had done, particularly one of a row of vines, a study of green done with such love of leaf and branch and sod and sky its value couldn't be mistaken, yet, because his father—perhaps with a slight frown or tilting of his head—told her it was not among her best, she had put it in a cupboard, and it had never been framed until after her death. Paintings, his father said, looked better unframed. "Let's wait till we have a bit more money before buying one," he would say, which meant never to everyone but him.

His father wrote and spoke about the value of spontaneity in art and literature and all things, but was he spontaneous? He seemed the opposite to Giacomo sometimes—very deliberate and willful. And how he wanted to escape his father's will. He still felt it upon him as he had when he was a child, a boy, a young man. His father's will shaping his life. His brother's life, too. At school, his brother had been good at all subjects, including mathematics, so his father must have a scientist in the family and had strongly advised him—and wasn't advice, especially the advice of someone whom you admired, harder to disobey than a command?—to study physics and mathematics at college, subjects for which he had no special gift. His brother hadn't, as a result, fared well at college. And as for Giacomo, when he was twenty-two and had been away from home, overseas, for seven years—it was wartime—his father had written, making it seem urgent that he come back immediately. "You are coming home to save your mother," one of his letters said. And Giacomo, who would have wished to delay his return another year—there was a girl, there were his studies, well begun—had gone back only to find that his father had exaggerated, sort of been carried away.

Then his father had a way of asking Giacomo to do things that instinctively made him wish to disobey. He seemed to like asking favors, to ask them for the sake of asking. Giacomo had never answered a flat no; he wasn't that familiar with his father. Recently, though, he had done something worse. His father had called to tell him once again about a cistern whose drainage had become a fixed idea with him. Giacomo had made the mistake of contradicting, and now his father, pencil and paper in hand, came after him so he would get a thorough understanding of his plan. But Giacomo, who had heard enough of it, went off, leaving his father in a rage. Never before had he refused to listen. Now, doing so, he experienced a strange sense of freedom, as though he had shaken off the bonds of childhood. For a moment, he felt almost snug and comfortable in his attitude toward his father. Perhaps it wasn't all unjustified, he thought, and old, childhood resentments came back to him. He remembered a fall from horseback when he was a boy: limping home, with a gaping wound about the knee that needed stitching, his father scolding him for it, and the words of his mother—soothing, like something cool upon a burn—and her taking him to the hospital, the doctor telling her it might be better if she left the room, her replying that she had once been a nurse, staying with him, holding him by the hand while the doctor put the stitches in. His father had scolded him, instead. No, he thought, perhaps I am not altogether in the wrong.

But seeing his father watch the sunset in the garden as he so often did, absorbed in light, a man whom beauty had always held in sway, or hearing him recite a poem—though now he rarely did—enunciating the words in all their clearness, slowly, in a voice that seemed ever on the verge of breaking yet never broke and that seemed to pick each nuance of rhythm and of meaning, Giacomo felt his old love, respect, and admiration come back full to overflowing as when he was a child and it seemed to him that his father never could be wrong—in the realm of the spirit, a man of mighty aims and wider grasp.

And chancing to meet him late at night going into the kitchen for food, looking so frail and thin in his pajamas and so old without his dentures, Giacomo felt ashamed of himself. Oh, his unfriendliness was revolting. That he should be distant and cold toward his father now when he was weak and wifeless, now when he was so old he had become almost childish in some ways—laughing and crying with ease. It was unforgivable, horrible, inhuman. If it hadn't been for his father, where would they be, Giacomo asked himself. If his father hadn't taken his family out of Italy in time, they might all have perished in a German concentration camp. And he had seen that his children learned English almost from babyhood. And he had never raised a hand against them. And he had been generous with those who needed money or lodging or employment.

Well, there was nothing for it but to change his attitude. He must make more of an effort. No week went by without Giacomo's telling himself. He would talk to his father as to a friend, about any subject that came to his mind. "What this town needs, I think," he said to him at lunch one day, trying to be nice, "is a newspaper. I'd like to start one."

"It would be a very bad idea," his father said.

"Why?"

"But it's obvious why," his father snapped with irritation and perhaps even dislike.

"Well, I wish you would explain it."

"But anyone can see that if there were only one newspaper in the country it would have a better chance of being a good one."

This wasn't like his father at all. He seemed only to want to contradict.

"I thought that to encourage writers and the arts, as well as trade, a local paper . . . " Giacomo didn't finish his sentence. Why should he? His father's face seemed full of aversion, as though Giacomo were saying something blasphemous.

The meal went on in silence. Giacomo looked up at his father. The lines of his face were still set in anger, and he was looking down at his plate, the segment nearest to him, almost at his napkin. No, one could not change, Giacomo thought. His father could not change. He himself could not change. Perhaps if one could fall into a state of oblivion one could change, but otherwise?

AND THEN CAME the evening when his father did not turn up for supper and Giacomo went to call him in his room. It wasn't nearly as bad as the earlier time, when he thought his father had had a stroke—after all, now he was conscious, his breathing was normal, he wasn't in a spasm, and he could speak. Yet Giacomo had the same feeling that the end had come. His father seemed so tenuously, so delicately attached to life, like down of a thistle in the wind. And when he spoke he was like a flame that wavered in the air this way and that, sometimes almost detached from the body that fed it.

It seemed as though he were living in another century and in another land. "We'll have to ask the Byzantine government," he said.

"What Byzantine government?" Giacomo asked.

"In Constantinople," his father replied, as if he found it odd for anyone to ask a question with such an obvious answer.

It was strange he should speak of the Byzantines. His father's ancestors were from Venice, and Giacomo sensed that his father was talking of the affairs of six or seven centuries ago.

To bring him back to this one, he began to speak to him, to explain just what had happened and to reassure him. He told his father that his memory would all come back to him in a little while, after he had drunk some coffee. And he went on to tell him who he was, and, when his wife appeared with a cup of coffee, who she was, and about the house, his fruit trees, his articles and books, the recent letters; he went over all his life with him, in a fashion.

Intent on reconnecting himself to the past and those around him, patiently, like someone threading beads, the present not quite with him, his father sat up on the bed and, speaking very gently, asked him questions. "Where is Mama?' he said, referring to his own wife.

For a second, Giacomo didn't answer. He had expected and feared the question. Then he said, "She died. You know, she died three years ago."

"Ah, yes," he said sadly, and for a moment father and son seemed not so much to look at one another as to survey the last days of her life.

"And you say we went to England?"

"Yes, do you remember, in 1938? You took us there."

"Yes. You children were so good on that crowded train."

"And when we got to England you saw a sign that read, 'Cross at your own risk,' and you said it was worth coming just to see that sign, and that in Italy it would have said, 'It is severely forbidden to cross.'"

His father smiled. "It was a sign of freedom."

"Yes."

"And then we came back here?"

"Yes, by boat, after the war. The bailiff met you in Naples, all the money he had for you stuffed under his garters, in his socks. He was afraid of thieves."

They laughed together. Laughter, it has the power to reconcile lost friends, to bridge the widest gaps.

"Your wife . . . tell me her name again."

"Jessie."

"Ah, yes, so dear," he said tenderly. He got up slowly and went to his desk for a pencil. He said he wanted to write the name down before he forgot it once more. He looked at the desk aimlessly, then pulled out the wrong drawer. "My little things," he said, "where are they?" He looked like a child whose toys a gust of wind has blown away.

Giacomo found a pencil for him, and his father wrote the name Jessie on a piece of paper. Next, he paused by the bookcase. All the books in it he had annotated, but now he looked at them as if for the first time.

"This one you wrote," Giacomo said.

His father looked at it closely. "This one I know. But the others . . . " He stroked his head as if to scold it. "And these are your poems," he said, seeing a flimsy little book with his son's name. "I remember the first one you wrote, about the stars, when you were ten. Strange, your mother's father, too, wrote about the stars—his best one."

"You see, you remember a lot."

"About the distant past. Such a long time . . . for you, too." He smiled, then, looking at him warmly, said, "Our Giacomo," and it was as it had been when Giacomo was a boy and his father used to look at him and say "Ajax," because he considered him generous and strong.

Strangely, now, Giacomo found that he *could* talk to his father, easily, affably, and with pleasure, and that his voice was gentle. When his father was well, he couldn't, but now he was reaching the secret, soft core—the secret, gentle, tender core that is in each of us. And he thought, *This* is what my father is really like; the way he is now, this is his real, his naked self. For a moment it has been uncovered; he is young again. This was the young man his mother had met and fallen in love with; this was the man on whose knees he had played, who had carried him on his shoulders up the hills, who had read to him the poems he liked so much. His other manner was brought on by age, by a hundred preoccupations, by the years, by the hardening that comes with the turning of the years.

Already, with coffee, with their talk, his father was recovering his memory. Soon he would be up and about, and soon Giacomo wouldn't be able to talk to him as he did now. But though he wouldn't, he would think of his father in the way he had been given back to him, the way he had been and somewhere—deep and secret and only to be uncovered sometimes—still was.

A Ceremony
of Innocence

THE THICK EVERGREENS screened Georgia Ann McCullum's front porch so well that Tisha did not see her sitting in the porch swing until she reached the top step—the eighth, because she had once measured her age by these steps. She had practiced the salutation "Mother" Georgia to pay honor to this distant cousin who had reached the highest point of distinction for a woman in Chute Bay. She had been made the "mother" of Chute Bay Memorial Baptist Church, which had been built by the people in the Bay on a pay-as-you-go basis during the Depression years.

Tisha stood quietly hugging herself in a full-length Natural Emba Autumn Haze mink coat as she waited for the old woman to recognize her. Even though it was a bright day, the temperature held at 23 degrees above zero and a stiff breeze blew in from the north.

The noise of a truck coming down Bay Road jostled the swinger from an apparent reverie. She slipped from the swing and started forward, then recognized Tisha. Their eyes met and held long enough for the old woman to make a good guess. She fumbled in her mind and grunted, then, caught by pain, she backed back to the swing to steady herself. The swing moved backward, almost causing her to miss her seat.

Tisha rushed to clasp her in a bear hug.

"Don't fall, Mother Georgia—please don't fall," she pleaded.

"Don't tell me," Mother Georgia said, "you Flora Dee's baby. Ain't you now?"

"Yes, Mother Georgia," she answered, and relaxed her grip, helping the old woman to set herself in the swing.

"This here Tisha. Sweet little Tisha. Just as pretty, too. You look good enough to eat. Your grandpa still call you his 'little spicy gal'?"

"Grandpa hasn't come close to me since I've been home, Mother Georgia."

"That's your own doings. But thang God. Thang God. Thang God. I talk to Him the other night 'bout you, and here He done sent you already. I ain't scared of you just 'cause you gone astray." She cradled Tisha in her arms and nuzzled her thin cheeks with a bottom lip packed hard with Railroad Mill snuff. Coins hit the porch and began to roll as they reeled in this odd pantomime of genuine affection. She finally held Tisha away at arm's length and gloating over her, told of the wonders that had come with the title "Mother" Georgia.

Old white men whose shirts she had ironed until arthritis twisted both of her wrists—who had brought shirts to her even though a one-day service laundry had opened in Crystal Hill—who brought handouts to supplement the $54.00 a month from the "government"—even they used the title of honor "Mother" Georgia, when they had for decades called her "Aunty."

After this rehearsal, Tisha began to pick up the coins from the floor. She found several nickels and a dime, but Mother Georgia said that that was not all.

"Don't bother yourself," she told Tisha, "go on in and make yourself at home. You needn't act like company, when this your second home. I'm slow but I'm coming."

Tisha walked into the front room, a room she knew by heart

before she left Chute Bay. She glanced about, noticing that it was the same. She waited a minute for Mother Georgia, then brushed the bottom of a chair with her fingers to test it for dust. Her fingertips were black with coal dust. She walked to the door to check on the old woman's delay. She did not want to be caught cleaning the chair. She walked to the door and looked out in time to see Mother Georgia crawling about slowly on her knees and fumbling up and down the porch planks with her drawn hands.

"Mother Georgia, can I help—?"

"No, Sugar, I got all but two pennies. Hope the Lord them two didn't roll off the porch. If it was Mr. Pogue' truck, I'd get my coal if I was a few cents short. But this truck want every cent. I don't know who it b'long to."

"Come on in, Mother Georgia," Tisha said. "I'll give you what you need for the coal man." She then went out and helped her up from the floor.

"Sugar, they got them ole engines what pull theirself. If they was still using coal like they used to, I'd be out there up and down them tracks with my bucket, picking me up all the coal I want."

"Yes ma'm," Tisha replied. "Now tell me now much the coal cost, and I'll sit out there and wait for the truck."

"No, Sugar. You so dressed up, he might not stop if he don't see me. You just sit tight, and soons he come I'm going to make up a great big fire in the heater. It ain't cold, is it? I got on plenty clothes, and you got on that big fine coat. Don't get hetted up 'cause I got to ask you for myself 'bout that Allie what Flora worried to death 'bout. She worried plumb stiff 'bout that God've yours, just like she can't put you back in your place. Humph. I said send her to me when she come home. I'll get her straight before she go back out yonder."

Tisha pat her feet as Mother Georgia talked, because her toes were getting stiff from cold. A minute later a truck pulled up, and she let Tisha give the driver $1.25 for a crocker sack of coal and a bunch of lightwood splinters. She built a fire in the heater with two splinters and a few lumps of coal. She washed her hands in a basin on the washstand, then sat down to watch Tisha.

"Lord, Sugar, you look good enough to bite on the jaw. The only thing got me bothered is what your ma told me 'bout that Allie. You know you got her nearly distracted? What's that, any-how, child—talking 'bout goin'ta serve Allie? That ain't no God. You know Mother Georgia ain't goin'ta tell you nothing wrong 'long's I had my hand on the gospel plough. That was 'fore they spanked your ma, so you know I'm a soldier. You got no business turning your back on God."

"Allah, Mother Georgia, is the true God. You see, I know He's the right God because of what He's done for me. Okay?" Tisha started to stand, but the old woman waved her back to her chair. "He helps us to have heaven right here on earth, and that's what I want because I can enjoy life every day of my life."

"What I'm telling you—that is, what Mother Georgia, am-bassador to Christ, is telling you, is that ain't no God you found up the road. Your ma learned you 'bout the right God from your cradle, and it ought to be good enough to take you to your grave. You see what He's done for me, don't you, child? That Allie you heard tell of way out yonder is just a make-shift God the crowd hark'ning after. And I'm trying to tell you better 'cause, you, Flora and every child she got rest close to my heart. We kin as cousins, but I been a mother to her and to y'all before I come a mother to the church. You better turn to the true and living God 'fore it's a day and hour and eternity too late."

Tisha started to let the argument rest, but she felt that she would be a shameful volunteer for Allah if she let this occasion pass without sharing her idea of his worth.

"I'm serving Allah," she persisted, "and I hope to serve Him better. I'm twenty-two now, and I hope to be that many times stronger in His grace before I'm twice that old."

"I'm going on these here knees, little Miss, to the Master I know who'll open your eyes. Look at me." Mother Georgia hoisted her huge frame from the rocker and fastened her sharp bird eyes on Tisha. "I'm seventy-six-odd years old. How you reckon I make it without the Lord? You see that sack of coal? The Lord sent it here. Let me tell you, the Pastor—I reckon you don't know Reverend Sarks—anyway, he come here faithful as the days is long and brings me ration just like he take it home. And Mr. Dwyer—I guess you forgot him—he sends me all the bones from his store to feed these six dogs I got on the yard for company. Some of them oxtails 'n stuff the dogs don't see 'cause I make me a pot've soup."

"Well, let's not get excited," Tisha said. "I brought a present for you. Let's look after that." Tisha handed her a small Christmas-wrapped package which the old woman shook.

"What these? Drawers?" she asked.

Tisha shook her head. "You see," she told Mother Georgia, "we don't have Christmas, but you do."

"You mean Allie don't let y'all have no Christmas? How do you do when you don't ever have no Christmas? How can you live with no Christmas?"

"Everyday ought to be important in this life." Tisha had lost her ardor.

"Oh, these them pretty head rags? Well, I'm going to wear this cotton one to Prayer Meeting and the silk one on Communion Sunday." She rewrapped the gift in the same paper.

"That will be nice." Tisha was pleased with her happiness over the small gift. It was one of the things she always cherished about Mother Georgia.

It was warm enough now for Tisha to remove her coat. The old woman got up to leave for the kitchen, but Tisha tried to persuade her to relax or, if she insisted on making coffee, to make it on the heater, but she would not listen.

"You're company now," she maintained, "and a fine lady at that, so I'll treat you like one, no matter if you did used to help me out. You make yourself at home now while I get straight in the kitchen. And you get up and turn that coat insadouter so's no smoke'll hit it."

"Yes ma'm," she answered.

TISHA SAT THERE remembering the room as she had known it years before. This room was full of furniture. There was an upright grand piano, a three-piece bedroom suite, a washstand, two rocking chairs, and a davenport with sugar-starched crocheted pieces on the arm rests. The center table held a large metal oil lamp on the top and a big family Bible on the bottom tier. The old green wool rug was practically eaten away from the floor, and the wallpaper of unidentified color was smoky and filled with rainwater circles.

There was an array of several pretty vases on the mantlepiece, of odd shapes and sizes, and pictures hung indiscriminately wherever a nail could be placed to hold them. High above the mantle was a picture of Cupid asleep, with the bow and arrow besides him. Glancing around the wall, she found the pictures of undertakers, ministers, church groups, family members, movie stars and flowers. There was a lone insurance policy hanging above the doorsill going to the middle room. She tried to evaluate the holdings of this room in terms of financial worth—the most valuable possessions in the house secured from a lifetime of satisfactory labor. They hardly added up to dollars and cents.

After a while Mother Georgia came in with a cup of coffee and a plate of cake on a tray.

"I made your coffee on the hot plate. I got 'lectric, you know," and she pointed to the bulb hanging on a suspended wire in the center of the room. "I have my lamp lighted half the time before I remember I can pull that little chain to get some light." She watched Tisha a minute, then encouraged her to eat the five slices of cake because she had baked the cakes herself. They were her specials: raisin, chocolate, pineapple, coconut and strawberry jelly.

"Mother Georgia," she said, "you remember the time I ate a whole plateful of cake when I was a child? Well, it was the best cake I'd ever had in my life at that time. And since then I've found out how to enjoy life the way I enjoyed that first plate of cake you gave me. As long as you enjoy this life, there's nothing to worry about."

"I don't want to spoil your appetite, but you're gone from your raising. You're caught in the web of sin. And you know what that mean. You sitting there all pretty, but you dying, Sugar." The old woman shook her head.

Dying! Tisha turned and looked at Georgia Ann McCullum. *She* was dying. The old woman was dying—dying as she had done every day of her life, though she was too good a minstrel man to know it. Her ugly life was death. She no doubt would have a beautiful funeral according to their pattern, with a nice long obituary, good remarks from the deacons, a wailing eulogy from the preacher and honest tears from unknown visitors at the grave; but her life was, and always had been, an ugly death.

"Thang God you come through, Sugar. Look—put your cake you left in a bag and take it home with you. And when you go back up the road, you'll remember what God has done for me and you'll forget about that Allie and the Mooselims. They'll run the world off the map if you not careful. You were raised to know that no colored folks can't rule the world by theirself. My folks told me white folks is a mess, but a nigger ain't nothing."

"Yes ma'm," Tisha said as she put on her coat to leave. She was not going to argue with the old lady because, more than anyone else, Mother Georgia had given her the final proof that she had chosen the right path—the path away from the religion of the Cross. God, the God of Mother Georgia, the God of her parents, the God who had let His only Son be crucified by wicked men, was uncaring. Then, as now, she told herself, if He was up there, He was oblivious of all the Georgia Ann McCullums in the universe.

She pulled the mink closer to her ears as she faced the cold, crisp air on the walk to her parents' home down Bay Road, happy in the thought that she had learned to praise Allah, who cared for His black children enough to help them find heaven on earth.

After
the Denim

EDITH PACKER had the tape cassette plugged into her ear, and she was smoking one of his cigarettes. The TV played without any volume as she sat on the sofa with her legs tucked under her and turned the pages of a magazine. James Packer came out of the guest room, which was the room he had fixed up as an office, and Edith Packer took the cord from her ear. She put the cigarette in the ashtray and pointed her foot and wiggled her toes in greeting.

He said, "Are we going or not?"

"I'm going," she said.

Edith Packer liked classical music. James Packer did not. He was a retired accountant. But he still did returns for some old clients, and he didn't like to hear music when he did it.

"If we're going, let's go."

He looked at the TV, and then went to turn it off.

"I'm going," she said.

She closed the magazine and got up. She left the room and went to the back.

He followed her to make sure the back door was locked and also that the porch light was on. Then he stood waiting and waiting in the living room.

It was a ten-minute drive to the community center, which meant they were going to miss the first game.

IN THE PLACE where James always parked, there was an old van with markings on it, so he had to keep going to the end of the block.

"Lots of cars tonight," Edith said.

He said, "There wouldn't be so many if we'd been on time."

"There'd still be as many. It's just we wouldn't have seen them." She pinched his sleeve, teasing.

He said, "Edith, if we're going to play bingo, we ought to be here on time."

"Hush," Edith Packer said.

He found a parking space and turned into it. He switched off the engine and cut the lights. He said, "I don't know if I feel lucky tonight. I think I felt lucky when I was doing Howard's taxes. But I don't think I feel lucky now. It's not lucky if you have to start out walking half a mile just to play."

"You stick to me," Edith Packer said. "You'll feel lucky."

"I don't feel lucky yet," James said. "Lock your door."

THERE WAS a cold breeze. He zipped the windbreaker to his neck, and she pulled her coat closed. They could hear the surf breaking on the rocks at the bottom of the cliff behind the building.

She said, "I'll take one of your cigarettes first."

They stopped under the street lamp at the corner. It was a damaged street lamp, and wires had been added to support it. The wires moved in the wind, made shadows on the pavement.

"When are you going to stop?" he said, lighting his cigarette after he'd lighted hers.

"When you stop," she said. "I'll stop when you stop. Just like it was when you stopped drinking. Like that. Like you."

"I can teach you to do needlework," he said.

"One needleworker in the house is enough," she said.

He took her arm and they kept on walking.

When they reached the entrance, she dropped her cigarette and stepped on it. They went up the steps and into the foyer. There was a sofa in the room, a wooden table, folding chairs stacked up. On the walls were hung photographs of fishing boats and naval vessels, one showing a boat that had turned over, a man standing on the keel and waving.

The Packers passed through the foyer, James taking Edith's arm as they entered the corridor.

SOME CLUBWOMEN sat to the side of the far doorway signing people in as they entered the assembly hall, where a game was already in progress, the numbers being called by a woman who stood on the stage.

The Packers hurried to their regular table. But a young couple occupied the Packers' usual places. The girl wore denims, and so did the long-haired man with her. She had rings and bracelets and earrings that made her shiny in the milky light. Just as the Packers came up, the girl turned to the fellow with her and poked her finger at a number on his card. Then she pinched his arm. The fellow had his hair pulled back and tied behind his head, and something else the Packers saw—a tiny gold loop through his earlobe.

JAMES GUIDED EDITH to another table, turning to look again before sitting down. First he took off his windbreaker and helped Edith with her coat, and then he stared at the couple who had taken their places. The girl was scanning her cards as the numbers were called, leaning over to check the man's cards too—as if, James thought, the fellow did not have sense enough to look after his own numbers.

James picked up the stack of bingo cards that had been set out on the table. He gave half to Edith. "Pick some winners," he said. "Because I'm taking these three on top. It doesn't matter which ones I pick. Edith, I don't feel lucky tonight."

"Don't you pay it any attention," she said. "They're just young, that's all."

He said, "This is regular Friday night bingo for the people of this community."

She said, "It's a free country."

She handed back the stack of cards. He put them on the other side of the table. Then they served themselves from the bowl of beans.

JAMES PEELED a dollar bill from the roll of bills he kept for bingo nights. He put the dollar next to his cards. One of the clubwomen, a thin woman with bluish hair and a spot on her neck—the Packers knew her only as Alice—would presently come by with a coffee can. She would collect the coins and bills, making change from the can. It was this woman or another woman who paid off the wins.

The woman on the stage called "I-25," and someone in the hall yelled, "Bingo!"

Alice made her way between the tables. She took up the winning card and held it in her hand as the woman on the stage read out the winning numbers.

"It's a bingo," Alice confirmed.

"That bingo, ladies and gentlemen, is worth twelve dollars!" the woman on the stage announced. "Congratulations to the winner!"

THE PACKERS played another five games to no effect. James came close once on one of his cards. But then five numbers were called in succession, none of them his, the fifth a number that produced a bingo on somebody else's card.

"You almost had it that time," Edith said. "I was watching your card."

"She was teasing me," James said.

He tilted the card and let the beans slide into his hand. He closed his hand and made a fist. He shook the beans in his fist. Something came to him about a boy who'd thrown some beans out a window. The memory reached to him from a long way off, and it made him feel lonely.

"Change cards, maybe," Edith said.

"It isn't my night," James said.

He looked over at the young couple again. They were laughing at something the fellow had said. James could see they weren't paying attention to anyone else in the hall.

Alice came around collecting money for the next game, and just after the first number had been called, James saw the fellow in the denims put down a bean on a card he hadn't paid for. Another number was called, and James saw the fellow do it again. James was amazed. He could not concentrate on his own cards. He kept looking up to see what the fellow in denim was doing.

"James, look at your cards," Edith said. "You missed N-34. Pay attention."

"That fellow over there who has our place is cheating. I can't believe my eyes," James said.

"How is he cheating?" Edith said.

"He's playing a card that he hasn't paid for," James said. "Somebody ought to report him."

"Not you, dear," Edith said. She spoke slowly and tried to keep her eyes on her cards. She dropped a bean on a number.

"The fellow is cheating," James said.

She extracted a bean from her palm and placed it on a number. "Play your cards," Edith said.

He looked back at his cards. But he knew he might as well write this game off. There was no telling how many numbers he had missed, how far behind he had fallen. He squeezed the beans in his fist.

The woman on the stage called, "G-60."
Someone yelled, "Bingo!"
"Christ," James Packer said.

A TEN-MINUTE BREAK was announced. The game after the break would be a Blackout, one dollar a card, winner takes all, this week's jackpot ninety-eight dollars.

There was whistling and clapping.

James looked at the couple. The fellow was touching the ring in his ear and staring up at the ceiling. The girl had her hand on his leg.

"I have to go to the bathroom," Edith said. "Give me your cigarettes."

James said, "And I'll get us some raisin cookies and coffee."

"I'll go to the bathroom," Edith said.

But James Packer did not go to get cookies and coffee. Instead, he went to stand behind the chair of the fellow in denim.

"I see what you're doing," James said.

The man turned around. "Pardon me?" he said and stared. "What am I doing?"

"You know," James said.

The girl held her cookie in mid-bite.

"A word to the wise," James said.

He walked back to his table. He was trembling.

When Edith came back, she handed him the cigarettes and sat down, not talking, not being her jovial self.

James looked at her closely. He said, "Edith, has something happened?"

"I'm spotting again," she said.

"Spotting?" he said. But he knew what she meant. "Spotting," he said again, very quietly.

"Oh, dear," Edith Packer said, picking up some cards and sorting through them.

"I think we should go home," he said.

She kept sorting through the cards. "No, let's stay," she said. "It's just the spotting, is all."

He touched her hand.

"We'll stay," she said. "It'll be all right."

"This is the worst bingo night in history," James Packer said.

THEY PLAYED the Blackout game, James watching the man in denim. The fellow was still at it, still playing a card he hadn't paid for. From time to time, James checked how Edith was doing. But there was no way of telling. She held her lips pursed together. It could mean anything—resolve, worry, pain. Or maybe she just liked having her lips that way for this particular game.

He had three numbers to go on one card and five numbers on another, and no chance at all on a third card when the girl with the man in denim began shrieking: "Bingo! Bingo! Bingo! I have a bingo!"

The fellow clapped and shouted with her. "She's got a bingo! She's got a bingo, folks! A bingo!"

The fellow in denim kept clapping.

It was the woman on the stage herself who went to the girl's table to check her card against the master list. She said, "This young woman has a bingo, and that's a ninety-eight-dollar jackpot! Let's give her a round of applause, people! It's a bingo here! A Blackout!"

Edith clapped along with the rest. But James kept his hands on the table.

The fellow in denim hugged the girl when the woman from the stage handed over the cash.

"They'll use it to buy drugs," James said.

THEY STAYED for the rest of the games. They stayed until the last game was played. It was a game called the Progressive, the jackpot increasing from week to week if no one bingoed before so many numbers were called.

James put his money down and played his cards with no hope of winning. He waited for the fellow in denim to call "Bingo!"

But no one won, and the jackpot would be carried over to the following week, the prize bigger than ever.

"That's bingo for tonight!" the woman on the stage proclaimed. "Thank you all for coming. God bless you and good night."

The Packers filed out of the assembly hall along with the rest, somehow managing to fall in behind the fellow in denim and his girl. They saw the girl pat her pocket. They saw the girl put her arm around the fellow's waist.

"Let those people get ahead of us," James said into Edith's ear. "I can't stand to look at them."

Edith said nothing in reply. But she hung back a little to give the couple time to move ahead.

Outside, the wind was up. James thought sure he could hear the surf over the sound of engines starting.

He saw the couple stop at the van. Of course. He should have put two and two together.

"The dumbbell," James Packer said.

EDITH WENT into the bathroom and shut the door. James took off his windbreaker and put it down on the back of the sofa. He turned on the TV and took up his place and waited.

After a time, Edith came out of the bathroom. James concentrated his attention on the TV. Edith went to the kitchen and ran water. James heard her turn off the faucet. Edith came to the room and said, "I guess I'll have to see Dr. Crawford in the morning. I guess there really is something happening down there."

"The lousy luck," James said.

She stood there shaking her head. She covered her eyes and leaned into him when he came to put his arms around her.

"Edith, dearest Edith," James Packer said.

He felt awkward and terrified. He stood with his arms more or less holding his wife.

She reached for his face and kissed his lips, and then she said good night.

HE WENT to the refrigerator. He stood in front of the open door and drank tomato juice while he studied everything inside. Cold air blew out at him. He looked at the little packages and the containers of foodstuffs on the shelves, a chicken covered in plastic wrap, the neat, protected exhibits.

He shut the door and spit the last of the juice into the sink. Then he rinsed his mouth and made himself a cup of instant coffee. He carried it into the living room. He sat down in front of the TV and lit a cigarette. He understood that it took only one lunatic and a torch to bring everything to ruin.

He smoked and finished the coffee, and then he turned the TV off. He went to the bedroom door and listened for a time. He felt unworthy to be listening, to be standing.

Why not someone else? Why not those people tonight? Why not all those people who sail through life free as birds? Why not them instead of Edith?

He moved away from the bedroom door. He thought about going for a walk. But the wind was wild now, and he could hear the branches whining in the birch tree behind the house.

He sat in front of the TV again. But he did not turn it on. He smoked and thought of that sauntering, arrogant gait as the two of them moved just ahead. If only they knew. If only someone would tell them. Just once!

He closed his eyes. He would get up early and fix breakfast. He would go with her to see Crawford. If only they had to sit with him in the waiting room! He'd tell them what was waiting for you after the denim and the earrings, after touching each other and cheating at games.

HE GOT UP and went into the guest room and turned on the lamp over the bed. He glanced at his papers and at his account books and at the adding machine on his desk. He found a pair of pajamas in one of the drawers. He turned down the covers on the bed. Then he walked back through the house snapping off lights and checking doors. For a while he stood looking out the kitchen window at the tree shaking under the force of the wind.

He left the porch light on and went back to the guest room. He pushed aside his knitting basket, took up his basket of embroidery, and then settled himself in the chair. He raised the lid of the basket and got out the metal hoop. There was fresh white linen stretched across it. Holding the tiny needle to the light, James Packer stabbed at the eye with a length of blue silk thread. Then he set to work—stitch after stitch—making believe he was waving like the man on the keel.

The Middle Drawer

THE DRAWER was always kept locked. In a household where the tangled rubbish of existence had collected on surfaces like a scurf, which was forever being cleared away by her mother and the maid, then by her mother, and, finally, hardly at all, it had been a permanent cell—rather like, Hester thought wryly, the gene that is carried over from one generation to the other. Now, holding the small, square, indelibly known key in her hand, she shrank before it, reluctant to perform the blasphemy that the living must inevitably perpetrate on the possessions of the dead. There were no revelations to be expected when she opened the drawer, only the painful reiteration of her mother's personality and the power it had held over her own, which would rise—an emanation, a mist, that she herself had long since shredded away, parted, and escaped.

She repeated to herself, like an incantation, "I am married. I have a child of my own, a home of my own five hundred miles away. I have not even lived in this house—my parents' house—for over seven years." Stepping back, she sat on the bed where her mother had died the week before, slowly, from cancer, where Hester had held the large, long-fingered, com-

petent hand for a whole night, watching the asphyxiating action
of the fluid mounting in the lungs until it had extinguished the
breath. She sat facing the drawer.

It had taken her all her own lifetime to get to know its full
contents, starting from the first glimpses, when she was just
able to lean her chin on the side and have her hand pushed away
from the packets and japanned boxes, to the last weeks, when
she had made a careful show of not noticing while she got out
the necessary bankbooks and safe-deposit keys. Many times
during her childhood, when she had lain blandly ill herself,
elevated to the honor of the parental bed while she suffered from
the "auto-intoxication" that must have been 1918's
euphemism for plain piggishness, the drawer had been opened.
Then she had been allowed to play with the two pairs of pearled
opera glasses or the long string of graduated white china beads,
each with its oval sides flushed like cheeks. Over these she had
sometimes spent the whole afternoon, pencilling two eyes and a
pursed mouth on each bead, until she had achieved an incredible string of minute, doll-like heads that made even her
mother laugh.

Once while Hester was in college, the drawer had been
opened for the replacement of her grandmother's great sunburst
pin, which she had never before seen and which had been in
pawn, and doggedly reclaimed over a long period by her mother.
And for Hester's wedding her mother had taken out the delicate
diamond chain—the "lavaliere" of the Gibson-girl era—that
had been her father's wedding gift to her mother, and the ugly,
expensive bar pin that had been his gift to his wife on the birth
of her son. Hester had never before seen either of them, for the
fashion of wearing diamonds indiscriminately had never been
her mother's, who was contemptuous of other women's display,
although she might spend minutes in front of the mirror debating a choice between two relatively gimcrack pieces of costume
jewelry. Hester had never known why this was until recently,
when the separation of the last few years had relaxed the tension

between her mother and herself—not enough to prevent explosions when they met but enough for her to see, obscurely, the long motivations of her mother's life. In the European sense, family jewelry was Property, and with all her faultless English and New World poise, her mother had never exorcised her European core.

In the back of the middle drawer, there was a small square of brown-toned photograph that had never escaped into the large, ramshackle portfolio of family pictures kept in the drawer of the old break-front bookcase, open to any hand. Seated on a bench, Hedwig Licht, aged two, brows knitted under ragged hair, stared mournfully into the camera with the huge, heavy-lidded eyes that had continued to brood in her face as a woman, the eyes that she had transmitted to Hester, along with the high cheekbones that she had deplored. Fat, wrinkled stockings were bowed into arcs that almost met at the high-stretched boots, which did not touch the floor; to hold up the stockings, strips of calico matching the dumpy little dress were bound around the knees.

Long ago, Hester, in her teens, staring tenaciously into the drawer under her mother's impatient glance, had found the little square and exclaimed over it, and her mother, snatching it away from her, had muttered, "If that isn't Dutchy!" But she had looked at it long and ruefully before she had pushed it back into a corner. Hester had added the picture to the legend of her mother's childhood built up from the bitter little anecdotes that her mother had let drop casually over the years.

She saw the small Hedwig, as clearly as if it had been herself, haunting the stiff rooms of the house in the townlet of Oberelsbach, motherless since birth and almost immediately stepmothered by a woman who had been unloving, if not unkind, and had soon borne the stern, *Haustyrann* father a son. The small figure she saw had no connection with the all-powerful figure of her mother but, rather, seemed akin to the legion of lonely children who were a constant motif in the literature that had been her own drug—the Sara Crewes and Little Dorrits, all those children who inhabited the familiar terror-struck dark that crouched under the lash of the adult. She saw Hedwig receiving from her dead mother's mother—the Grandmother Rosenberg, warm and loving but, alas, too far away to be of help—the beautiful, satin-incrusted bisque doll, and she saw the bad stepmother taking it away from Hedwig and putting it in the drawing room, because "it is too beautiful for a child to play with." She saw all this as if it had happened to her and she had never forgotten.

Years later, when this woman, Hester's step-grandmother, had come to the United States in the long train of refugees from Hitler, her mother had urged the grown Hester to visit her, and she had refused, knowing her own childishness but feeling the resentment rise in her as if she were six, saying, "I won't go. She wouldn't let you have your doll." Her mother had smiled at her sadly and had shrugged her shoulders resignedly. "You wouldn't say that if you could see her. She's an old woman. She has no teeth." Looking at her mother, Hester had wondered what her feelings were after forty years, but her mother, private as always in her emotions, had given no sign.

There had been no sign for Hester—never an open demonstration of love or an appeal—until the telephone call of a few months before, when she had heard her mother say quietly, over the distance, "I think you'd better come," and she had turned away from the phone saying bitterly, almost in awe, "If she *asks me* to come, she must be dying!"

Turning the key over in her hand, Hester looked back at the composite figure of her mother—that far-off figure of the legendary child, the nearer object of her own dependence, love, and hate—looked at it from behind the safe, dry wall of her own "American" education. We are told, she thought, that people who do not experience love in their earliest years cannot open up; they cannot give it to others; but by the time we have learned this from books or dredged it out of reminiscence, they have long since left upon us their chill, irremediable stain.

If Hester searched in her memory for moments of animal maternal warmth, like those she self-consciously gave her own child (as if her own childhood prodded her from behind), she thought always of the blue-shot twilight of one New York evening, the winter she was eight, when she and her mother were returning from a shopping expedition, gay and united in the shared guilt of being late for supper. In her mind, now, their arrested figures stood like two silhouettes caught in the spotlight of time. They had paused under the brightly agitated bulbs of a movie-theatre marquee, behind them the broad, rose-red sign of a Happiness candy store. Her mother, suddenly leaning down to her, had encircled her with her arm and nuzzled her, saying almost anxiously, "We do have fun together, don't we?" Hester had stared back stolidly, almost suspiciously, into the looming, pleading eyes, but she had rested against the encircling arm, and warmth had trickled through her as from a closed wound reopening.

After this, her mother's part in the years that followed seemed blurred with the recriminations from which Hester had retreated ever farther, always seeking the remote corners of the household—the sofa-fortressed alcoves, the store closet, the servants' bathroom—always bearing her amulet, a book. It seemed to her now, wincing, that the barrier of her mother's dissatisfaction with her had risen imperceptibly, like a coral cliff built inexorably from the slow accretion of carelessly ejaculated criticisms that had grown into solid being in the heavy fullness of time. Meanwhile, her father's uncritical affection, his open caresses, had been steadiness under her feet after the shifting waters of her mother's personality, but he had been away from home on business for long periods, and when at home he, too, was increasingly a target for her mother's deep-burning rage against life. Adored member of a large family that was almost tribal in its affections and unity, he could not cope with this smoldering force and never tried to understand it, but the shield of his adulthood gave him a protection that Hester did not have. He stood on equal ground.

Hester's parents had met at Saratoga, at the races. So dissimilar were their backgrounds that it was improbable that they would ever have met elsewhere than in the somewhat easy social flux of a spa, although their brownstone homes in New York were not many blocks apart, his in the gentility of upper Madison Avenue, hers in the solid, Germanic comfort of Yorkville. By this time, Hedwig had been in America ten years.

All Hester knew of her mother's coming to America was that she had arrived when she was sixteen. Now that she knew how old her mother had been at death, knew the birth date so zealously guarded during a lifetime of evasion and so quickly exposed by the noncommittal nakedness of funeral routine, she realized that her mother must have arrived in 1900. She had come to the home of an aunt, a sister of her own dead mother. What family drama had preceded her coming, whose decision it had been, Hester did not know. Her mother's one reply to a direct question had been a shrugging "There was nothing for me there."

Hester had a vivid picture of her mother's arrival and first years in New York, although this was drawn from only two clues. Her great-aunt, remarking once on Hester's looks in the dispassionate way of near relations, had nodded over Hester's head to her mother. "She is dark, like the father, no? Not like you were." And Hester, with a naïve glance of surprise at her mother's sedate pompadour, had eagerly interposed, "What was she like, Tante?"

"*Ach*, when she came off the boat, *war sie hübsch!*" Tante had said, lapsing into German with unusual warmth, "Such a color! Pink and cream!"

"Yes, a real Bavarian *Mädchen*," said her mother with a trace of contempt. "Too pink for the fashion here. I guess they thought it wasn't real."

Another time, her mother had said, in one of her rare bursts of anecdote, "When I came, I brought enough linen and underclothing to supply two brides. At the convent school where I was sent, the nuns didn't teach you much besides embroidery, so I had plenty to bring, plenty. They were nice, though. Good, simple women. Kind. I remember I brought four dozen handkerchiefs, beautiful heavy linen that you don't get in America. But they were large, bigger than the size of a man's handkerchief over here, and the first time I unfolded one, everybody laughed, so I threw them away." She had sighed, perhaps for the linen. "And underdrawers! Long red flannel, and I had spent months embroidering them with yards of white eyelet work on the ruffles. I remember Tante's maid came in from the back yard quite angry and refused to hang them on the line any more. She said the other maids, from the houses around, teased her for belonging to a family who would wear things like that."

Until Hester was in her teens, her mother had always employed young Germans or Czech girls fresh from "the other side"—Teenies and Josies of long braided hair, broad cotton ankles and queer, blunt shoes, who had clacked deferentially to her mother in German and had gone off to marry their waiter's and baker's apprentices at just about the time they learned to wear silk stockings and "just as soon as you've taught them how to serve a dinner," returning regularly to show off their square, acrid babies. "Greenhorns!" her mother had always called them, a veil of something indefinable about her lips. But in the middle drawer there was a long rope of blond hair, sacrificed, like the handkerchiefs, but not wholly discarded.

There was no passport in the drawer. Perhaps it had been destroyed during the years of the first World War, when her mother, long since a citizen by virtue of her marriage, had felt the contemporary pressure to excise everything Teutonic. "If that nosy Mrs. Cahn asks you when I came over, just say I came over as a child," she had said to Hester. And how easy it had been to nettle her by pretending that one could discern a trace of accent in her speech! Once, when the family had teased her by affecting to hear an echo of "puplic" in her pronunciation of "public," Hester had come upon her, hours after, standing before a mirror, color and nose high, watching herself say, over and over again, "Public! Public!"

Was it this, thought Hester, her straining toward perfection, that made her so intolerant of me, almost as if she were castigating in her child the imperfections that were her own? "Big feet, big hands, like mine," her mother had grumbled. "Why? Why? When every woman in your father's family wears size one! But their nice, large ears—you must have *those!*" And dressing Hester for Sunday school she would withdraw a few feet to look at the finished product, saying slowly, with dreamy cruelty, "I don't know why I let you wear those white gloves. They make your hands look clumsy, just like a policeman's."

It was over books that the rift between Hester and her mother had become complete. To her mother, marrying into a family whose bookish traditions she had never ceased trying to undermine with the sneer of the practical, it was as if the stigmata of that tradition, appearing upon the girl, had forever made them alien to one another.

"Your eyes don't look like a girl's, they look like an old woman's! Reading! Forever reading!" she had stormed, chasing Hester from room to room, flushing her out of doors, and on one remote, terrible afternoon, whipping the book out of Hester's hand, she had leaned over her, glaring, and had torn the book in two.

Hester shivered now, remembering the cold sense of triumph that had welled up in her as she had faced her mother, rejoicing in the enormity of what her mother had done.

Her mother had faltered before her. "Do you want to be a dreamer all your life?" she had muttered.

Hester had been unable to think of anything to say for a moment. Then she had stuttered, "All you think of in life is money!," and had made her grand exit. But huddling miserably in her room afterward she had known even then that it was not as simple as that, that her mother, too, was whipped and driven by some ungovernable dream she could not express, which had left her, like the book, torn in two.

Was it this, perhaps, that had sent her across an ocean, that had impelled her to perfect her dress and manner, and to reject the humdrum suitors of her aunt's circle for a Virginia bachelor twenty-two years older than herself? Had she, perhaps, married him not only for his money and his seasoned male charm but also for his standards and traditions, against which her railings had been a confession of envy and defeat?

So Hester and her mother had continued to pit their implacable difference against each other in a struggle that was complicated out of all reason by their undeniable likeness—each pursuing in her own orbit the warmth that had been denied. Gauche and surly as Hester was in her mother's presence, away from it she had striven successfully for the very falsities of standard that she despised in her mother, and it was her misery that she was forever impelled to earn her mother's approval at the expense of her own. Always, she knew now, there had been the lurking, buried wish that someday she would find the final barb, the homing shaft, that would maim her mother once and for all, as she felt herself to have been maimed.

A few months before, the barb had been placed in her hand. In answer to the telephone call, she had come to visit the family a short time after her mother's sudden operation for cancer of the breast. She had found her father and brother in an anguish of helplessness, fear, and male distaste at the thought of the illness, and her mother a prima donna of fortitude, moving unbowed toward the unspoken idea of her death but with the signs on her face of a pitiful tension that went beyond the disease. She had taken to using separate utensils and to sleeping alone, although the medical opinion that cancer was not transferable by contact was well known to her. It was clear that she was suffering from a horror of what had been done to her and from a fear of the revulsion of others. It was clear to Hester, also, that her father and brother had such a revulsion and had not been wholly successful in concealing it.

One night she and her mother had been together in her mother's bedroom. Hester, in a shabby housegown, stretched out on the bed luxuriously, thinking of how there was always a certain equivocal ease, a letting down of pretense, an illusory return to the irresponsibility of childhood, in the house of one's birth. Her mother, back turned, had been standing unnecessarily long at the bureau, fumbling with articles upon it. She turned slowly.

"They've been giving me X ray twice a week," she said, not looking at Hester, "to stop any involvement of the glands."

"Oh," said Hester, carefully smoothing down a wrinkle on the bedspread. "It's very wise to have that done."

Suddenly, her mother had put out her hand in a gesture almost of appeal. Half in a whisper, she asked, "Would you like to see it? No one has seen it since I left the hospital."

"Yes," Hester said, keeping her tone cool, even, full only of polite interest. "I'd like very much to see it." Frozen there on the bed, she had reverted to childhood in reality, remembering, as if they had all been crammed into one slot in time, the thousands of incidents when she had been the one to stand before her mother, vulnerable and bare, helplessly awaiting the cruel exactitude of her displeasure. I know how she feels as if I were standing there myself, thought Hester. How well she taught me to know!

Slowly her mother undid her housegown and bared her breast. She stood there for a long moment, on her face the looming, pleading look of twenty years before, the look it had once shown under the theatre marquee.

Hester half rose from the bed. There was a hurt in her own breast that she did not recognize. She spoke with difficulty.

"Why . . . it's a beautiful job, Mother," she said, distilling the carefully natural tone of her voice. "Neat as can be. I had no idea . . . I thought it would be ugly." With a step toward her mother, she looked, as if casually, as the dreadful neatness of the cicatrix, at the twisted, foreshortened tendon of the upper arm.

"I can't raise my arm yet," whispered her mother. "They had to cut deep. . . . Your father won't look at it."

In an eternity of slowness, Hester stretched out her hand. Trembling, she touched a tentative finger to her mother's chest, where the breast had been. Then, with rising sureness, with infinite delicacy, she drew her fingertips along the length of scar in a light, affirmative caress, and they stood eye to eye for an immeasurable second, on equal ground at last.

IN THE COLD, darkening room, Hester unclenched herself from remembrance. She was always vulnerable, Hester thought. As we all are. What she bequeathed me unwittingly, ironically, was fortitude—the fortitude of those who have had to live under the blow. But pity—that I found for myself.

She knew now that the tangents of her mother and herself would never have fully met, even if her mother had lived. Holding her mother's hand through the long night as she retreated over the border line of narcosis and coma into death, she had felt the giddy sense of conquering, the heady euphoria of being still alive, which comes to the watcher in the night. Nevertheless, she had known with sureness, even then, that she would go on all her life trying to "show" her mother, in an unsatisfied effort to earn her approval—and unconditional love.

As a child, she had slapped at her mother once in a frenzy of rebellion, and her mother, in reproof, had told her the tale of the peasant girl who had struck her mother and had later fallen ill and died and been buried in the village cemetery. When the mourners came to tend the mound, they found that the corpse's offending hand had grown out of the grave. They cut if off and reburied it, but when they came again in the morning, the hand had grown again. So, too, thought Hester, even though I might learn—have learned in some ways—to escape my mother's hand, all my life I will have to push it down; all my life my mother's hand will grow again out of the unquiet grave of the past.

It was her own life that was in the middle drawer. She was the person she was not only because of her mother but because, fifty-eight years before, in the little town of Oberelsbach, another woman, whose qualities she would never know, had died too soon. Death, she thought, absolves equally the bungler, the evildoer, the unloving, and the unloved—but never the living. In the end, the cicatrix that she had, in the smallest of ways, helped her mother to bear had eaten its way in and killed. The living carry, she thought, perhaps not one tangible wound but the burden of the innumerable small cicatrices imposed on us by our beginnings; we carry them with us always, and from these, from this agony, we are not absolved.

She turned the key and opened the drawer.

V

NADINE GORDIMER

Enemies

WHEN MRS. CLARA HANSEN travels, she keeps herself to herself. This is usually easy, for she has money, has been a baroness and a beauty, and has survived dramatic suffering. The crushing presence of these states in her face and bearing is nearly always enough to stop the loose mouths of people who find themselves in her company. It is only the very stupid, the senile, or the self-obsessed who blunder up to assail that face, withdrawn as a castle, across the common ground of a public dining room.

Last month, when Mrs. Hansen left Cape Town for Johannesburg by train, an old lady occupying the adjoining compartment tried to make of her apologies, as she pressed past in the corridor loaded with string bags and paper parcels, an excuse to open one of those pointless conversations between strangers which arise in the nervous moments of departure. Mrs. Hansen was giving last calm instructions to Alfred, her Malay chauffeur and manservant, whom she was leaving behind, and she did not look up. Alfred had stowed her old calf cases from Europe firmly and within reach in her compartment, which, of course, influence with the reservation office had ensured she would have to herself all the way. He had watched her put away in a special pocket in her handbag, her train ticket, a ticket for her de luxe bed, a book of tickets for her meals. He had made sure that she had her two yellow sleeping pills and the red pills for that feeling of pressure in her head, lying in cottonwool in her silver pillbox. He himself had seen that her two pairs of spectacles, one for distance, one for reading, were in her overnight bag, and had noted that her lorgnette hung below the diamond bow on the bosom of her dress. He had taken down the folding table from its niche above the washbasin in the compartment, and placed on it the three magazines she had sent him to buy at the book-stall, along with the paper from Switzerland that, this week, had been kept aside, unread, for the journey.

For a full fifteen minutes before the train left, he and his employer were free to ignore the to-and-fro of voices and luggage, the heat and confusion. Mrs. Hansen murmured down to him; Alfred, chauffeur's cap in hand, dusty sunlight the colour of beer dimming the oil shine of his black hair, looked up from the plat-form and made low assent. They used the half-sentences, the hesitations, and the slight changes of tone or expression of people who speak the language of their association in the coun-try of their own range of situation. It was hardly speech; now and then it sank away altogether into the minds of each, but the sounds of the station did not well up in its place. Alfred dangled the key of the car on his little finger. The old face beneath the toque noted it, and the lips, the infinitely weary corners of the eyes drooped in the indication of a smile. Would he really put the car away into the garage for six weeks after he'd seen that it was oiled and greased?

Unmindful of the finger, his face empty of the satisfaction of a month's wages in advance in his pocket, two friends waiting to be picked up in a house in the Malay quarter of the town, he said, "I must make a note that I mustn't send Madam's letters on after the twenty-sixth."

"No. Not later than the twenty-sixth."

Did she know? With that face that looked as if it knew everything, could she know, too, about the two friends in the house in the Malay quarter?

She said—and neither of them listened—"In case of need, you've always got Mr. Van Dam." Van Dam was her lawyer. This remark, like a stone thrown idly into a pool to pass the time, had fallen time and again between them into the widening hiatus of parting. They had never questioned or troubled to define its meaning. In ten years, what need had there ever been that Alfred couldn't deal with himself, from a burst pipe in the flat to a jammed fastener on Mrs. Hansen's dress?

Alfred backed away from the ice-cream carton a vendor thrust under his nose; the last untidy lump of canvas luggage belonging to the woman next door thumped down like a dusty animal at Mrs. Hansen's side; the final bell rang.

As the train ground past out of the station, Alfred stood quite still with his cap between his hands, watching Mrs. Hansen. He always stood like that when he saw her off. And she remained at the window, as usual, smiling slightly, inclining her head slightly, as if in dismissal. Neither waved. Neither moved until the other was borne out of sight.

When the station was gone and Mrs. Hansen turned slowly to enter her compartment to the quickening rhythm of the train, she met the gasping face of the old woman next door. Fat overflowed not only from her jowl to her neck, but from her ankles to her shoes. She looked like a pudding that had risen too high and run down the sides of the dish. She was sprinkling cologne onto a handkerchief and hitting with it at her face as if she were trying to kill something. "Rush like that, it's no good for you," she said. "Something went wrong with my son-in-law's car, and what a job to get a taxi! *They* don't care—get you here today or tomorrow. I thought I'd never get up those steps."

Mrs. Hansen looked at her. "When one is no longer young, one must always give oneself exactly twice as much time as one needs. I have learned that. I beg your pardon." And she passed before the woman into her compartment.

The woman stopped her in the doorway. "I wonder if they're

serving tea yet? Shall we go along to the dining car?"

"I always have my tea brought to me in my compartment," said Mrs. Hansen, in the low, dead voice that had been considered a pity in her day but that now made young people who could have been her grandchildren ask if she had been an actress. And she slid the door shut.

Alone, she stood a moment in the secretive privacy, where everything swayed and veered in obedience to the gait of the train. She began to look anxiously over the stacked luggage, her lips moving, but she had grown too set to adjust her balance from moment to moment, and suddenly she found herself sitting down. The train had dumped her out of the way. Good thing, too, she thought, chastising herself impatiently—counting the luggage, fussing, when in ten years Alfred's never forgotten anything. Old fool, she told herself, old fool. Her ageing self often seemed to her an enemy of her real self, the self that had never changed. The enemy was a stupid one, fortunately; she merely had to keep an eye on it in order to keep it outwitted. Other selves that had arisen in her life had been much worse; how terrible had been the struggle with some of *them!*

She sat down with her back to the engine, beside the window, and put on her reading glasses and took up the newspaper from Switzerland. But for some minutes she did not read. She heard again inside herself the words *alone, alone,* just the way she had heard them fifty-nine years ago when she was twelve years old and crossing France by herself for the first time. As she had sat there, bolt upright in the corner of a carriage, her green velvet fur-trimmed cloak around her, her hamper beside her, and the locket with the picture of her grandfather hidden in her hand, she had felt a swelling terror of exhilaration, the dark, drowning swirl of cutting loose, had tasted the strength to be brewed out of self-pity and the calm to be lashed together out of panic that belonged to other times and other journeys approaching her from the distance of her future. *Alone, alone.*

This that her real self had known years before it happened to her—before she had lived the journey that took her from a lover, or those others that took her from the alienated faces of madness and death—that same self remembered years after those journeys had dropped behind into the past. Now she was alone, lonely, lone—whatever you liked to call it—all the time. There is nothing of the drama of an occasion about it, for me, she reminded herself dryly. Still, there was no denying it, *alone* was not the same as *lonely;* even the Old Fool could not blur the distinction of that. The blue silk coat quivered where Alfred had hung it, the bundle of magazines edged along the table, and somewhere above her head a loose strap tapped. She felt again aloneness as the carapace that did not shut her off but shielded her strong sense of survival—against it, and all else.

She opened the paper from Switzerland, and, with her left foot (the heat had made it a little swollen) up on the seat opposite, she began to read. She felt lulled and comfortable and was not even irritated by the thuds and dragging noises coming from the partition behind her head; it was clear that that was the woman next door—*she* must be fussing with her luggage. Presently a steward brought a tea tray, which Alfred had ordered before the train left. Mrs. Hansen drew in her mouth with pleasure at the taste of the strong tea, as connoisseurs do when they drink old brandy, and read the afternoon away.

SHE TOOK her dinner in the dining car because she had established in a long experience that it was not a meal that could be expected to travel train corridors and remain hot, and also because there was something shabby, something *petit bourgeois,* about taking meals in the stuffy cubicle in which you were also to sleep. She tidied her hair around the sides of her toque—it was a beautiful hat, one of four, always the same shape, that she had made for herself every second year in Vienna—took off her rings and washed her hands, and powdered her nose, pulling a critical, amused face at herself in the compact mirror. Then she put on her silk coat, picked up her handbag, and went with upright dignity, despite the twitchings and lurchings of the train, along the corridors to the dining car. She seated herself at an empty table for two beside a window, and, of course, although it was early and there were many other seats vacant, the old woman from the compartment next door, entering five minutes later, came straight over and sat down opposite her.

Now it was impossible not to speak to the woman and Mrs. Hansen listened to her with the distant patience of an adult giving half an ear to a child, and answered her when necessary, with a dry simplicity calculated to be far above her head. Of course, Old Fool was tempted to unbend, to lapse into the small boastings and rivalries usual between two old ladies. But Mrs. Hansen would not allow it and certainly not with this woman—this acquaintance thrust upon her in a train. It was bad enough that, only the week before, Old Fool had led her into one of these pathetic pieces of senile nonsense, cleverly disguised—Old Fool could be wily enough—but, just the same, unmistakably the kind of thing that people found boring. It was about her teeth. At seventy-one they were still her own, which was a self-evident miracle. Yet she had allowed herself, at a dinner party given by some young friends who were obviously impressed by her, to tell a funny story (not quite true, either) about how, when she was a weekend guest in a house with an oversolicitous hostess, the jovial host had hoaxed his wife by impressing upon her the importance of providing a suitable receptacle for their guests's teeth when she took them out overnight. There was a glass beside the jug of water on the bedside table; the hostess appeared, embarrassedly, with another. "But, my dear, what is the other glass for?" The denouement, laughter, etc. Disgusting. Good teeth as well as bad aches and pains must be kept to oneself; when one is young, one takes the first for granted, and does not know the existence of the others.

So it was that when the menu was held before the two women Mrs. Hansen ignored the consternation into which it seemed to plunge her companion, forestalled the temptation to enter, by contributing her doctor's views, into age's passionate preoccupation with diet, and ordered fish.

"D'you think the fish'll be all right? I always wonder, on a train, you know ... " said the woman from the next compartment.

Mrs. Hansen merely confirmed her order to the waiter by lowering her eyes and settling her chin slightly. The woman decided to begin at the beginning, with soup. "Can't go far wrong with soup, can you?"

"Don't wait, please," said Mrs. Hansen when the soup came.

The soup was watery, the woman said. Mrs. Hansen smiled her tragic smile, indulgently. The woman decided that she'd keep Mrs. Hansen company, and risk the fish, too. The fish lay beneath a pasty blanket of white sauce and while Mrs. Hansen calmly pushed aside the sauce and ate, the woman said, "There's nothing like the good, clean food cooked in your own kitchen."

Mrs. Hansen put a forkful of fish to her mouth and, when she had finished, spoke at last. "I'm afraid it's many years since I had my own kitchen for more than a month or two a year."

"Well, of course, if you go about a lot, you get used to strange food, I suppose. I find I can't eat half the stuff they put in front of you in hotels. Last time I was away, there were some days I didn't know what to have at all for lunch. I was in one of the best hotels in Durban and all there was was this endless curry—curry this, curry that—and a lot of dried-up cold meats."

Mrs. Hansen shrugged. "I always find enough for my needs. It does not matter much."

"What can you do? I suppose this sauce is the wrong thing for me, but you've got to take what you get when you're travelling," said the woman. She broke off a piece of bread and passed it swiftly around her plate to scoop up what was left of the sauce. "Starchy," she added.

Mrs. Hansen ordered a cutlet, and, after a solemn study of the menu, the other woman asked for the item listed immediately below the fish—oxtail stew. While they were waiting she ate bread and butter and shifting her mouthful comfortably from one side of her mouth to the other, accomplished a shift of her attention, too, as if her jaw and her brain had some simple mechanical connection. "You're not from here, I suppose?" she asked, looking at Mrs. Hansen with the appraisal reserved for foreigners and the licence granted by the tacit acceptance of old age on both sides.

"I have lived in the Cape, on and off, for some years," said Mrs. Hansen. "My second husband was Danish, but settled here."

"I could have married again. I'm not boasting, I mean, but I did have the chance, if I'd've wanted to," said the woman. "Somehow, I couldn't face it, after losing my first—fifty-two, that's all, and you'd have taken a lease on his life. Ah, those doctors. No wonder I feel I can't trust them a minute."

Mrs. Hansen parted the jaws of her large, elegant black bag to take out a handkerchief; the stack of letters that she always had with her—new ones arriving to take the place of old with every airmail—lay exposed. Thin letters, fat letters, big envelopes, small ones; the torn edges of foreign stamps, the large, sloping, and small, crabbed hands of foreigners writing foreign tongues. The other woman looked down upon them like a tourist, curious, impersonally insolent, envious. "Of course, if I'd been the sort to run about a lot, I suppose it might have been different. I might have met someone really *congenial*. But there's my daughters. A mother's responsibility is never over—that's what I say. When they're little, it's little troubles. When they're grown up, it's big ones. They're all nicely married, thank God, but you know, it's always something—one of them sick, or one of the grandchildren, bless them . . . I don't suppose you've got any children. Not even from your first, I mean?"

"No," said Mrs. Hansen. "No." And the lie, as always, came to her as a triumph against that arrogant boy (Old Fool persisted in thinking of him as a gentle-browed youth bent over a dachshund puppy, though he was a man of forty-five by now) whom truly she had made, as she had warned she would, no son of hers. When the lie was said it had the effect of leaving her breathless, as if she had just crowned a steep rise. Firmly and calmly, she leaned forward and poured herself a glass of water, as one who has deserved it.

"My, it does look fatty," the other woman was saying over the oxtail, which had just been placed before her, "My doctor'd have a fit if he knew I was eating this." But eat it she did, and cutlet and roast turkey to follow. Mrs. Hansen never knew whether or not her companion rounded off the meal with rhubarb pie (the woman had remarked, as she saw it carried past, that it looked soggy), because she herself had gone straight from cutlet to coffee, and, her meal finished, excused herself before the other was through the turkey course. Back in her compartment, she took off her toque at last and tied a grey chiffon scarf around her head. Then she took her red-and-gold Florentine leather cigarette case from her bag and settled down to smoke her nightly cigarette while she waited for the man to come and convert her seat into the de luxe bed Alfred had paid for in advance.

IT SEEMED to Mrs. Hansen that she did not sleep very well during the early part of the night, though she did not quite know what it was that made her restless. She was awakened, time and again, apparently by some noise that had ceased by the time she was conscious enough to identify it. The third or fourth time this happened, she woke to silence and a sense of absolute cessation, as if the world had stopped turning. But it was only the train that had stopped. Mrs. Hansen lay and listened. They must be at some deserted siding in the small hours; there were no lights shining in through the shuttered window, no footsteps, no talk. The voice of a cricket, like a fingernail screeching over glass, sounded, providing, beyond the old woman's closed eyes, beyond the dark compartment and the shutters, a landscape of grass, dark, and telephone poles.

Suddenly the train gave a terrific reverberating jerk, as if it had been given a violent push. All was still again. And in the stillness, Mrs. Hansen became aware of groans coming from the other side of the partition against which she lay. The groans came, bumbling and nasal, through the wood and leather; they sounded like a dog with its head buried in a cushion, worrying at the feathers. Mrs. Hansen breathed out once, hard, in annoyance, and turned over; the greedy old pig, now she was suffering agonies of indigestion from that oxtail, of course. The groans continued at intervals. Once there was a muffled tinkling sound, as if a spoon had been dropped. Mrs. Hansen lay tense with irritation, waiting for the train to move on and drown the woman's noise. At last, with the shake that quickly settled into a fast clip, they were off again, lickety-lack, lickety-lack, past (Mrs. Hansen could imagine) the endless telephone poles, the dark grass, the black-coated cricket. Under the dialogue of the train, she was an unwilling eavesdropper to the vulgar intimacies next door; then either the groans stopped or she fell asleep in spite of them, for she heard nothing till the steward woke her with the arrival of early-morning coffee.

MRS. HANSEN sponged herself, dressed, and had a quiet breakfast, undisturbed by anyone, in the dining car. The man sitting opposite her did not even ask her so much as to pass the salt. She was back in her compartment, reading, when the ticket examiner came in to take her ticket away (they would be in Johannesburg soon), and of course, she knew just where to lay her hand on it, in her bag. He leaned against the doorway while she got it out. "Hear what happened?" he said.

"What happened?" she said uncertainly, screwing up her face because he spoke indistinctly, like most young South Africans.

"Next door," he said. "The lady next door, elderly lady. She fierce little faith that, having been denied the early joys of motherhood, she was at least entitled to escape its later pangs. While her friends had been confined to the nursery, she had been more actively engaged in what she had dared to call "real life," and if this had provided a poorer show than the shining faces and curly hair of progeny, it ought, now that those faces had lost their glow and that hair its fresh abundance, to supply the compensation of an old age that refused to be relegated to the shelf of fruitless nostalgia and of rejected participation. Agnes was not yet prepared to admit that she was not still alive.

The "real life" in which she and Percy had been such close partners had been largely the life of his law firm, Lynne, Travers, Platt & O'Shea, on Court Street, one of the biggest in Brooklyn, rivaling all but the very biggest across the East River. The Lynnes had constantly entertained the partners and associates in their commodious, comfortable, old-fashioned apartment overlooking Prospect Park. Agnes had come to think of herself as a kind of office mother, giving quiet tips to the over-ambitious partners, helping the wives of the younger associates to find apartments and doctors and baby sitters, making herself available at teatime on weekends to lonely bachelor clerks. She had even fostered a romance between one of the loneliest of the latter and the almost old-maid daughter of a senior partner which had resulted in a surprisingly happy marriage.

But best of all had been the firm itself. Lynne, Travers had been a happy association of dedicated men. At least, so Agnes had seen it, or tried to see it. The partners had been gentlemen in the truest old sense of that now scorned word, united in their trust as well as in their affection. There had been no squabbles over dividing profits, no wrangling over precedence in the firm name, no squeezing out of old and failing members. The indigent client had received the same quality of service as the rich one, and both time and money had been liberally contributed to Legal Aid.

Oh, of course, it had not been all *that* perfect. Far from it!

died last night."

"She died? That woman died?" She stood up and questioned him closely, as if he were irresponsible.

"Yes," he said, checking the ticket on his list. "The bed boy found her this morning, dead in her bed. She never answered when the steward came round with coffee, you see."

"My God," said Mrs. Hansen. "My God. So she died, eh?"

"Yes, lady." He held out his hand for her ticket; he had the tale to tell all up and down the train.

With a gesture of futility, she gave it to him.

After he had gone, she sank down on the seat, beside the window, and watched the veld go by, the grasses streaming past in the sun like the long black tails of the widow birds blowing where they swung upon the fences. She had finished her paper and magazines. There was no sound but the sound of the hurrying train.

WHEN THEY REACHED Johannesburg she had all her luggage trimly closed and ready for the porter from the hotel at which she was going to stay. She left the station with him within five minutes of the train's arrival, and was gone before the doctor, officials, and, she supposed, newspaper reporters came to see the woman taken away from the compartment next door. What could I have said to them? she thought, pleased with her sensible escape. Could I tell them she died of greed? Better not to be mixed up in it.

And then she thought of something. Newspaper reporters. No doubt there would be a piece in the Cape papers tomorrow. ELDERLY WOMAN FOUND DEAD IN CAPE—JOHANNESBURG TRAIN.

As soon as she had signed the register at the hotel she asked for a telegram form. She paused a moment, leaning on the marble-topped reception desk, looking out over the heads of the clerks. Her eyes, which were still handsome, crinkled at the corners; her nostrils lifted; her mouth, which was still so shapely because of her teeth, turned its sad corners lower in her reluctant, calculating smile. She printed Alfred's name and the address of the flat in Cape Town, and then wrote quickly, in the fine hand she had mastered more than sixty years ago: "It was not me. Clara Hansen."

LOUIS AUCHINCLO

Suttee

AGNES LYNNE considered that, at sixty-seven, she w young to be widowed, but she was surprised to find how ma of her contemporaries had preceded her to this condition. was as if, while Percy had been alive, the widows had tried camouflage their state of bereavement, rounding up a brother nephew or cousin to accompany them to dinner at the Lynnes or at least, if they had to come alone, making as much noise two, but that now that Agnes was one of them, they could rela and admit the pleasures as well as the necessities of a purely fe male society, positively flaunting their assumption that she, lik themselves, was henceforth dependent on the matinee, the bridge table, the book class, the garden tour. They beckoned to her, with a hint of grimness behind their friendliness, a note of subdued triumph in their very sympathy, like shades of the dead welcoming a soul newly arrived from our warm planet at the dreary realms of Pluto.

Agnes rebelled against what they so evidently deemed her doom. Having been childless, she could not join in their desolate, endless chatter about absent and indifferent children, and more absent and more indifferent grandchildren. She had a

Agnes was not so fatuous as to suppose so, and if she had been, Percy, in the terrible misanthropic moods that had followed his rare drinking bouts, would have enlightened her. In a single one of these he used to be able to destroy the work of years. He would become sullen, bitter, vindictive. He would refuse to stay home, despite her begging, and would go to the office to taunt the clerks for their supposed laziness and stupidity. At times he had seemed to show a streak of near sadism. After the fit had passed, he had been disarmingly apologetic, and Agnes had usually managed to visit the bruised young men and to heal their wounds with the old saw about bark and bite, but for all his charm and for all her sympathy, these outbreaks had produced some permanent alienations.

Percy's last illness had been frightful, a culmination of all the most terrible of his depressions. The great, gaunt, fuliginous man had lain motionless on his hospital bed, his face turned sullenly away from visitors. But at the very end, just when she had thought that she could not bear it, just when it had seemed too hideously much that their whole life together should be smirched with this final gloom, he had turned and roughly seized her hand and pressed it until it hurt and then had hoarsely blessed her for forty-five years of patience and love. Oh, the difference that had made! She still ached in her heart at the thought of it, or rather at the thought of how long and hideously she would have ached without it. If their reach had exceeded their grasp, at least they had reached. And if he had found it difficult to love, at least he had tried.

And now she was left, stunned and groggy with the sense of all that was over. Not only was Percy over, and their life together over, but so was the firm itself, or at least the firm in any shape that she cared to recognize as such. It was not that she had been unprepared for change, even for annihilation. She had read "Ozymandias" and knew about those vast and trunkless legs of stone standing in the desert. But what she had not been prepared for was the speed with which the past could be wrapped up and put away. She had thought it might be decades, at least years. She had not dreamed that it might be a matter of months.

Yet so it was. Old Mr. Bry, who had been Percy's guide and mentor, had died at ninety; then Judge Satler, then Percy—all within thirteen months. In the same period Kings Long Island Trust Company, Percy's favorite client, had been merged with a Manhattan bank and lost to the latter's Wall Street counsel. And then the firm itself had joined up with a smaller firm and had acquired seven new partners, five of whom had never even met Percy. One miserable little year of death and mergers, and the whole character of a grand old law partnership was lost! Each time that Agnes, as executrix of her husband's will, went down to Court Street, there would like as not be a receptionist at the desk who did not even know her. "Mrs. Linn? L-i-n-n? Is that right?" It was worst when these girls were polite, solicitous. Agnes would have rather faced some blunt old dragon, waving her away with a snarl of "Scat, has-been!"

Determined to avoid both the altered firm and the beckoning widows, she found a temporary solace in a new friend, Ada Koepel. Ada, a tall, trim woman, with faded beauty, very gray, always in black, was also a widow and also the widow of a lawyer—Mr. Koepel had been a surrogate and a leader in Jewish philanthropies—but, like Agnes, she eschewed the company of bereaved females. They had met, not through what they had lost but through what they still had—their poodles—in Prospect Park, and they had slipped into the habit of meeting at the same bench, by the Botanic Gardens, at eleven. Ada Koepel lived alone—her two married daughters had moved to the West Coast—but she was devoid of the usual desperation. She seemed to accept the sun and the grass and the park as her natural companions. But Agnes soon discovered that the park Ada, so calm and seemingly gentle, had a lively counterpart in the Ada of the Brooklyn Library, the Ada of the Philharmonic. If she was quiet in Prospect Park, it was because she needed the rest.

"You'll find that what gets you through is your intellect," Ada summed up one day, when she had completed what must have been a silent "diagnosis" of her new friend. Or had it been a testing period? "You must read with me, my dear. And don't tell me that it's a 'passive' occupation. Reading is only the converse to writing. Where would Shakespeare be without *us?*"

"You don't mean to compare a reader with a writer? A great writer? A writer like Shakespeare?"

"Why not? Appreciation completes the artistic process. Perfect appreciation is just as rare as perfect writing. I don't, mind you, say that mine is perfect. I'm not such an ass. But one can try."

Oh, yes, Ada, when she wanted, had the tone of a leader! She led Agnes now, to the library, to lectures, to museums, to concerts. To the latter such things had always been a fringe to life, an attractive fringe, to be sure, but nothing more. Now she tried to learn to respect the great reality that they were to Ada. But where she decidedly did not follow her new friend was in the latter's attitude toward the world of law in which both their husbands had been so importantly engaged. Ada cast an eye on this world which to Agnes was too cool, too balanced, too distinctly appraising. Ada's greatest principle in life, it sometimes seemed to Agnes, was to be "taken in" by nothing—but the sonnets of Shakespeare and the fugues of Bach.

Ada was not, for example, suitably impressed by the great "public spirit" of the old firm of Lynne, Travers, even when Agnes had broadly hinted how much of that spirit had been directly infused from the late Percy Lynne.

"Well, in the 'great old days,' as you call them," Ada wanted to know, "didn't your husband's firm discriminate against Jews?"

"Oh, I doubt that," Agnes answered, much embarrassed. "I just don't think Jewish boys cared to go into that kind of firm. At least in those days."

"What kind of firm?"

"Well . . . a non-Jewish firm."

"You mean it just used to happen that way? The Jews wanted to be with Jews and the Gentiles with Gentiles?"

Agnes, at this, was decidedly disappointed in her new friend. She had not believed that Ada would be so narrowly partisan. It was not, of course, that her tone was disagreeable. Ada's voice was as soft as ever. But the laughter behind it, if heard, would have been mocking. Agnes had sadly to conclude that Ada was never going to concede that Percy and his partners had lived on a higher moral plane than other lawyers. Certainly, she had to admit to herself, if Ada had heard any of the anti-Jewish stories that Percy had loved to tell, she would not. Ada would never have understood that a certain kind of jovial, conversational anti-Semitism had been a harmless trait in Percy and his friends. They had roasted Jews the way they had roasted Catholics—it had been a social habit, a men's convention, lacking in taste perhaps, but having nothing to do with any real animus, certainly having nothing to do with discriminations or persecutions. Had Percy not arranged the election of the first Jew to his fraternity at Yale?

"I don't think you understand the kind of firm Percy's was," Agnes told her friend with dignified regret. "He and his partners would never have held race or religion against their fellow men."

"Against their fellow clubmen," Ada corrected her. "I'm sorry, Agnes, but there are some things you have to be Jewish to understand. I am perfectly willing to concede that your husband and his partners were honest and industrious men, and in some ways high-minded. They trusted each other, but they kept 'each other' to a very small group. I know something about that, dear. Judge Koepel used to tell me."

Agnes was so indignant that she did not care if she was offensive. "Judge Koepel, I'm sure, knew everything."

"Ah, now you're cross, and there's no point in talking when one is cross." Ada rose and called her poodle which she had let off the leash. She and Agnes had picked that bench because the policeman on the beat winked at this. "Let us change the subject. But just before we do so, let me assure you that I'm not being superior. Judge Koepel was no more public-spirited than anyone in Mr. Lynne's firm. Perhaps he was a tiny bit clearer on some of the issues, that's all."

Agnes might have succumbed to the widows after this altercation had not a third diversion unexpectedly offered itself. Upon her return from the park on the day of her difference with Ada, she found a letter from Decius Blount, now senior partner of Percy's firm, asking if he could call upon her the following afternoon. But much more important even than this pleasant prospect was the gracious paragraph that ended his letter:

> I know that I must not lose touch with you. Now that I occupy the chief administrative position of the firm, I shall have a constant need of your advice and encouragement. You are the repository of all the old spirit and spark that made us great. Alas, we look about in vain for that today. If you would coach me—if you would simply talk to me, say, one day a week, or even a month, about yourself and Percy and all the wonderful things you planned together, I know that I should approach my task with a lighter heart and a bigger hope.

Agnes, standing by the window and looking out over darkening Prospect Park, put the letter to her heart and wept.

DECIUS BLOUNT, who was a rather boyish fifty, with soft brown eyes and soft brown hair, the latter only very lightly touched with gray, would have been almost good-looking had he not been a bit too short, a bit too plump and a good deal too mannered. Agnes could never forget Percy's crude expression that he sat in a drawing room chair as if he had "a bug up his ass." Poor Decius tried desperately to make up for his self-consciousness by arraying his round, plump body in beautiful tweeds and by soldering up his natural furtiveness in late-

Victorian pomposity. But when he played with his watch chain, when he complimented Agnes on her tea, when he admired any of the rather indifferent trinkets that sparsely furnished the living room (Agnes and Percy had cared little for bibelots), he suggested a Cruikshank drawing of one of Dickens' parlor hypocrites.

Yet, as Agnes well knew, mannerisms could be very misleading, and they were never more so than in the case of Decius Blount. He was one of those brilliant, effeminate men who study, from childhood, how to adapt themselves to the world of their more masculine fellows and end by dominating it. In the Middle Ages he would have been a political prelate; in the Ottoman court a eunuch and vizier; in our own, he was a lawyer. So thorough had been his understanding of every partner and client of Percy's firm that on the latter's death his succession had been as unquestioned as it had been surprising. Percy had always told Agnes that Decius was a "frustrated pansy," but Agnes, as a woman, suspected that he was simply an inhibited male.

If Percy had regarded Decius, as a lawyer, with his rare admiration and, as a human being, with his much commoner contempt, Decius had returned good for good and good for bad. He had consistently worshiped Percy in every capacity, and if the latter's widow occasionally and uneasily suspected that, like most worshipers, Decius subconsciously preferred to have the founder of the cult dead and freed from the faults of clay, she nonetheless appreciated a zeal that did not seem to have notably survived in her husband's other erstwhile admirers. To hear Decius praise Percy was a greater pleasure than any matinee that the widows could offer.

"What Percy understood," he told her that afternoon, pacing from the fireplace to the window and back, "was that a law firm is something much more than its clients' problems. In a way, you might say, the latter exist *for* the firm, as cases exist to make up law. The practice of any profession is an art, and the joint practice of it by a group of dedicated men can be the greatest art of all. Ah, but they must be dedicated, that's the point! They must be dedicated to something higher than the client, something higher than mere monetary reward!"

And what was better even than all of this, what was almost enough, in fact, to make a life out of a widowhood, was the astonishing revelation of his absolute determination to see her regularly. His note had not been flattery, after all; it had not even been politeness. Decius Blount had simply made up his mind that he must draw inspiration from the distinguished dead through *her* medium. He wanted his "day" in her week; he insisted upon coming to her, directly from the office, at six o'clock every Wednesday. He would hold the firm under her regency, as she would hold her regency under the shade of Percy. The past would not be dead. It should direct the living!

The only thing that she worried about was that Decius might ruin it all by too much solemnity. But even this fear proved unfounded.

"You know, Agnes," he told her, as early as their third Wednesday, "there is no reason that you should always be the one to entertain me. Suppose next Wednesday you come to my apartment? And not just for tea, but for dinner?"

Decius' apartment was unexpectedly charming, with a fine view of the harbor. It was on the top floor of an old brownstone mansion on Brooklyn Heights, and its walls were covered with his collection of baroque eighteenth-century stage designs. A grinning, white-coated Japanese houseboy served them steak and Burgundy, ice cream and champagne. Agnes became a little bit tipsy and listened with the greatest sympathy as Decius held forth on his lonely boyhood and his poor sad tubercular mother. Only with coffee did she suffer the dampening thought that this long dead parent must have been her own age. But when she mentioned this, Decius was unexpectedly explicit in his denial.

"Oh, Mummie was ages older than you, Agnes. You're only

sixty-eight, and Mummie would have been ninety-three. She was forty-two, you see, when I was born. I really belong in your generation. You could be my older sister."

"Well, yes—I suppose."

"And what's more I *feel* we're the same generation. Don't you? Don't you think we talk as contemporaries?"

Agnes was going to pass this off with a shrug, but Decius was much too serious. His eyes were fixed on her, and for once he sat still, making none of his usual nervous gesticulations. Even in the gentle haze which the wine had created, she could sense his force.

"It's not only a question of age, Decius," she answered, with a rueful note. "A bachelor always has his life more or less ahead of him, while a widow has hers behind. So even if you were sixty-eight, and I—what are you? Fifty-one?—I'd still be the elder."

"Not all widows feel that way!"

"Indeed they don't. There are widows and widows. I'm the old-fashioned kind. The best of me was buried with Percy."

Decius rose at this, very solemnly, and, leaning down, kissed her hand. It was all very embarrassing, but it was still not quite as embarrassing as she had thought it was going to be.

"God bless you, Agnes. What is left of you is better than what any of the rest of us have. So long as we've got you, we'll get by."

Agnes could think of nothing to say, so she made a vague murmuring noise, and Decius resumed his seat. After a tense, stiff little pause he continued, but in a more relaxed tone than she would have thought, under the circumstances, possible.

"It's not just as a member of the firm that I need you, Agnes. It's much more personal than that. I need you to be my friend." Decius' face was actually serene, in the style of some very shy people when they manage at last to talk intimately. "I've had few friends in my life. Almost none, really. As a boy I was weak physically. I didn't get my strength till college. I was afraid of girls, and the other boys made fun of me. After Mother died I turned entirely into myself and my work. In the firm I admired some of the older partners, particularly Percy, but I was never intimate with any of them. Maybe they didn't want to be. Maybe I didn't know how. Anyway, I was always alone. But now that you're alone, too, I thought we might be friends. Real friends. You wouldn't be always expecting those other things of me, the way younger women do. Lord, you wouldn't believe what some of them will do to get a man! And I wouldn't be expecting anything of you but the chance to take you out to dinner and the theater. Why couldn't we have a wonderful, happy friendship? Oh, Agnes, please say yes! I need you so!"

"But, my poor boy," Agnes cried, taking both his outstretched hands in hers, "do you think it's such a favor for a lonely old widow to agree to be taken out to dinner by an attractive, successful man? By a leader of the bar? Why, Decius, you've got it all mixed up. I'd be honored and flattered to be your friend!"

After this their Wednesday evenings became more festive. Decius would take her to dine in Manhattan in restaurants like the Pavillon or Voisin's, and order fine dishes and great wines. Agnes had never been much interested in these, but Decius was a decided gourmet, and she was already learning to humor him. Their conversation, a bit to her surprise, even a bit to her disappointment, rarely struck again the intense personal note that he had sounded on the night of their dinner at his apartment. They talked now continually about the office, even more than she had done with Percy: which clerks should be promoted, which partners should be retired, which clients were more trouble than they were worth. Decius had soon brought her up to date with the events that had occurred since Percy's death. He made them come alive because he saw them as a drama. He seemed to see the firm, she gradually made out, as a kind of oriental court of which he was sultan, a wise young sultan of emancipated ideas, but surrounded by stealthy courtiers who, if not constantly watched, would converge upon him and knife him and fling his corpse in the Bosporus, giving over the empire to rapine and lawlessness. Agnes even began to see that it might be the function of Percy Lynne's widow to keep this obsession from getting out of control.

"Has it ever occurred to you that they may be afraid of *you?*" she asked him once.

His eyes narrowed. "They?"

"Everyone you fear. Anyone you fear. You can be quite formidable, my dear. I'm very glad that you're on my side."

The pale distant look in his brown eyes immediately softened. "Oh, you'll never have to worry about that," he said quickly.

Not all their evenings were so exclusive. From time to time Decius entertained other partners and their wives, and Agnes had the opportunity, in the case of those who had come into the firm after Percy's death, to catch up with the missing characters of the drama. Soon all the partners, taking their cue from Decius that Agnes' mourning did not exclude social life, invited her to their own parties. She found that on these occasions she and Decius were treated as a couple, and she began, in this rather curious sense, to occupy again the social position in the firm that she had lost with Percy's death. But she was not at all sure that she liked it.

In particular, she was embarrassed by Decius' public attitude toward her. She did not so much mind the excessive flattery of his demeanor to her: the little toasts at dinner parties after rapping his fork on his glass, the appeals down the table to her wisdom and judgment, the hushing of other people when she was talking, but she did mind his possessiveness. He always insisted on bringing her to a party and on taking her home, on putting on her coat and taking it off, on maneuvering her about as if she were an adored but petulantly exacting sovereign and he a wily and admiring premier, Victoria and Disraeli. But when she finally spoke to him about this, at one of their restaurants, she was startled to find that he was not in the least embarrassed. On the contrary, he seemed suddenly to spring into action, like a sailor long trained for combat, at the bell for battle stations.

"There's only one solution to this," he exclaimed in a high tense tone, imperially signaling to the waiter for two more cocktails. "We must marry. That's all there is to it. We must marry, and why not?"

"For God's sake, why?" she cried aghast.

"Listen to me, Agnes. I've thought it all out. Listen to me and be quiet." They were side by side on a bench seat, their backs to the wall, and he stared across the room into the huge mirror opposite as he talked. "I'm not intruding on your duties to Percy. I should not be so presumptuous. They are sacred to me. The marriage would be in name only, of course. Oh, I should venerate you like a vestal virgin! But such a union would at least enable me to give you my name and home and your proper position as senior partner's wife again. Oh, Agnes, let me take care of you! I think I might almost be able to make you happy again. Don't say anything tonight. Don't say anything for weeks. But think it over. Think it over carefully. I've deserved that much."

"But you dear crazy boy, how would you look, married to an old woman!"

"You're not an old woman."

"People would say so."

"Who cares what people say?"

"Oh, Decius, you're sweet!" Agnes closed her eyes and gasped at the sudden stroke of her headache. Then, just as suddenly, the pain passed, and her eyes were full of tears. "What would Percy say?"

"Do you know something? I think Percy would approve. I think somewhere he's watching us right now! I think he *wants* you to be looked after."

Again Agnes closed her eyes as she seemed to hear the whole dining room reverberate with her late husband's high screechy laugh. "I wonder," she murmured faintly.

"Look how I've upset you. I'm a brute! I promise not to mention the subject again tonight. And neither do you. You're to consider it, that's all. Just to contemplate it, that's all."

"But Decius . . . "

"Not another word! Ah, good, here come our cocktails."

WHEN AGNES, the next morning, was considering whose advice she might seek, she was not surprised to discover that the only name that survived all objections was Ada Koepel's. All of the people she knew best in the world were connected in one way or another with Lynne, Travers, and it was out of the question to consult any of them. Besides, Ada was freer than most of preconceived notions. She found her at ten o'clock at their old meeting place.

"Well?" Ada asked, with a cryptic smile, when Agnes had finished her story.

"*Well?* What do you mean, Ada, well? What should I *do?*"

"Of course, you must realize that any widow who advised you to turn him down would be instantly accused of rank envy. As a chance, it's a near miracle."

"Ah, but Ada, what do you and I have to do with vulgar attitudes? The question is: what is my duty?"

"Duty? Does the situation present one?"

"Of course it does! Would Percy want me to preserve his firm by marrying and guiding Decius? Or would he feel that I had simply made myself ridiculous?"

"Percy is dead," Ada said drily. "I think we had better consider what *you* want."

"But it's not what I want, or even what Percy wants, really. It's what's right!"

"I see." Ada's face was inscrutable. "Well, then, what Mr. Blount proposes seems to me entirely fitting. You have told me how he feels about his law firm. It's precisely the way you feel.

Indeed, from what you tell me, I don't see why you and the gentleman are not in total agreement about everything. I suggest that this marriage was made in heaven!"

"Except that it wouldn't be really a marriage," Agnes corrected her, a bit shocked by the levity of Ada's tone. "I hoped I had made that clear."

"You implied that it wouldn't be consummated," Ada said, with a crudeness that Agnes found in poor taste. "But it seems to me it's still a marriage. What else would you call it?"

"A partnership."

"Oh, Agnes, you and your partnerships! I'm afraid they're beyond me."

"But you must see, Ada, that Percy was my husband, for ever and ever, the way . . . " She knew that Judge Koepel's name had been Abraham, but she did not know by what diminutive Ada might have addressed him. "The way Judge Koepel was yours," she ended lamely.

"Then what are we discussing?"

"The form of a marriage. The form of a marriage to carry on the substance of all that Percy believed in."

Ada now really stared at her. "You're beyond everything, Agnes. You and all the good women like you. But have it your way, by all means. Marry Mr. Blount for Percy's sake and live happily ever after!"

"But do you really mean that?"

"I really mean it. I may find your motives bizarre, but I thoroughly applaud your actions. What would you like for a wedding present? Oh, I beg your pardon. It's not really a wedding, is it? What would you like for a partnership present?"

Agnes was not much satisfied with this, but she decided ultimately—after some days' consideration—that Ada, for all her sarcasm, did basically approve of the union. Ada obviously thought very little of her—that had been evident from the beginning. How much, after all, did she really think of Ada? The point of their friendship had been in the new lights that each could provide the other. And what more valuable light could Ada provide than the revelation that, silly as Agnes Lynne might be, she would be no sillier as Agnes Blount?

For a week she saw no one at all, not even Decius. She walked with her poodle in parts of Prospect Park where she would not be apt to encounter Ada and went over her albums at night. She reviewed the photographs of every trip that she had made with Percy and read all the clippings from newspapers and bar journals about his accomplishments and awards. Yet she could never bring herself to see the shade of her husband as taking any attitude but a ribald one about her contemplated step. She even at times had an uncomfortable glimpse of him sitting beside Ada on that park bench. Wasn't it possible that he and Ada would have hit it off? Wasn't it even possible that he might be speaking to her through Ada?

Never! She was standing before the marble statue of Mowgli in the Elephant House when the cold common sense of this negative answer rattled through her. *That* was what Ada had meant when she had said that Percy was dead! That the decision to remarry was hers, not his! The fact that Percy mocked her and had always done so, that Ada mocked her and would continue to do so had little to do with the separate and distinct question of the duty of Percy's widow. What *she* had to consider was how her marriage would strike the world. For even, if she decided, with both Ada and Percy against her, that it was her duty to Percy's firm to marry Decius and guide him as senior partner, she had still to contend with the fact that if the world laughed at her, the world might foil her plan. For how could she help anyone, let alone a law firm, if she were a figure of fun? Ah, but she would not be—*that* was what she finally took from Ada—if the world were *ignorant* of her motive! The world would forgive love, at any age, in any old fool; it would never forgive self-sacrifice. If she were to marry Decius and marry him, according to her plan, successfully, she would have to keep her mouth shut about why she was doing it.

When she had finally thought it all through, she left the zoo and went directly home. She telephoned Decius and asked him to take her out to dinner. When he inquired which of their restaurants she would prefer, she named the most expensive and knew that in doing so, she had informed him that her answer would be affirmative.

SHE TOLD HIM with the first cocktail. She came straight out with it and hoped that she had succeeded in sounding gay. Decius turned pink. He insisted on kissing her hand and ordering champagne. She was almost afraid that he would leap to his feet and appeal to a roomful of strangers to drink their health.

"May we go to Venice on our honeymoon?" he asked excitedly. "I have always thought Venice the most romantic place in the world. Oh, Agnes, what a life we are going to have!"

He drank steadily through the evening, while Agnes took token sips to accompany him. Cocktails were followed by champagne and that by many brandies. She had never seen him in such a mood. His nervousness and excitement boiled over the brim of his normal discipline and seemed to inundate her with monologue. One subject triggered off another, but all were about Decius Blount and his long unhappy past and his long, now happy future. Nobody had understood him before Agnes, not even his sacred mother, who now, it appeared, had been rather an old bitch. He had never had a girl friend; he had never, he managed to imply, any relations whatever with women. There had been two or three men, including Percy, whom he had liked and admired, but none of them had really cared for him. But now, with Agnes . . . well, people would *see* what he had in him! His talk seemed to intoxicate him more than the wine or brandy, but this intoxication did not in the least affect his articulation or the lucidity of his thoughts. On the contrary, he seemed to have been totally released from his old formal and a bit formidable self. He seemed younger, brighter, more ebullient. He was the least bit like—and the thought struck her with something like dismay—a poet, a Shelley, a bright-eyed idealist. He, Decius Blount! At fifty-one!

"Oh, my dearest, I feel I know everything tonight!" he exclaimed. "And that I can tell you everything, too. You're not like other women because you don't expect things of me, if you see what I mean. And for that very reason you're the one woman in the world to whom I might be everything. Because we've promised each other no love, it's precisely what may be in store for us. Because to me you've been a priestess at the altar, you may be the one woman I'm destined to possess!" At this point Agnes' obvious disquietude briefly penetrated even his mist. "But never mind that now, dearest. I see that the priestess is alarmed. Which is, of course, the very thing to most excite the moral acolyte. No need to think of that till Venice!"

He was good to his resolution, however drunk, and did not revert to the subject, nor, needless to say, did Agnes. When she finally induced him to take her home, he was still in the same golden mood, and when she allowed him to kiss her good night in the taxi, gently but definitely refusing to let him come up with her, she was sure that he would go to a bar, perhaps to several. But he was better off alone, and certainly so was she. She knew what a night lay ahead of her.

After only an hour of anguished sobbing, however, she was able to dry the tears of mortification and take her seat at Percy's desk. There, looking over the moonlit park, she wrote what she hoped was a beautiful letter to Decius, breaking off their engagement and wishing him a happy and fruitful life with the younger woman "whom I feel confident that you will now find and whom I know that you richly deserve." After making a fair copy she went down herself to the lobby to mail it. At four in the morning she was able at last to sleep.

The next day in the park, as she told Ada the story, she felt that her conduct had been correct. It seemed to her that it had been both dignified and kind. Of course, it did not come to her as a surprise that Ada should take a less elevated view of the matter, but it certainly came as a shock, and finally as an outrage, that Ada should actually rail at her. She would not have believed that the woman could have been such a fishwife!

"When we first met," Ada exclaimed, in a tone that verged on the strident, "you complained about other widows because they were so removed from what you called 'life.' I thought that possibly we meant the same thing by the term, or at least something not too different. Indeed, I hoped it might prove the basis for a mutual sympathy. But now I see that I was very much misguided. For when life, poor wretched substance that it may be, dares at last to reveal itself to you—to Agnes Lynne—in any other form than a romantic illustration for the children's book, you beg off. Oh, Agnes, I have no patience with you! None! You and your kind are simply impossible. What in the name of Venus is your old body good for but to give some satisfaction to that poor frustrated man? Why are you always chattering about that law firm? *He's* the one who needs you. You ought to be proud!"

Agnes stared at the stranger beside her for a long moment and then slowly shook her head.

"I guess there are differences of opinion that are not arguable," she said sadly. "Even if you should be right it's much too late for me to learn. I think I must make do with myself as I am. For as long as may be necessary. Which I hope will not be long." She rose.

"Oh, Agnes, do sit down. I can't bear that high, injured look. Let's discuss this like two rational human beings!"

"How can we, when only one is present? Good day, Ada."

And as she moved away, she saw, ahead of her, unavoidable now, the widows looming.

RICHARD STERN

Dr. Cahn's Visit

"HOW FAR is it now, George?"

The old man was riding next to his son, Will. George was his brother, dead the day after Franklin Roosevelt.

"Almost there, Dad."

"What does 'almost' mean?"

"It's Eighty-sixth and Park. The hospital's at Ninety-ninth and Fifth. Mother's in the Klingenstein Pavilion."

"Mother's not well?"

"No, she's not well. Liss and I took her to the hospital a couple of weeks ago."

"It must have slipped my mind." The green eyes darkened with sympathy. "I'm sure you did the right thing. Is it a good hospital?"

"Very good. You were on staff there half a century."

"Of course I was. For many years, I believe."

"Fifty."

"Many as that?"

"A little slower, pal. These jolts are hard on the old man." The cabbie was no chicken himself. "It's your ride."

"Are we nearly there, George?"

"Two minutes more."

"The day isn't friendly," said Dr. Cahn. "I don't remember such—such—"

"Heat."

"Heat in New York." He took off his gray fedora and scratched at the hairless liver-spotted skin. Circulatory difficulty left it dry, itchy. Scratching had shredded and inflamed its soft center.

"It's damned hot. In the nineties. Like you."

"What's that?"

"It's as hot as you are old. Ninety-one."

"Ninety-one. That's not good."

"It's a grand age."

"That's your view."

"And Mother's eighty. You've lived good, long lives."

"Mother's not well, son?"

"Not too well. That's why Liss and I thought you ought to see her. Mother's looking forward to seeing you."

"Of course. I should be with her. Is this the first time I've come to visit?"

"Yes."

"I should be with her."

The last weeks had been difficult. Dr. Cahn had been the center of the household. Suddenly, his wife was. The nurses looked after her. And when he talked, she didn't answer. He grew angry, sullen. When her ulcerous mouth improved, her voice was rough and her thought harsh. "I wish you'd stop smoking for five minutes. Look at the ashes on your coat. Please stop smoking."

"Of course, dear. I didn't know I was annoying you." The ash tumbled like a suicide from thirty stories, the butt was crushed into its dead brothers. "I'll smoke inside." And he was off, but, in two minutes, back. Lighting up. Sometimes he lit two cigarettes at once. Or lit the filtered end. The odor was foul, and sometimes his wife was too weak to register her disgust.

They sat and lay within silent yards of each other. Dr. Cahn was in his favorite armchair, the *Times* bridge column inches from his cigarette. He read it all day long. The vocabulary of the game deformed his speech. "I need some clubs" might mean "I'm hungry." "My spades are tired" meant he was. Or his eyes were. Praise of someone might come out "He laid his hand out clearly." In the bedridden weeks, such mistakes intensified his wife's exasperation. "He's become such a penny-pincher," she said to Liss when Dr. Cahn refused to pay her for the carton of cigarettes she brought, saying, "They can't charge so much. You've been cheated."

"Liss has paid. Give her the money."

"Are you telling me what's trump? I've played this game all my life."

"You certainly have. And I can't bear it."

In sixty marital years, there had never been such anger. When Will came from Chicago to persuade his mother into the hospital, the bitterness dismayed him.

It was, therefore, not so clear that Dr. Cahn should visit his wife. Why disturb her last days? Besides, Dr. Cahn seldom went out anywhere. He wouldn't walk with the black nurses (women whom he loved, teased, and was teased by). It wasn't done. "I'll go out later. My feet aren't friendly today." Or, lowering the paper, "My legs can't trump."

Liss opposed his visit. "Mother's afraid he'll make a scene."

"It doesn't matter," said Will. "He has to have some sense of what's happening. They've been the center of each other's lives. It wouldn't be right."

The hope had been that Dr. Cahn would die first. He was ten years older, his mind had slipped its moorings years ago. Mrs. Cahn was clearheaded, and, except near the end, energetic. She loved to travel, wanted especially to visit Will in Chicago—she had not seen his new apartment—but she wouldn't leave her husband even for a day. "Suppose something happened." "Bring him along." "He can't travel. He'd make an awful scene."

Only old friends tolerated him, played bridge with him, forgiving his lapses and muddled critiques of their play. "If you don't understand a two bid now, you never will." Dr. Cahn was the most gentlemanly of men, but his tongue roughened with his memory. It was as if a lifetime of restraint were only the rind of a wicked impatience.

"He's so spoiled," said Mrs. Cahn, the spoiler.

"Here we are, Dad."

They parked under the blue awning. Dr. Cahn got out his wallet—he always paid for taxis, meals, shows—looked at the few bills, then handed it to his son. Will took a dollar, added two of his own, and thanked his father.

"This is a weak elevator," he said of one of the monsters made to drift the ill from floor to floor. A nurse wheeled in a stretcher and Dr. Cahn removed his fedora.

"Mother's on eight."

"Minnie is here?"

"Yes. She's ill. Step out now."

"I don't need your hand."

Each day, his mother filled less of the bed. Her face, unsupported by dentures, seemed shot away. Asleep, it looked to Will as if the universe leaned on the crumpled cheeks. When he kissed them, he feared they'd turn to dust, so astonishingly delicate was the flesh. The only vanity left was love of attention, and that was part of the only thing that counted, the thought of those who cared for her. How she appreciated the good nurses, and her children. They—who'd never seen before their mother's naked body—would change her nightgown if the nurse was gone. They brought her the bedpan and, though she usually suggested they leave the room, sat beside her while, under the sheets, her weak body emptied its small waste.

For the first time in his adult life, Will found her beautiful. Her flesh was mottled like a Pollock canvas, the facial skin trenched with the awful last ditches of self-defense, but her look melted him. It was human beauty.

Day by day, manners that seemed as much a part of her as

her eyes—fussiness, bossiness, nagging inquisitiveness—
dropped away. She was down to what she was.

Not since childhood had she held him so closely, kissed his
cheek with such force. "This is mine. This is what lasts," said
the force.

What was she to him? Sometimes, little more than the old organic scenery of his life. Sometimes she was the meaning of it.
"Hello, darling," she'd say. "I'm so glad to see you." The
voice, never melodious, was rusty, avian. Beautiful. No actress
could match it. "How are you? What's happening?"

"Very little. How are you today?"

She told her news. "Dr. Vacarian was in, he wanted to give
me another treatment. I told him, 'No more.' And no more
medicine." Each day, she had renounced more therapy. An unspoken decision had been made after a five-hour barium treatment which usurped the last of her strength. (Will thought that
might have been its point.) It had given her her last moments of
eloquence, a frightening jeremiad about life dark beyond belief,
nothing left, nothing right. It was the last complaint of an old
champion of complaint, and after it, she had made up her mind
to go. There was no more talk of going home.

"Hello, darling. How are you today?"

Will bent over, was kissed and held against her cheek.
"Mother, Dad's here."

To his delight, she showed hers. "Where is he?" Dr. Cahn
had waited at the door. Now he came in, looked at the bed, realized where he was and who was there.

"Dolph, dear. How are you, my darling? I'm so happy you
came to see me."

The old man stooped over and took her face in his hands. For
seconds, there was silence. "My dearest," he said; then, "I
didn't know. I had no idea. I've been so worried about you. But
don't worry now. You look wonderful. A little thin, perhaps.
We'll fix that. We'll have you out in no time."

The old man's pounding heart must have driven blood

through the clogged vessels. There was no talk of trumps.

"You can kiss me, dear." Dr. Cahn put his lips on hers.

He sat next to the bed and held his wife's hand through the low rail. Over and over he told her she'd be well. She asked about home and the nurses. He answered well for a while. Then they both saw him grow vague and tired. To Will he said, "I don't like the way she's looking. Are you sure she has a good doctor?"

Of course Mrs. Cahn heard. Her happiness watered a bit, not at the facts, but at his inattention. Still, she held on. She knew he could not sit so long in a strange room. "I'm so glad you came, darling."

Dr. Cahn heard his cue and rose. "We mustn't tire you Minnie, dear. We'll come back soon."

She held out her small arms, he managed to lean over, and they kissed again.

In the taxi, he was very tired. "Are we home?"

"Almost, Dad. You're happy you saw Mother, aren't you?"

"Of course I'm happy. But it's not a good day. It's a very poor day. Not a good bid at all."

Sleep It Off, Lady

ONE OCTOBER afternoon Mrs. Baker was having tea with Miss Verney and talking about the proposed broiler factory in the middle of the village where they both lived. Miss Verney, who had not been listening attentively, said, "You know Letty, I've been thinking a great deal about death lately. I hardly ever do, strangely enough."

"No dear," said Mrs. Baker. "It isn't strange at all. It's quite natural. We old people are rather like children, we live in the present as a rule. A merciful dispensation of providence."

"Perhaps," said Miss Verney doubtfully.

Mrs. Baker said "we old people" quite kindly, but could not help knowing that while she herself was only sixty-three and might, with any luck, see many a summer (after many a summer dies the swan, as some man said), Miss Verney, certainly well over seventy, could hardly hope for anything of the sort. Mrs. Baker gripped the arms of her chair. "Many a summer, touch wood and please God," she thought. Then she remarked that it was getting dark so early now and wasn't it extraordinary how time flew.

Miss Verney listened to the sound of the car driving away,

went back to her sitting-room and looked out of the window at the flat fields, the apple trees, the lilac tree that wouldn't flower again, not for ten years they told her, because lilacs won't stand being pruned. In the distance there was a rise in the ground—you could hardly call it a hill—and three trees so exactly shaped and spaced that they looked artificial. "It would be rather lovely covered in snow," Miss Verney thought. "The snow, so white, so smooth and in the end so boring. Even the hateful shed wouldn't look so bad." But she'd made up her mind to forget the shed.

Miss Verney had decided that it was an eyesore when she came to live in the cottage. Most of the paint had worn off the once-black galvanized iron. Now it was a greenish colour. Part of the roof was loose and flapped noisily in windy weather and a small gate off its hinges leaned up against the entrance. Inside it was astonishingly large, the far end almost dark. "What a waste of space," Miss Verney thought. "That must come down." Strange that she hadn't noticed it before.

Nails festooned with rags protruded from the only wooden rafter. There was a tin bucket with a hole, a huge dustbin. Nettles flourished in one corner but it was the opposite corner which disturbed her. Here was piled a rusty lawnmower, an old chair with a carpet draped over it, several sacks, and the remains of what had once been a bundle of hay. She found herself imagining that a fierce and dangerous animal lived there and called aloud: "Come out, come out, Shredni Vashtar, the beautiful." Then rather alarmed at herself she walked away as quickly as she could.

But she was not unduly worried. The local builder had done several odd jobs for her when she moved in and she would speak to him when she saw him next.

"Want the shed down?" said the builder.

"Yes," said Miss Verney. "It's hideous, and it takes up so much space."

"It's on the large side," the builder said.

"Enormous. Whatever did they use it for?"

"I expect it was the garden shed."

"I don't care what it was," said Miss Verney. "I want it out of the way."

The builder said that he couldn't manage the next week, but the Monday after that he'd look in and see what could be done. Monday came and Miss Verney waited but he didn't arrive. When this had happened twice she realized that he didn't mean to come and wrote to a firm in the nearest town.

A few days later a cheerful young man knocked at the door, explained who he was and asked if she would let him know exactly what she wanted. Miss Verney, who wasn't feeling at all well, pointed, "I want that pulled down. Can you do it?"

The young man inspected the shed, walked round it, then stood looking at it.

"I want it destroyed," said Miss Verney passionately, "utterly destroyed and carted away. I hate the sight of it."

"Quite a job," he said candidly.

And Miss Verney saw what he meant. Long after she was dead and her cottage had vanished it would survive. The tin bucket and the rusty lawnmower, the pieces of rag fluttering in the wind. All would last forever.

Eyeing her rather nervously he became businesslike. "I see what you want, and of course we can let you have an estimate of the cost. But you realize that if you pull the shed down you take away from the value of your cottage?"

"Why?" said Miss Verney.

"Well," he said, "very few people would live here without a car. It could be converted into a garage easily or even used as it is. You can decide of course when you have the estimate whether you think it worth the expense and... the trouble. Good day."

Left alone, Miss Verney felt so old, lonely and helpless that she began to cry. No builder would tackle that shed, not for any price she could afford. But crying relieved her and she soon felt quite cheerful again. It was ridiculous to brood, she told herself. She quite liked the cottage. One morning she'd wake up and know what to do about the shed, meanwhile she wouldn't look at the thing. She wouldn't think about it.

But it was astonishing how it haunted her dreams. One night she was standing looking at it changing its shape and becoming a very smart, shiny, dark blue coffin picked out in white. It reminded her of a dress she had once worn. A voice behind her said: "That's the laundry."

"Then oughtn't I to put it away?" said Miss Verney in her dream.

"Not just yet. Soon," said the voice so loudly that she woke up.

SHE HAD DRAGGED the large dustbin to the entrance and, because it was too heavy for her to lift, had arranged for it to be carried to the gate every week for the dustmen to collect. Every morning she took a small yellow bin from under the sink and emptied it into the large dustbin, quickly, without lingering or looking around. But on one particular morning the usual cold wind had dropped and she stood wondering if a coat of white paint would improve matters. Paint might look a lot worse, besides who could she get to do it? Then she saw a cat, as she thought, walking slowly across the far end. The sun shone through a chink in the wall. It was a large rat. Horrified, she watched it disappear under the old chair, dropped the yellow bin, walked as fast as she was able up the road and knocked at the door of a shabby thatched cottage.

"Oh Tom. There are rats in my shed. I've just seen a huge one. I'm so desperately afraid of them. What shall I do?"

When she left Tom's cottage she was still shaken, but calmer. Tom had assured her that he had an infallible rat poison, arrangements had been made, his wife had supplied a strong cup of tea.

He came that same day to put down the poison, and when afterwards he rapped loudly on the door and shouted: "Everything under control?" she answered quite cheerfully, "Yes, I'm fine and thanks for coming."

As one sunny day followed another she almost forgot how much the rat had frightened her. "It's dead or gone away," she assured herself.

When she saw it again she stood and stared disbelieving. It crossed the shed in the same unhurried way and she watched, not able to move. A huge rat, there was no doubt about it.

This time Miss Verney didn't rush to Tom's cottage to be reassured. She managed to get to the kitchen, still holding the empty yellow pail, slammed the door and locked it. Then she shut and bolted all the windows. This done, she took off her shoes, lay down, pulled the blankets over her head and listened to her hammering heart.

> *I'm the monarch of all I survey.*
> *My right, there is none to dispute.*

That was the way the rat walked.

In the close darkness she must have dozed, for suddenly she was sitting at a desk in the sun copying proverbs into a ruled book: "Evil Communications corrupt good manners. Look before you leap. Patience is a virtue, good temper a blessing," all the way up to Z. Z would be something to do with zeal or zealous. But how did they manage about X? What about X?

Thinking this, she slept, then woke, put on the light, took two tuinal tablets and slept again, heavily. When she next opened her eyes it was morning, the unwound bedside clock had stopped, but she guessed the time from the light and hurried into the kitchen waiting for Tom's car to pass. The room was stuffy and airless but she didn't dream of opening the window. When she saw the car approaching she ran out into the road and waved it down. It was as if fear had given her wings and once more she moved lightly and quickly.

"Tom, Tom."

He stopped.

"Oh Tom, the rat's still there. I saw it last evening."

He got down stiffly. Not a young man, but surely surely, a kind man? "I put down enough stuff to kill a dozen rats," he said. "Let's 'ave a look."

He walked across to the shed. She followed, several yards behind, and watched him rattling the old lawnmower, kicking the sacks, trampling the hay and nettles.

"No rat 'ere," he said at last.

"Well there was one," she said.

"Not 'ere."

"It was a huge rat," she said.

Tom had round brown eyes, honest eyes, she'd thought. But now they were sly, mocking, even hostile.

"Are you sure it wasn't a pink rat?" he said.

She knew that the bottles in her dustbin were counted and discussed in the village. But Tom, who she liked so much?

"No," she managed to say steadily. "An ordinary colour but very large. Don't they say that some rats now don't care about poison? Super rats."

Tom laughed. "Nothing of that sort round 'ere."

She said: "I asked Mr. Slade, who cuts the grass, to clear out the shed and he said he would but I think he's forgotten."

"Mr. Slade is a very busy man," said Tom. "He can't clear out the shed just when you tell him. You've got to wait. Do you expect him to leave his work and waste his time looking for what's not there?"

"No," she said, "of course not. But I think it ought to be done." (She stopped herself from saying: "I can't because I'm afraid.")

"Now you go and make yourself a nice cup of tea," Tom said, speaking in a more friendly voice. "There's no rat in your shed." And he went back to his car.

Miss Verney slumped heavily into the kitchen armchair. "He doesn't believe me. I can't stay alone in this place, not with that monster a few yards away. I can't do it." But another cold voice persisted: "Where will you go? With what money? Are you really such a coward as all that?"

AFTER A TIME Miss Verney got up. She dragged what furniture there was away from the walls so that she would know that nothing lurked in the corners and decided to keep the windows looking onto the shed shut and bolted. The others she opened but only at the top. Then she made a large parcel of all the food that the rat could possibly smell—cheese, bacon, ham, cold meat, practically everything . . . she'd give it to Mrs. Randolph, the cleaning woman, later.

"But no more confidences." Mrs. Randolph would be as sceptical as Tom had been. A nice woman but a gossip, she wouldn't be able to resist telling her cronies about the giant, almost certainly imaginary, rat terrorizing her employer.

Next morning Mrs. Randolph said that a stray dog had upset the large dustbin. She'd had to pick everything up from the floor of the shed. "It wasn't a dog" thought Miss Verney, but she only suggested that two stones on the lid turned the other way up would keep the dog off.

When she saw the size of the stones she nearly said aloud: "I defy any rat to get that lid off."

MISS VERNEY had always been a careless, not a fussy, woman. Now all that changed. She spent hours every day sweeping, dusting, arranging the cupboards and putting fresh paper into the drawers. She pounced on every speck of dust with a dustpan. She tried to convince herself that as long as she kept her house spotlessly clean the rat would keep to the shed, not to wonder what she would do if, after all, she encountered it.

"I'd collapse," she thought, "that's what I'd do."

After this she'd start with fresh energy, again fearfully sweeping under the bed, behind cupboards. Then feeling too tired to eat, she would beat up an egg in cold milk, add a good deal of whisky and sip it slowly. "I don't need a lot of food now." But her work in the house grew slower and slower, her daily walks shorter and shorter. Finally the walks stopped. "Why should I bother?" As she never answered letters, letters ceased to arrive, and when Tom knocked at the door one day to ask how she was: "Oh I'm quite all right," she said and smiled.

He seemed ill at ease and didn't speak about rats or clearing the shed out. Nor did she.

"Not seen you about lately," he said.

"Oh I go the other way now."

When she shut the door after him she thought: "And I imagined I liked him. How very strange."

"NO PAIN?" the doctor asked.

"It's just an odd feeling," said Miss Verney.

The doctor said nothing. He waited.

"It's as if all my blood was running backwards. It's rather horrible really. And then for a while sometimes I can't move. I mean if I'm holding a cup I have to drop it because there's no life in my arm."

"And how long does this last?"

"Not long. Only a few minutes I suppose. It just seems a long time."

"Does it happen often?"

"Twice lately."

The doctor thought he'd better examine her. Eventually he left her room and came back with a bottle half full of pills. "Take these three times a day—don't forget, it's important. Long before they're finished I'll come and see you. I'm going to give you some injections that may help, but I'll have to send away for those."

As Miss Verney was gathering her things together before

leaving the surgery he asked in a casual voice: "Are you on the telephone?"

"No," said Miss Verney, "but I have an arrangement with some people."

"You told me. But those people are some way off, aren't they?"

"I'll get a telephone," said Miss Verney making up her mind. "I'll see about it at once."

"Good. You won't be so lonely."

"I suppose not."

"Don't go moving the furniture about, will you? Don't lift heavy weights. Don't . . . " ("Oh Lord," she thought, "is he going to say 'Don't drink!'—because that's impossible!") . . . "Don't worry," he said.

When Miss Verney left his surgery she felt relieved but tired and she walked very slowly home. It was quite a long walk for she lived in the less prosperous part of the village, near the row of council houses. She had never minded that. She was protected by tall thick hedges and a tree or two. Of course it had taken her some time to get used to the children's loud shrieking and the women who stood outside their doors to gossip. At first they stared at her with curiosity and some disapproval, she couldn't help feeling, but they'd soon found out that she was harmless.

The child Deena, however, was a very different matter.

Most of the village boys were called Jack, Willie, Stan and so on—the girls' first names were more elaborate. Deena's mother had gone one better than anyone else and christened her daughter Undine.

Deena—as everyone called her—was a tall plump girl of about twelve with a pretty, healthy but rather bovine face. She never joined the shrieking games, she never played football with dustbin lids. She apparently spent all her spare time standing at the gate of her mother's house silently, unsmilingly, staring at everyone who passed.

Miss Verney had long ago given up trying to be friendly. So

much did the child's cynical eyes depress her that she would cross over the road to avoid her, and sometimes was guilty of the cowardice of making sure Deena wasn't there before setting out.

Now she looked anxiously along the street and was relieved that it was empty. "Of course," she told herself, "it's getting cold. When winter comes they'll all stay indoors."

Not that Deena seemed to mind cold. Only a few days ago, looking out of the window, Miss Verney had seen her standing outside—oblivious of the bitter wind—staring at the front door as though, if she looked hard enough, she could see through the wood and find out what went on in the silent house—what Miss Verney did with herself all day.

ONE MORNING soon after her visit to the doctor Miss Verney woke feeling very well and very happy. Also she was not at all certain where she was. She lay luxuriating in the feeling of renewed youth, renewed health, and slowly recognized the various pieces of furniture.

"Of course," she thought when she drew the curtains. "What a funny place to end up in."

The sky was pale blue. There was no wind. Watching the still trees she sang softly to herself: "The day of days." She had always sung "The day of days" on her birthday. Poised between two years—last year, next year—she never felt any age at all. Birthdays were a pause, a rest.

In the midst of slow dressing she remembered the rat for the first time. But that seemed something that had happened long ago. "Thank God I didn't tell anybody else how frightened I was. As soon as they give me a telephone I'll ask Letty Baker to tea. She'll know exactly the sensible thing to do."

Out of habit she ate, swept and dusted but even more slowly than usual and with long pauses, when leaning on the handle of her tall, old-fashioned, carpet sweeper she stared out at the trees. "Goodbye summer. Goodbye goodbye," she hummed.

But in spite of sad songs she never lost the certainty of health, of youth.

All at once she noticed, to her surprise, that it was getting dark. "And I haven't emptied the dustbin."

She got to the shed carrying the small yellow pail and saw that the big dustbin wasn't there. For once Mrs. Randolph must have slipped up and left it outside the gate. Indeed it was so.

She first brought in the lid, easy, then turned the heavy bin onto its side and kicked it along. But this was slow. Growing impatient, she picked it up, carried it into the shed and looked for the stones that had defeated the dog, the rat. They too were missing and she realized that Mrs. Randolph, a hefty young woman in a hurry, must have taken out the bin, stones and all. They would be in the road where the dustmen had thrown them. She went to look and there they were.

She picked up the first stone and, astonished at its weight, immediately dropped it. But lifted it again and staggered to the shed, then leaned breathless against the cold wall. After a few minutes she breathed more easily, was less exhausted, and the determination to prove to herself that she was quite well again drove her into the road to pick up the second stone.

After a few steps she felt that she had been walking for a long time, for years, weighed down by an impossible weight, and now her strength was gone and she couldn't any more. Still, she reached the shed, dropped the stone and said: "That's all now, that's the lot. Only the yellow plastic pail to tackle." She'd fix the stones tomorrow. The yellow pail was light, full of paper, eggshells, stale bread. Miss Verney lifted it. . . .

SHE WAS SITTING on the ground with her back against the dustbin and her legs stretched out, surrounded by torn paper and eggshells. Her skirt had ridden up and there was a slice of stale bread on her bare knee. She felt very cold and it was nearly dark.

"What happened," she thought, "did I faint or something? I

must go back to the house."

She tried to get up but it was as if she were glued to the ground. "Wait," she thought. "Don't panic. Breathe deeply. Relax." But when she tried again she was lead. "This has happened before. I'll be all right soon," she told herself. But darkness was coming on very quickly.

Some women passed on the road and she called to them. At first: "Could you please . . . I'm so sorry to trouble you . . . " but the wind had got up and was blowing against her and no one heard. "Help!" she called. Still no one heard.

Tightly buttoned up, carrying string bags, heads in headscarves, they passed and the road was empty.

With her back against the dustbin, shivering with cold she prayed: "God, don't leave me here. Dear God, let someone come. Let someone come!"

When she opened her eyes she was not at all surprised to see a figure leaning on her gate.

"Deena! Deena!" she called, trying to keep the hysterical relief out of her voice.

Deena advanced cautiously, stood a few yards off and contemplated Miss Verney lying near the dustbin with an expressionless face.

"Listen Deena," said Miss Verney. "I'm afraid I'm not very well. Will you please ask your mother—your mum—to telephone to the doctor. He'll come I think. And if only she could help me back into the house. I'm very cold. . . . "

Deena said: "It's no good my asking mum. She doesn't like you and she doesn't want to have anything to do with you. She hates stuck up people. Everybody knows that you shut yourself up to get drunk. People can hear you falling about. 'She ought to take more water with it,' my mum says. Sleep it off, lady," said this horrible child, skipping away.

Miss Verney didn't try to call her back or argue. She knew that it was useless. A numb weak feeling slowly took possession of her. Stronger than cold. Stronger than fear. It was a great unwillingness to do anything more at all—it was almost resignation. Even if someone else came, would she call again for help. Could she? Fighting the cold numbness she made a last tremendous effort to move, at any rate to jerk the bread off her knee, for now her fear of the rat, forgotten all day, began to torment her.

It was impossible.

She strained her eyes to see into the corner where it would certainly appear—the corner with the old chair and carpet, the corner with the bundle of hay. Would it attack at once or would it wait until it was sure that she couldn't move? Sooner or later it would come. So Miss Verney waited in the darkness for the Super Rat.

IT WAS THE POSTMAN who found her. He had a parcel of books for her and he left them as usual in the passage. But he couldn't help noticing that all the lights were on and all the doors open. Miss Verney was certainly not in the cottage.

"I suppose she's gone out. But so early and such a cold morning?"

Uneasy, he looked back at the gate and saw the bundle of clothes near the shed.

He managed to lift her and got her into the kitchen armchair. There was an open bottle of whisky on the table and he tried to force her to drink some, but her teeth were tightly clenched and the whisky spilled all over her face.

He remembered that there was a telephone in the house where he was to deliver next. He must hurry.

In less time than you'd think, considering it was a remote village, the doctor appeared and shortly afterwards the ambulance.

Miss Verney died that evening in the nearest hospital without recovering consciousness. The doctor said she died of shock and cold. He was treating her for a heart condition, he said.

"Very widespread now—a heart condition."

WALLACE E. KNIGHT

The Resurrection
Man

ALVA MASON once had an opportunity to go to work in Indianapolis, but he turned the offer down after he looked at a map and saw the lines that reached from town to town. They were straight, or almost so; there was no interference from nature.

"I could have gone with the biggest rope dealer in Indianapolis," he said. "They said, Come on, Alvie, use your thick head, and I told them that if Warren Gamaliel Harding himself said, Come on, Alvie, take the job and sell rope, I'd tell him, No Sir."

Man needs something ungiving behind him to back him up. That's what Alva Mason thought, and it was an idea he lived with even though he compromised with it. He worked for a wholesale hardware dealer in a town on the Ohio for forty years, living most of the time in an apartment over a grocery store. It was all right for him and Kate; the porch along the side was cool, and there was a place out back for a garden. It was enough to know that only twenty miles away was an unassailable mountain that he could get to if he ever needed to, and he could put his back up against it.

You know how time passes. They quit using wagons and bought trucks. Alva went to the bank one morning for Mr. Pemberton and it was closed; the cashier stood on the roof and shouted down to the crowd that he'd remember every damn soul who didn't trust him. On September 1, 1939, Alva was inventorying bolts, and on Pearl Harbor Day he had come in to watch a boy load copper wire for the mines. He heard on the radio, a plastic Zenith. And Kate died during the big December snow of 1950, when there were only two ruts on River Street.

When Alva retired, the Pemberton boy had said, "Alvie, what are you going to do out there all by yourself?"

"Well," he had said, "I'm going to take it easy." And that's what Alva Mason did, in his covert way, on his eighty-five acres against Ten Pole Mountain, beginning in 1957.

He had a two-room rough-cut house, stained deep brown. The well, good most of the time, was hand-dug, and when it went dry, there was still a spring. Every week or so he'd walk out and get coffee, bacon, cigars, and candy, and on check weeks he'd buy a newspaper and kerosene.

Please keep in mind that Alva Mason was not alone or without friends; he never missed the Labor Day party for retirees, and whenever one of the Bingham kids from down the creek came by, Alva talked to him until he left. Once or twice the Hatchers—from the store—came out to go hunting, and Alva led them right up to the deer and pointed.

There aren't many people who understand a frontier. Days come and brighten and glow and fade, and there is a loose rattle of limbs or the soft brushing of milkweed to listen to, as the season offers. Nothing much happens if you don't let small things bother you, and that's enough.

All at once Alva Mason was very old, a lean greasy man with white hair, white beard, a black ulcer growing beside his nose, and days passing in front of him with such ease that he hardly noticed.

He talked to himself. He used the battery radio only in the

evening to get the news, which he'd grumble about, shaking his head. He wasn't really surprised or even concerned about the things he heard—after all, he knew people and he knew the world. He'd shake his head because that's what people do when they hear about plane crashes, wars, and floods.

He ate a lot of oatmeal and applesauce and greens.

He'd sing sometimes, until it bothered him to hear his own old voice quaver and the tune wander away.

All in all he was unconcerned with time and change and the seasons, as he liked the things he saw on Ten Pole Mountain and was ready for as much of it as he could get, if it came with sense and good health.

"The only thing I worry about," Alva once told Audrill Bingham, "is that maybe I'll get to be a bother to somebody. I'd rather be dead than trouble."

"Alvie," said Audrill, "you know you're welcome as beans at our place. You can come live in our back bedroom any day in the world, long as you want. You know I'll look up the hollow for you; you get the poorlies and I'm carrying you out of here and keeping you long as you want."

Alva appreciated it and said so, but he wasn't going to get sick on anybody, he vowed. He knew he had the capacity to die when he had to, right off, without clawing for time.

"Thank you, Audrill," he said. "I'll be no trouble to you, though."

To assure this, Alva went to work in the spring, before the dogwood was out, even though he felt fine.

He borrowed a post-hole digger at Anderson's store, carried it home, and dug a hole just below the slipbank, where the hill was almost perpendicular. He made it nearly two feet in diameter and eight feet deep—a terrible labor that took him a week and hurt cruelly. Four feet he dug in two days, but then he had to lie on his stomach by the hole, thrusting the digger down, catching dirt, compacting it, pulling the tool up with breathless care, dumping it. His heart pounded powerfully with each repeating of the process, and often he'd lose loose dirt back down the hole. He'd get five scoops and rest, five more and rest, feeling the earth's dampness, desperate to finish and finally be done, down to eight feet on a two-by-four he'd marked off and kept beside him.

Alva rested a week and figured what to do next.

He took a day and tamped the hole until its walls were firm and the bottom was flat and solid. It was a good place, all right, dirt all the way, left there in the hollow a speck at a time over eons, soil laced with sandstone above it in the bank, often moist but never muddy. When he had finished he covered the hole with a plywood sheet so nothing would fall in.

He took his time. He was busy for a while spading the garden plot and planting tomatoes and half-runners, and June had come before he got back to the next steps.

On the bank above the hole he rigged a length of chicken wire, and lined the wire with three layers of painters' drop cloths that had been neatly folded in the shed for years. He tied the ends with heavy rope to saplings up the hill, so that the wire and canvas hung like a hammock against the bank. Then he shoveled all the loose dirt from the hole into the hammock until it curved heavily down, and he carried rocks and added them, and wheeled in more dirt, until finally there was a pendulous burden above the plywood cover that swelled threateningly. There were tons, leaning against the hill, held back from Alva's pit gently and precariously. He made it neat, raking away unsightly clods, and planted rye grass on it.

In the evenings, before he went to bed, Alva would walk out and inspect his handiwork. At several points he drove stakes into the bank, just below the wire netting, which settled gently and rested there as the days passed.

He went to Pemberton's one morning, riding into town with the mailman, and waited until just a couple of the fellows were in the store.

"Alvie, Alvie," said Boob Camper, "Alvie, I haven't seen you in years. Lord God, Alvie, you're looking good."

Herb Hatcher came over from the dark corner behind the revolving nail bin. "Thought you was dead, Alvie," he said, grinning. "Old Boob took up a collection, anyway. You get your flowers, Alvie?"

It took time to get rid of Herbie, but finally just the two of them were there, across the counter, Boob and Alva.

"I want a whole bunch of things, Boob," Alva said hesitantly. "I'm going to clear out a place, and I need some batteries for a bell, and damned if I don't have to have a clock, too." He got out a list.

Six sticks of dynamite, three blasting caps, fine copper wire, a brush hook, two dry-cell batteries, alarm clock, screen-door spring, whetstone.

Boob became serious. "Now, Alvie, that's a young man's list," he said. "You can't carry all that, much less use it. You'll break your fool back."

"I got a boy to help me," Alva answered, just as he had prepared to answer. "We're going to blow out three stumps so I won't have to climb around them anymore. I'm getting so I want things easy."

So Boob got everything together happily, glad to help out, gave Alva a twenty percent discount, gave him a cold root beer out of the dispenser, and carried the stuff over to the newspaper office so that Alva could ride back with the routeman when the first edition was out.

"You're a kind man, Boob. You come by and I'll make you some corn bread."

"I'll do that, Alvie. I'll hold you to that. I'll even carry old Pemberton out and let him watch me eat."

Odd, thought Alva, how young Pemberton had become old Pemberton. He couldn't be over fifty.

He carried the packages from the road all the way up the hollow and up the hill in one trip, fearful to leave anything behind. When he had put everything away he went to bed and slept until the next morning was half gone.

Plans that are carefully made needn't be hurried. Alva didn't feel that he had to hurry, although he watched the black place on his cheek grow and felt around it gingerly, and felt his chest analytically when his heart pounded, and noted precisely how his knees pained when he walked up-hill. And so he laid his garden by, and laid in food and wood and kerosene for the winter, shot rabbits from the front porch, and at Christmas drank half a bottle of old wine.

One weekend when snow was on the ground he got out the things from the store—everything but the brush hook and spring, which he really hadn't needed—and made the exploder.

What else would you call it? Its function was to explode.

He took a board and tacked the feet of the new alarm clock onto it. He taped three sticks of dynamite to the other end of the board, which was only about two feet long, and then between the clock and dynamite pounded in two circles of finishing nails. He measured the circles with the base of a dry-cell battery; the nails made cradles in which the batteries could stand, side by side.

Alva frowned. He should have taken the glass off the clock-face first. He broke it with a tack hammer and tested the hands. Everything was fine. He swept up.

Finally he arranged the copper wire, and as he did this he found himself wary and expectant. Once he was sure he heard something outside, but of course there was nothing—just the snow, unmarked except by birds and rabbits and the smoothing of the wind.

He linked the batteries, and led one wire to the dynamite and let its loose end dangle where the blasting cap would be. He took another strand and twisted it twice around the hour hand of the clock. His touch was delicate. He measured and left some to spare; the wire extended from the dynamite to the clock hand and then off, pointing with the hand, into space. He took a final strand, hooked it to a battery terminal, and let it reach out, feeling. Then he tested and twisted and balanced and presently was sure that at four o'clock, on that day when it was needed, the ex-

ploder would be rigged right, so that the hand's descending wire
would touch the waiting, reaching battery wire and the circuit
would be complete and a shock could fly across the clock and to
the dynamite, an instant destructive surge. He tested the exploder again and again, with pride, and then put it away, with
the caps and extra dynamite, in the warm cabinet by the fireplace.

By God, thought Alva Mason, if I don't lose my mind or get
so sick I can't crawl, I've done it. I've taken care of myself and
nobody can say he had to take me off my mountain and take care
of me!

That night he went out and looked up at the mountain,
through the spiny hardwood black on snow toward the places
where the rock outcropped and the sky met it. It was bitter and
he didn't stay out long, but he felt exuberance. This is a marvelous place to die, beyond all the lights of towns and people's
fencerows, out where I can face directly whatever there is to
face, and tip my hat and disappear with nobody calling after me.

He shivered and went inside, and as he closed the door and
stuffed a rug up against the crack and turned the lamp down he
thought about how he had buried Kate in town and he was
sorry.

The long wait bothered him this year. He got out to the town
only once in February and twice in March. Instead of doing
things in the afternoons he found himself dozing, occasionally
until the fire went out. He'd wake up cold and eat something out
of a can and go to bed. He hadn't remembered being afraid until
one black night two dogs came barking insistently onto the
porch, and somehow this terrified him; it was as if he were a
child again, dogs of unimaginable fierceness were at the door,
scraping and nosing at it, and no one could drive them away.
He wept, and then wondered at it.

He went without shaving until the place by his nose, spreading across his cheek, was half hidden, but from it he could now
feel tense lines of pain. He found new hurtings in his side and

under one arm. It was a winter full of things he had never known before. Spring would not start.

Finally, though, the rains began, and presently May arrived, swelling and loud.

Alva began to watch each morning carefully. This is the month, he told himself; I'm almost sure this is the month.

But May passed, and a week of June. It rained one afternoon when Alva was out in the garden. He kept hoeing until the earth was slick and sticky, and then he got down and pulled weeds from the beet rows. When he went inside he was soaked and coughing, and he sat down, wet, and coughed and cried. He ached all the way through his body. His cheek burned deep; he could feel the shape of his face from the pain. He pulled a blanket over himself and slept.

Good morning, God; this is the big day!

But nobody says that. This is the day I breathe through vomitus until I can't; this is the day my mouth flops open and hangs open, and my eyes open and glaze. It's time for the lake of sputum inside me to hold me under, for my heart to spit and sputter, for my bowels to spit and sputter, for hope to shut down, for ice to take my hands and feet and freeze me until I freeze all over.

Alva got up slowly and went to the cabinet and got out the board and the rest that went with it—clock, dynamite, wire, blasting caps, batteries. He gouged into one of the dynamite sticks with an ice pick until he could force the cap into it. Then he carried the things out, the whole kit, to the hole he had dug, and sat down under the bulging net that hung above the hole and hooked the exploder up, exactly, until each part was ready, and the hour hand was armed with its pointing, gently bobbing wire. The clock was at ten, he wound it. At four its hand would reach over and close the circuit, wire to wire, set the dynamite off, sunder the screen and canvas hammock and shatter the whole impending rig so that tons of earth and stone would fall, perhaps setting off a larger slide but even so, obliterating the hammock, the hole, and Alva in it dead. Alva had until four o'clock to die.

I'll set my mind to it and go fast, he said, and get this pain done. I'm tired.

He took a long look around, checking off last things.

He sighed. I ought to close up, he told himself, and so he arose and walked slowly to the house. He was ready to pull the door shut and a new thought came, and then another. Damn it, he said.

Now he had to go inside and poke through the cupboard until he found a pencil and cardboard and the old candy jar with the glass top. He tore a piece of cardboard and wrote on it: "These are the remains of Alva G. Mason. I died of old age. Very truly yours, Alva G. Mason." He put the note inside the jar and pushed the top down hard. Then, on what was left of the cardboard, he printed carefully—"Gone for a while."

The door, when he shut it, latched satisfyingly. Alva hooked his farewell on a nailhead where the wind couldn't reach it and then walked slowly back to the hole, carrying the candy jar.

I don't know why I didn't think of these things before.

I'm not going to do anything else.

He pushed back the plywood cover and let his legs dangle in the hole for a moment. He looked far down the valley and then up the hill and then at the clock on its board nestled under the hammock of earth and then back at the sky and pushed forward. He slid and skidded and fell.

Surprisingly, there was time to think about falling. Alva realized how his legs were bent and how the candy jar fell with him, from his lap; his arms were flailing awkwardly, and then he tipped until his forehead touched dirt and scraped and burned. Then he hit bottom, jammed down in a gasping, fearful heap, and he was crying.

He waited. He shut his eyes and let one shoulder into the dirt, propping so that his legs could be tested. He did this very slowly, sobbing, tears smearing his face. Then, sternly, he became analytical, checking one leg and then the other, his arms, his scratched forehead, even the scalding wetness of his ulcerated cheek. Beneath him he noted the candy jar, unbroken.

I'm all right, Alva Mason gasped. He felt triumph. Made it!

Then, in the damp, one minute, two, three minutes in the grave, the old pains came back and terrible tiredness; Alva realized once more that he had come to die. He went to work on it.

First, I'll pray some. He prayed, mentioning Kate and the hope of seeing her soon, and suggesting that someone be sent to get the tomatoes before the weeds choked them.

Now I'll slow myself down. He did this by breathing slower and slower and shallower, until he felt that his lungs were no longer functioning. He found this helped quiet his heart, too; the pounding slowed to a weak plodding.

But how my legs hurt! They were bent and there was no way to ease them, no stretching or relaxing. Alva pushed his elbows out and tried to let them bear his weight. No respite came.

Death, come here and lay me down to sleep. Stop my thinking. Make my blood be still.

After a while Alva Mason dozed, and he dreamed about crawling into the niche at the back of the springhouse while his father called and called for him. He was small and angry and bitter, as he had just been whipped for leaving the chicken house door ajar all night, and he wouldn't answer. Father drew closer and Alva crouched further back in the corner behind the milk cans, and their wetness covered him. He bent into an angry ball, expecting to be found and ready to leap out and run off ahead of Father, who now was worried and apologetic. He heard Alvie! Alvie! Alvie! and the sound of his name was hateful. He wanted to die in the springhouse and let his father find his body there, cold and wet and undefeated.

Then he woke up, and immediately he was aware that he was alive and old and the voice of his father was a phantom unheard in half a century.

Well, said Alva, damn it to hell, what am I going to do now?

He began an inventory of things and parts. Legs, painful. Heart, beating away. Arms, OK now that I've undoubled them. Head, scraped but that's all. Guts—hungry.

That's awful, Alva moaned. I didn't ever expect to get hungry.

He waited as long as he could, and then he had to admit it. I'm just not going to die yet. He moaned again.

Would you look at that. I'm buried and I'm not going to die. Got my tombstone in a candy jar and my dust in a hole in the ground and I'm hungry. Oh, damn it.

He looked up and reached up and his fingers touched the rim of the hole he'd dug, but he couldn't touch grass. He stretched, but he couldn't bend his fingers and get a grip. Above he saw the sky divided; half was blue, and half was darkened by the sagging hammock of dirt he'd built, and the arc of sunlight reaching down the hole was shallow. The sun was off toward the West. What time was it?

Alva, how long was I asleep? I don't know, Alva, have I been dead and buried and is this judgment time? No, hell no! I was asleep. How long? Perhaps an hour, maybe just a minute. Maybe it's getting on toward four o'clock.

God, said Alva, this is no way to take an old man. I wanted to die by myself. Don't scare me. No tricks. He said these things despairingly.

But there was nothing for him to do now except get out, and Alva began thinking about how he'd do it. This was new; he'd only planned dying.

First he tried to dig his toes into the side of the hole so that he could inch upward, but the earth was tamped and pounded and too firm. He could take only a half-step and then fall back; he did this over and over.

Then he stopped and thought, and systematically went through his pockets hoping he'd find his knife. He had a box of matches and a pencil, nothing more. He pulled his belt off, arduously, and tried to dig a toehold with the buckle. It was thin,

and after ten painful minutes he realized that he was not suc-
ceeding.

I am going to feel the weight of the explosion for only a second. Probably I'll never hear it. I'll get squashed down, and the
earth will fall. Any second. He felt like crying again, but didn't.

Underfoot Alva felt the candy jar, square and hard; it was between his heels, and he had been stepping around it. It was like
a rock; a rock against dirt.

Bending his head forward, pulling back his body, Alva could
see it, and tentatively he pushed at the jar with one foot. He
turned it with a toe so that it was upright on the floor of the hole
and then he brought down his heel on the lid, as hard as he was
able, grunting, forcing the beveled lid tighter into the jar. He
stomped and stomped again, and on the third time the glass
shattered. Alva stood with broken glass around his feet.

Now he bent as far as he could, thrusting one hand down between his knees into the narrowness of the hole, straining
against its sides, feeling, and two fingers found a shard of glass
and seized it. He gripped tight and pulled up and it cut his fingertips, but now he had it, and it was a large, heavy, marvelously
sharp piece, a glass tool that could cut rapidly and easily.

Alva dug a groove for one foot, and above it a second one, and
then a third. He cut steps, and when he had made four he
pushed the raw glass into the earth in front of him so that it
couldn't fall back. Then, cautiously, he stepped and slid upward, pushing his back against dirt, prying and grunting until
his head and then his arms and then half of him to the waist
were above ground. He flopped onto the grass, puffing, and
pushed on until he knew he would not fall back.

The sun was hot. Alva felt its strength. It gave him strength.

He crawled and then was free of the hole, an old dirt-streaked
porcupine bleeding, heaving, a bony old man with tear stains
going down into his beard. He looked at the clock. It was almost
two.

Alva rolled onto his back and for a long time he looked, and his mind said nothing. The world was silent and motionless and without glare or luster, and only the clock minutes descending, time disappearing.

But he heard a bird, and black ants began climbing on his hand, running frantically between his fingers, and he heard the flat mechanical ticking of the clock, and he had to get up. After he had done this and his sore hands were moving easily again, Alva carefully pushed the wires of the exploder apart and eased the cap from the dynamite. He kept the kit intact and carried it, like a tray, back to the house.

I'm going to get sick if I don't eat something. I'll make some soup and then I'll wash up good and go to bed.

From the end of the porch he looked up toward the top of Ten Pole Mountain.

I don't think I could have had a better place to live, said Alva Mason, if I had searched all over the world. This place is going to be here forever.

Now he felt pretty good.

Mr. Arcularis

M R. ARCULARIS stood at the window of his room in the hospital and looked down at the street. There had been a light shower, which had patterned the sidewalks with large drops, but now again the sun was out, blue sky was showing here and there between the swift white clouds, a cold wind was blowing the poplar trees. An itinerant band had stopped before the building and was playing, with violin, harp, and flute, the finale of "Cavalleria Rusticana." Leaning against the window-sill—for he felt extraordinarily weak after his operation—Mr. Arcularis suddenly, listening to the wretched music, felt like crying. He rested the palm of one hand against a cold window-pane and stared down at the old man who was blowing the flute, and blinked his eyes. It seemed absurd that he should be so weak, so emotional, so like a child—and especially now that everything was over at last. In spite of all their predictions, in spite, too, of his own dreadful certainty that he was going to die, here he was, as fit as a fiddle—but what a fiddle it was, so out of tune!—with a long life before him. And to begin with, a voyage to England ordered by the doctor. What could be more delightful? Why should he feel sad about it and want to cry like a baby?

In a few minutes Harry would arrive with his car to take him to the wharf; in an hour he would be on the sea, in two hours he would see the sunset behind him, where Boston had been, and his new life would be opening before him. It was many years since he had been abroad. June, the best of the year to come—England, France, the Rhine—how ridiculous that he should already be homesick!

There was a light footstep outside the door, a knock, the door opened, and Harry came in.

"Well, old man, I've come to get you. The old bus actually got here. Are you ready? Here, let me take your arm. You're tottering like an octogenarian!"

Mr. Arcularis submitted gratefully, laughing, and they made the journey slowly along the bleak corridor and down the stairs to the entrance hall. Miss Hoyle, his nurse, was there, and the Matron, and the charming little assistant with freckles who had helped to prepare him for the operation. Miss Hoyle put out her hand.

"Goodbye, Mr. Arcularis," she said, "and *bon voyage.*"

"Goodbye, Miss Hoyle, and thank you for everything. You were very kind to me. And I fear I was a nuisance."

The girl with the freckles, too, gave him her hand, smiling. She was very pretty, and it would have been easy to fall in love with her. She reminded him of someone. Who was it? He tried in vain to remember while he said goodbye to her and turned to the Matron.

"And not too many latitudes with the young ladies, Mr. Arcularis!" she was saying.

Mr. Arcularis was pleased, flattered, by all this attention to a middle-aged invalid, and felt a joke taking shape in his mind, and no sooner in his mind than on his tongue.

"Oh, no latitudes," he said, laughing. "I'll leave the latitudes to the ship!"

"Oh, come now," said the Matron, "we don't seem to have hurt him much, do we?"

"I think we'll have to operate on him again and *really* cure him," said Miss Hoyle.

He was going down the front steps, between the potted palmettos, and they all laughed and waved. The wind was cold, very cold for June, and he was glad he had put on his coat. He shivered.

"Damned cold for June!" he said. "Why should it be so cold?"

"East wind," Harry said, arranging the rug over his knees. "Sorry it's an open car, but I believe in fresh air and all that sort of thing. I'll drive slowly. We've got plenty of time."

They coasted gently down the long hill toward Beacon Street, but the road was badly surfaced, and despite Harry's care Mr. Arcularis felt his pain again. He found that he could alleviate it a little by leaning to the right, against the arm-rest, and not breathing too deeply. But how glorious to be out again! How strange and vivid the world looked! The trees had innumerable green fresh leaves—they were all blowing and shifting and turning and flashing in the wind; drops of rainwater fell downward sparkling; the robins were singing their absurd, delicious little four-noted songs; even the street cars looked unusually bright and beautiful, just as they used to look when he was a child and had wanted above all things to be a motorman. He found himself smiling foolishly at everything, foolishly and weakly, and wanted to say something about it to Harry. It was no use, though—he had no strength, and the mere finding of words would be almost more than he could manage. And even if he should succeed in saying it, he would then most likely burst into tears. He shook his head slowly from side to side.

"Ain't it grand?" he said.

"I'll bet it looks good," said Harry.

"Words fail me."

"You wait till you get out to sea. You'll have a swell time."

"Oh, swell! . . . I hope not. I hope it'll be calm."

"Tut tut."

When they passed the Harvard Club Mr. Arcularis made a slow and somewhat painful effort to turn in his seat and look at it. It might be the last chance to see it for a long time. Why this sentimental longing to stare at it, though? There it was, with the great flag blowing in the wind, the Harvard seal now concealed by the swift folds and now revealed, and there were the windows in the library, where he had spent so many delightful hours reading—Plato, and Kipling, and the Lord knows what—and the balconies from which for so many years he had watched the Marathon. Old Talbot might be in there now, sleeping with a book on his knee, hoping forlornly to be interrupted by anyone, for anything.

"Goodbye to the old club," he said.

"The bar will miss you," said Harry, smiling with friendly irony and looking straight ahead.

"But let there be no moaning," said Mr. Arcularis.

"What's *that* a quotation from?"

" 'The Odyssey.' "

In spite of the cold, he was glad of the wind on his face, for it helped to dissipate the feeling of vagueness and dizziness that came over him in a sickening wave from time to time. All of a sudden everything would begin to swim and dissolve, the houses would lean their heads together, he had to close his eyes, and there would be a curious and dreadful humming noise, which at regular intervals rose to a crescendo and then drawlingly subsided again. It was disconcerting. Perhaps he still had a trace of fever. When he got on the ship he would have a glass of whisky. . . . From one of these spells he opened his eyes and found that they were on the ferry, crossing to East Boston. It must have been the ferry's engines that he had heard. From another spell he woke to find himself on the wharf, the car at a standstill beside a pile of yellow packing cases.

"We're here because we're here because we're here," said Harry.

"Because we're here," added Mr. Arcularis.

He dozed in the car while Harry—and what a good friend Harry was!—attended to all the details. He went and came with tickets and passports and baggage checks and porters. And at last he unwrapped Mr. Arcularis from the rugs and led him up the steep gangplank to the deck, and thence by devious windings to a small cold stateroom with the solitary porthole like the eye of a Cyclops.

"Here you are," he said, "and now I've got to go. Did you hear the whistle?"

"No."

"Well, you're half asleep. It's sounded the all-ashore. Goodbye, old fellow, and take care of yourself. Bring me back a spray of edelweiss. And send me a picture postcard from the Absolute."

"Will you have it finite or infinite?"

"Oh, infinite. But with your signature on it. Now you'd better turn in for a while and have a nap. Cheerio!"

Mr. Arcularis took his hand and pressed it hard, and once more felt like crying. Absurd! Had he become a child again?

"Goodbye," he said.

He sat down in the little wicker chair, with his overcoat still on, closed his eyes, and listened to the humming of the air in the ventilator. Hurried footsteps ran up and down the corridor. The chair was not too comfortable, and his pain began to bother him again, so he moved, with his coat still on, to the narrow berth and fell asleep. When he woke up, it was dark, and the porthole had been partly opened. He groped for the switch and turned on the light. Then he rang for the steward.

"It's cold in here," he said. "Would you mind closing the port?"

THE GIRL who sat opposite him at dinner was charming. Who was it she reminded him of? Why, of course, the girl at the hospital, the girl with the freckles. Her hair was beautiful, not quite red, not quite gold, nor had it been bobbed; arranged with a sort of graceful untidiness, it made him think of a Melozzo da Forli angel. Her face was freckled, she had a mouth which was both humorous and voluptuous. And she seemed to be alone.

He frowned at the bill of fare and ordered the thick soup.

"No hors d'oeuvres?" asked the steward.

"I think not," said Mr. Arcularis. "They might kill me."

The steward permitted himself to be amused and deposited the menu card on the table against the water bottle. His eyebrows were lifted. As he moved away, the girl followed him with her eyes and smiled.

"I'm afraid you shocked him," she said.

"Impossible," said Mr. Arcularis. "These stewards, they're dead souls. How could they be stewards otherwise? And they think they've seen and known everything. They suffer terribly from the *déjà vu*. Personally, I don't blame them."

"It must be a dreadful sort of life."

"It's because they're dead that they accept it."

"Do you think so?"

"I'm sure of it. I'm enough of a dead soul myself to know the signs!"

"Well, I don't know what you mean by that!"

"But nothing mysterious! I'm just out of hospital, after an operation. I was given up for dead. For six months I had given *myself* up for dead. If you've ever been seriously ill you know the feeling. You have a posthumous feeling—a mild, cynical tolerance for everything and everyone. What is there you haven't seen or done or understood? Nothing."

Mr. Arcularis waved his hands and smiled.

"I wish I could understand you," said the girl, "but I've never been ill in my life."

"Never?"

"Never."

"Good God!"

The torrent of the unexpressed and inexpressible paralyzed him and rendered him speechless. He stared at the girl, wondering who she was and then, realizing that he had perhaps stared too fixedly, averted his gaze, gave a little laugh, rolled a pill of bread between his fingers. After a second or two he allowed himself to look at her again and found her smiling.

"Never pay any attention to invalids," he said, "or they'll drag you to the hospital."

She examined him critically, with her head tilted a little to one side, but with friendliness.

"You don't *look* like an invalid," she said.

Mr. Arcularis thought her charming. His pain ceased to bother him, the disagreeable humming disappeared, or rather, it was dissociated from himself and became merely, as it should be, the sound of the ship's engines, and he began to think the voyage was going to be really delightful. The parson on his right passed him the salt.

"I fear you will need this in your soup," he said.

"Thank you. Is it as bad as that?"

The steward, overhearing, was immediately apologetic and solicitous. He explained that on the first day everything was at sixes and sevens. The girl looked up at him and asked him a question.

"Do you think we'll have a good voyage?" she said.

He was passing the hot rolls to the parson, removing the napkins from them with a deprecatory finger.

"Well, madam, I don't like to be a Jeremiah, but—"

"Oh, come," said the parson, "I hope we have no Jeremiahs."

"What do you mean?" said the girl.

Mr. Arcularis ate his soup with gusto—it was nice and hot.

"Well, maybe I shouldn't say it, but there's a corpse on board, going to Ireland; and I never yet knew a voyage with a corpse on board that we didn't have bad weather."

"Why, steward, you're just superstitious! What nonsense!"

"That's a very ancient superstition," said Mr. Arcularis. "I've heard it many times. Maybe it's true. Maybe we'll be wrecked. And what does it matter, after all?" He was very bland.

"Then let's be wrecked," said the parson coldly.

Nevertheless, Mr. Arcularis felt a shudder go through him on hearing the steward's remark. A corpse in the hold—a coffin? Perhaps it was true. Perhaps some disaster would befall them. There might be fogs. There might be icebergs. He thought of all the wrecks of which he had read. There was the *Titanic,* which he had read about in the warm newspaper room at the Harvard Club—it had seemed dreadfully real, even there. That band, playing "Nearer My God to Thee" on the after-deck while the ship sank! It was one of the darkest of his memories. And the *Empress of Ireland*—all those poor people trapped in the smoking room, with only one door between them and life, and that door locked for the night by the deck steward, and the deck steward nowhere to be found! He shivered, feeling a draft, and turned to the parson.

"How do these strange delusions arise?" he said.

The parson looked at him searchingly, appraisingly—from chin to forehead, from forehead to chin—and Mr. Arcularis, feeling uncomfortable, straightened his tie.

"From nothing but fear," said the parson. "Nothing on earth but fear."

"How strange!' said the girl.

Mr. Arcularis again looked at her—she had lowered her face—and again tried to think of whom she reminded him. It wasn't only the little freckle-faced girl at the hospital—both of them had reminded him of someone else. Someone far back in his life: remote, beautiful, lovely. But he couldn't think. The meal came to an end, they all rose, the ship's orchestra played a feeble fox-trot, and Mr. Arcularis, once more alone, went to the bar to have his whisky. The room was stuffy, and the ship's engines were both audible and palpable. The humming and throbbing oppressed him, the rhythm seemed to be the rhythm of his own pain, and after a short time he found his way, with slow steps, holding on to the walls in his moments of weakness and dizziness, to his forlorn and white little room. The port had been—thank God!—closed for the night; it was cold enough anyway. The white and blue ribbons fluttered from the ventilator, the bottle and glasses clicked and clucked as the ship swayed gently to the long, slow motion of the sea. It was all very peculiar—it was all like something he had experienced somewhere before. What was it? Where was it? . . . He untied his tie, looking at his face in the glass, and wondered, and from time to time put his hand to his side to hold in the pain. It wasn't at Portsmouth, in his childhood, nor at Salem, nor in the rose garden at his Aunt Julia's, nor in the schoolroom at Cambridge. It was something very queer, very intimate, very precious. The jackstones, the Sunday-school cards which he had loved when he was a child. . . . He fell asleep.

THE SENSE OF TIME was already hopelessly confused. One hour was like another, the sea looked always the same, morning was indistinguishable from afternoon—and was it Tuesday or Wednesday? Mr. Arcularis was sitting in the smoking room, in his favorite corner, watching the parson teach Miss Dean to play chess. On the deck outside he could see the people passing and repassing in their restless round of the ship. The red jacket went by, then the black hat with the white feather, then the purple scarf, the brown tweed coat, the Bulgarian mustache, the monocle, the Scotch cap with fluttering ribbons, and in no time at all the red jacket again, dipping past the windows with its own peculiar rhythm, followed once more by the black hat and the purple scarf. How odd to reflect on the fixed little orbits of these things—as definite and profound, perhaps, as the orbits of the stars, and as important to God or the Absolute. There was a kind of tyranny in this fixedness, too—to think of it too much made one uncomfortable. He closed his eyes for a moment, to avoid seeing for the fortieth time the Bulgarian mustache and the pursuing monocle. The parson was explaining the movements of knights. Two forward and one to the side. Eight possible moves, always to the opposite color from that on which the piece stands. Two forward and one to the side: Miss Dean repeated the words several times with reflective emphasis. Here, too, was the terrifying fixed curve of the infinite, the creeping curve of logic which at last must become the final signpost at the edge of nothing. After that—the deluge. The great white light of annihilation. The bright flash of death. . . . Was it merely the sea which made these abstractions so insistent, so intrusive? The mere notion of *orbit* had somehow become extraordinarily naked; and to rid himself of the discomfort and also to forget a little the pain which bothered his side whenever he sat down, he walked slowly and carefully into the writing room, and examined a pile of superannuated magazines and catalogues of travel. The bright colors amused him, the photographs of remote islands and mountains, savages in sampans or sarongs or both—it was all very far off and delightful, like something in a dream or a fever. But he found that he was too tired to read and was incapable of concentration. Dreams! Yes, that reminded him. That rather alarming business—sleep-walking!

Later in the evening—at what hour he didn't know—he was telling Miss Dean about it, as he had intended to do. They were sitting in deck chairs on the sheltered side. The sea was black, and there was a cold wind. He wished they had chosen to sit in the lounge.

Miss Dean was extremely pretty—no, beautiful. She looked at him, too, in a very strange and lovely way, with something of inquiry, something of sympathy, something of affection. It seemed as if, between the question and the answer, they had sat thus for a very long time, exchanging an unspoken secret, simply looking at each other quietly and kindly. Had an hour or two passed? And was it at all necessary to speak?

"No," she said, "I never have."

She breathed into the low words a note of interrogation and gave him a slow smile.

"That's the funny part of it. I never had either until last night. Never in my life. I hardly ever even dream. And it really rather frightens me."

"Tell me about it, Mr. Arcularis."

"I dreamed at first that I was walking, alone, in a wide plain covered with snow. It was growing dark, I was very cold, my feet were frozen and numb, and I was lost. I came then to a signpost—at first it seemed to me there was nothing on it. Nothing but ice. Just before it grew finally dark, however, I made out on it the one word 'Polaris.' "

"The Pole Star."

"Yes—and you see, I didn't myself know that. I looked it up only this morning. I suppose I must have seen it somewhere? And of course it rhymes with my name."

"Why, so it does!"

"Anyway, it gave me—in the dream—an awful feeling of despair, and the dream changed. This time, I dreamed I was standing *outside* my stateroom in the little dark corridor, or *cul-de-sac*, and trying to find the door-handle to let myself in. I was in my pajamas, and again I was very cold. And at this point I woke up. . . . The extraordinary thing is that's exactly where I was!"

"Good heavens. How strange!"

"Yes. And now the question is, *Where had I been?* I was frightened, when I came to—not unnaturally. For among other things I *did* have, quite definitely, the feeling that I *had been* somewhere. Somewhere where it was very cold. It doesn't sound very proper. Suppose I had been seen!"

"That might have been awkward," said Miss Dean.

"Awkward! It might indeed. It's very singular. I've never done such a thing before. It's this sort of thing that reminds one—rather wholesomely, perhaps, don't you think?"—and

Mr. Arcularis gave a nervous little laugh—"how extraordinarily little we know about the workings of our own minds or souls. After all, what *do* we know?"

"Nothing—nothing—nothing—nothing," said Miss Dean slowly.

"*Absolutely* nothing."

Their voices had dropped, and again they were silent; and again they looked at each other gently and sympathetically, as if for the exchange of something unspoken and perhaps unspeakable. Time ceased. The orbit—so it seemed to Mr. Arcularis—once more became pure, became absolute. And once more he found himself wondering who it was that Miss Dean—Clarice Dean—reminded him of. Long ago and far away. Like those pictures of the islands and mountains. The little freckle-faced girl at the hospital was merely, as it were, the stepping stone, the signpost, or, as in algebra, the "equals" sign. But what was it they both "equaled"? The jackstones came again into his mind and his Aunt Julia's rose garden—at sunset; but this was ridiculous. It couldn't be simply that they reminded him of his childhood! And yet why not?

They went into the lounge. The ship's orchestra, in the oval-shaped balcony among faded palms, was playing the finale of "Cavalleria Rusticana," playing it badly.

"Good God!" said Mr. Arcularis, "can't I ever escape from that damned sentimental tune? It's the last thing I heard in America, and the last thing I *want* to hear."

"But don't you like it?"

"As music? No! It moves me too much, but in the wrong way."

"What, exactly, do you mean?"

"Exactly? Nothing. When I heard it at the hospital—when was it?—it made me feel like crying. Three old Italians tootling it in the rain. I suppose, like most people, I'm afraid of my feelings."

"Are they so dangerous?"

"Now then, young woman! Are you pulling my leg?"

The stewards had rolled away the carpets, and the passengers were beginning to dance. Miss Dean accepted the invitation of a young officer, and Mr. Arcularis watched them with envy. Odd, that last exchange of remarks—very odd; in fact, everything was odd. Was it possible that they were falling in love? Was that what it was all about—all these concealed references and recollections? He had read of such things. But at his age! And with a girl of twenty-two! It was ridiculous.

After an amused look at his old friend Polaris from the open door on the sheltered side, he went to bed.

The rhythm of the ship's engines was positively a persecution. It gave one no rest, it followed one like the Hound of Heaven, it drove on, out into space and across the Milky Way and then back home by way of Betelgeuse. It was cold there, too. Mr. Arcularis, making the round trip by way of Betelgeuse and Polaris, sparkled with frost. He felt like a Christmas tree. Icicles on his fingers and icicles on his toes. He tinkled and spangled in the void, hallooed to the waste echoes, rounded the buoy on the verge of the Unknown, and tacked glitteringly homeward. The wind whistled. He was barefooted. Snowflakes and tinsel blew past him. Next time, by George, he would go farther still—for altogether it was rather a lark. Forward into the untrodden! as somebody said. Some intrepid explorer of his own backyard, probably, some middle-aged professor with an umbrella: those were the fellows for courage! But give us time, thought Mr. Arcularis, give us time, and we will bring back with us the night-rime of the Obsolute. Or was it Absolete? If only there weren't this perpetual throbbing, this iteration of sound, like a pain, these circles and repetitions of light—the feeling as of everything coiling inward to a center of misery. . . .

Suddenly it was dark, and he was lost. He was groping, he touched the cold, white, slippery woodwork with his fingernails, looking for an electric switch. The throbbing, of course, was the throbbing of the ship. But he was almost home—almost home. Another corner to round, a door to be opened, and there he would be. Safe and sound. Safe in his father's home.

It was at this point that he woke up: in the corridor that led to the dining saloon. Such pure terror, such horror, seized him as he had never known. His heart felt as if it would stop beating. His back was toward the dining saloon; apparently he had just come from it. He was in his pajamas. The corridor was dim, all but two lights having been turned out for the night, and—thank God!—deserted. Not a soul, not a sound. He was perhaps fifty yards from his room. With luck he could get to it unseen. Holding tremulously to the rail that ran along the wall, a brown, greasy rail, he began to creep his way forward. He felt very weak, very dizzy, and his thoughts refused to concentrate. Vaguely he remembered Miss Dean—Clarice—and the freckled girl, as if they were one and the same person. But he wasn't in the hospital, he was on the ship. Of course. How absurd. The Great Circle. Here we are, old fellow . . . steady round the corner . . . hold hard to your umbrella. . . .

In his room, with the door safely shut behind him, Mr. Arcularis broke into a cold sweat. He had no sooner got into his bunk, shivering, than he heard the night watchman pass.

"But where"—he thought, closing his eyes in agony—"have I been? . . . "

A dreadful idea had occurred to him.

IT'S NOTHING SERIOUS—how could it be anything serious? Of course, it's nothing serious," said Mr. Arcularis.

"No, it's nothing serious," said the ship's doctor urbanely.

"I knew you'd think so. But just the same—"

"Such a condition is the result of worry," said the doctor. "Are you worried—do you mind telling me—about something? Just try to think."

"Worried?"

Mr. Arcularis knitted his brows. *Was* there something? Some little mosquito of a cloud disappearing into the southwest, the northeast? Some little gnat-song of despair? But no, that was all over. All over.

"Nothing," he said, "nothing whatever."

"It's very strange," said the doctor.

"Strange! I should say so. I've come to sea for a rest, not for a nightmare! What about a bromide?"

"Well, I can give you a bromide, Mr. Arcularis—"

"Then, please, if you don't mind, give me a bromide."

He carried the little phial hopefully to his stateroom, and took a dose at once. He could see the sun through his porthole. It looked northern and pale and small, like a little peppermint, which was only natural enough, for the latitude was changing with every hour. But why was it that doctors were all alike? And all, for that matter, like his father, or that other fellow at the hospital? Smythe, his name was. Doctor Smythe. A nice, dry little fellow, and they said he was a writer. Wrote poetry, or something like that. Poor fellow—disappointed. Like everybody else. Crouched in there, in his cabin, night after night, writing blank verse or something—all about the stars and flowers and love and death; ice and the sea and the infinite; time and tide—well, every man to his own taste.

"But it's nothing serious," said Arcularis, later, to the parson. "How could it be?"

"Why, of course not, my dear fellow," said the parson, patting his back. "How could it be?"

"I know it isn't and yet I worry about it."

"It would be ridiculous to think it serious," said the parson. Mr. Arcularis shivered; it was colder than ever. It was said that they were near icebergs. For a few hours in the morning there had been a fog, and the siren had blown—devastatingly—at three-minute intervals. Icebergs caused fog—he knew that.

"These things always come," said the parson, "from a sense of guilt. You feel guilty about something. I won't be so rude as to inquire what it is. But if you could rid yourself of the sense of guilt—"

And later still, when the sky was pink:

"But is it anything to worry about?" said Miss Dean. "Really?"

"No, I suppose not."

"Then don't worry. We aren't children any longer!"

"Aren't we? I wonder!"

They leaned, shoulders touching, on the deck-rail, and looked at the sea, which was multitudinously incarnadined. Mr. Arcularis scanned the horizon in vain for an iceberg.

"Anyway," he said, "the colder we are the less we feel!"

"I hope that's no reflection on *you*," said Miss Dean.

"Here . . . feel my hand," said Mr. Arcularis.

"Heaven knows, it's cold!"

"It's been to Polaris and back! No wonder."

"Poor thing, poor thing!"

"Warm it."

"May I?"

"You can."

"I'll try."

Laughing, she took his hand between both of hers, one palm under and one palm over, and began rubbing it briskly. The decks were deserted, no one was near them, everyone was dressing for dinner. The sea grew darker, the wind blew colder.

"I wish I could remember who you are," he said.

"And you—who are you?"

"Myself."

"Then perhaps *I* am yourself."

"Don't be metaphysical!"

"But I *am* metaphysical!"

She laughed, withdrew, pulled the light coat about her shoulders.

The bugle blew the summons for dinner—"The Roast Beef of Old England"—and they walked together along the darkening deck toward the door, from which a shaft of soft light fell across the deck-rail. As they stepped over the brass door-sill Mr. Arcularis felt the throb of the engines again; he put his hand quickly to his side.

"*Auf wiedersehen*," he said. "*Tomorrow and tomorrow and tomorrow.*"

MR. ARCULARIS was finding it impossible, absolutely impossible, to keep warm. A cold fog surrounded the ship, had done so, it seemed, for days. The sun had all but disappeared, the transition from day to night was almost unnoticeable. The ship, too, seemed scarcely to be moving—it was as if anchored among walls of ice and rime. Monstrous that, merely because it was June, and supposed, therefore, to be warm, the ship's authorities should consider it unnecessary to turn on the heat! By day, he wore his heavy coat and sat shivering in the corner of the smoking room. His teeth chattered, his hands were blue. By night, he heaped blankets on his bed, closed the porthole's black eye against the sea, and drew the yellow curtains across it, but in vain. Somehow, despite everything, the fog crept in, and the icy fingers touched his throat. The steward, questioned about it, merely said, "Icebergs." Of course—any fool knew that. But how long, in God's name, was it going to last? They surely ought to be past the Grand Banks by this time! And surely it wasn't necessary to sail to England by way of Greenland and Iceland!

Miss Dean—Clarice—was sympathetic.

"It's simply because," she said, "your vitality has been lowered by your illness. You can't expect to be your normal self so soon after an operation! When *was* your operation, by the way?"

Mr. Arcularis considered. Strange—he couldn't be quite sure. It was all a little vague—his sense of time had disappeared.

"Heavens knows!" he said. "Centuries ago. When I was a tadpole and you were a fish. I should think it must have been at about the time of the Battle of Teutoburg Forest. Or perhaps when I was a Neanderthal man with a club!"

"Are you sure it wasn't farther back still?"

What did she mean by that?

"Not at all. Obviously, we've been on this damned ship for ages—for eras—for aeons. And even on this ship, you must remember, I've had plenty of time, in my nocturnal wanderings, to go several times to Orion and back. I'm thinking, by the way, of going farther still. There's a nice little star off to the left, as you round Betelgeuse, which looks as if it might be right at the edge. The last outpost of the finite. I think I'll have a look at it and bring you back a frozen rime-feather."

"It would melt when you got it back."

"Oh, no, it wouldn't—not on *this* ship!"

Clarice laughed.

"I wish I could go with you," she said.

"If only you would! If only—"

He broke off his sentence and looked hard at her—how lovely she was, and how desirable! No such woman had ever before come into his life; there had been no one with whom he had at once felt so profound a sympathy and understanding. It was a miracle, simply—a miracle. No need to put his arm around her or to kiss her—delightful as such small vulgarities would be. He had only to look at her, and to feel, gazing into those extraordinary eyes, that she knew him, had always known him. It was as if, indeed, she might be his own soul.

But as he looked thus at her, reflecting, he noticed that she was frowning.

"What is it?" he said.

She shook her head, slowly.

"I don't know."

"Tell me."

"Nothing. It just occurred to me that perhaps you weren't looking quite so well."

Mr. Arcularis was startled. He straightened himself up.

"What nonsense! Of course, this pain bothers me—and I feel astonishingly weak—"

"It's more than that—much more than that. Something is worrying you horribly." She paused, and then with an air of challenging him, added, "Tell me, did you—"

Her eyes were suddenly asking him blazingly the question he had been afraid of. He flinched, caught his breath, looked away. But it was no use, as he knew; he would have to tell her. He had known all along that he would have to tell her.

"Clarice," he said—and his voice broke in spite of his effort to control it—"it's killing me, it's ghastly! Yes, I did."

His eyes filled with tears, he saw that her own had done so also. She put her hand on his arm.

"I knew," she said. "I knew. But tell me."

"It's happened twice again—*twice*—and each time I was farther away. The same dream of going round a star, the same terrible coldness and helplessness. That awful whistling curve. . . . " He shuddered.

"And when you woke up"—she spoke quietly—"where were you when you woke up? Don't be afraid!"

"The first time I was at the farther end of the dining saloon. I had my hand on the door that leads into the pantry."

"I see. Yes. And the next time?"

Mr. Arcularis wanted to close his eyes in terror—he felt as if he were going mad. His lips moved before he could speak, and when at last he did speak it was in a voice so low as to be almost a whisper.

"I was at the bottom of the stairway that leads down from the pantry to the hold, past the refrigerating plant. It was dark, and I was crawling on my hands and knees . . . *crawling on my hands and knees!* . . . "

"Oh!" she said, and again, "Oh!"

He began to tremble violently; he felt the hand on his arm trembling also. And then he watched a look of unmistakable horror come slowly into Clarice's eyes, and a look of understanding, as if she saw. . . . She tightened her hold on his arm.

"Do you think. . . . " she whispered.

They stared at each other.

"I know," he said. "And so do you. . . . Twice more—three times—and I'll be looking down into an empty. . . . "

It was then that they first embraced—then, at the edge of the infinite, at the last signpost of the finite. They clung together desperately, forlornly, weeping as they kissed each other, staring hard one moment and closing their eyes the next. Passionately, passionately, she kissed him, as if she were indeed trying to give him her warmth, her life.

"But what nonsense!" she cried, leaning back, and holding his face between her hands, her hands which were wet with his tears. "What nonsense! It can't be!"

"It is," said Mr. Arcularis slowly.

"But how do you know? . . . How do you know where the—"

For the first time Mr. Arcularis smiled.

"Don't be afraid, darling—you mean the coffin?"

"How could you know where it is?"

"I don't need to," said Mr. Arcularis. . . . "I'm already almost there."

BEFORE THEY SEPARATED for the night, in the smoking room, they had several whisky cocktails.

"We must make it gay!" Mr. Arcularis said. "Above all, we must make it gay. Perhaps even now it will turn out to be nothing but a nightmare from which both of us will wake! And even at the worst, at my present rate of travel, I ought to need two more nights! It's a long way, still, to that little star."

The parson passed them at the door.

"What! turning in so soon?" he said. "I was hoping for a game of chess."

"Yes, both turning in. But tomorrow?"

"Tomorrow, then, Miss Dean! And goodnight!"

"Good night."

They walked once round the deck, then leaned on the railing and stared into the fog. It was thicker and whiter than ever. The ship was moving barely perceptibly, the rhythm of the engines was slower, more subdued and remote, and at regular intervals, mournfully, came the long reverberating cry of the foghorn. The sea was calm, and lapped only very tenderly against the side of the ship, the sound coming up to them clearly, however, because of the profound stillness.

" 'On such a night as this—' " quoted Mr. Arcularis grimly.

" 'On such a night as this—' "

Their voices hung suspended in the night, time ceased for them, for an eternal instant they were happy. When at last they parted it was by tacit agreement on a note of the ridiculous.

"Be a good boy and take your bromide?" she said.

"Yes, mother, I'll take my medicine!"

IN HIS STATEROOM, he mixed himself a strong potion of bromide, a very strong one, and got into bed. He would have no trouble in falling asleep; he felt more tired, more supremely exhausted, than he had ever been in his life; nor had bed ever seemed so delicious. And that long, magnificent, delirious swoop of dizziness . . . the Great Circle . . . the swift pathway to Arcturus. . . .

It was all as before, but infinitely more rapid. Never had Mr. Arcularis achieved such phenomenal, such supernatural, speed. In no time at all he was beyond the moon, shot past the North Star as if it were standing still (which perhaps it was?), swooped in a long, bright curve round the Pleiades, shouted his frosty greetings to Betelgeuse, and was off to the little blue star which pointed the way to the Unknown. Forward into the untrodden! Courage, old man, and hold on to your umbrella! Have you got your garters on? Mind your hat! In no time at all we'll be back to Clarice with the frozen rime-feather, the time-feather, the snowflake of the Absolute, the Obsolete. If only we don't wake . . . if only we needn't wake . . . if only we don't wake in that—in that—time and space . . . somewhere or nowhere . . . cold and dark . . . "Cavalleria Rusticana" sobbing among the palms; if a lonely . . . if only . . . the coffers of the poor—not coffers, not coffers, not coffers, Oh, God, not coffers, but light, delight, supreme white and brightness, whirling lightness above all—and freezing—freezing—freezing . . .

AT THIS POINT in the void the surgeon's last effort to save Mr. Arcularis's life had failed. He stood back from the operating table and made a tired gesture with a rubber-gloved hand.

"It's all over," he said. "As I expected."

He looked at Miss Hoyle, whose gaze was downward, at the basin she held. There was a moment's stillness, a pause, a brief flight of unexchanged comment, and then the ordered life of the hospital was resumed.

TEXT AND COVER DESIGN BY TREE SWENSON.

COVER ART IS BY HELEN BYERS.

EHRHARDT AND PERPETUA TYPES SET BY THE TYPEWORKS.

BOOK MANUFACTURE BY EDWARDS BROTHERS.

Other Books in

The Graywolf Short Fiction Series